Table of Contents

Chapter 1 – Saturday 24ᵗʰ August 1940

The bomber exploded in a blossom of orange flame. Jack's Spitfire shot into the rapidly expanding fireball, then out into clear blue sky, miraculously untouched by any of the hurtling debris.

His body ached. He craved rest. But tracer rounds flashed overhead and a blow to the kidneys made him flinch in expectation of worse to come.

'Fool. Never relax.'

He smashed the stick hard right, pulled into a tight turn and looked over his shoulder.

A Messerschmitt 109.

'Pull, Jack, pull.'

And he did, fighting to remain conscious as the g force mounted. Only when his Spitfire began to vibrate like a car driving on cobbles did he ease the back pressure a smidgen.

'That's it, Jack. That's it.'

He was flying *on the buffet*, turning at the maximum rate.

The German was trying to do the same. But his Messerschmitt shuddered, stalling again and again. It was losing lift, and speed, dropping back. The hunter was becoming the hunted.

'Hold it there, Jack. Hold it there.'

As he closed on the 109's tail, his thumb stroked the gun button.

'Another few seconds.'

Just as he was about to fire, the 109 rolled hard left.

'Bad choice, Butt.'

Arms aching, Jack reversed his own turn and pulled his gunsight ahead of the Messerschmitt.

'Try this for size.'

He fired a two second burst. The 109's engine cowling belched a cloud of white vapour.

'And this.'

The cloud ignited. Writhing tongues of flame licked the enemy fighter's fuselage and canopy. It rolled on its back and pitched into a steep dive. Jack checked his rear view mirror and followed, his thumb still poised over the gun button.

But the 109 had become a flaming meteorite.

Jack's mood changed. Through the flames, he caught glimpses of the other pilot, struggling to release his canopy.

'Come on, come on. You can do it.'

Just as it seemed the German's efforts had failed, the angular perspex cover flew open. The man emerged, but wreathed in fire, tumbling through the air, arms and legs flailing.

Jack levelled, grimacing as he watched pilot and aircraft in their fiery descents. No parachute appeared, and the smaller object soon became a tiny dot. It had disappeared from view long before the Messerschmitt hit the green fields of Kent in a billowing mushroom of oily black smoke and flame.

He looked around. Thirty seconds ago, the sky had been full of wheeling and diving machines. Now, nothing but a few decaying vapour trails.

Any sense of achievement had long since evaporated. He felt tired, deflated, horrified at what he'd just done to another young man; horrified also that he'd have no hesitation in doing the same in a few hours' time.

Oblivious to the beauty of the shimmering orange globe hanging in the early morning haze, Jack sighed wearily, turned his Spitfire through 180 degrees and began a slow, lonely, descent towards Biggin Hill.

One hundred and fifty miles away, Alex stood in front of the hall mirror.

Over the last three days, he wasn't sure what had been worse, his mother's raw emotion, his father's exaggerated displays of manly indifference or his own futile attempts to smile and be his old self.

Although the photograph on the table was only 15 months old, the tall, blond-haired, boy in the picture no longer existed. He'd grown another inch, ditched his school uniform and become an RAF officer, a pilot who'd already lost three friends to flying accidents.

If that wasn't enough to banish the innocence of schooldays, he was also steeling himself for the greatest challenge of his life, something he dreaded but was drawn to in equal measure. Was he man enough to face what lay ahead?

'You look very smart, son,' his mother said.

Despite his anxiety, Alex's chest puffed with pride. The wings above the left breast pocket of his newly-tailored uniform of soft blue barathea still dazzled him.

His father opened the front door.

He'd tried to dissuade them from accompanying him to the station, but they'd insisted. And, as they stepped out into the warm sunshine and set off down Gravel Hill, he was glad they were with him.

Carrying a battered brown suitcase each, he and his father walked either side of his mother, towering over her.

It was market day and they stopped every few yards to exchange pleasantries with some acquaintance or other, his parents finding some excuse to draw attention to his wings, just in case the person had failed to notice. Not that that was likely. Everyone in Ludlow must know their son was a Royal Air Force pilot, and soon to be a fighter pilot.

At the station, carriage doors slammed. Self-consciously, Alex eased himself clear of his mother's embrace.

'Just you be careful, son,' she sobbed, dabbing her eyes with a small white handkerchief.

His father, standing stiffly at her side, shook his hand. 'Oh, he'll be fine, won't you, Alex?' The voice seemed to have lost some of its earlier confidence.

'Of course, Dad. I'll be fine.'

Trying to look more relaxed than he felt, he turned his back and boarded the train. It pulled away almost immediately, leaving no time for the things he really should have said. Hoping they knew anyway, he leaned out and waved until his carriage entered the tunnel and the smoke drove him back inside.

Jack undid the third button and slipped his hand under Gwen's blouse. His excitement mounted as he stroked over her breast, delighting at its softness through the smooth, silky material of her slip. Her breath caught as he reached the hardening bud of a nipple. Cupping his hand, he…

'You'll be joining B Flight.'

He screwed his eyes closed and tried to stay with the daydream. Her breasts…

'Your flight commander will be Flight Lieutenant Waters.'

It was hopeless. The more he tried to shut out the words, the more impossible it became. Giving in to the inevitable, he sighed, opened his eyes and drew his wiry frame up the battered leather armchair.

Ten yards away, towards the end of the dispersal hut, two young men stood to the side of the Adjutant's desk. Jack surveyed them with a mixture of curiosity and pity while the fatherly administrator, George Evans, a moustachioed veteran of The Great War, bombarded them with the minutiae of squadron routine, details that would soon lose all significance in the confusion of daily life, and death.

Like Jack, both were sergeants, three chevrons adorning each arm just below the shoulders of their off the peg uniforms of coarse blue material. One was about Jack's age, early 20s, while the other looked no more than 18. But most importantly, each wore a pilot's badge on his left breast.

The Squadron badly needed replacements. Yesterday, a new boy who'd stood in the same place had failed to come back.

The Adjutant mirrored his own thoughts.

'I'm afraid you won't get much time to settle in before you're in the thick of it.'

'That's fine by me,' sprouted the younger sergeant, looking round self-consciously to judge the effect of his bravado.

Jack tried not to be too cynical at the parade ground smartness and enthusiasm. It could have been him four months ago.

'Good, that's the ticket', George encouraged. 'But I'll try and keep their hands off you for the rest of the morning at least.'

Jack felt a nudge at his elbow and looked across at a scruffy individual reclining wearily in the battered armchair next to his.

'Pound to a penny they don't last the next three days, old boy.'

He was inclined to agree. It would be a minor miracle if both the new arrivals survived their first week, and it wouldn't be unheard of for both of them to fall by the wayside. But he tried to be a bit more positive.

'Oh, give them a break will you, Binky. We survived, didn't we?'

'Suppose you're right, my fine Welsh wizard, but we seem to be falling fast at the moment.'

Not for the first time, Jack was struck by the contrast between his harsh Barry accent and Flying Officer Clifford Binkman's cut glass delivery. He decided not to mention how close he'd just come to adding to the growing list of casualties. If the 20mm cannon shell that had embedded itself in his seat armour had exploded… But he was surprised at his friend's public display of pessimism. He was usually so upbeat.

'Still, mustn't dwell on things must we? Onward and upward and all that.'

Binky's attempt to reassert his usual optimism sounded decidedly half-hearted. Jack looked on with genuine concern as the handsome young Cambridge graduate slumped back in his chair and closed his eyes.

Roused out of his own torpor for the moment, he watched George Evans lead the two new pilots through the door to the adjoining locker room.

He ran a hand through his unruly black hair - must find time for a haircut - and looked around.

The wooden hut was a mess, the air thick with blue cigarette and pipe smoke, the flaking cream paint largely hidden behind heavily laden shelves, groaning clothes hooks, and more posters than it was possible to read in a morning. Seven or eight leather arm chairs lined each side wall. All contained recumbent figures dressed in a variety of flying kit, most with their feet resting on a line of cluttered low tables running down the centre of the room. To one end, behind the Adjutant's desk, half a dozen camp beds were occupied by more prone figures.

At this time of year, no-one wore the bulky flying suits provided. They preferred to fly in their uniforms, some in their blue jackets, some just in shirt sleeves. Trousers were mostly tucked into high leather flying boots, although a few wore ordinary uniform shoes. And all wore silk scarves, not as sartorial statements, but to prevent their collars shrinking and throttling them if they ended up in the sea, or chafing as they turned their heads, trying to spot the enemy.

Over shirt or jacket, they wore Mae West life preservers. A few, like Jack, were lucky to have the German equivalent, greatly prized because they inflated when you hit the water. The RAF version had to be blown up, not easy when treading water in wet clothes, incredibly difficult if injured, and bloody impossible if you happened to be unconscious.

They looked a rag-tag outfit, but they had been up since 4 am. The first scramble hadn't come until 7.30, about an hour later than usual, and the second was now long overdue.

Grateful for the respite, most were sleeping, trying to sleep, or pretending to sleep, much as Jack had been a few minutes previously. Others played cards or dominoes, and a few were reading; although, if you watched them for long enough, you noticed that not many pages were turned.

At the far end of the room, just outside the offices of the squadron and flight commanders, was the Ops

Desk. Sitting atop it, amongst a jumble of paperwork, was the device that ruled their lives: the big black Ops Phone.

Its ring could send some round the back of the hut to be sick. At the least, its strident alarm set their hearts racing, and Jack didn't believe anyone could sleep beyond its first ring. He certainly couldn't.

Grimacing at the sight of the telephone orderly removing a grubby forefinger from his nose, he sank back and tried to resurrect the memory of his last few hours with Gwen.

The phone rang.

The 12 Mark I Spitfires of No 646 Squadron Royal Air Force climbed out of the haze into the bright blue of another beautiful summer day. At that moment, Jack would not have wished himself anywhere else in the world.

The aircraft surrounding him were all elegant curves, sunlight glinting off rounded perspex canopies and camouflaged metal surfaces. The nine to his front were in vics of three, the wingmen sitting just to either side of the tailplanes of their section leaders. Red Section sat 150 yards ahead, with Yellow 50 yards behind them, then Green, just 50 yards ahead of his own propeller spinner.

Over his shoulders, behind the aesthetic sweep of his Spitfire's elliptical wings, sat the two wingmen of his own Blue Section.

As sometimes happened on such occasions, he was overwhelmed, reduced almost to tears. Who wouldn't feel privileged to be surrounded by such machines at such a moment in history?

And all were piloted by men he was proud to serve

alongside. Even where differences in rank or character made friendship impossible, there was a strong sense of camaraderie. They were all intent on protecting the towns and villages below them from an enemy that had already laid waste to much of Europe. Jack knew. He'd seen it with his own eyes.

The CO's confident voice crackled in his headset. 'Bastion, this is Dragon Leader, passing angels one two.'

'Roger, Dragon Leader. This is Bastion. Maintain heading. One hundred plus bandits, angels one five, approaching Dover.'

Good, Jack thought. Plenty of time to get above them.

Height was all-important. They could convert it to speed, diving down on the bombers, firing a short burst and climbing again to dive in a second time, all before the enemy fighters intervened. At least, that was the theory.

In practise, before the second attack, and sometimes before the first, they were likely to be bounced themselves.

In the Spitfire to Jack's rear right, Pilot Officer Johnny Thwaite stared straight ahead, as if in a daze.

'Blue Two,' he admonished gently, gesturing his wingman to keep his eyes moving.

Johnny had only been with them five days and seemed to be finding it all too much.

'Roger, Blue Leader. Sorry.'

Such a lonely, timid, voice. Jack felt sorry for the young man, but he had to buck his ideas up. It wasn't just his life that depended on it.

Pilot Officer Piers White, sitting out to the left, was much more competent, and confident, although he'd only been with them a few days longer than Johnny. Acting as weaver, he was manoeuvring at the rear, quartering the sky for the enemy while the rest of the Squadron concentrated on holding formation. Arse-end Charlie was a position of trust, but a vulnerable one; they were usually the first to be attacked.

As expected, Piers's head and eyes were in constant motion. Good. At this time of day, he'd be paying special attention to the area to his right, to the south, looking with watering eyes for the Hun in the sun. Jack gave him a thumbs-up. The young man returned the gesture, his eyes creasing above his oxygen mask in what Jack knew was a broad smile.

'Bastion, this is Dragon Leader,' the CO's voice broke in again. 'Tally-ho, tally-ho, one hundred plus bandits, eleven o'clock, slightly high.'

'Roger, Dragon Leader. Remember, priority to the bombers, and watch out for Snappers. Good luck, Bastion out.'

Jack gestured his two wingmen to keep their eyes moving. The rest of the Squadron would probably be looking towards the bombers, oblivious of anything else, such as roving enemy fighters. But even he couldn't resist a quick glance to the left.

'Cripes!'

It was 100 plus all right, in a formation several miles long, stepped up in waves from front to back, the larger silhouettes of the bombers shepherded by groups of the smaller Snappers – single-engined Messerschmitt Bf 109Es.

Until a week ago, the German fighters would probably have been high above, ready to dive down, spitting death and destruction from their nose-mounted machine guns and wing-mounted cannons. But in the last few days, they'd been flying close escort to the bombers, weaving around at a similar height, and there seemed to be many more of them. They'd forfeited the element of surprise, but made it harder to get at the bombers, as Jack had found earlier that morning.

He looked away to quarter the sky. The CO had taken advantage of the sun, climbing them to the south and turning above the rear left quarter of the enemy formation. Ideally placed.

'Dragon, line abreast, line abreast, go.'

Jack eased Blue Section to the left of the Squadron, set his engine rpm to 2650, pressed the emergency boost override, switched his reflector sight on, set his gun button to fire, lowered his seat a notch and tightened his seat straps.

'Not long now, Jack.'

He often talked to himself. It might seem daft, but it helped him stay calm.

Not that he didn't feel the familiar butterflies as the moment of combat approached. Ignoring them, he looked to left and right, giving his section a confident thumbs-up.

Piers looked relaxed, but Johnny made even his nod of acknowledgement seem hesitant. Too late for any more encouragement though. The nose of the CO's Spitfire dipped.

'Dragon, here we go chaps. Good luck all.'

Alex looked out of the carriage window at the rolling green countryside of Herefordshire. He tried to recall the scene 18 months before, during his first journey to London.

More barbed wire this time. And more uniforms. But otherwise, not much seemed to have changed.

Perhaps that was what the war was really about; making sure people out here wondered what all the fuss was.

He still couldn't resist looking at his reflection, admiring the wings on his chest. He'd never felt like this, so proud of anything he'd done, of anything he'd possessed. He also enjoyed the way other people looked at him, with a sense of approval he'd never experienced before. He was tempted to undo his top button and declare himself a fighter pilot, but that would be too much. He'd done nothing yet to earn such a display.

And would he make a good fighter pilot?

His 13 hours of Spitfire flying on the Operational Training Unit had gone well. The aircraft was a delight in the air, but a handful to land and manoeuvre on the ground.

And the cockpit was a bit cosy for someone of his stature. But he could fly competently in formation, and knew some basic tactics, although they'd been given little weapons training, so he had no idea whether he'd be able to shoot down enemy bombers, let alone fighters. Most importantly, though, he had no idea how he'd react to combat.

As they steamed into Abergavenny, the countryside became more rugged, almost threatening, the sombre hills mirroring, or precipitating, darker thoughts.

Would he fall prey to cowardice?

Until he answered that question, he didn't deserve anyone's admiration, and he certainly couldn't undo his top button.

Dragon were diving on the rear of the formation of twin-engined Dornier 17 bombers. Jack picked one to the rear left and wound the type's wingspan into his gunsight. Looking around again, he felt exhilaration and pride. They may be vastly outnumbered, but their Spitfires couldn't look more heroic, bobbing gently up and down like cavalry chargers racing over the turf.

The bombers started to grow menacingly in his windshield. Flashes of tracer streaked ahead of some of the other Spitfires.

'Far too early,' he tutted.

Getting in close was the key, as they'd learned over Dunkirk. But it took nerve, and none of them had been taught much about gunnery.

He held his fire. They had only 14 seconds of ammunition. There was no point in wasting it. Taking a last look round, he saw the 109s to the left break towards them.

'Dragon, Snappers left, 10 o'clock.'

They'd also been spotted by the bombers. Deadly rods of light arced towards him, setting out slowly, but speeding up as they approached, and then flashing past. In a few seconds, the sky was full of them. He tried to forget the swarm of invisible but equally deadly machine gun bullets accompanying each brightly glowing tracer round. It wasn't easy.

Much of the fire was coming from the upper turret of his chosen target. He felt the usual twinge of fear in the pit of his stomach, but waited for the bomber's wingspan to grow until it touched the two vertical lines of his gunsight - 250 yards. Even then, he still waited.

'Until... Until...Now.'

At about 100 yards, he pressed the gun button.

The firing of the eight, wing-mounted, .303 machine guns assailed his senses. A loud pneumatic hiss and metallic clattering were accompanied by tooth-rattling vibration and the acrid smell of cordite. His ammunition sparked on the Dornier. Bits flew off its slim fuselage and wings. It grew to fill his canopy.

'Bloody hell, Jack!'

He pushed the stick forward. The Spitfire rocked violently, but flew straight on. Just as he was about to raise his arms to cover his face, its nose dipped and it dived under the bomber's looming tailplane and out of the turbulent slipstream. The negative g caused his engine to cough and forced his head up into the roof of the canopy along with all the dust and debris from the cockpit floor. As the engine recovered, he shook himself and looked around.

Nothing on his tail yet, but a 109 was closing on Johnny.

'Johnny, break, break, Snapper on your tail.'

There was nothing else he could do. He watched just long enough to see the young officer turn right, but oh so lethargically.

What next?

The battle was raging, the sky full of jinking aircraft, trails of vapour, smoke and flame. A Dornier and a Spitfire were falling. His earphones were filled with swearing shouts and screams of pain.

Shutting out the sounds, he pulled out of his dive, welcoming the return of positive g. Another quick look round. Every second aircraft seemed to be a Messerschmitt, but there was still nothing on his tail. The bombers held formation 500 yards above. He picked one, another Dornier, and climbed towards it. Tracer spat at him from its lower gun.

'That's not very friendly, is it?'

Waiting until he was well inside 250 yards again, Jack pressed the gun button. His rounds smashed into the bomber's left wing and fuselage. The left propeller wound down and the gunner fell forward over his gun, its barrel pointing uselessly upwards.

Using the last of his excess energy, he banked to the right to fly under the bomber's belly, so close he could see oily smudges flowing back from individual rivets and fastenings. Once clear, he reversed the turn to look down on his prey.

The Dornier was dropping from the formation, smoke trailing from its left engine.

'Now what, Jack?'

The bomber may have been mortally damaged, in which case, there was no use in expending more time and energy in pursuit. But it could also be trying to sneak home at low level, something he couldn't allow.

A stream of tracer threaded towards him from the rear upper gun.

'That does it.'

He rolled in for a rear quarter attack, aiming a long burst at the right wing and front fuselage. The Dornier's perspex canopy shattered and a finger of smoke and flame appeared from under the cowling of the right engine.

They were both dropping below the mêlée now, and Jack realised his enemy was probably beaten. As usual on such occasions, he felt an immediate change of mood.

Now the Dornier posed no personal threat and seemed highly unlikely to make it across the Channel, his murderous intent gave way to concern for the safety of its crew. It was a fragile change. If the aircraft recovered, or its guns started firing, he'd have no hesitation in giving it another burst of machine gun fire. But, for the moment, he willed any surviving crew members to escape what was rapidly becoming a burning wreck.

'Come on lads, get the hell out of there.'

Flames from the burning engines licked along the fuselage. But the aircraft still seemed to be under control. Somewhere in that metal oven, a very brave man was wrestling to keep his aircraft stable enough for his crew to escape.

A pair of legs appeared in the bottom hatch.

'Yes, that's it.'

A body dropped into the air. Thinking back to the morning, Jack held his breath, but after only a short wait, he was relieved to see the billowing silk of an unfurling parachute.

'Come on, the rest of you?'

Another pair of legs appeared.

'Yes.'

But, as the shout left his lips, the bomber rolled onto its back and settled into a steeply spiralling descent, wreathed in smoke and flames. The pilot had lost his battle for control. Jack pictured the scene in the bomber and winced.

He watched the plummeting fireball for a short while, but saw no more legs, or parachutes.

'Quiet' the young officer said, adjusting his sling and fixing the two sergeant pilots with piercing blue eyes. Startled at their guide's sudden intensity, the NCOs obeyed without question, realising as they did so that a hush had fallen. The groundcrew, until now working noisily on the few aircraft not in the air, had fallen into silent inactivity, eyes turned expectantly to the south east.

The unmistakable sound of a Merlin engine

signalled the impending return of the Biggin Hill fleet – the Hurricanes of 32 Squadron and Spitfires of 629 Squadron had scrambled soon after 646. The sergeants sensed excitement in those around them, but also concern, a feeling that intensified when they heard a loud backfire.

'There it is,' a lone voice shouted as a Spitfire appeared over the hedge, streaming white vapour.

NCOs barked orders, and there was frenzied activity as tradesmen rushed to ground equipment and fuel bowsers.

'Sorry, chaps,' the young officer said, never taking his eyes off the stricken aircraft. 'Better leave it there. I'd just about finished anyway.'

'Thanks, sir. I think I got most of it,' the younger sergeant piped up, trying to maintain his earlier bravado. He stepped out of the cockpit and followed the other two down the wing.

The older sergeant jumped to the ground and wondered whether he should help the officer. But the young man, probably no more than 18 or 19 years old, leapt to the ground unaided, gingerly supporting his left arm with his good hand. He winced in pain, but quickly recovered his composure and led them the short distance to the group of chairs outside the dispersal hut. There, he turned, and the two sergeants followed suit.

The officer was finding it hard to believe that, until a few days ago, he'd been part of the tableau unfolding before them. The sergeants were only too aware that they soon would be.

The backfiring Spitfire touched down and was chased across the airfield by a fire truck, an ambulance and a three-ton lorry carrying two lines of bouncing men. In other circumstances, the similarity to a scene from a silent movie might have evoked laughter, but not today.

The aircraft came to rest, and, as the various vehicles disgorged their occupants, its propeller slowed to a stop. After a short delay, the canopy was thrown back and the pilot stood up and waved. At that point, the ambulance crew lost interest. They jumped back in their vehicle and drove away. The vapour had cleared, but the fire crew kept their hoses pointed at the engine, and the occupants of the three-ton truck milled around.

The two sergeants looked at one another. They were just about to break the nervous silence when the sound of more Merlin engines drew their eyes back to the south east. The noise level rose steadily until a gaggle of Spitfires and Hurricanes appeared, some overhead the airfield, others landing on the runway and the grass to either side.

It all looked pretty chaotic, but as each aircraft reached the end of its landing run, it turned unhurriedly left or right and taxyed towards the dispersal pens, and the waiting groundcrew. The Spitfires weaved extravagantly from side to side as they lurched across the grass.

'You can forget most of what they taught you at the OTU,' the young officer said, looking earnestly at both of them in turn. 'But you better remember to weave the nose when you taxy. After the raid last Sunday, an NCO from the other side of the airfield taxyed straight into a bomb crater. Wrote his kite off. Made him very popular I can tell you. The old man's hearing the charge today.'

The two NCOs were unsure what to say in reply,

but their discomfort was short-lived. The officer pointed.

A Hurricane trailing sinister black smoke crossed low over the hedge. It landed heavily, bounced into the air and crashed down again, slewing to the left. Its undercarriage collapsed and it careered sideways, sending up clods of earth and a cloud of dust. When it came to a halt, flames rose from the engine cowling just ahead of the cockpit. The canopy was open, but the pilot's head was bent forward, resting on the instrument panel. They watched in horror as the fire intensified and still he failed to move.

Other aircraft landed to either side as the fire tender, ambulance and more three-ton trucks threaded their way towards it. Soon, the burning Hurricane was lost to sight in a ring of vehicles, but a pall of smoke rose ominously above the tarpaulin cover of one of the trucks. After an agonising delay, the ambulance drove away towards the far side of the airfield.

Meanwhile, the Spitfires of 646, Dragon Squadron, had been taxying towards the small group of watchers. They were nearing their E pens – roofless oblong sanctuaries, with high blast walls on three sides, and a central wall dividing them into two protective bays.

Two groundcrew met each Spitfire, grasped the wingtips, walked alongside for a short distance and helped turn them through ninety degrees and halt, their tails pointing into the opening of a bay.

Propellers wound down and stopped to the accompaniment of loud backfires, while clouds of smoke belched from stub exhausts lining engine cowlings. More groundcrew gathered along the leading edges of the wings and the aircraft were pushed back into their pens, accompanied by much arm-waving and shouts of 'Brakes on', and 'Brakes off'.

Slowly, the pilots stepped out of their cockpits. All seemed to take a few moments to look round, before waddling down the wing, jumping to the ground, taking off their parachutes and hanging them over wing or tailplane. After brief exchanges with their groundcrew, they walked with varying degrees of urgency towards the pen nearest the dispersal hut, 50 yards from the onlookers.

A flight lieutenant leaned against the end of a blast wall, smoking a pipe and holding a clipboard.

Probably no older than 40, he looked positively ancient compared with the young men that soon surrounded him. They all seemed to talk at once, some using their arms expansively, others laughing noisily or hooting in derision. Somehow, despite the press of bodies, the unflappable flight lieutenant managed to give each a little time, writing calmly, and occasionally tapping the clipboard with the stem of his pipe as if making some point, or seeking clarification.

One by one, figures left the group and made their way towards the dispersal hut. A few nodded at the young officer and sergeants as they passed, then either walked into the hut or flopped into the chairs in the fresh air. All were grubby, their faces sweat-stained, bearing marks where oxygen masks had fitted around noses and chins. To a man, they looked weary.

Most of the pens were occupied now, groundcrew moving purposefully around the resident aircraft. But the sergeants noticed that one pen was empty. Two men stood outside, heads turned to the south east.

It was just after 12.30pm.

Jack threw his gloves into a seat and turned to face the

young man he'd followed into the dispersal hut, now perching on the edge of the Ops Desk.

'I'd seen Johnny with a 109 on his tail, so when I saw a Spit going down, I thought it must be him, until just now that is. I hope it wasn't Binky. He hasn't come back yet, has he?'

'No,' the officer replied, running a hand through his curly brown hair and preening his short moustache.

Flight Lieutenant Mike 'Muddy' Waters was the same age as Jack, 22, a Cranwell-trained officer with six months' front line experience, and already a flight commander.

'But there were other squadrons about, Jack.'

'Yes, I know. Just have to wait and see. Could do without the loss of experience, though, couldn't we?'

'I know. There aren't many of us old stagers left.'

Yet again, Jack found it incredible that anyone could think of him, of them, as old stagers. Binky had said as much earlier. He hoped his friend's sense of foreboding hadn't been prophetic. When people began to believe something bad was about to happen, it often did.

Muddy continued, 'I'll speak to the CO and pick someone to take Binky's section. Just in case. And I think we'll have to take one of the new sergeants as well.'

'I thought you might say that. Poor bastards. Did you see them? They're looking shell-shocked already.'

'I know. I was hoping to leave them 'til tomorrow. I've had a look at their reports and neither of them has more than 15 hours on type. But what can we do? I'll take the older one.' He broke off to look at a piece of paper on the desk. 'Thomson, Sergeant Thomson. Not that age makes any difference up there.'

He looked at Jack, adopting a more sympathetic tone. 'How's Johnny Thwaite coping?'

Before Jack could answer, the CO came into the room followed by a noisy group of pilots, all jostling one another playfully, full of banter, as if they'd just come back from an enjoyable football match.

'Okay, Muddy. I suppose we'd better have a little chat,' the Squadron Commander said as he swept past the Ops Desk and disappeared into his office without breaking stride.

'Right, sir.' Muddy leapt playfully to attention, winked at Jack and followed the CO, closing the door behind him.

Squadron Leader Gerry Parr was their third CO in as many months, and the best. He was enthusiastic without being reckless, and he had good tactical awareness, unlike his two predecessors, who hadn't lasted long, partly because of their weakness in that area. Unfortunately, they'd taken some good men with them.

Jack would never understand why they brought in squadron commanders with little or no front line experience. Some had flown nothing but a desk for years. Why not promote the best flight commanders? It was the same with tactics. Why persist with old-fashioned vics of three, when they knew the Luftwaffe's pairs or 4s were much more efficient? But then, being only a humble sergeant, he wasn't paid to decide such things. It all seemed daft though, if not downright dangerous.

Anyway, Squadron Leader Parr was good. Jack just hoped he managed to stay healthy. They could do with some continuity.

His musing was ended by the sight of Johnny

Thwaite walking into the hut. The thin, fair-haired, young man looked pale and distracted, almost stumbling, as if in a daze. There was no doubt he was trying, but he just wasn't cut out for this life, either physically or temperamentally.

Not for the first time that day, Jack felt both pity and concern. And right now, the young man needed support. But, although Jack was his section leader, he didn't think he was the best person to step in. He looked around and made eye contact with Piers, sitting on the edge of an armchair.

Unlike Johnny, Piers seemed to be revelling in the challenges of combat. He was also an astute young man, and Jack had to do no more than raise an eyebrow and nod towards Johnny for the other to nod in return and move off.

He watched Piers intercept his charge and turn him round to walk into the fresh air. 'Come on, old boy, let's find the NAAFI wagon and get a cup of tea.'

Nicely done, Jack thought. And I hope it works, because I don't think the day's over yet!

He jumped as the Ops Phone rang.

Aircraftman Hopkins reached for the large black handpiece, raised it to his ear, listened intently and put it back in its cradle. 'The NAAFI wagon's been delayed over the other side. Should be here in about 15 minutes.'

He ducked as a large book sailed over his head.

The phone had rung another half dozen times for relatively trivial reasons before Jack moved outside to try and escape its harsh trilling. He was unsuccessful. Even though its ring was now much quieter, it wasn't the volume that set his nerves on edge; it was the expectation, the fear of what its message would be.

It was hard to explain. Once airborne, he felt fine; more than that, he felt as if he was where he should be, where he belonged. He didn't forget the dangers. He just accepted them and got on with the job in hand.

But that wasn't the same as saying he wanted to go into combat. On the ground, waiting for the phone to ring, hearing it, then he felt fear.

There was another reason for moving outside today though. He was watching Piers and Johnny, sitting together on the grass, a little removed from the rest of the group. You wouldn't exactly describe it as an animated conversation, but they were talking, and Piers had even managed to get Johnny to smile on occasion.

It was strange how two people of similar age and background could react to events so differently. They were both 19 and boyish in appearance, but Piers, dark haired and handsome, looked relaxed and self-assured. He used his hands expressively and smiled frequently, whereas Johnny, although less ashen than before, still looked tired and strained, especially so when the phone rang.

Eventually, Piers clapped his friend on the back, rose and walked away, throwing a parting remark over his shoulder. Spotting Jack, he responded to another minimalist head movement and walked over, squatting on the grass next to his section leader's chair and lighting a cigarette.

'He's alright, I think. He's just having trouble sleeping and, well let's face it, none of us knew what to expect, did we?'

Piers raised the cigarette to his lips and Jack was surprised to see a slight tremor in his hand. There was also an underlying tension in his face that he hadn't noticed before.

'No. You're right, but thank you. I thought it would be better if one of his friends had a chat, rather than me bumble over and put my foot in it. And how are you feeling?'

'A bit tired actually, but,' and he smiled disarmingly, dark eyes holding Jack's in a firm gaze, 'I'll be fine.'

Jack believed him.

'Okay. Thanks again. I think you'll be arse-end Charlie for the next scramble as well, so just be ready. Keep those eyes moving.'

The arrival of lunch provided a chance for Jack to have a few words with Johnny, without making either of them feel too uncomfortable.

Afterwards, he remained concerned. The young man was edgier than Piers had admitted. But was it enough to take the matter further, to recommend resting him? If he did that, no matter how careful he was, he risked labelling Johnny as LMF – lacking moral fibre – and that would be grossly unfair. He just shouldn't have been sent to a fighter squadron.

After agonising briefly, he decided to give the young officer another chance. So, he confined himself to offering a few gentle words of advice, before returning to his chair to shut his eyes for as long as the Luftwaffe would allow.

After several minutes of unproductive musing on the absence of Binky and the rest of the day's events, he managed to drag his thoughts back to Gwen.

It had been just over a week ago, the second night of his 48-hour pass.

He'd picked her up from her parents' house on

Barry Island, overlooking the docks. They'd known one another for years, been going out for three of them, and he knew that everyone, including Gwen, was expecting an engagement announcement soon.

She looked stunning, a Welsh beauty, raven hair falling down in waves to frame a face with a complexion as smooth and white as porcelain. She was wearing a white blouse, a dark skirt and heels, the combination serving to show off her curvy figure, at least until her mother intervened.

'Don't forget your coat. It'll be chilly later.'

He'd tried to engage in some preliminary petting in the cinema, but to no avail. Gwen had been too determined to resist all but an arm around her shoulders and a few furtive pecks on the cheek.

'Stop it, Jack. There's too many people.'

So he'd manoeuvred her to somewhere much quieter: on the beach just in front of the western shelter on Whitmore Bay.

'Come on, Gwen, it's not cold. Let's put our coats on the sand.'

'All right, but not for long. I don't know what's got into you tonight.'

The war and the stark realisation of his own mortality; that was what had got into him. So many things he wanted to do before he died, and top of the list at that particular moment was make love to Gwen.

'Look, Gwen, it's a beautiful night. Come down here and look at the stars.'

He lay unthreateningly on his back, hands behind his head.

It was a beautiful, starry night, the headlands to left and right silhouetted against the dark sky, their gun installations silent for the moment, their barrage balloons grounded.

'It is lovely,' she said in a soft tone, and he pictured her lips, sensuous and curved, free of lipstick but cherry red nonetheless.

He heard her lie next to him. 'Why can't you just work on the docks like your dad did?'

Because I joined the RAF, and I'm fighting in a war, he thought tetchily. She'd been asking a lot of similar questions in her letters.

'I know, dear, I know. It's just the war.'

He leaned over, placed an arm around her waist and kissed her before she could make further comment. Slightly to his surprise, she yielded to his embrace and he prolonged the kiss. Her lips were as soft as he'd imagined. He edged his hand upward. She tensed, but didn't resist. His confidence grew and his heart raced.

He stroked her breasts through the thin material of her blouse. She emitted a contented sigh and her lips parted. He felt the tip of her tongue…

Bugger!

There was no ignoring Hopkins' shouts and the accompanying ringing of the ship's bell, a memento of some vessel the Squadron had sunk in the last war.

'Dragon scramble, one hundred plus bandits, angels fifteen, North Foreland. Dragon scramble.'

For the third time that day, Jack found himself racing across the grass.

As Alex's train approached Paddington, concerns about his bravery or lack of it were eased into the background.

Like many a Shropshire lad before him, he was marvelling at the sheer size of the capital. They'd hit the outskirts miles back. Hereford, Newport, Swindon and Reading were big, but this was something else.

After the visit to the RAF selection centre on Kingsway 18 months before, he should have been more blasé, but he was still overawed. It was a shame he wouldn't get to see much of the city this time.

He stepped from the train into the grubby grandeur of Paddington station, slightly discomfited by the crush of people squeezing along the platform and into the main concourse. He'd have preferred to take a taxi, or walk, as he had on his last visit, but time was tight, and he found himself at the top of the steps leading to the Underground. After a slight hesitation, he plunged down.

The journey was pretty amazing. The unremitting crowds of people; the size of the brightly tiled spaces and pedestrian tunnels; the steeply sloping escalators and the depth to which they descended; the rush of air as the trains approached, and the screech as they halted alongside the platform; the jostling throng exiting and boarding; the crush once inside; the whirr of the motors; and the jarring acceleration that shot them into the dark at such speed. The whole experience was just so different from the sedate walk through Ludlow a few hours earlier.

And, to his eyes, when he climbed the final flight of stairs to the surface again, he could have been back in Paddington. But it was Victoria, and he set off to find his train.

They pulled out into the sunlight and Alex looked back, hoping that he'd get to visit the city again before too long, maybe even sample some of the night life.

To the east, he noticed swirling white patterns in the bright blue sky, as if a child had scribbled with a crayon. He tried to imagine what it must be like to be up there among – making - those vapour trails. But it was impossible.

His mood darkened again.

'Dragon, this is Bastion, bandits angels one five, now in your twelve o'clock, approximately fifteen miles.'

'Roger, Bastion, this is Dragon Leader, still looking.'

No time to get above the enemy this time, Jack thought. It would have to be a head-on attack. Not for the faint-hearted, but often very effective. Most bombers lacked frontal armour, so there was nothing but perspex between the crew and your bullets.

You still had to have energy though. If you met them in the climb, at slow speed, you'd be sitting ducks. The previous two COs had never grasped this fundamental point. Thankfully, this one had. With the help of a switched on Controller, he'd flown some weaving turns to position them with the sun behind, maybe even a thousand feet in hand.

Blue Section was at the rear again, the rest of the Squadron slightly above and ahead. Jack looked out to either side. Piers, weaving gently, appeared cool and confident, head and eyes in constant motion, but Johnny still looked pensive. Perhaps he shouldn't have given him the benefit of the doubt. Too late now.

'Okay, Blue Two?' he prodded.

Johnny managed a thumbs-up, but Jack sensed fear and confusion in his eyes.

He was pondering whether there was anything else he could do, when he spotted a slight darkening beyond the Spitfires in front, like a fuzzy swarm of bees against the blue sky.

'Dragon Leader, this is Blue Leader, possible

bandits, 11 o'clock slightly high.'

'Roger, Blue Leader, thank you. Looking.'

They all loved the unhurried courtesy with which Squadron Leader Parr completed even the most fraught of exchanges. A great calming influence.

'Dragon, line abreast, line abreast, go.'

Jack felt the usual prickling of anticipation as he positioned his section to the left of the line. By the time he returned his gaze to the front, the nebulous swarm had become a rectangular phalanx of small black shapes. He was just about to make another report when the CO's voice piped in.

'Bastion, this is Dragon Leader, tally-ho, one hundred plus bandits, five miles, slightly low. Going in.'

'Roger, Dragon Leader. Good luck, Bastion out.'

'So, here we are again,' Jack said as he looked along the line, 'twelve against a hundred.'

As on previous occasions, the odds did nothing but increase his resolve. Whether others felt the same he couldn't say, but to his way of thinking, the more there were, the more they could shoot down. The CO obviously felt the same.

'Dragon, in we go lads. Plenty to go round so don't be greedy. Good luck.'

The nose of the CO's aircraft dipped and they followed him into a shallow dive.

Jack could see only bombers, but the Snappers would be out there somewhere, all the more dangerous for not being seen. He looked behind. All clear. They were accelerating, closing at over 500 miles an hour. Things would happen fast.

How could he explain any of this to Gwen, and what would she make of it if he did?

He wound the wingspan of the Junkers 88s into the gunsight and positioned his thumb over the gun button. No tracer yet. The sun was a marvellous ally.

Jack picked a bomber and watched it grow behind the gunsight information projected onto the small glass circle in front of the bulletproof windscreen. Tracer shot ahead of other aircraft in the formation, but he forced himself to wait. Only when his bomber pilot was clearly visible, shouting at who knew what, did he open fire.

His airframe shuddered with the recoil and his rounds hit the target. To prevent his Spitfire doing the same, he pushed the stick. Dust and debris rose from the cockpit floor. The sky darkened, filled with the perspex nose of the bomber. He held his breath.

There was no impact, but a flash to his right suggested that not everyone had been so lucky. Collision was an ever-present danger at such high closing speeds, especially for the overly-brave, or the inexperienced. He turned his head. A Spitfire wing cart-wheeled out of a fireball.

'Poor bastard.'

But even now, he found himself admiring the elegance of the wing as it dropped alongside the other debris.

Whose was it?

Surely Johnny Thwaite had been too far away? He jinked to throw off any attacking fighters and spotted his wingman's Spitfire in a shallow dive to the right. His relief was short-lived. A Messerschmitt 109 was closing on it from behind.

For the second time in two missions, Jack shouted, 'Break, Johnny, break, Snapper on your tail.'

Nothing. If Johnny had heard the warning, he was

frozen into immobility.

'Damn.'

Grunting against the g, Jack turned sharply right to engage the 109. Luckily its pilot seemed intent on stalking Johnny to the exclusion of all else. Keen not to make the same mistake, Jack looked round. Two 109s sat high to his right.

'Better turn under them, Jack.'

But what about Johnny?

The Messerschmitt pilot leaned forward as if urging his machine to close more quickly. If he fired, he couldn't miss the unsuspecting British pilot.

'For fuck's sake, Johnny, break right, Snapper on your tail.'

Perhaps the swearing broke the spell, but whatever it was, Johnny's head swivelled and his Spitfire started a lazy turn to the right. It was far too sedate to throw off his pursuer, but it could buy some time as the Messerschmitt pilot adjusted his aim.

Still the German hadn't looked to his left, and Jack was closing. He stole a quick glance above him.

'Bugger.'

The two Messerschmitts were diving.

His stomach cramped. He had to turn into them or he was dead meat. Probably too late to save Johnny anyway, and no-one would ever know.

At least one of them might live to fight another day.

Disowning such cold logic, he rolled out of his turn and headed for his wingman's pursuer. The distance was against him, but there was no more time. Estimating the lay off, Jack pressed the gun button.

The Messerschmitt flew into his line of tracer. Belatedly, the German's head snapped left. Jack's snapped right, just as his world tumbled.

By the time the taxi dropped Alex outside the main gates of RAF Biggin Hill, he was feeling nervous and lonely. He tried not to show it, but the response of the stick-thin, middle-aged, airman behind the guardroom desk did nothing to raise his spirits.

'Sorry sir,' he said, in a rasping, 60-a-day, Cockney accent. 'We weren't expecting you.'

Alex wasn't surprised. He hadn't known where he was going himself until 48 hours previously. He must have looked disappointed though, because the airman seemed moved to expand.

'Don't worry though, sir, it's not you. We hardly get anybody we're expecting these days. Especially pilots. Just turn up out of the blue, if you don't mind the pun, sir?'

Alex smiled weakly, unsure what to do now. He sensed it was too late to arrive at his new squadron, and in any case he didn't have to be there until 8.30 the next morning. So... His next question was pre-empted.

'I'll get a car to take you to the Officers' Mess, sir, if that's alright?'

Alex still wasn't used to receiving deference from anyone, especially someone older.

'Thank you, that's very helpful.'

The next few minutes dragged interminably, and he was very glad when the car arrived. And thank goodness for the Women's Auxiliary Air Force. The young WAAF driver was so much prettier than the leather-faced man in the Guardroom, and she seemed genuinely impressed that he was joining 646 Squadron. During the short drive, her warm smile raised his spirits, and made him blush.

The Officers' Mess had the look of a large country

house. Feeling out of his depth again, Alex waved farewell to his driver and stepped into a cavernous reception area, panelled in dark wood. Another young WAAF stood behind an impressive wooden counter.

'Sorry, sir, we weren't expecting you.'

Alex smiled. He sensed he was going to get used to those words.

'If you'll give me a minute though, sir, I'll see what I can do.'

She was short and dark, a similar age to him, with a broad northern accent, possibly Lancashire or Yorkshire, but then again, possibly not. Until 15 months previously, he'd heard little beyond his own Shropshire burr; since, he'd heard a confusing array of accents. But, if it wasn't Scouse, Brummie or Geordie, he was usually at a loss to identify it with any accuracy.

Putting his cases down, he strolled around looking at the pictures on the walls. Most were of silver biplanes flying past large country houses.

They seemed to represent some long distant era, but the Hurricanes and Spitfires had only appeared over the last couple of years.

'Sir?'

Alex turned. 'Yes.'

'I'll put you in a room with Pilot Officer Barratt. He's on 646 as well. I'll get somebody to carry your bags and show you the way.'

'Thank you.' He gave the girl a grateful smile.

'If you'd like to warn in, sir, I'll go and find somebody.'

Alex took out his pen and wrote in the leather-bound Warning–In Book on the counter. Pilot Officer A E Lowe; warning in, from Dinner 24 August until further notice; Living in; Posted in.

That was it. He'd arrived. He doubted the rest of the process would be as painless.

The WAAF returned with an airman in tow. Without making eye contact or uttering a word, the young man walked towards Alex, picked up the cases, turned about, and set off.

Alex thanked the receptionist and made off in pursuit.

Jack was trapped in a violent maelstrom, his body smashing painfully against every metal surface in the cockpit. It felt as if his Spitfire was tumbling through the air like the wing he'd seen earlier. His head and stomach were also spinning in confusion, the motion so disorientating that there were no visual clues beyond alternating light and dark.

Have I been unconscious? he thought. And if so, for how long?

The ground!

Fighting against the erratic g forces, and the urge to panic, he reached up and followed the cockpit arch to the canopy handle. He grabbed it and tugged. To his great relief, the canopy eased back and away.

'Bless you, Brummie,' he thanked his airframe fitter for his pedantic greasing and polishing of the canopy rails.

His head was upright now. Glimpses of blue sky and dark earth flashed past. But the motion was still too violent to allow him to focus. Thoughts of the ground galvanised him again. He lowered his hand to locate and remove the seat harness pin.

What if the eccentric motion trapped him in his seat?

He needn't have worried. With the pin out, he shot from the cockpit like a champagne cork from a bottle. He carried on tumbling though, and imagined the ground rushing up to meet him. Keeping his right arm close to his body, he located the D-ring and pulled. There was a tremendous jolt and the parachute webbing dug into his groin.

A new fear. Would his violent motion wrap him up in the parachute lines and stop the canopy opening? But, remarkably quickly, he found himself comforted by a gentle swaying motion, and looked up to see the silk fully deployed above him.

He was bruised, confused and motion sick, but, miraculously, still alive. He was also higher than he'd feared, perhaps 3,000 feet. Even so, at the rate he'd been falling, he'd have been little more than 15 seconds from death. There were a couple of fires on the ground, perhaps the remains of his tumbling tomb, but once again, he was alone in the sky.

The hot sweat coating his body was cooling in the airflow. He shivered and wondered if anyone had seen what had happened. The impacts had felt like gunfire, but the dramatic results more like the aftermath of a collision. And what about Johnny?

'Come on, Jack, no time for that.'

About 1,000 feet to go. Better get ready for touchdown. This was his first attempt at a parachute descent - they received no training - but he felt extremely lucky to be given the opportunity, whatever the outcome.

Light wind, so little drift, and it looked as if he was descending into a large field next to some farm buildings. Handy if he broke something when he hit the ground.

There was a large wood to his right, but he seemed to be well clear of it, and he'd be very unlucky to land in one of the trees dotting the hedgerows. There didn't seem to be any other obstacles.

At about 400 feet, he heard voices. Out to his left, a group of ten or 12 men were running towards him. He suddenly felt very vulnerable. Several thoughts collided. Had German bombers crashed nearby; or could they see the German writing on his Mae West, a gift from Binky; and were they armed, ready to shoot first and make enquiries later?

He beamed a friendly smile and thought about shouting, but decided that his Welsh accent drifting on the air might do more harm than good. Better to hold his tongue until he was safely on the ground. On second thoughts, if he was knocked out and they read the writing on his Mae West…

'RAF. Welsh. RAF.'

The grass came up fast and hit him hard. His legs crumpled, his chin hit his chest and he fell forward. He was winded, but didn't seem to have broken anything. After a few seconds, he groaned and rolled onto his back.

A tall bearded man stood over him brandishing a fearsome pitchfork. Before Jack could gather enough breath to speak, the face broke into a broad smile.

'Don't look so worried, Taffy, we heard you the first time.'

'You look a bit lost. Can I help?'

Alex had been ambling uncertainly down the corridor, following the smell of toast. He'd hoped to bump into someone eventually, but hadn't expected it to be a tall young WAAF officer. As usual in the presence of a pretty girl, he felt himself blush.

'Oh, Hello. Well yes. To tell the truth, I am a bit lost. I've only just arrived and I didn't expect it to be quite so quiet.'

'Isn't always, but it seems to have turned into a really busy day, so the pilots are all over at the squadrons, or airborne of course.'

The voice was pure public school. Alex still felt self-conscious about his own accent, especially the rounded r's he produced saying words like farm, bar or car. Not that the attractive young lady looked at all judgemental.

She continued. 'They're likely to be busy for some time yet I should think. Sophie Preston-Wright by the way. I work in the Sector Headquarters.'

She smiled and held out a pale, delicate, hand.

Alex felt himself blush even more deeply. He reached out and gave the hand a gentle squeeze.

'Alex Lowe. Pleased to meet you. I've just been posted in to 646 Squadron.'

'Oh well, you'll soon find out what I mean by busy then.'

He thought he spotted a hint of pity in her tone, and in her eyes. Pretty grey eyes, shining from a thin face framed by short black hair. Why couldn't he think of anything to say? Not just anything clever, but anything at all.

She seemed not to notice. 'There were a few of us in for tea and toast, but it's finished now I'm afraid. And I don't suppose you'll get another chance for a while, unless the weather breaks. Never many pilots in the Mess on a beautiful day like today. They'll be quite late back as well I should think.'

They stood facing each other, Alex still trying to

think of something to say.

'Well, the anteroom is just round the corner on the right, if you don't mind the smell of toast. Nice to meet you.'

And she was off, walking purposefully up the corridor.

'Nice to meet you too,' Alex shouted to her receding back.

He kicked himself for being so tongue-tied. He'd always been the same, but it had rarely seemed to matter so much before. Sophie Preston-Wright was a stunner, about his age or a bit older, and she must be all of five foot nine.

He walked on and looked in on the anteroom. It was comfortably furnished with dark wood coffee tables and plush leather armchairs, but it was depressingly empty, so he decided to retreat to his new room and unpack before dinner.

The ruddy cheeked farmer brushed off another of Jack's apologies for disrupting their routine.

'Don't worry. The lads here are only too glad of the break. Isn't that right, lads?'

He raised his glass in Jack's direction.

Jack acknowledged the cheers and gap-toothed grins. Most of 'the lads' were about 50 years old, more like a pirate crew than a group of farm labourers. But there was no doubting their contentment at his arrival, and the glasses of home made cider.

And he was enjoying himself as well, despite the discovery of a new bruise every time he moved. Not that he'd moved much since telephoning Biggin Hill. He was beginning to feel quite at home seated in a large carver in the stone-flagged kitchen. It was developing into quite a party.

Just as he was thinking that things could hardly be better under the circumstances, the farmer's short round wife appeared, bearing a plate of bread and ham.

It was always a bit nerve-wracking waiting to meet a new room-mate. Alex looked around at the utilitarian furnishings: two beds, two chests of drawers, two wardrobes, a table under the single window and two upright chairs. He was lounging on the bed that hadn't been covered in clothing, when the door opened. He jumped to his feet.

A young man entered. He was about Alex's age, blond-haired and blue-eyed as well, but several inches shorter, and with his left arm in a sling.

'Oh, hello,' he said cheerily, moving forward. 'Oliver Barratt, but everyone calls me Olly.'

'Alexander Lowe,' and, as they shook hands, 'Alex.'

'Welcome, Alex. I see you've managed to find somewhere to put your things. I hope I wasn't taking up too much room? I've been on my own for a couple of nights.'

'No, no, it was fine.'

'Are you staying or just passing through?'

'Staying I hope. I'm posted to 646 Squadron.'

'Ah, a jolly good choice if I may say so, old boy,' Olly said with a cut glass accent and a smile.

'Yes, the receptionist said you were on 646.'

'I am,' he said, looking down at his sling. Although I haven't been much use to them lately.'

'Is it painful?' Alex asked sympathetically.

'Not too bad now thanks,' the shorter man said, his mood darkening a little. 'A bit bloody frightening at the time though, I can tell you. Still, plenty of time for that.'

He looked up, smiling again as he changed the subject. 'What time do you have to report in the morning?'

'Not till eight thirty.'

'Oh good. That's when I'm pitching in. We'll leave a message for Jenkins to wake us both at seven, if that's all right with you?'

'Sounds fine,' Alex replied, relieved that more housekeeping details were falling into place.

'Then I suppose I'll have to put up with you being woken at four every morning.'

'Is it that early?'

'Fraid so, old boy, but Jenkins's tea will wake you up, don't you worry. Then you'll meet the rest in the dining room and get transport over with them. But you can come with me tomorrow.'

Leaning back and patting his stomach, Jack smiled gratefully at the farmer's wife. 'Thank you, Mrs Cleaver, but I couldn't eat another mouthful.'

He was overcome at their hospitality. While they'd continued to consume Farmer Cleaver's stocks of cider, his wife had laid on a magnificent meal. And not only for him, but the pirate crew as well. Between them, they must have eaten the couple out of house and home.

The farmer raised his glass for another in what was turning out to be a long succession of toasts. 'And here's to Fighter Command.'

The dining room was almost empty and they had a table to themselves. Alex discovered that Olly had been only a few weeks ahead of him in training, and they discussed their experiences, even discovering some mutual friends and acquaintances.

Afterwards, they moved into the anteroom and settled back into leather armchairs, ordering beers from the white-jacketed steward. As the man walked away, Alex looked around, disappointed not to see Sophie Preston-Wright in this room either.

He decided to broach the subject of Olly's sling. 'You said you'd tell me how you ended up like that?'

His new friend rubbed his arm. 'I did, didn't I? Not a very gallant or glorious story I'm afraid.'

His youthful face became more serious than Alex had seen it to date. 'It was a week ago, my third day on the Squadron. We'd flown twice the day before on convoy patrols, but hadn't seen any action. On the third morning, we were scrambled to meet an incoming raid.

'It's funny, but if you're like me, you'll find that time moves really slowly when you're waiting, and then it all happens too fast. One minute I was sitting there, then I was running across the grass, then in the air, then somebody shouted tally-ho, and I was heading into my first combat. Trouble was, my brain was still on the ground trying to catch up.'

The steward returned. They took their beers from the silver tray and thanked him as Olly signed his bar book. The man walked away and resumed his station by the anteroom door.

'Cheers.' Olly raised his glass and took a sip, before continuing. 'My section leader says he saw a Messerschmitt 110, but I'll have to take his word for it. I never saw anything, and it was all over before he could shout a warning.

'It seems a shell hit my glycol and oil tanks and the engine seized pretty shortly afterwards. I was braced for more, but they only made the one pass, then high-tailed it. Classic fighter pilot stuff.

'So I was left with a stationary propeller, while the rest of the squadron carried on regardless. Never saw another aircraft for the rest of the trip. I was going to jump, but apart from the engine, everything else seemed fine, so I decided to stick with it.'

He lifted his sling an inch or two. 'Might have been better under a brolly I suppose. But who knows, could have broken my bloody neck?

Alex smiled at the familiar jargon, and they both took another sip of beer.

'Anyway, couldn't see an airfield, so I picked a large field and headed for that.

'Went swimmingly until I touched down, wheels up so I didn't flip over and all that. But I must have been going a bit fast, or landed a bit long, because I hit the far hedge, clipped a tree and spun round. Cracked my arm in the process.

'Luckily, there was no fire and I managed to get out. Just a few bruises apart from this. And the kite wasn't too bad either, all things considered. The farmer was none too happy about his hedge, but you can't please everyone, can you?'

He patted his arm again. 'The Doc says I should have the sling off in a few days, and I could be back on ops next week. In the meantime, I nursemaid the new boys. Suspect I'll be looking after you tomorrow.'

Good, Alex thought. It would be nice to see at least one familiar face.

Jack's car had failed to arrive on time, and the farmer

had opened more cider while they waited. Two hours later, with the vehicle and driver in the lane, they were all a little the worse for wear; all bar the farmer's wife that is. Jack could see that her patience was wearing thin, guest or no guest.

In the lane, he steadied himself against the gatepost and, with as much formality as he could muster, said, 'Thank you for your hospitality.'

'That's quite alright,' the farmer replied.

Then, holding his hands up as if it was the first time he'd made the pun that evening, he giggled, 'Drop in any time'.

Jack made to laugh, but the sight of the farmer's wife rolling her eyes cut him short.

She was unwilling to admonish her husband in front of a guest, but there'd be harsh words once he'd gone, of that Jack was sure.

'I know, but thank you anyway,' he persisted. 'And especially you, Mrs Cleaver, for that marvellous meal.' He bowed.

The charm worked and Mrs Cleaver managed a smile.

'Just you keep givin' it to them Gerries,' Mr Cleaver sprayed through his bushy beard as Jack ducked into the car.

The couple moved into the lane and waved as the driver pulled away. Jack leaned out of the passenger window and, watching them recede into the gathering gloom, he waved in return.

There was a sudden commotion behind Alex. He turned to see a group of young men streaming noisily into the room. Olly rose from his chair, and he did the same, moving round to stand next to his room mate and face the newcomers.

A few acknowledged Olly and nodded at Alex as they passed the steward, inundating him with impatient orders for beer. They formed two distinct groups.

Olly leaned in towards Alex, 'Some are 646, but most are 32. Don't know many of them. You'll find we're pretty tribal, although I'm not sure whether I'm part of the tribe yet.'

As if in answer, a flight lieutenant with brown curly hair, a neat moustache and a pipe, shouted from the smaller group, 'Come on, Olly, come and join us, and bring your friend with you.'

Olly led them over.

'This is Alex Lowe. He'll be joining us tomorrow.'

There was a chorus of hellos.

'Hello,' Alex said self-consciously as he came to a halt next to the flight lieutenant. There were six in the group, a couple about his age, the others a few years older, but none beyond their early twenties he guessed. They looked dishevelled, their uniforms creased and their faces grubby, the darker haired sporting a hint of stubble. And despite their smiles, they all looked desperately tired, careworn beyond their years.

Was that what being in combat did to you?

He could sense them appraising him, but even as he blushed, he realised it wasn't his physical appearance they were interested in. They were asking the same questions he was asking of himself. Would he fit in? Did he have what it took? He felt the pressure ratchet up another notch.

'Are you coming down the pub, Olly?' one of the younger ones asked, breaking the silence with a marked antipodean twang.

'Not tonight, Smithy, thanks. Going to give the arm

a rest.'

'A poor excuse, mate, but I'll let you off just this once.'

Given the time and the way they looked, Alex was amazed they were contemplating going out. The steward arrived with a tray of beer and there was a brief hiatus as they claimed their drinks.

The flight lieutenant raised his tankard. 'Welcome to 646 Squadron, Alex.'

The others, including Olly, followed suit, and Alex blushed in acknowledgement, noting that all bar Olly took long draughts from their beers, sighing appreciatively as they lowered their glasses.

They weren't going to last long at that rate.

Formalities concluded, the rest of the group fell into more general chatter. After taking a long draw on his pipe and exhaling reflectively towards the ceiling, the flight lieutenant turned to Alex.

'The CO, Squadron Leader Parr, will speak to you tomorrow if he's got time, Alex, but I'm Mike Waters. I'm going to be your flight commander, for my sins.'

'Pleased to meet you, sir.'

'Never mind the sir, Alex, you're not in training now. Everyone calls me Muddy. You can do the same.'

'Sorry si.. Muddy.' They both smiled.

'How many hours have you got?'

'One hundred and eighty; one hundred and five solo,' Alex said with some pride.

'And on the Spit?'

'Thirteen.'

The flight commander drew on his pipe again, suddenly looking even more tired. He seemed to disappear into a reverie that Alex was reluctant to interrupt, but it lasted no more than a moment or two, and he snapped out of it as quickly as he'd drifted in.

'Well, that's good. Haven't had your reports yet. Probably won't see them for a day or two if past experience is anything to go by. Is there anything you think we should know?'

He took another long draught of beer, and Alex answered as honestly as he could. 'No, nothing really. I had a few problems with instrument flying and navigation early on, but nothing since then. I came out of advanced training as above average, and everything went pretty well at Aston Down.'

'Good. Unfortunately, you'll find we don't do things quite the way they do on the OTU, but you'll soon get the hang of it. Anyway, enough shop for one night. Apologies if I'm not around to say hello first thing tomorrow, but if it's anything like today, we'll probably be airborne when you pitch up.'

He drained his tankard. 'Anyway, good to have you aboard, Alex. Now if you'll excuse me, I'm going for a bath before we hit the bright lights. You're welcome to join us if you like. If not, see you tomorrow.'

As he walked out, putting his tankard on the steward's tray, he shouted over his shoulder, 'Transport in thirty minutes.'

The others downed their beers and followed in a noisy gaggle, leaving Alex and Olly standing several yards from the 32 Squadron group. They'd settled into armchairs, as if preparing for a longer stay.

'Where do they get the stamina from? They all look absolutely bushed, and if they've got to be up at four again tomorrow...?'

'I know. I can't keep up, and I'm not flying three or four times a day. Or perhaps that's why I can't keep up. I think they just need to unwind, and it sounds as if they've had a hard day. You're not going with them then?'

Alex shrugged. 'No, I took it as a rhetorical invitation. But I'd certainly like to have found out about their day.'

'I know, but I'm not sure they'd tell you much until you're one of the group. I found that when I first arrived. But I've just discovered that a couple of the chaps are missing, section leaders both of them. And two others bought it this afternoon.'

'I'm glad I didn't ask then. No wonder they go out for a beer.'

'Yes. You'll be doing it yourself in a few days no doubt.' Olly drained his tankard. 'Now, I'm going to have one more before turning in. Would you like one?'

'Well, Sergeant Williams, you've picked up an impressive range of bruises, but I don't think anything's broken.'

Jack had sobered up a fair bit during the drive to Biggin Hill. Driving in the blackout was a sobering thing anyway, being driven even worse, and it had been a slow journey. The Medical Officer's thorough prodding had seen off any residual effects of the cider, apart from a slight headache.

'I think you might be alright tomorrow, but I suggest you get a good night's sleep at least and see how you are in the morning. I'll get a message to the squadron that you won't be in until nine; that'll give you time to get in touch if there's a problem. You'll be bloody stiff if nothing else. Get back to me if you can't face sitting in a cockpit for a few days.'

'Thanks, Doc,' Jack winced as he swung his legs

off the bed. 'But I'm sure I'll be fine.'

He wasn't sure at all, but a lie in would be welcome and, as the MO had said, he'd see how he felt in the morning.

It was 11 o'clock by the time he got to his room in the Sergeants' Mess. He lay back and tried to ignore the loud snores and grunts of his roommates.

Was Binky similarly tucked up in the Officers' Mess, he wondered?

Chapter 2 – Monday 26th August 1940

Alex sprinted over the grass with the others.

All morning, he'd wondered if they could see how nervous he was, how he'd jumped every time the big black phone rang. Well, it didn't matter now. They were about to find out exactly what he was made of.

By the time he reached his pen, he was breathing heavily and had broken into a red-faced sweat. Occupying the centre of the small space was a Spitfire, rocking gently at low revs. He stopped at the left wingtip. Hands trembling, he donned his parachute and looked up at the machine he was about to board. For a moment, his breathless anxiety gave way to a feeling of immense pride, and responsibility. His aircraft. And his groundcrew.

Sandyman, his engine fitter, was sitting in the cockpit looking back at him. Mead, his airframe rigger, removed the starter plug and waved a greeting as he pulled the trolley clear.

Until joining the Squadron, Alex's biggest fear had been returning home to his parents in disgrace. Now, it was letting down the two young men before him. It was they he'd have to face first, and fear of failing them far exceeded fear of the enemy.

But that was probably because he couldn't yet envisage the enemy, or the reality of combat. All that would change in the next few minutes.

He waddled into the slipstream, parachute pack dangling beneath his bottom, and climbed onto the wing. Approaching the open cockpit, his nostrils flared at the familiar aroma of exhaust fumes.

Sandyman jumped out onto the other wing and turned to give him a gap-toothed grin.

Alex hesitated for a moment, then stepped in through the small cockpit door, sat, lifted the flying helmet from the stick and put it on.

Mead, who'd followed him up the wing, shut the door, and then he and Sandyman passed Alex the shoulder straps of his Sutton harness. Still breathing heavily, he fought to steady his hands long enough to insert the pin connecting the shoulder to the leg straps. By the time he'd done it, the two tradesmen were back on the ground, looking up at him. He took a deep breath and waved his hands in front of his face, the signal for them to remove the wheel chocks.

Only now did he look beyond the boundaries of the pen to take in the wider scene. The other Spitfires were on the move, weaving from side to side over the tufted grass.

Was he really going to join them?

He could see nothing to the front of his aircraft's long nose, and the cockpit suddenly seemed dark, claustrophobic and full of strange smells. Fighting off a rising sense of panic, he craned his neck towards the fresh air, took another deep breath and looked out to the right of the hazy propeller disc. His section leader, Sergeant Williams, Jack, taxyed past and gave him a thumbs-up. He returned the gesture, immediately feeling more relaxed for even this minimal display of control over his limbs. Piers taxyed past with a cheery wave.

Pulse racing, Alex opened the throttle. The engine roared and the aircraft rocked more violently.

He released the brakes and the Spitfire eased forward. Sandyman and Mead walked alongside, holding the wingtips.

When they'd cleared the pen, they waved him away

with forelock-touching salutes and smiles. Alex waved in return, trying to look more confident than he felt as they disappeared behind him.

Fittingly for the new boy, he was last in the line of 12 aircraft. He swung his Spitfire's nose from side to side to keep the others in sight, and was just beginning to feel more relaxed when they began turning into wind and forming vics of three in preparation for take off.

So little time. He looked around the cockpit, checking that all was as it should be.

Jack's Spitfire swung to the right and trundled forward a short distance before stopping 50 yards behind the third vic. Alex turned right and stopped with his left wingtip about ten yards to the right of Jack's tailplane. He was Blue 2. Piers, Blue 3, had now taken up a mirror image position on Jack's left.

Alex was still flustered, his heart jumping in his chest. It was all happening so fast. But any hope of a few seconds' respite was dashed by the CO's voice in his headset.

'Dragon, here we go.'

Feeling things running away from him, Alex opened the throttle and fought to stay in formation with Jack, Piers and the other nine aircraft, bouncing over the grass ahead of him.

Jack watched the section in front, rudders flicking as pilots fought the torque to keep their Spitfires in a straight line. The speed built up, the tailwheels of the lead aircraft lifted and they leapt into the air. He eased the stick forward to raise his own tailwheel and looked out to his right.

Good. Alex was holding in nicely.

He liked the new boy and hoped he'd last longer than some of the others, like Johnny. He hadn't found out about him until he'd entered the smoky atmosphere of his flight commander's office at 9 o'clock the day before, stiff and sore as the MO had warned.

'Ah, Jack, good of you to join me,' Muddy had joked, taking the pipe from his mouth.

'Well, you know how it is, Muddy,' he said wearily, slipping into their usual familiarity.

Rank etiquette could be difficult for outsiders to understand, but the protocol for NCOs using the first names of officers could be unfathomable even to those in the Service. It depended on so many factors: personality, experience, mutual respect, common sense. Jack had joined 646 at the same time as Muddy and Binky. They'd all had their first experience of combat over Dunkirk, and they'd become firm friends. It was the officers who'd told him to use their first names when they were alone, and Muddy had insisted he continue even when he became a flight commander.

'I thought I'd have a leisurely lie in and breakfast in bed.'

'Good for you, but I'm afraid the Hun decided to hold the war up until you arrived. How're you feeling?'

'Bit stiff, but I'll be all right. How did the rest of yesterday go?'

'A bit bloody really.' The flight commander adopted a more sombre tone. 'Johnny didn't make it I'm afraid.'

'Oh.' It was a disappointment, but not a surprise. 'That's a shame. I was trying to get a Snapper off his tail when my world fell apart.'

The young flight lieutenant drew on his pipe. 'You

must have succeeded then, because he landed after that. You had your tail shot off by the way. Smithy saw what was left of your kite falling away. Very impressive he said, but he didn't see a parachute. And we didn't get your message yesterday afternoon, so we didn't know you were alive until the boys came in this morning. No, we were scrambled again and Johnny disappeared before we got to height. Piers said he kept dropping back in the climb. He tried to chivvy him on, but he didn't seem to be listening. Then he saw some Snappers above, and next time he looked back, he was gone. We don't really know what happened, but the wreck was found near Maidstone. No news of anyone being picked up yet, I'm afraid.'

'Don't suppose there will be either,' Jack said sadly. 'As soon as I saw his face before we dived in, I knew I should have asked you to take him off ops.'

'It's no good blaming yourself, Jack. Perhaps I should have made time for that chat we were going to have, but…

'Okay, Muddy, I get the message. Heard anything from Binky?'

'Yes. Hit by return fire from a Dornier we think. Managed to bale out, but he's badly burned I'm afraid. Critical, and they're not sure whether he's going to pull through.'

'Where is he?'

'East Grinstead. I'll give you the details later if you like.'

'Yes please.'

They all dreaded fire; after all, they were sitting right behind the fuel tanks, and burns were a certainty if they were hit and didn't bale out straight away. He'd heard of pilots carrying a pistol to finish themselves off if they were trapped in a fire. Even he wasn't sure he'd want to survive if he was badly burned.

He resolved to visit his friend at some stage, burns or no burns.

'Just before I was hit, I thought I saw the aftermath of a collision?'

Muddy Waters blew a long stream of blue smoke into the fug already swirling around the office ceiling.

'Yes. Sgt Thomson.'

And, in answer to Jack's raised eyebrow. 'The older of the two that arrived yesterday morning.'

'First bloody trip! They don't stand a chance, do they?'

'Seems not, but it's not just the new boys copping it, witness you and Binky. And let's face it, we need them. I don't know how we're going to carry on if we keep losing pilots at this rate. Thank goodness you're alright, or we'd be looking for another section leader – not that I don't value you as a human being as well, old boy.'

'Thank you very much' Jack said in mock appreciation, and they both laughed.

'Anyway, I've given Green Section to Smithy. I know he's even less experienced than usual, but we'll just have to make the best of it. Speaking of which, your new Blue 2 is Pilot Officer Alex Lowe. You can't miss him, he's seven foot tall. Well, six foot three at least, blond hair, blue eyes, that sort of thing. Not sure how he fits in a Spit, but he's managed it for all of thirteen hours, one hundred and eighty in total.'

Jack looked to his right and smiled at the eccentric porpoising of Alex's Spitfire. As if it wasn't difficult enough flying a formation take off with only 13 hours on type, once airborne, you had to swap hands and pump the undercarriage up manually. It could take a long time before you were able to pump with your right hand and hold the stick still with your left. Some never managed it. Alex looked composed though, and his aircraft settled as soon as the gear was up.

The CO's voice crackled in Jack's headset, 'Bastion, Dragon squadron airborne.'

'Roger, Dragon. This is Bastion, vector one zero zero, one hundred bandits approaching Dover Folkestone, angels one seven.'

Alex was relieved to be flying at the back of the squadron. It meant that few eyes witnessed the meal he'd made of retracting the undercarriage. He put his right hand back on the stick, moved his left over to the throttle and steadied the yo-yoing. Then, as Jack had told him, he eased out to a wider position, allowing him to look for enemy aircraft as well as formate on his leader.

Like so many things he'd been told in the last two days, it made perfect sense, even if it did contradict much of what he'd been taught in flying training, where tight formation flying was the pinnacle of achievement.

His first day had turned out much as Olly had predicted. First, he'd spent an hour or so with the Adjutant. The kindly old gent had shown him round and helped him fill in a blizzard of forms. Then, he'd had arrival interviews, first with the CO, a wiry, dark-haired squadron leader who oozed a sense of calm authority, then his flight commander, the pipe-smoking flight lieutenant he'd met in the bar the previous evening.

They'd said similar things – 'Welcome to the

Squadron… fine bunch of chaps… don't worry too much… soon pick things up… any problems give me a shout.'

Most importantly though, they'd told him he was to join Blue Section under Sergeant Jack Williams, one of the most experienced pilots on the Squadron.

But it was Olly that grabbed him as he came out of the flight commander's office. He showed him how to prepare his Spitfire for a quick getaway and took him to be issued with his flying kit. And when Alex had loaded the jumble of equipment and clothing into his newly-allocated locker, his new friend held out a navy and white silk scarf.

'You better have this as well.'

'No, I couldn't, Olly.' Alex blushed at the thoughtfulness of the gesture. 'I'll get one next time I go shopping.'

'Don't be daft. You'll have no skin on your neck after the first trip if you stick to that collar, and it'll throttle you if you end up in the sea. Anyway, you should jump at the chance to wear Bedford School colours.'

'I'm not so sure about that,' Alex scoffed playfully, 'but thanks anyway.'

Ludlow Grammar School colours were more flamboyant: bright crimson, navy and light blue stripes, but he didn't think they'd had a silk scarf.

And finally, he'd met Jack. The sergeant pilot was lounging in a deckchair outside a Spitfire pen, enjoying the sun. As he approached, Jack made an exaggerated display of trying to get his wiry frame out of the deckchair, before falling back in defeat.

'Excuse me if I don't get up, sir, but now I'm in this contraption, I'm not sure I can get out.'

Alex had heard about Jack's ordeal. He laughed at the performance and gestured the man to remain in his seat. 'It's quite all right….' He suddenly realised he wasn't sure how to address the person before him. After a self-conscious pause, he rounded off with, '…Sergeant Williams.'

He lowered himself to the grass in front of the deckchair, sensing the man's dark eyes appraising him. 'It looks as if you're in pain.'

'Oh, it's not so bad. Well certainly not as bad as it could have been.'

It was a Welsh accent, but not very broad.

'You must be Pilot Officer Lowe?'

'Yes. Alex Lowe,' he said, feeling himself colour. He wished he knew what the rank etiquette on the squadron was. It had all been very formal in flying training. He'd always used the rank and surname of his NCO instructors, and they'd always called him sir, even though they were the ones teaching him to fly.

'Jack Williams, sir.' The Welshman held out his hand. 'You can call me Jack, and I'll call you sir, for a while at least.' He smiled.

Alex reached forward and shook the outstretched hand. Beneath an unruly mop of curly black hair, his section leader had a thin face with high cheekbones and a square jaw. He also had a prominent broken nose, a feature that seemed to make him more rather than less handsome. The man was only a few years older, but Alex sensed a wealth of experience and a quiet confidence that immediately put him at ease.

'Thank you – Jack.' He laughed nervously. 'There are so many things I haven't a clue about.'

'Don't worry, sir, no doubt the CO and Flight Lieutenant Waters have already said you'll soon get the hang of it.'

They'd gone on to talk for hours. The only scramble had been late in the afternoon, and it had been for A Flight only, so he hadn't had to fly on his first day.

But he was flying now, his field of view dominated by Spitfires, gently bobbing around as they maintained formation. It was just after midday, and apart from some very high cloud, it was bright and clear, sunshine glinting on the metal and perspex of the aircraft ahead.

Much to his relief, his heart rate and breathing had slowed, and the rising sense of panic that had threatened to overwhelm him had subsided. Nonetheless, he was still worried about what was to come.

What was to come?

Jack had told him to forget the fighter attack profiles he'd learnt on the Operational Training Unit. Over Dunkirk, they'd discovered it was better to make the first attack from above, with sections alongside one another if possible, in line abreast.

And once the first contact was over, it was every man for himself. If you could, you climbed again and attacked in slow time, but the enemy fighters were likely to have intervened before then, so you were more likely to end up firing on targets of opportunity as they flashed past.

Alex was sure it was good advice, but he felt his fragile confidence seeping away as he tried to envisage the reality of implementing it.

'Blue 2. Keep those eyes moving.'

He'd let his thoughts overwhelm him. He gave Jack a thumbs-up and renewed his search for enemy aircraft.

Jack smiled. Alex had positively jumped at the sound of his callsign. Looked steady enough now though, holding formation 20 yards away, eyes quartering the sky. What with his lack of mobility, and Ginge being away, Jack didn't think he'd ever spent so much time with a new boy. The young officer had seemed quite content to sit there, and he'd given him as much gen as he could without them getting airborne. Piers had joined them for much of the time.

'Dragon, this is Bastion, bandits in your ten o'clock, angels one seven.'

Good, Jack thought. Once again, they were down sun of the bandits, and they were climbing above them.

Although Jack had warned him to keep his eyes looking for wandering fighters, Alex couldn't resist glancing to the left. He immediately wished he hadn't.

They were stalking a huge rectangular formation of what looked like hundreds of dark shapes, some bigger than others, but all equally sinister, invaders, intent on wreaking destruction on the peaceful countryside below.

What use were their 12 Spitfires against such numbers?

His stomach tightened, and he was steeling himself to make a sighting report to the leader, when the CO's voice broke in.

'Bastion, this is Dragon Leader. Tally ho, tally ho. More like one hundred and fifty though, repeat one hundred and fifty bandits, ten o'clock, slightly low.'

'Roger, Dragon Leader, this is Bastion, understand one hundred and fifty. Good luck. Bastion out.'

Alex was impressed at the calmness of both voices, although the Controller must be under less pressure, sitting in the Sector Headquarters, looking at attractive WAAFs like Sophie. A brief image of the tall WAAF officer flashed into his mind. They'd had another quick chat the previous evening, nothing consequential, but thinking of her made him even more determined not to fail.

They turned left to position above and behind the enemy and he recalled more of his section leader's words. 'You don't necessarily have to shoot them down, just get among them. Scatter them. Stop them hitting their targets, or at least reduce their accuracy. You could even make them jettison their bombs early.'

Sweat tickled Alex's brow and top lip as he tried to imagine the reality of getting amongst them.

'Dragon, line abreast, line abreast, go.'

The sections in front moved to left and right and eased forward. Unbidden, he edged closer to his leader, now guiding Blue Section to the extreme left of the line.

So this was it. Again, he relied on Jack's advice to prepare himself and his aircraft for the imminent combat: rpm to 2650, emergency boost override, reflector sight on, gun button to fire, lower the seat a notch and tighten the straps. Finally, on his own initiative, he checked his oxygen for about the tenth time; apparently, not switching it on was one of the easier methods to lose consciousness and become a statistic.

More words of wisdom rushed to the fore. 'Never relax. Never fly in a straight line. Keep looking around. Weave like mad if something latches onto you. Fly the aircraft to its limits.'

Once again, he didn't doubt the advice, only his ability to carry it out. And would his limits coincide with those of his Spitfire? He was about to find out.

'Dragon, here we go, good luck lads, and save some for me.'

Alex smiled, relaxing a little at the CO's words. The noses of the aircraft to either side of him dipped. He eased the stick forward to follow suit, relieved that his main emotion seemed to be excitement rather than fear.

Sophie watched the counters being moved across the plotting table by her WAAFs. She didn't usually take much notice of which squadrons were going into action, preferring to stay focused on the overall picture and make sure 'her girls' were doing their jobs properly.

Of course, she couldn't totally forget that the pilots she met in the Mess were attacking vast formations of German aircraft. And sometimes, screams from the Ops Room speaker brought the harsh reality to the fore. It could be immensely moving, especially when you recognised the voice, then went on to see an empty place at dinner. But generally, she was able to distance herself from the detail of the constant radio chatter. Not today, though, for some reason.

She'd been spending a lot of time with 629 lately, but Bunter was becoming a pain. Just because their parents knew each other, he seemed to think he could monopolise her. But it wasn't his squadron's Soho callsign that made her ears prick up. It was 646 Squadron: Dragon.

Even after the briefest of chats the previous evening, she couldn't help thinking about the tall, blushing, pilot. Was he getting his first taste of combat? If so, she hoped he'd come through unscathed.

With their dark paint schemes and black crosses, the phalanx of twin-engined Heinkel 111 bombers looked as evil as Alex had imagined. In contrast, the Spitfires diving alongside him looked magnificent. He knew he was on the side of right.

He wound the 111's wingspan into his reflector sight. They were diving at over 400 miles an hour, the fastest he'd ever flown. Tracer shot ahead of the Spitfire on his right.

A bit early, he thought. His gunsight confirmed it. They were closing remarkably quickly, but were still not at 250 yards. Despite his eagerness, he followed Jack's advice and held his fire.

An urgent voice. 'Snappers four o'clock high.'

He swung his head. Four Messerschmitt 109s. Rods of light. Growing. Flashing past. The size of light bulbs. He froze, his mind overwhelmed by the sudden onset, the immediacy of the threat. For the first time in his life, he knew what it was to be paralysed with gut-wrenching fear.

A sickening thump. A jagged hole in his right wingtip. Should he pull toward the fighters?

The bombers!

To his front, a terrified Heinkel top gunner. The man raised his arms.

Alex pulled and waited, flinching. Somehow, the impact never came. He soared upwards. A Spitfire canopy almost stroked his right wingtip. The other pilot's startled expression mirrored his own.

The violent manoeuvre had disorientated him, the g drawing the blood from his brain, dimming his vision and making him see stars. He recognised the tingling cold sweat and dry mouth of approaching airsickness, a sensation he hadn't experienced since his first attempts at aerobatics many months earlier. The screams in his headset only added to his confusion and rising sense of panic.

He took a deep breath and forced his eyes to focus ahead, hoping for a few seconds' respite. A dark shape appeared in his peripheral vision. He looked right. Three hundred yards away, a twin engined Messerschmitt 110 was lining up for an attack.

Alex pulled hard right.

Jack witnessed Alex's near collision with the Heinkel as he flashed beneath his own target.

He was sure he'd hit the bomber, but there'd been no visible signs of damage. Safely past, he looked for Alex again, but could see no sign of him, or Piers for that matter. He hoped he wouldn't lose another wingman, but there was nothing he could do for them now, so he concentrated on his own battles.

His limbs still ached from his buffeting two days before, but he ignored the pain as he weaved aggressively in and out of the enemy formation. He failed to latch on to any one target, firing his guns in short bursts as fighters and bombers appeared ahead of him. He'd followed the formation for about 20 miles inland before his ammunition gave out and he dived for the relative safety of a low level transit back to Biggin Hill.

Alex woke with his head down, almost between his knees.

Where was he?

His mouth was dry and he felt like death. But what

was that noise?

Frantic shouts and, an…an engine.

The Messerschmitt? Where was the Messerschmitt?

Wincing in pain, he sat up and opened his eyes. His head was spinning, but so was the world outside. Fast. Too fast to think clearly or focus on anything. Nothing made sense. Why not just lean back and close his eyes?

Spinning?

The ground!

Finally jolted into lucidity, he realised the true danger. He was plummeting earthwards. Had been for some time. He looked ahead and grasped the controls.

'Spinning right. Full left rudder. Stick forward.'

The green fields kept spinning. He was on the verge of panic. Then, with a violent jolt, the rotation stopped. Still with no idea of how far above the ground he was, he closed his eyes and pulled, groaning against the g, fighting not to retch.

When he felt himself soaring upwards, he opened his eyes, and then the canopy, gulping fresh air. He looked at the altimeter. Ten thousand feet.

When he'd pulled to avoid the Messerschmitt, he must have blacked out. And he'd fallen 7,000 feet while unconscious, or struggling to regain consciousness. A few seconds more and he'd have had too little height to recover from the spin, or take to his parachute. It was a minor miracle he'd survived long enough to wake up; he must have been a sitting duck.

But what a cock-up. He'd been in combat for no more than a few seconds before he'd fallen out of it, and he hadn't fired a single round of ammunition.

For a fleeting moment, he toyed with the idea of firing his guns and concocting a story of a prolonged battle with the fighter that had holed his wing. Given the chaos up there, the chances of being caught in a lie seemed pretty remote.

But no. It wasn't him.

He just hoped he wasn't sick all over the cockpit. That really would put the seal on a perfect start to life as a fighter pilot.

He still felt weak and vulnerable. His hands were shaking and cold sweat coated his body. The chatter in his headset had ceased, and the sky was empty, but…?

Where am I?

The ground seemed completely featureless and another wave of panic threatened.

Then he spotted a large town. A bit of a long shot given his lack of local knowledge, but it could be Ashford. He checked his directional gyro and compass, and set what he hoped was a sensible heading for Biggin Hill.

Crestfallen at his abject failure, he started a gentle descent. The countryside trundled past, its verdant beauty lost to his depression. Just as new doubts were surfacing, he spotted what he was fairly sure was Maidstone, out to the right, and then Sevenoaks appeared on the nose. More confident of his navigation at last, his mind raced ahead to the next problem: landing. It was another skill he hadn't totally mastered yet.

Joining the circuit at Biggin Hill, he was surprised to find himself in the company of other aircraft. He'd thought they would all be home by now, waiting to hear his tale of humiliation. But there were other Spitfires, and Hurricanes, some still in the air, some landing, and others taxying across the airfield.

Oh for the luxury of a few practice approaches. But

this was not the time, so he set himself up on a curving final approach, taking care to identify his intended touchdown point before it disappeared under the high nose as he lined up.

Relax, he told himself unsuccessfully.

The hedge passed beneath – a little too close for comfort. He closed the throttle and held on for what turned out to be a reasonable three-pointer.

Reaching the end of his landing run, he turned to follow another Spitfire towards the waiting groundcrew.

'Flaps up and radiator shutter open' he said aloud, as if seeking verbal evidence of his own existence.

He'd survived his first scramble – just!

Jack turned off the landing area just behind Alex, very relieved to see him. But he could tell from the youngster's body language that all was not well. He vowed to give him as much support as he could over the next few hours.

As Alex approached the pen he'd left less than an hour earlier, his two groundcrew jogged out to grab his wingtips. Sandyman was a stocky, rugby playing Welshman with prematurely receding brown curly hair, and Mead, a tall, red-haired Liverpudlian, mad on football. Both were smiling now, Mead pointing at the jagged hole in his right wingtip.

What were they going to think of him when they heard how he'd performed?

He swung the Spitfire round to point away from the pen, applied the brake and answered Sandyman's throat-cutting signal by pulling the engine cut out. After a few backfires, the propeller stopped, and the cockpit filled with fumes. Alex leaned back and ran his hand over his face, letting the sudden silence wash over him.

'Brakes off. *Brakes off.'*

From the exasperated tone, he realised he must have dozed off. Sure enough, when he looked out, more groundcrew had appeared. They were leaning against the leading edges of the wings looking up at him.

'Brakes off,' he shouted, releasing the brakes and staying alert as he was pushed back into the pen.

'Brakes on.'

'Brakes on,' he replied immediately.

By the time he'd removed his headset, Sandyman was leaning over to take his shoulder straps.

'That must have made your eyes water, sir,' he smiled, pointing towards the wingtip.

'Yes, it certainly woke me up.' A bad choice of words he realised, as he'd put himself to sleep very shortly afterwards.

'Everything alright apart from that, sir?'

'Yes thanks, Sandyman. She was fine.'

'Good, and Scouse says he'll probably be able to patch the hole up 'til cease flying, if he gets time before the next shout, that is.'

The next shout. He suddenly realised he might have to do all this again, and sooner rather than later. His heart sank.

'Well, you'll have pleased the armourers at least,' the engine fitter said cheerily.

They'd spotted the strips of material glued over the gun holes to stop moisture getting in.

'Yes. I'm afraid I didn't get a single shot off,' Alex said sheepishly.

'Not to worry, sir. It looks to me as if you're lucky

to be here at all.'

The Welshman seemingly refused to have his spirits dampened, or to be anything other than positive about his pilot's performance.

'I suppose you're right, Sandyman. Thanks.'

Alex watched the engine fitter scamper down the wing. Perhaps the groundcrew were trained in psychology. It would have been all too easy for them to crush his confidence altogether, but they'd managed to raise his spirits. Not that they'd have thought it if they'd heard the weary sigh as he climbed out of the cockpit. The movement brought on a fresh bout of queasiness.

Jack stopped outside his pen to wait for Alex. New boys always took a bit longer to unstrap and sort things out with the groundcrew. Most of the others were already milling round the Intelligence Officer, standing in his usual spot, clipboard at the ready.

When Alex eventually appeared, he turned paler with every step of his approach, about as far from the blushing complexion of the day before as could be imagined. Even his lips were white, and he looked as if he was about to throw up.

'All right, sir?' Jack asked, trying to hide the concern in his voice.

'Actually, Jack, I feel a bit sick.'

'That's okay, sir. I bet it's a fair while since you manoeuvred like that. Just hold it here for a few seconds. There's no rush.'

He watched Alex lean against the blast wall, then tried to strike a positive note.

'You did well to miss that Heinkel.'

'Thanks, but I'm afraid I made a mess of everything

after that.'

Oh dear. He really was down, but at least he looked a bit less pale.

'Why, what happened, sir?'

'I'm pretty sure I blacked out.'

'Bloody frightening, isn't it?'

'Yes.' There was a short pause. 'Have you done it then, Jack?'

'Oh yes. On my second trip over Dunkirk. I woke up twitching and wondering where the hell I was. Luckily, I couldn't have been out long. How about you?'

'I don't know, but it must have been a while. I woke up in a spin, and I didn't recover till ten thousand feet.'

Jack was quietly pleased. Alex's conversation was becoming more animated and some colour had returned to his cheeks.

'Wow. Sounds much worse than mine.'

'I don't mind telling you, I was scared to death.'

'I'm not surprised, sir. Do you feel up to a stroll?' He held his arm out towards the Intelligence Officer, 100 yards away.

'Yes, I feel a bit better now, thanks.'

They set off at a slow pace, the blond-haired officer towering five inches above the dark-haired NCO.

'When did you black out?' Jack asked.

'Not long after I avoided the Heinkel. I spotted a 110 about to take a shot, so I pulled. And that was that.'

'It's amazing what adrenalin can do. You were probably still doing about four hundred miles an hour, and a good hefty tug at that speed racks up the g in no time. It'll knock you out before you know what's happening.'

'As I found out.' Alex smiled for the first time.

Jack looked up into his face. 'You've done really well to make it back in one piece after an experience like that, sir. Well done.'

He patted the young man's shoulder lightly, and repeated, 'Well done.'

They were within yards of the pipe-smoking Nick Hudson, and Jack made a final, conspiratorial, remark. 'But it sounds to me as if you don't have much to tell the IntO, do you?'

Sitting on the grass outside the dispersal hut, Alex related his experience to Olly and Piers. By the time he'd finished, even he thought some of it sounded funny, and he was feeling much better. The story drew another unexpected response, this time from Piers.

'I almost blacked out once,' he said, flicking the ash from his cigarette. 'Saw nothing but stars for a while, even after I eased the pull. I was shit scared, I can tell you. The last thing I'd seen was a 109. But I don't think he could take the g either, or didn't trust his kite. They say the wings snap off if they pull too hard.'

Olly joined in, a wicked grin on his face. 'Even so, I guess the trick is not to pull so hard you end up unconscious, and in a spin, isn't that right, Alex?'

He gave Alex a playful push and they all laughed.

'Seriously though,' Piers continued, stubbing the cigarette out on the grass, 'a lot of the old hands say they've done the same. They reckon quite a few that buy it in the early trips have probably blacked out, and either crashed or been shot down. So, I guess we must be among the lucky ones.'

'Didn't feel very lucky at the time,' Alex joked.

What with Jack's little chat, and this talk with his

new friends, he was feeling much more sanguine about his first combat. But he was dreading what the second might hold.

'Well, let's hope you both stay lucky,' Olly piped, seeming to capture the change of mood.

'And you, when you stop malingering with that bloody sling.'

Piers refused to be serious, and Alex joined in the laughter.

'Just wait 'til the doc takes it off. I'll teach you to call me a malingerer.'

Jack sensed he didn't need to worry too much about Alex. The young man had suffered a rude awakening, but, joking with Piers and Olly Barratt, he looked okay for now. It might be different if something similar happened during his next sortie, but they'd cross that bridge when they came to it.

At least he looked better than the young sergeant who'd been so full of bravado when he'd arrived three days ago. Like Alex, he'd just had his first contact with the enemy, but he was still ashen. Dusty Miller was trying to engage him in conversation, but didn't seem to be having much success.

Not my concern, thank goodness, Jack thought, feeling guilty at his sense of relief.

He turned and walked away from the dispersal hut, wincing with each step. He'd proved he could fly with his aches and pains, but he still wasn't up to running, so he hobbled over to sit outside his pen, and to consider his domestic predicament.

After their thorough blooding over Dunkirk, the Squadron had been sent to recover and rebuild at Pembrey, in south west Wales. It had been close enough to Barry Island for him to spend much more time with Gwen than over the previous three years. But the proximity hadn't strengthened their relationship in the way he'd assumed.

It wasn't Gwen's fault. She was still a great girl, beautiful and bubbly. It was him. He'd changed, first with pilot training, then with flying in combat. He'd also decided that, if he survived, he would make a career of the RAF. But all she wanted was for him to get a regular job in Barry. That way, she wouldn't have to leave her family and friends.

He'd begun to realise there was a widening gulf in their aspirations, but just how wide only became apparent that night on the beach. What a night! He imagined himself back on the sand of Whitmore Bay, leaning over Gwen, eyes becoming accustomed to the dark.

He revelled in the sight and the softness of her breasts, while her little gasps of excitement added to his arousal. His doubts about the strength of their relationship were evaporating. Perhaps they were made for one another after all.

After several enjoyable minutes, he became bolder and played a hand slowly down her body. She stiffened slightly, but he continued, stroking over her stomach, lower and lower, until his fingers rested between her thighs. Her legs eased apart and he felt a palpable sense of triumph. He cupped his hand, teasing his fingers against the thin material of her skirt.

'That's enough of that, Jack!'

She brushed his hand away and sat up. Before he could react or remonstrate, she was on her feet and dusting herself down.

'There'll be plenty of time for that sort of thing.'

He felt a flash of anger.

'For you maybe, but not for me.'

He regretted it as soon as he'd said it. But at least when she asked what he meant, he'd be able to give her an idea of the dangers he was about to face. Surely, then she'd understand.

But the question never came, and her next words served only to underline how different they were in aspiration and temperament.

'Don't be so stupid, Jack. I don't know what's come over you lately. There'll be plenty of time for... for that sort of thing when you come back to Barry.'

Didn't she realise he had to experience 'that sort of thing' now, because he might never get another chance? Although ops from Pembrey had had their moments, they were nothing compared to what he was about to face. He might not survive the next day, let alone until they found time to be married. As to what they were doing, she'd spat out the words as if it was the most sordid activity in the world, instead of the most wonderful.

But he knew he could never put any of these thoughts into words. Not to Gwen anyway.

And there was more. He wanted to shout, I'm not coming back to Barry.

Oh, there was nothing wrong with Barry. He would have said the same wherever he'd lived. He just needed to get away, to forge a life beyond the narrow boundaries of his home town.

He'd known in that moment that Gwen could never be part of his life. Even if he pretended otherwise and persuaded her to follow him to wherever he happened to be based, she'd be miserable, pining for the familiarity of Barry Island and its folk.

Now, outside the pen, he regretted not trying to talk things through at the time. But he'd reasoned that his anger was partly born of sexual frustration, while the last thing he'd wanted was to end his leave with a row. So, he'd walked Gwen home in silence.

It had been an unsatisfactory parting, and it would take time to sort out, because he didn't want to break up by letter or telephone. He owed it to her to make it face to face.

Sitting in the sun next to his Spitfire, he wondered when that would be. The sooner the better, because only then could he imagine himself losing his virginity, something he was even more desperate to do after that night on the beach.

Alex was scared.

He'd perked up on the ground, but now they were airborne again, he felt sick. And this time, he was sure it was nothing to do with motion or claustrophobia. It was a physical manifestation of the fear that had come over him as soon as he'd clipped the oxygen mask over his mouth.

Jack's Spitfire was just ahead and to his left, and the Welshman was looking back at him. He tried to make his eyes smile.

He'd even managed to eat some lunch, but the meal didn't seem such a good idea now. It was threatening to reappear. He swallowed hard.

His first experience of combat had been so brief it hardly seemed to count, but it had lasted long enough for him to become all too aware of the pace at which things developed.

He doubted he'd ever be able to cope. After all, he'd been paralysed with fear at the sight of the first

Messerschmitt, convinced he was about to die, but unable to do anything about it. And although he'd managed to move eventually, it had only been just in time to avoid a collision with the bomber he was meant to be attacking.

The only positive thing was his speedy reaction to the sight of the second Messerschmitt, the 110; but even that didn't stand up to close scrutiny. Blacking out and falling from the fray without firing a shot were hardly grounds for self-congratulation.

So, he seemed to have plenty to be fearful about.

'Dragon, this is Bastion, one hundred and fifty bandits, angels one five, approaching Margate. Vector one zero zero.'

One hundred and fifty! He looked at the 11 Spitfires ahead and to his left.

'Bastion, this is Dragon Leader, roger, passing angels one two.'

The two voices sounded completely untroubled by the ludicrous odds. Didn't the Controllers ever say ten bandits, or twelve?

Suddenly, the Spitfire 50 yards ahead banked sharply right and entered a descending turn, falling rapidly away from the formation.

'Green 2, where are you going?' snapped an Australian voice.

'S-sorry, Green Leader,' a frightened falsetto replied. 'H-high oil temperature and engine vibration. Returning to base.'

After a short pause, the Australian came back, still sounding tetchy, 'Roger, Green 2.'

Then, as if undergoing a change of heart, he took on a more sympathetic tone. 'Good luck.'

There was no reply from Green 2.

Alex watched Sergeant Ellis's Spitfire diving away. For the briefest of moments, he wondered whether he should follow and seek the sanctuary of Biggin Hill himself. But it was only a fleeting thought. His fear of failure was still stronger than his fear of the enemy, or perhaps he wasn't brave enough to admit his frailty and run away.

'Blue 2.'

He gave an immediate thumbs-up to acknowledge the gentle rebuke. He was desperate not to let Jack and the others down, but he was even less sure than three hours ago that he could succeed.

'Come on, Alex, pull yourself together.'

He took a series of deep breaths and, as he continued to look for enemy aircraft, he tried to appreciate the beauty around him: the Spitfires moving gently up and down in the watery sunlight, the green of the countryside, church spires and towers marking the villages and towns.

But the bubbling fear kept his sickness to the fore, while his palms oozed sweat and his hands shook. He swallowed hard and cursed his weakness.

Jack could only guess at the turmoil in Alex's mind. The eyes never lied, and he could tell the young man was fighting an inner battle.

He had periods of apprehension himself, but he was fortunate that he only seemed to experience gut-wrenching fear when he was threatened with imminent destruction.

And even then, he'd so far managed to avoid the torpor or paralysis that some seemed to exhibit. He hoped it stayed that way.

At least Alex hadn't chickened out when he'd heard

the odds, unlike Green 2. It was a harsh judgement to make on Smithy's new wingman, but Jack had recognised a familiar quality in the young sergeant's voice. He'd heard it several times before. The cracking timbre was the outward sign of a fear that could no longer be contained, that had become so overpowering the sufferer had to turn his back on the enemy, and his comrades, and run.

And yet it was not contempt that Jack felt, but pity. It could happen to anyone, at any time, and sometimes it happened to the very best.

He looked back at Alex, holding his Spitfire in perfect formation, its clean lines framed against a background of startling white cumulus. Hopefully, he'd be able to overcome, or at least contain, his fear.

Sophie felt the tremor from the first bomb even before the Controller ordered them to put on their tin helmets. She also sensed a tightening in her stomach. You felt so helpless. The Sector HQ was better protected than some buildings on the Station, but it wouldn't survive a direct hit.

Or a near miss, she mused, as another tremor caused a fall of dust from the thick concrete ceiling.

Her girls were still raking counters over the map as if nothing untoward was happening. She felt a flush of pride. It wasn't only the pilots who faced danger and showed bravery. Thinking of the aircrew brought her focus back to the plotting table.

The counter for the massive raid, Hostile 24, was being closed on by several Fighter Command squadrons. But way in front of the rest was Dragon. They were likely to meet the enemy very soon. She wondered whether Alex was with them again.

From the little Alex knew about it, the Controller and the CO seemed to be climbing them in text book fashion between the enemy formation and the sun. This looked more promising. But then came a warning shout.

'Snappers, seven o'clock high, coming in.'

Another voice shouted, 'Dragon, break break.'

Spitfires flew in all directions: Jack almost straight up, Piers up and left. Beyond them, a dozen 109s, diving down, firing as they came. Alex rolled left and pulled, grunting at the onset of g. His vision dimmed. His head and limbs became lead weights.

He was scared, although not paralysed this time. But he'd pulled straight into the buffet. His Spitfire shuddered around him. The left wing dropped. Another spin.

A dark shape flashed past. He centralised the controls, but his aircraft continued to rotate. Panic threatened. Then, a sudden jolt, and the rolling motion ceased. Upside down.

'Behind you Smithy…Break left Boy…' The frantic calls added to his disorientation.

Blocking them out, he rolled upright. Cold steak pie and carrots rose into the back of his throat. He swallowed, wincing at the sour taste and looked around. To his front, an enormous formation of bombers, all black crosses and swastikas. To his right, more Messerschmitts, dozens of them. No tracer yet.

'Get out of here, Alex.'

He rolled hard right, pulled, then levelled the wings and shot beneath the bomber stream. He was breathing fast, hyperventilating. Trickles of cold sweat ran down his body.

Fighting to control his breathing, he tried to ignore the large shapes passing menacingly above. In the distance, aircraft dropped from the formation trailing smoke. Smaller shapes chased them down, threading in and out, like tiny bees attacking a swarm of invading hornets. A confusing cacophony of cries assailed his ears.

Pinpoints of light set out from two of the nearest bombers. Instinctively, he pulled up, then realised what was above him. By some miracle, he shot through a gap and found himself a couple of hundred feet above the marauders.

'This is ridiculous' he admonished. 'You still haven't fired a shot.'

Smarting at his inadequacy, he picked a Dornier passing a few hundred yards ahead, and pushed in for an attack on its rear left quarter. He estimated the deflection, eased the dot in the centre of the reflector sight just ahead of the bomber's nose, and pressed the gun button.

The violence of the juddering, the noise, like the ripping of thick material, and the acrid smell of cordite, all took him by surprise. But he was elated. At last, he'd fired his guns.

The air around him filled with tracer.

What now?

He slammed the stick to the right and pulled.

Determined not to black out or lose control this time, he played the g.

But his arms were already beginning to ache, and it was all he could do to keep his head up and moving.

A Messerschmitt 109, 200 yards ahead. Alex fired a short burst. The 109 sped from view, followed by a Hurricane, its guns spitting tracer at the German fighter.

Feeling hot and queasy, he rolled out, passed behind the Hurricane and looked around. The sky above was empty, but below, the battle was continuing. The bomber formation was streaming away to his left. There were a few gaps, but it still seemed remarkably intact considering the number of fighters wheeling in and out, firing and being fired at.

I could sneak away now, he thought. He'd fired his guns, and he had something to tell the Intelligence Officer this time.

But no, he couldn't do it. Setting his jaw, he moved the stick briskly to the left, rolled through 120 degrees and pulled down towards the bombers.

Jack pulled straight up to escape the Messerschmitt attack. But it wasn't long before his speed washed off and he had to lower the nose again. Expecting to be hit at any moment, he rolled left and looked around. To his surprise and relief, he hadn't been followed.

Then, a thousand feet below, he saw a lone Spitfire flying toward the bomber stream, a large formation of Messerschmitt 109s to its right. Somehow, he knew it was Alex, and it seemed inevitable that he'd lose another wingman.

It was probably a futile gesture, but nonetheless, he rolled inverted, pulled down and made to shout a warning. Even as he did so, the Spitfire turned and shot under the bomber stream.

'Clever boy, Alex, clever boy.'

Attacking the mass of fighters suddenly seemed suicidal, so he rolled back to the right and dived behind them. As he passed a few hundred feet above, two turned towards him, but he plunged past before they could bring their guns to bear.

Picking a Dornier on the edge of the bomber formation, he set himself up for a beam attack. Like most in Fighter Command, he'd never been taught the art of deflection gunnery. But he'd done a fair bit of shooting before he became a pilot, and perhaps because of this, he seemed able to judge the lay off required to hit a fast moving target. He didn't find it easy, especially when the target was side on like now, but he enjoyed more success than most.

The bomber was probably doing over 200 miles an hour, so he aimed well ahead of its nose.

'That's it, Jack, about there.'

He waited until it was no more than 200 yards ahead, then jabbed the gun button with his thumb.

'Take that, you bastard.'

And he meant it. How dare they come over here, treating Britain like every other country between Poland and The Channel? He'd bloody well show 'em.

His Spitfire juddered as the ammunition set off, seemingly into thin air ahead of the Dornier. But, a few moment's later, impacts raked the bomber's side. He pushed to fly beneath it, pleased at hitting the target, but with no idea of the damage caused. It was often the way.

Below the bomber stream, the combat was ranging far and wide.

What a spectacle! If he survived, would he be able to bring such scenes to mind in the future? Or would he have the opposite problem, images of men and aircraft plummeting in flames haunting him for the rest of his life?

No time for such reveries now though. Somewhere out there, his fellow pilots were fighting - and dying, often in the most horrific ways. He hoped Alex and Piers weren't among them.

In between spikes of extreme terror, Alex had been in a state of simmering fear since the first Messerschmitts had jumped them. But now, as he closed on the bomber formation, he seemed to be in control of events. Or was he?

A sudden sense of danger made his skin crawl. There was nothing in his rear view mirror, but he was sure something was out there. He weaved from side to side, looking above and behind, then below.

'I knew it.'

Two 109s were climbing towards him. They must have dived and pulled up to attack from below, because they were closing fast. He couldn't outrun them and they'd soon be in a position to fire.

He resisted the urge to push into a dive. His carburettor-fed engine would cough, possibly stop, whereas the Germans' fuel-injected engines would continue to give full power as they swooped to finish him off.

'Come on, Alex, do something.'

He rolled briskly left, presenting himself in upper plan view, but gambling that they'd take a few seconds to react.

Tracer surrounded him, pointing to the folly of his choice, but he pulled hard to maintain positive g and dived back towards them. He also fed on rudder to make his turn as eccentric as possible.

'Whooa!'

He fought to regain control as his aircraft corkscrewed and skidded above the Messerschmitts. Looking back, he watched them turn to follow.

'Damn!'

He was in big trouble. Running away rankled, but it seemed the only sensible thing to do. Pressing on the already fully open throttle, he arrowed into an almost vertical dive.

The Messerschmitts were also diving, one to either side of his slipstream. First one and then the other opened fire.

Feeling airsick again, Alex tried for all he was worth to out-manoeuvre them. But, as the speed built up, so did the airflow forces on the controls. Eventually, pull as he might, he couldn't get his Spitfire to react.

The patchwork of fields below was growing in size. Tracer continued to flash past.

'Hold your nerve, Alex, hold it.'

The airspeed was off the clock, the competing whines of airflow and engine increasing to an ear-splitting crescendo.

'Yes.'

One of the Messerschmitts was pulling away, but the other was still intent on pursuit.

The ground was now approaching at an alarming rate. It was level or fly into it. Alex pulled, but the control forces were too high and nothing happened.

Gritting his teeth, he pulled again. The altimeter wound rapidly through 5,000 feet. Still the controls refused to respond.

Another rod of tracer flashed past, but being hit now seemed the least of his worries.

Putting his feet on the straining bars on top of the rudder pedals, he pulled again, muscles aching and sweat seeping from every pore. Imperceptibly, the nose began to rise. Eventually, it reached 45 degrees but he was still plummeting down. He kept pulling. Trees and buildings rushed up. He wasn't going to make it.

Looking around for the last time, he could just make out the Messerschmitt, still in a much steeper dive. Ignoring the pain in his forearms, he pulled with renewed vigour. The nose finally rose above the horizon, but the ground still climbed to meet him. A tree-top flashed past. He was sinking inexorably towards the grass, flinching in anticipation.

His Spitfire levelled. But was it too late? A hedge flashed beneath. A rise in the ground or a tree would kill him. Unseen, a farmer waved a fist as his orderly line of cows scattered.

The world was streaking past at an incredible rate. Five hundred miles an hour at 20 feet. A church steeple. Alex exerted more pressure on the control column and the Spitfire soared upwards.

When he was sure he was high enough to avoid any immediate obstacles, he levelled. His clothes were soaked in sweat and he ached all over. He'd never felt so tired, so completely drained, physically and mentally.

How did anybody do this all the time?

But the ordeal wasn't over. Fighting to overcome the extreme lethargy that had enveloped him, he tried to work out where he was.

Jack had damaged another bomber before he was set on by the fighter screen. He managed to evade the first two 109s, then latched onto a 110 attacking a Hurricane.

The Messerschmitt 110 was a formidable adversary. It had a top speed of about 350 miles an hour, bristled with machine guns and cannons to the front, and had a machine gunner in the rear of the two-man cockpit. But if you could attack it from behind and below…

He rolled right and eased beneath the twin tail of the two-engined fighter. The Hurricane, ignorant of its pursuer, flew straight on. Luckily, the 110 did the same.

'That's it, nice and steady.'

He eased the gunsight onto the Messerschmitt. The Hurricane started a lazy turn. Jack pressed his gun button before the 110 could follow. His De Wilde ammunition sparked on its underbelly.

'Bloody hell!'

The German fighter emitted a jet of lurid flame. He must have hit a fuel tank.

The Hurricane continued its gentle turn, still oblivious of events unfolding behind it.

'You owe me one,' Jack shouted as he turned the opposite way.

Before he lost sight of the Messerschmitt, it exploded, wings and fuselage folding upwards into the mushrooming cloud of smoke and flames. The crew had not escaped.

'To climb or not to climb?'

Alex suspected the second Messerschmitt had hit the ground, or pulled its wings off in a futile attempt to avoid doing so. But he couldn't be sure, and his best chance of evading it, or any other enemy aircraft stooging around, was to stay at low level.

'A few hundred feet should do it.'

He settled just clear of the tree tops and, as his speed reduced, opened the cockpit, gulping fresh air in an effort to clear his head and cool down. He also began weaving and scanning the sky. There were vapour trails high above, but nothing at his level. Not that he could see far. He was so low that every fold in the earth obscured his view.

'Now, where are you this time, Alex?'

They'd been attacked just to the south of Margate, and after his quick foray north towards the bombers, he was pretty sure he'd been diving away south or south west.

'Go west, young man.'

Feeling tired, sore and lonely, he turned a few degrees north onto a westerly heading and hoped that something familiar would show up.

After the encounter with the 110, Jack found himself alone again. If he could have spotted another target, he would have chased it, but he couldn't, and he still ached. Better to nurse himself home and live to fight another day.

He was just to the south of Chatham, so he headed into the west in a gentle weaving descent, keeping a good lookout for other aircraft. He saw none until he was closer to Biggin Hill. Smoke rose from the airfield.

'Bloody hell, sir, what you been up to this time?' Sandyman asked as he removed Alex's shoulder straps.

Alex was too tired to work out what his engine fitter meant, so he countered with a simple, 'Why?'

'Because your back end looks like a sieve, sir. It's a wonder you've still got a tailplane. Must have given you quite a fright?'

Until he climbed out, Alex could only guess at the

damage he'd sustained.

'Yes, I suppose it did. Is it that bad?'

'Well, sir, let's just say you better take your helmet and parachute back to the hut with you this time.'

With the Welshman's cryptic message ringing in his ears, Alex climbed wearily out of the cockpit and looked back along the fuselage. Gosh. There were jagged wounds all along the left hand side of the rear fuselage and tailfin, and his tailplane was peppered with tens of golf-ball sized holes.

As he rolled the headset off, he heard a Liverpudlian accent.

'Better take that with you, sir.'

Alex decided not to point out that his rigger was the second person to offer that advice in as many seconds. 'Yes, I think you're probably right, Mead.'

'Don't worry though, sir, they'll have a spare out before you can shake a stick.'

Trying not to show how much the thought of another scramble horrified him, Alex pointed onto the airfield, where a working party was busy shovelling soil into a large hole.

'Looks as if you've had a bit of excitement yourselves?'

'Yes, sir. The Gerries heard you were away. Didn't turn out too bad though. Most fell outside the wire. But it's bloody scary sitting in a shelter, I can tell you.'

'Yes, I can imagine. I think I'd rather be up there.' He pointed to the heavens.

'That's what I thought, sir, until I saw the state of your kite.'

They both smiled as Alex hefted the parachute onto his shoulder and walked out of the pen.

Jack closed the door to Muddy's office, turned and saluted.

'Hello, Jack. Take a seat.'

'Thanks, I will,' He lowered himself gingerly into an adjacent chair.

'How's Alex?' the officer asked.

'Oh, all right I think. A bit ashen again, but he was joining in some of the banter when I left him. The thing that worries him most is that he might have shot down a Hurricane.'

'Which would be a shame,' the flight commander joined in with a wry grin, 'because it sounds as if he's unlikely to have hit anything else?'

'No, unless it was false modesty, it does sound a bit unlikely. Why are we still not taking gunnery seriously, Muddy?'

'No time for that one now, Jack, I'm afraid. What I really called you in for was to say they've found Johnny Thwaite's body. Sorry.'

'Bloody shame, but we…'

There was a knock at the door.

'Come in.'

Instinctively, Jack stood up as the door opened. Flying Officer Greg Smith walked in.

'Not interrupting anything, am I?' he said, in the now familiar twang.

They were becoming quite a cosmopolitan group, Jack thought. Only a handful of the original Auxiliary squadron of affluent friends had survived the Dunkirk campaign. In place of those killed, wounded or captured, there was a small, but increasing, number of NCOs, like himself and Ginge, a Canadian, an Australian and a Pole, as well as many more Regular and Volunteer Reserve officers than would have been around before May. All the Auxiliary squadrons had suffered the same fate.

'No, Jack and I had just about finished.'

Jack turned towards the stocky Australian. 'Sorry to hear about Ellis, sir.'

'Thanks, Jack. Sounds as if he'd nearly made the airfield. Bounced by a couple of 109s with the bombers that hit this place. Anyway, we won't have to investigate his engine problems now, will we?'

Jack was glad he hadn't said it, even if he'd been thinking it.

'No you're right, Smithy,' the flight commander said, blowing a smoke ring to the ceiling. After a short silence, he continued, 'Okay. Thanks, Jack. And by the way, the CO wants to see you.'

'Wo-ho, what you been up to, Jack?' Smithy hooted.

Jack answered with a look of mild bemusement and a shrug. He saluted Muddy and left.

Why would the CO want to see him?

He turned right, walked behind Hopkins, sitting at the ops desk, and knocked on the CO's office door.

'Come in.'

Jack stepped in and saluted.

'Ah, Sergeant Williams. Thank you for coming.'

A bit formal, Jack thought.

The Squadron Leader sat behind a desk buried under a mountain of paperwork. Jack didn't envy him having to keep up with all the admin, and lead the Squadron in the air. The poor man looked old beyond his years today, and deathly tired.

'Sorry to hear about Thwaites, Jack. Never easy when you lose one of your section. Just trying to write a letter to his parents. Damned difficult though. He'd been around for such a short time. Never really got to know him.'

Now that was one of the things Jack definitely didn't envy the CO: writing letters of condolence. And when he'd finished Johnny's, he'd have to start Sergeant Ellis's. It irked him that he still didn't know the lad's first name, although it hardly seemed to matter any more.

The CO sighed and seemed to perk up a bit, a thin smile creasing his otherwise care-worn features. 'But don't worry, I haven't called you in to help me write letters. I'm pleased to tell you you've been awarded the DFM.'

The Distinguished Flying Medal. That would cost him a few beers.

'Well done, Jack. Well deserved. Now,' the smile disappeared again, 'sorry to make it so rushed, but I'd like to try and finish this before the next shout. And ask the Adj to step in would you, please?'

Jack saluted, smiling at the politeness of the order. He exited the office to be greeted by a group of smiling pilots, tunelessly humming the RAF March Past.

'Piss off, you lot,' he shouted.

Alex lay back against the side of the three-tonner. Although the third scramble had ended with a speedy return to base, the tension of waiting, and the fear of taking part, had eaten through his final reserves of physical and mental strength. Following the recall message, he'd struggled to stay awake long enough to pull off a successful landing. And after another, thankfully short, agonising, wait, they'd finally been stood down at 8.30 pm.

Despite the banter and name calling, he decided not to join the rest of them in the pub. He didn't know where they found the energy, and he didn't really care. He just needed his bed.

The lorry pulled up outside the Mess. He lowered himself to the ground and followed the others into the building. When they turned into the bar, he carried on, followed by a good-natured chorus of cat-calls. Waving over his shoulder, he turned the corner into the corridor leading to his room.

'Sophie. What a surprise,' he said truthfully.

'A pleasant one, I hope?'

He dreaded to think what he looked like, but she looked marvellous. WAAF uniforms did nothing for most girls, but Sophie was so tall and slim she made the regulation blue skirt and jacket look elegant and feminine. Her short dark hair bounced as she walked and her cheeks revealed little dimples when she smiled, as she did now.

'We always seem to meet in the corridor,' he said, blushing, his tiredness banished for the time being.

'I know, we must try and meet somewhere else next time.'

'I'd like that,' he said, blushing even more.

A plump red face popped round the corner.

'Come on, Soph, we're off.'

'Alright, Bunter,' she said, looking stern and sounding a bit put out. 'I'm coming.'

She turned back to Alex, her face and voice softening. 'Sorry, Alex. I've got to go. Nice to meet you again.'

'And you,' he said.

With a smiling backward glance, she turned the corner and disappeared.

Chapter 3 - Tuesday 27th August 1940

'Four o'clock, sir. Four o'clock.'

Alex knew the man wouldn't give up until convinced he wasn't just going to roll over and go back to sleep.

'Four o'clock, sir.'

'All right, Jenkins.' He hoped he didn't sound too tetchy, but he'd only just dropped off.

'Your tea's on the side, sir.'

'All right!' Definitely sounding tetchy, Alex.

He sensed someone standing over him. Only when he made to sit up did he hear footfalls easing away. His bedside light was already on, and, as he opened his eyes, a brylcreemed head disappeared through the partially open door.

'Thank you, Jenkins,' he shout-whispered. 'Sorry.'

'That's all right, sir.'

The door closed with a click. They must get used to people being irritable at four in the morning.

Olly still seemed to be sleeping soundly. What he'd give to be allowed the same luxury.

After speaking to Sophie, he'd come straight to bed, desperate for sleep. But, although he'd hardly been able to keep his eyes open before slipping beneath the sheets, when he had, he'd found himself just lying there. It had been a complete waste of time. Might as well have gone to the pub. Perhaps that's why they all did it.

His mind had been too awash with the experiences of his first day in combat; some positive, like the Spitfires glinting in the sun, or the camaraderie with his fellow pilots and groundcrew; but most negative, nightmares in which he either relived what had happened, or, even worse, suffered through what might have been.

When not being hit by the glowing tracer arcing towards him, he imagined himself trapped in his cramped cockpit after blacking out. Sometimes, he just plummeted into the ground without regaining consciousness. And sometimes, he woke enveloped in flame, his flesh burning as the ground rushed up and he tried to open a canopy that refused to budge.

Plummeting into the ground had been a theme with endless variations: from a spin, from a precipitous dive, or simply because he was lost and had run out of fuel.

Any one of these scenarios would have been enough to disturb his sleep, but he experienced them all several times in subtly different guises. And every time he managed to drop off, he jolted into wakefulness in a state of sweat-drenched panic.

In the most vivid and disturbing nightmare, he was explaining to the parents of a young Hurricane pilot why he'd shot down and killed their son. And the couple confronting him in their grief were his own parents.

Was it just three nights since he'd slept so soundly in his bedroom in Ludlow?

And all this was the result of just one day in combat. What would he be like after a week, or a month? Did you get used to it, or did every new experience add to the library of horrors until life became one long nightmare?

Alex shivered and took a sip of the dark brown liquid Jenkins had placed on his bedside table. Shivering again, as much from the taste of the tea as the cold, he got out of bed, picked up his wash bag and padded barefoot along the icy floor to the ablutions.

Jack woke with a crashing hangover. Ginge had returned from leave and they'd gone to the bar for a quiet drink. All too quickly, it had turned into a celebration for his DFM, which had moved to the pub, and then to a house where they'd carried on drinking. Any excuse!

'Come on, you lazy bastard,' a Geordie accent assailed him. 'If I can get up, so can you. It's your fuckin' fault anyway, ya shite.'

Despite the pain in his head, Jack smiled. Ginge had a lovely turn of phrase.

They'd been on the same apprentice entry at Halton, where they'd been acquaintances, rather than friends. But, after a couple of years at different bases, and 18 months' flying training at different units, they'd ended up on 646 together, just in time for Dunkirk. The Halton connection had drawn them together, and they'd been firm friends ever since.

Jack opened one eye. No more than a foot away was a freckly face, sporting an impish grin.

'Don't you breathe on me,' Jack shouted, leaping out of bed to avoid one of Ginge's favourite alarm calls. He instantly wished he hadn't moved so fast, and held his head in his hands.

'I thought that might shift ya, ya lazy Welsh bastard. Ya've missed a treat though. A whiff of last night's pickled eggs. I can taste 'em.' He gave a loud belch, of which he seemed immensely proud.

Fully awake now, but still horribly hung over, Jack headed for the washroom.

Alex had thought he looked a little tired as he washed

and shaved. But most of those at the breakfast table resembled extras in a Bella Lugosi vampire film: the undead, blank eyes staring out of sunken grey sockets. And he wasn't the only one to have ordered toast from the steward, but been unable to face it when it arrived. At his table, only Muddy Waters, Piers and a bear of a Canadian, nicknamed Grizzly, seemed able to eat.

Alex sipped his tea and fought the gagging reflex. Would he ever be able to eat and drink again without feeling sick?

The meal was taking place in silence, the officer pilots of 646 Squadron sitting at two tables in the corner of the dining room. The officer pilots of 32 and 629 Squadrons had gravitated to what he guessed were their regular tables. They seemed no less zombie-like, and no sparkling conversation or banter drifted over.

In his own group, the Pole, known as S to Z because his name was unpronounceable, was wearing his uniform over his pyjamas, the striped collar clearly visible above the neckline of his jacket. Smithy and another young pilot officer he knew only as Boy, looked as if they'd slept in their uniforms; and a flying officer he'd met only briefly, Birdy, still was asleep, his head resting on the table, his smiling mouth blowing little bubbles. The exhibition briefly raised everyone's spirits, until Birdy coughed and sat up with a start, a look of profound disappointment clouding his features when he realised where he was.

A steward strode in, coughed to gain their attention, and announced, 'Transport for 32 and 646.'

Hoping he encountered no obstacles before his eyes became accustomed to the gloom, Alex walked away from the dispersal hut. It was overcast, no moon or stars to be seen, and the grass was damp from recent rain. Apart from his muffled footfalls, the only noises were occasional shouts from the various aircraft pens, and the odd clank of metal on metal from the same source. It was too early even for the birds.

This wasn't a scene he'd envisaged when he'd decided to become a fighter pilot. In fact, little of what he'd experienced to date was as he'd imagined. Just as he felt himself descending into another anguished debate on whether he was cut out for his chosen path, a loud metallic churning made him jump.

A starter had engaged in the pen to his left. Flashes of flame shot from stub exhausts along the nose of the resident Spitfire. The propeller turned over and the whole machine quivered, the engine bursting into life amid clouds of exhaust fumes. Alex watched for a few seconds, then walked on.

The engine of his own Spitfire started just as he walked into its pen. Unnoticed, he stood to one side and watched his groundcrew follow their morning routine. Mead stood to the front right of the propeller disc, while Sandyman sat in the cockpit. After a few moments, they exchanged hand signals and the Merlin engine roared.

The Spitfire bounced against the chocks and Alex picked up slight changes in engine note as Sandyman checked the magnetos, first at high power, then again at lower revs. Finally, the engine was throttled back to idle for a few seconds before the propeller stopped amid more gouts of flame and smoke.

But there was no return to silence. All around the airfield, other Merlin engines were following the same sequence.

'Morning, sir,' Mead smiled as he turned to see

Alex walking towards him.

'Good morning, Mead. How are you?'

'As well as can be expected at five in the morning, sir.'

'I know what you mean,' Alex laughed and nodded at the Spitfire. 'How is she?'

'This one's fine, sir. 'Fraid you won't see the other one for a few days.'

Alex doubted whether he'd get the other aircraft again anyway. He hadn't been around long enough to merit his own airframe. One day perhaps.

Sandyman bounded up, looking far too chipper for the time of day.

'Mag drops are fine, sir, and she's running as sweet as a nut.'

'Thanks, Sandyman, I heard. Well, I'll just set myself up then.'

It all sounded far too formal and stilted, he realised, but chatting unselfconsciously to his groundcrew was one of the many skills he had yet to learn. It must be so much easier for someone like Jack, who'd been a tradesman himself until a few months ago.

He placed his parachute on the left wingtip and climbed onto the wing. His mood darkened as he approached the cockpit and squatted down to lean in. The confined space, its textures and smells, rekindled the images of the previous day, and his recent nightmares. He felt sick.

Standing upright, he held onto the rear view mirror protruding above the canopy arch and fought to regain his composure. Slowly, the dizziness and sickness passed. Bracing himself, he took a deep breath and leaned down again, determined to overcome his fear.

He concentrated on formulating his own morning

routine, draping his helmet over the stick, and connecting the RT lead and oxygen hose. Looking around, he checked that the oxygen and fuel tanks were full and the brake pressure was okay. Feeling calmer for the completion of the mundane but vital tasks, he carried on, setting full right rudder trim and the elevator trim to one degree nose heavy.

His Spitfire was now ready for the first scramble of the day. Was he?

Jack waited impatiently for his engine fitter to jump out of the cockpit.

'Come on, Stokesy.'

As soon as the man was clear, he connected the oxygen, put the mask to his face and took several deep breaths. It was the best known cure for a hangover, and he guessed he wasn't the only pilot at this and many other RAF airfields gulping large lungfuls of oxygen in the pre-dawn. Were the Germans doing the same on the other side of the Channel, he wondered?

'Yow look good, Sarge,' his rigger said cheerily as Jack stepped gingerly from the wing.

'Thanks, Brummie. Where did you get your medical degree?'

'Smeddick University, Sarge.' He seemed pleased with his speedy riposte and gave Jack a gap-toothed grin. 'Congratulations on the gong by the way.'

'Thanks, Brummie. Now if you can manage without my normal sparkling conversation this morning, I'm going to find somewhere to put my head down until breakfast, or the dawn patrol.'

'Okay, Sarge. Let's hope it's breakfast, eh?'

Jack walked back to the dispersal hut. All the camp beds were occupied, so he found an armchair, lay out with his legs on a low table and closed his eyes.

Alex walked towards the corner of the pen. Sandyman and Mead were sitting on pieces of ground equipment, eating sandwiches. They stood at his approach. Blushing, he waved them down, then sat on a starter trolley facing them.

Deeply aware of how forced it must all seem, he asked, 'Which part of Wales do you come from, Sandyman?'

'Pwll, sir.'

The engine fitter smiled at Alex's obvious bemusement. 'Don't worry, sir, I won't ask you to pronounce it. It's a little place between Llanelli and Pembrey.'

'Oh, thank you. Must have been handy over the last few months?'

'Yes, it was great, sir. I'd never been so close to home before, and…'

'Oh no, you've started something now, sir,' Mead jumped in. 'You hadn't got anything planned for the rest of the morning, had you?'

'Well, that rather depends on the Gerries, doesn't it?'

'Yes, sir,' the Liverpudlian smiled conspiratorially. He was in his late twenties, perhaps five years older than Sandyman.

'I know yesterday was probably a bit of a trial, getting shot up and all that, but I reckon you'll be praying for a scramble just to get away from us in another five minutes.'

Sandyman wore an expression of mock exasperation.

'Why, what have I let myself in for?' Alex played

along.

'A fate worse than death, sir. We've been putting up with it ever since we left Pembrey.'

'Have you finished then, Scouse?'

'Just warning the young officer what to expect, Sandy.'

'Come on, Sandyman. You'll have to tell me now,' He was genuinely enjoying the double act, but was also grateful for the tacit acknowledgement that the previous day had been difficult. He wondered how many other young pilots they'd seen come and go.

'You'll be disappointed after all that build up, sir. I was only going to say I got married just before we left.'

He rummaged in his overall pocket.

'Here we go, sir. Brace yourself.'

The engine fitter gave the rigger a playful nudge as he took a creased photograph from a wallet.

An attractive, dark haired young woman in a flowered dress stood in a garden next to a clothes line.

'She's very pretty, Sandyman.'

'Thank you sir. Megan, her name's Megan.'

Alex was wondering what else to say, when Mead butted in again.

'Until now, you was the only person in Kent not to have seen that photo, sir.'

They all laughed.

'Are you married then, Mead?'

With the dawn, the sky had failed to lighten beyond dark grey. Silver sheets of rain pulsed across the airfield, driven on by a stiff southerly wind. Biggin Hill was on a plateau atop the North Downs – it was known as Biggin on the Bump – and today, it seemed to be reaching up to the cloudbase.

Alex now understood why such foul weather was loved by fighter pilots. Although the enemy might try to sneak in some reconnaissance sorties, even the odd small raid, they were unlikely to mount any major operations. So, given the number of squadrons available, there was a fair chance one of the others would be called into action. And if the rain persisted, they might even be stood down early.

Most of his fellow pilots had gained a few hours extra sleep, or, in his case, fitful rest. He hadn't yet perfected the art of napping in an armchair in a room full of shuffling bodies. From the loud snores, and worse, he was in the minority though.

Breakfast had arrived by truck at 8.00am, but he'd managed only to nibble at a bacon sandwich, and sip at another cup of disgusting tea.

Jack, in contrast, had slept for another three hours and eaten heartily. He felt much better for it.

Now, an hour or so later, they and the rest of the pilots were waiting in the smoke-filled atmosphere of the hut for the CO to address them.

Squadron Leader Gerry Parr stood in front of the Adjutant's desk, appraising them with piercing brown eyes.

In contrast to most of his squadron, he looked well groomed, his hair neatly brushed, his uniform freshly pressed, and, although unable to hide the bags under his eyes, he appeared relaxed, at ease with the pressures of command. He coughed to gain their attention, waited patiently for the hubbub to subside, then started in a deep, confident, voice.

'Some of you may know that I went to a meeting at Group last night.'

There were groans from some in the armchairs, and from others lurking in the smoke at the back of the room. Meetings at Uxbridge often heralded bad news.

'Don't worry, nothing too painful, but some important things came out, and from a meeting with the Station Commander this morning.'

More groans. The CO laughed and turned to his flight commanders, leaning against the desk to either side of him. Muddy raised his eyes in mock exasperation and smiled back, a thin stream of blue smoke rising from the bowl of his pipe. To the other side, Flight Lieutenant 'Freddie' Fowler looked tense, a little tic pulsing in the corner of his eye. Alex had noticed it the day before. It made him glad he was in Muddy's Flight.

Jack also noticed the tic. It had developed the moment they'd been told of the move from Pembrey to Biggin Hill. Freddie had been shot down twice over Dunkirk, the first time ending up in the sea, the second, on the beach, where he'd spent two nights before escaping on one of the last transports to leave. After the first bale out, he'd been only too eager to regale them with his story. After the second, he'd remained silent. They'd all known it was a bad sign.

The CO turned back to face them. 'The AOC confirmed what most of you will already have noticed. The Hun have started going for our airfields. Apart from our glancing blow yesterday, they've given Manston, Kenley, North Weald and Debden a real pasting.

'And they're flying more devious tracks, making it difficult for the Controllers. That's why we're being launched later and struggling to get above the bombers. As a result, I think we'll probably end up flying more frontal attacks.'

A few groans.

'Not everyone's cup of tea, I know, but you've seen how effective they can be. Believe me, Gerry likes them even less than we do.'

Alex felt the CO's eyes rest on his for a moment. Until then, he'd felt as if the Squadron Commander's words were aimed only at the more experienced men in the room. Now, although the eye contact had been fleeting, he knew they were also meant for him. It gave him a real boost, validation that he belonged.

Jack was also touched by the CO's gaze, and he too felt his spirits lift. The man had an ability to engage and inspire that some of the other COs had lacked.

'You'll also have noticed more Snappers about, and that they're sticking to the bomber stream. It means they've lost the advantage of height, but they've also made it harder for us to get at the bombers, and they're getting through. So the message is, and I know you've heard it before, concentrate on the bombers.'

The CO smiled as he addressed the few rumbling murmurs of discontent. 'I know, I know. Easier said than done, but there it is. Try and avoid getting tangled up in the fighter screen.

'Now, if they get to us first, it's a different kettle of fish of course. But therein lies another problem. I'm grateful to Piers for his warning yesterday, but we've got to have more eyes looking out for their fighters.'

Jack nodded at a smiling Piers, then felt the CO's eyes rest on him again.

'I know some of you want to go over to flying in pairs, and I tend to agree in principle, but now is not the time.'

Jack had been one of the strongest advocates of the

German system. Their basic formation was a widely spaced pair, the wingman slightly behind and above or below his leader, depending on the position of the sun. It allowed them to keep a good look out for one another, and to turn in and engage anyone attacking either of them. The pairs could also slot easily into larger formations of four or more. All in all, they were much more flexible than Fighter Command's tightly packed triangular vics of three.

They should have changed while they were at Pembrey, but Squadron Leader Parr hadn't been in charge then, and more conservative voices had won out. Jack could see why the CO was reluctant to make such a radical change now, in the full heat of battle, and with so many new faces about. Nonetheless, he sensed a hint of apology in the eyes before they moved on.

'What we're going to do is widen our vics to 50 yards spacing, so we can all keep a good lookout, rather than fixate on keeping formation. We'll maintain that spacing until we close up for an attack. I still want a tail-end Charlie, but let's all get our heads moving.

'Right, on the subject of airfields.' He paused, as if conducting some internal debate, then carried on in a more conspiratorial tone. 'Between you and me, the AOC's really fed up with 12 Group. He's asked them to watch our backs while we're up, but they spend so long forming their bloody 'big wing' that by the time they arrive, the bombers have hit and are halfway back across the Channel. He's had another go at Leigh Mallory, but I wouldn't hold your breath.

'Anyway, back to the point. It's bad enough losing pilots in the air, but we can't afford to lose them on the ground. So, 32's replacements, 79, are going to Hawkinge, and 629 are going to detach daily to operate from Gravesend. We're going to stay here, but the Station Commander has decided to move us off base, out of the Messes. I'm not sure where to yet, or when, but it's likely to be sooner rather than later, so keep your ears open.'

'I volunteer to live in the bar of the White Hart, sir,' a Geordie accent piped up.

'I thought you already did, Sergeant Clough,' the CO shot straight back to much general laughter.

'Okay chaps. A fair bit to mull over there, and I know you'll have lots of questions, but I'm afraid I'm going to have to run again, so I'll hand over to the flight commanders to go over the detail. Carry on.'

They all stood up and the CO walked through the room to his office.

The 'quick chat' in the flight commander's office took the whole morning. Discussions roamed far and wide, and by the time they adjourned for lunch, Alex felt much wiser on a range of topics, from battle tactics to Mess bills.

After lunch, with the weather still dank, he and Piers made for the Ops Block, on a visit arranged by Muddy as part of their ongoing education. Alex hoped to see Sophie, but was surprised when she was the first person he saw as they made a noisy entrance through a sticking door. He had time for no more than a blushing nod of acknowledgement before an authoritative voice made them turn.

The appearance of the squadron leader pilot sitting on the platform was a shock for which Alex was not prepared. He knew that injured aircrew sometimes became controllers, but he hadn't given much thought to what injuries they might have suffered.

The face before them resembled a mask. The skin was a mosaic of colours, from cream, through light purple, to blood red; it looked thin, almost translucent where it was drawn tightly over forehead, cheekbones and chin, like the skin of a haggis. The ears were small and wrinkled, like the knots sealing party balloons, and there was a thin, pinched nose and a mouth that seemed almost to fray at the edges. The poor man had no hair, no eyebrows and no eyelashes, but his dark eyes sparkled expressively.

'Welcome, chaps. You must be Pilot Officers White and Lowe?'

Even though the face gave an impression of great age, the voice was youthful. Its owner continued without waiting for them to confirm their identities.

'Good to see you. It's not every day we get a couple of young pilots in here. I'm Squadron Leader Rice, today's Duty Controller, Bastion to you when you're airborne.

'Sorry if I've startled you.' He pointed at his face with hands that were also badly burned. 'Brush with the Hun over Scotland last November. If you think this is bad, you should have seen me then!'

His attempt at a disarming smile was accompanied by a sweep of the arm that absolved them of the need to reply, and allowed them to turn their eyes away.

'Welcome to the Sector Operations Room for Charlie Sector.'

Before them was a spacious, brightly lit room with a high, concrete-beamed ceiling. Almost filling the floor space was a large table covered with a map of south eastern England, northern France and the Low

Countries. Around the table, mostly seated, were about a dozen young WAAFs in light blue shirts and black ties. Most seemed to be knitting, stopping only briefly to look up at the two young men.

The Controller was still smiling as they turned back. He and three other men sat overlooking the map from a raised platform, like a magistrate's bench. He extended an arm towards Sophie and a WAAF flight sergeant, sitting behind a small table to the right hand side of the platform.

'Assistant Section Officer Preston-Wright, why don't you give these two the conducted tour? I'm sure they'd much rather look at you than me.'

The pain behind the self-deprecating words could only be guessed at, but, after giving the Controller a weak smile, Alex turned gratefully to face Sophie. She stood and walked towards them, and he felt an immediate lift in his spirits. She really was tall, a good two inches taller than Piers.

It was Sophie's turn to blush as she held out her hand. 'Hello, Alex, and…?'

'Oh, Piers White. Nice to meet you.'

'Sorry. I didn't realise you two hadn't met,' Alex blurted.

He admired Sophie's pretty smile and dimpled cheeks, and noted that Piers held her hand for longer than seemed strictly necessary.

Squadron Leader Kelvin Rice also noticed. He'd fallen in love with Sophie on seeing her for the first time three weeks previously, and had been tortured by his proximity to her ever since. She didn't turn away in horror like some women he met, but he feared she would never look on him with anything other than sympathetic concern.

Piers continued to play the simpering buffoon. 'You know what it's like, so many beautiful girls and so little time,' he said, before finally relinquishing his grip.

Sophie blushed more deeply, and Alex saw some of the WAAFs exchange knowing looks and giggles. They were enjoying their officer's discomfort, but lowered their heads to concentrate on their knitting as she turned to look over the map.

'Right, as Squadron Leader Rice said, this is the Sector Operations Room for the Biggin Hill Sector. You're probably most interested in how we control you in the air, but I'll give you a bit of gen on the system as a whole, if you like?'

'Yes please, Sophie,' Piers jumped in.

'Okay. Don't be afraid to interrupt if I'm teaching you to suck eggs, and feel free to ask questions as we go.'

She commenced a well-rehearsed narrative.

'The operators at the RDF stations watch raids form up over France and the Low Countries and track them to the coast. Over land, the Observer Corps take over with their binoculars, if cloud cover permits. Both outfits pass their reports to Bentley Priory. Bentley filters out any rubbish, then plots the raids on a table, just like this, only showing the whole country.'

She paused, and they nodded their understanding.

'Bentley then pass the information to Group at Uxbridge, and to us and the six other Sector Airfields: Debden, Hornchurch, Kenley, North Weald, Northolt and Tangmere.'

Alex was impressed with Sophie's knowledge, but also with the confident way it was being presented.

She swept her arm over the table. 'And we produce

our map, a replica, for our sector, of what they have at Bentley Priory and Uxbridge.'

'Must be mayhem in here when it's busy?' Piers piped.

He'd noticed that despite his best efforts to capture those sparkling grey eyes, she addressed most of her words to Alex. Kelvin Rice had also noticed, and was quietly pleased that the tall, modest, young pilot seemed to be up-staging his brash companion.

Sophie smiled, 'Yes, it does get a bit hectic, but fortunately it's very quiet at the moment. There's only this one hostile on the map.' She pointed at a black counter just inland of the coast by Hastings. 'We think it's a lone reconnaissance, and Group have asked Tangmere to intercept it.'

She pointed at a red counter on the coast further to the west.

A pretty blonde on the far side of the table stood, reached out with a croupiers' rake and pulled the black counter towards her.

'This is probably a good time to go through the process.'

Sophie pointed at the far wall directly opposite the Controller's platform.

'You can see that the five minute periods on the face of the clock are painted either red, yellow or blue. Now, as the counters are raked on to the map, the direction arrow is given the colour of the period the minute hand is sweeping. So the Controller can tell how old the information on the plotting table is, and we make sure it's never more than 15 minutes old.

'Angela has probably just been given an update on our hostile through her headphones.'

Angela picked up the black counter and smiled at

Piers, who beamed back.

There was a cough, and Alex glanced back to catch the flight sergeant giving the young WAAF a disapproving glare. Angela's smile disappeared, replaced by a look of deep concentration. A dark haired WAAF next to her leaned over and raked in the red counter.

Sophie continued. 'Angela's counter has a plaque with a large letter H for hostile, a plot number, an estimate of the number of aircraft in the raid and their height, and the minute hand of the clock is now in the blue sector.'

Angela pushed the black counter and a blue arrow out onto the map, and Sophie continued. 'This is Hostile zero seven, one aircraft at twenty thousand feet, and you can see that it's turned round and headed back out to sea. The weather really must be bad.'

The red counter was also pushed onto the map, further along the coast between Tangmere and Hastings.

'And there's an F for friendly section of three aircraft, passing ten thousand feet heading towards the hostile. I suspect they'll get pancaked shortly, but let's pretend the hostile was a big raid heading inland. The Group Controller at Uxbridge watches it and tries to work out where it's heading. Then he consults his tote boards, like those under the clock.'

Three white boards, one for each of the Biggin Hill squadrons, stood about four feet tall and nine inches wide. Lines of black writing, like identical shopping lists, ran from top to bottom of each, with one item on each list illuminated from behind by a small bulb. For 646 and 79 Squadrons, a line near the top reading '30 minutes' was lit. For 629 Squadron, it was the next line down, '15 minutes'.

'At Uxbridge of course, the AOC has a set of these for all seven sector airfields, and for things like the anti-aircraft and searchlight batteries, and the barrage balloons. So, he can see at a glance who's available, at standby, airborne, engaging the enemy, or coming back to land, or refuelling. All manner of things. And from that, he decides which of the Sector stations should react to a particular raid, and with how many aircraft or squadrons. Then, his Controllers get on the blower to ours.'

Sophie pointed back at Kelvin Rice, who made a seated bowing motion. 'And the Sector Controller or his assistant passes the message to the squadron ops desks, either here or at the satellite airfields.'

She kept her eyes on Kelvin Rice. 'I think you're better qualified to explain the next bit, sir?'

He knew his plastic surgery hadn't yet reached the stage where he could display much beyond a frown or a smile, so Sophie couldn't see the admiration or longing he felt. Probably just as well really.

'Thank you, Section Officer Preston-Wright. That was splendid as usual.'

She smiled at him and walked back towards her desk.

Alex watched her for a short while, then turned to face the Controller. He already found the man's appearance less disconcerting, and he sought and maintained eye contact as the squadron leader continued.

'I'll have been watching the raiders coming in, and I should have an idea of their heading and how fast they're travelling. So, when you get the message to get airborne, I should be able to give you a heading to fly, as well as the number of bandits you can expect to see, and at what height. As the counters get updated, I update your instructions. I can handle two squadrons, but if a third gets airborne, I hand it over to my assistant.'

He nodded at the flight sergeant pilot to his right. Alex couldn't help wondering what injury, if any, he'd sustained.

'The brown jobs on my left,' Kelvin Rice said pointing a gnarled hand at an Army officer and NCO seated next to him, 'look after the airfield defences. If a raid's headed our way, they warn their gunners, and we keep them updated on what you're up to. That way, they shouldn't take pot shots when you come back to land. Touch wood, they haven't done it yet, but you never know. They're a trigger-happy bunch.'

He smiled at the two soldiers who rolled their eyes good naturedly. They'd heard it all before.

'Now, once your CO sights the bandits and calls tally-ho, I take a back seat, unless I need to tell you to break off for some reason, or warn you of more bandits. But when the action's over, I'm here to provide help if you need it; say, if you find yourself stuck above cloud, or temporarily unaware of your position.'

Alex wished he'd thought of that the day before, although he'd been so low on both occasions that he doubted they'd have picked up his transmissions. Something to bear in mind for the future though.

'And of course, while all this is going on, the staff in here are updating the map and the tote boards, receiving information from Group and passing it the other way. So, to answer your earlier question again, Piers, on a busy day, you'd find everyone in here talking at once, either on the telephone or the radio, or both, and all to different people. Complete bloody bedlam.'

He pointed to the desk at the side, where Sophie had re-taken her seat. 'Section Officer Preston-Wright and the flight sergeant keep an eye on the girls and bring on subs when it all gets too much. But most of the time, we're just one big happy family.' He raised his voice. 'Aren't we, girls?'

The 'girls' offered a world weary, 'Yes, sir', in well-rehearsed unison, much to the Controller's delight.

'See what I mean?'

Alex and Piers walked into the fresh air and returned the salute of the sentry.

It had stopped raining, but the threat was still present in the dark grey clouds scurrying past on the wind.

'I'm in love, Alex.'

'Yes. She's lovely, isn't she?' Alex said wistfully. 'But I'm afraid she's taken.'

'Sorry? How do you know that?'

'She went out with the 629 boys last night, with a chap called Bunter.'

'Drat. I thought we'd sort of connected.'

'You connected all right. I thought you were never going to let go of her hand.'

'What?' Piers shot back, looking perplexed.

'I thought you were going to keep hold of her hand for the whole briefing. I think Sophie did too.'

'Sophie?'

Now it was Alex's turn to look perplexed. 'Yes, Sophie. Who else would we be talking about?'

'The pretty little blonde with the rake of course. Angela.'

'Oh, I'm sorry. I thought you meant Sophie.'

'No. nice enough girl, I grant you. But she's taken, so I gave up on her straight away.

'Yes. It's a shame isn't it? This Bunter's a lucky chap.'

'Alex, you really are a stupid old duffer!'

'How was Crispy?'

Alex wondered whether he would ever again understand anything that was said to him. He was still trying to digest what Piers had said about Sophie.

Adopting the inquisitive tone that seemed to have become his stock in trade, he looked at his flight commander and sought clarification. 'Sorry?'

Muddy put his pen down and eyed them both from behind his desk. 'How was Crispy Rice, the Sector Controller?'

They both cringed.

'I know. Not my name for him. Blame the CO. He was a flight commander on a Hurricane squadron at Turnhouse last November when Squadron Leader Kelvin Rice took over. At the time, he was the youngest CO in Fighter Command, just 23 I think the Boss said. Bloody handsome as well.

'Didn't last the first week though. Shot down by a Snapper near Rosyth. They still have no idea how he got out of the kite and pulled his D-ring. Landed in the oggin, and picked up by one of the warships they were protecting. Lucky to land in the sea by all accounts. Cooled the burns. And they say the salt helps.'

'We haven't seen him round the Mess,' Piers interrupted.

'No, you wouldn't. He goes back to East Grinstead every night. Still living in the hospital I think. He'll be getting treatment for years. Anyway, enough of this. Was it a worthwhile visit?'

Alex nodded politely, but Piers spoke up again. 'Yes and no, Muddy. I can see it can be useful to put a face to the voice of the Controller. But, in this case, I'm not sure it's a face I want in my head when I go into combat!'

It was dropping dark as Jack got out of the car, feeling a bit bemused by it all. The CO had warned that the move off base could happen sooner rather than later, but no-one had expected it to be that night.

He lifted his kitbags from the boot, slammed it shut and banged on the side rear window, shouting his thanks as the driver pulled away.

Number 5 was a small house in the middle of a terrace mirrored on the other side of the road. A three foot high wooden gate was set in a low wall topped with railings. Both the gate and the railings were tatty, barely covered with peeling flecks of dark paint. Tall, unkempt, hedges glowered over a tiny front garden, and the front door and window frames displayed more flaking paint.

'Good luck, Sarge.'

Jack waved as the car drove back down the street and turned left for the airfield.

'I think I might need it,' he sighed, already wishing he'd been allowed to stay in the Mess and take his chance with the bombers. The general air of decay didn't bode well, and he wondered where Ginge had ended up.

Oh well, here goes.

He unlatched the gate, picked up his bags and gave it a nudge with his knee. It dropped away from the top hinge and wouldn't budge with either another gentle prod, or a more determined kick.

'What the fu...!'

Sighing mightily, he dropped his bags, opened the gate, brought them through and closed it again using both hands. By the time he knocked on the door, he was not in the best of moods.

Chapter 4 – Wednesday 28ᵗʰ August 1940

Alex headed back to the dispersal hut. He'd set up his Spitfire for the first launch of the day and spent a few minutes talking to Sandyman and Mead. It was a clear, chilly, morning with the stars dimming as the first hint of daylight tinted the eastern horizon.

'Hello, sir.'

A shadowy figure walked out of the gloom.

'Oh, hello, Jack. Where did you end up then?'

'A bijou little terraced house in Keston, sir. And how about you? Some bloody great palace, I expect.'

'Well, actually, Jack, it is rather grand. Sambrook House, near Tatsfield.'

'Ooh, Sambrook House. Sounds a bit posher than 5 Keston Avenue.

'Yes. I'm sorry. It does, doesn't it?'

Alex still wondered why he'd been given a commission when most of his contemporaries had been made NCOs. And why was he enjoying higher status, better pay and conditions than some of the men he was fighting alongside, even the man he was following into battle? It didn't make sense.

'You seem very chipper if I may say so, sir.'

'Yes, I do feel a lot better today thanks.'

It was partially true. He'd been plagued by nightmares again, scenes from his first day in combat intermingling with images of Crispy Rice, frantically trying to escape his burning aircraft, then falling through the air, grasping for his parachute D-ring with claw-like hands.

So, chipper was a bit strong, but he was more in control, or was he just learning to hide his true feelings?

And there had been more positive things to mull over, such as Piers's idea that Sophie held a torch for him, that she hadn't been able to keep her eyes off him in the Ops Room. He thought it had been the other way round, to the point where he'd found it hard to concentrate on what she was saying rather than just admiring her. There was so much to admire.

But he knew so little about girls. There'd been the annual dance with the High School, but he'd been far too shy to walk across the floor and ask anyone to dance. And now they'd moved out of the Mess, he had no idea when he'd get the chance to meet Sophie again anyway. And then there was Bunter.

'You look a bit better as well, Jack.'

'Yes. I escaped the evil influence of Ginge Clough and had a quiet night.'

They walked into the dispersal hut and Jack put a finger to his lips. Alex nodded, and they went their separate ways, stepping around and over slumbering figures.

Jack liked Alex, and could see why he'd impressed the Selection Board enough to be given a commission. Despite his youthful appearance and shyness, he was imposing physically, and exuded an air of quiet courage and determination that had already earned him the genuine respect of some of the hardest judges around: his groundcrew.

Most new boys would have gone to pieces if they'd experienced what Alex had during his first two flights.

Even some of the old stagers would probably have struggled to cope. It was early days, but he seemed to be made of the right stuff. Jack expected him to go from strength to strength, if he survived.

He settled down in an armchair and closed his eyes.

The door into a brightly lit hall is opened by a voluptuous woman in a diaphanous nightgown, her face in shadow. Jack's eyes take in the smooth skin of her neck, then admire her breasts, the curves and dark aureolae just visible beneath the thin material, nipples pushing forward. Lower still, the hint of a dark triangle nestling atop long, shapely, legs.

She raises her arms, the nightgown opens and Jack falls into her embrace, the warmth of her soft flesh contrasting his coldness. He nestles his face against her shoulder and slides his hands inside the gown.

'A Flight scramble, three bandits, angels two five, approaching Deal. A Flight scramble.'

Bugger, bugger, bugger. He can't even make love in his dreams.

Must have been enjoying himself though, because he hadn't heard the phone.

The last of A Flight were just disappearing through the door. Slowly, his eyes adjusted to the glare outside the gloomy hut. The sky was blue. He glanced at the clock above the Ops Desk. Six twenty five. A Flight would probably be in vain pursuit of an enemy reconnaissance aircraft, and when it reported good weather, they'd have another busy day.

He sat up. A few others did the same, but no-one spoke. Some were still slumbering, or pretending to. He shut his eyes and thought back to the previous night.

A woman had opened the door. And she had been standing in a hall bathed in light. But she hadn't been wearing a diaphanous gown, or anything remotely like it. It had been a blue housecoat.

'Please, come in,' she said, waving him forward with a hint of impatience.

She shut the door behind him and leaned against it, heaving a sigh of relief.

'Sorry to be so short,' she smiled. 'The ARP Warden lives on the other side of the road, and he loves nothing more than to tick me off about breaking the blackout.'

'Sorry, I wasn't thinking.'

This was a lie. His mind had been whirring madly since she'd opened the door. He hadn't expected his new landlady to be young, and attractive.

A few moments later, he was sitting in a small front room. In marked contrast to the outside of the house, it was neat and tidy. A highly polished sideboard stood along the back wall opposite a fireplace. In front of the brightly glowing fire, Jack sat on one of two small armchairs with floral fabric covers and antimacassars. Between the chairs was a small table. Above the fire, to either side of an elliptical mirror, hung seascapes and paintings of ships. Similar artwork adorned the other three walls, and the knick-knacks on the mantelpiece also had a maritime theme.

A photograph on the sideboard seemed to offer some explanation. Two young people smiled out: a bride with a bouquet, and a groom in the uniform of a Merchant Navy officer.

He stood up as the young woman in the photograph came in with a tea tray.

'That's a lovely fire, Mrs Spencer.'

'Thank you, Sergeant Williams. It's already getting quite chilly in the evenings, so I thought I'd try and warm the place up a bit. And please, call me Caroline. Mrs Spencer makes me sound like a seaside landlady.'

Jack estimated she was in her early 20s, and she'd shed her housecoat to reveal a trim figure that was about as far from the stereotypical seaside landlady as you could imagine.

'Well, thank you, Caroline, it's very welcoming. And I think you'd better call me Jack. I'm not sure what Sergeant Williams makes me sound like.'

'All right, Jack. Thank you. Now how do you like your tea?'

She had a lovely smile. Her wavy dark hair was short, worn just above the collar of a purple blouse that was complemented by a narrow black skirt. Catching himself appraising her physical attributes, he reminded himself she was a married woman.

He decided to break the silence as she poured the tea. 'Is your husband at sea?'

To that point, he'd picked up no underlying sadness in her demeanour, but now a cloud passed across her face, momentarily dimming the bright sparkle in her dark brown eyes. She lowered the teapot and looked towards the sideboard.

'You could say that. Alfie was killed when his ship was sunk off the coast of Nova Scotia five months ago. Lost with all hands I think the term is.'

'I'm very sorry, and very sorry I asked.'

'It's alright, Jack.' Her eyes were glassy, but there were no tears. 'I like to talk about it. Most people pretend it hasn't happened, and it gets a bit wearing after a while.

'You see, we'd only been married a month, and we'd met only a month before that. In Town.'

She spoke BBC English, with no hint of accent Jack could pinpoint.

'And with the war and everything, we decided to

marry straight away.'

He tried desperately to think of something to say as she added two spoonfuls of sugar to his tea and handed him the cup and saucer.

'Is this your home village?'

'No, no. I come from North London. But Alfie had grown up in this house, and… It's a long story, but his parents died just before the war began, and we moved in after we married. I've just about finished tidying up the inside, but the front's still a bit of a mess I'm afraid.'

Before Jack could express understanding, or commiserate further, she moved on, seeming to speak as much to herself as to him.

'We never really got to know each other. He spent most of our marriage at sea. It's still hard to know whether we did the right thing.'

Jack thought about Gwen and the temptation to marry in haste because of the war, but he decided not to mention it. 'I'm sorry, I can't think of anything clever to say. I usually can.'

He smiled at her and she smiled back.

'No. I'm sorry. It's not the easiest of subjects, is it? But we had to talk about it some time. This is just a bit earlier than I'd expected.'

He wondered why she was still in this house and not with her family. But before he could think of another question, Caroline turned the tables.

'Now, what about you? You must have a wife or a girlfriend at home?'

He was taken unawares.

'No, neither.'

It was the first time he'd acknowledged this to anyone, perhaps even to himself.

From then on, they talked about more mundane things, such as what his routine was likely to be. When they'd finished their tea, Caroline offered to show him to his room.

Despite his determination not to, he couldn't help admiring the shapely calves as she led the way up the stairs. She stopped on the small landing and pointed to the nearer of two white doors.

'This will be your room. I hope you find it suitable?'

'I'm sure I will.'

'And please excuse me if I don't get up at four in the morning to wave you off.' She smiled, 'Good night, Jack.'

'Good night, Caroline.'

Not for the first time, Caroline Spencer wondered whether it had been a good idea to volunteer use of her spare room to RAF Biggin Hill. But she'd wanted to share the ghosts with someone else. And, until now, it had been the disruption to her routine that had made her doubt the wisdom of the move, not the likelihood of tongues wagging. She'd expected an older man, even a woman, not a handsome young pilot. A very pleasant, handsome young pilot.

The neighbours were bound to talk. Perhaps she should ask for a different lodger.

Alex felt sorry for A Flight. They'd barely had time to eat breakfast before they were scrambled again. But this time, B Flight were with them. It was 8.45.

He found strapping in and preparing to taxy easier, but his trepidation seemed just as great, perhaps greater. He knew what to expect now, and his mind was less occupied on the minutiae. More time to think.

Waving off Sandyman and Mead, he fell in behind Jack and Piers. He felt sick, and despite the cold blast through the open canopy, he could already feel sweat prickling his upper lip. Perhaps this feeling would always be with him now, and he'd just have to get used to it. He swallowed, trying to moisten his mouth and rid it of the metallic tang, the taste, he now knew, of fear.

Jack's Spitfire turned into wind and stopped behind the other three sections. Piers passed behind it to line up on the left. Alex turned and positioned himself to his section leader's right. There was a nerve-jangling pause. He looked to a small, battered, green caravan, and waited for the aldis lamp signal to release them.

'Come on, Bastion,' the CO's voice growled.

'Patience, Dragon.'

The distortion on the HF radio was too great for Alex to recognise the Controller as Crispy Rice, but the image of the poor man's face came to him anyway. Perhaps that was why some squadrons discouraged burns victims from visiting.

A small green circle shone from the caravan.

'Dragon, here we go.'

Alex watched the CO's section edge forward and looked to Jack, opening the throttle only when his section leader's Spitfire began to move.

The Merlin engine growled as he advanced the throttle to match Jack's acceleration.

Using brake and large rudder pedal movements, he fought to keep straight, relaxing only as the speed increased and smaller rudder deflections were required. They started to bounce across the grass, the ailerons and elevators gaining authority.

Jack's tailwheel lifted and Alex eased the stick forward to raise his own, seeing Piers do the same. In his peripheral vision, the section ahead leapt into the air. A few seconds later, Jack's mainwheels left the ground, and, with an almost imperceptible backward pressure on the stick, he too was airborne.

'Bastion, this is Dragon Leader, twelve aircraft airborne.'

'Roger, Dragon, this is Bastion, vector one zero zero, one hundred plus bandits, angels one five, approaching Deal.'

From the longer transmission, he was sure it was Crispy. Why had he been drawn into using that horrible nickname with its associated graphic image?

Jack's mainwheels began to retract and Alex resigned himself to ten seconds of yo-yoing as he pumped up his own landing gear. He wasn't disappointed. But he was pleased to see that Piers was also porpoising, as were some of the others in the formation. One day he'd be rock steady, like Jack.

With both hands restored to their rightful positions, he eased away from his section leader's aircraft and concentrated on maintaining a good lookout. The other sections were also more widely spaced, as the CO had briefed, their triangular vics staggered alternately to right and left to allow a better view of the surrounding airspace.

Blue Section were still at the back, but somebody had to hold the short straw.

'Dragon, this is Bastion, bandits easing north, vector zero nine zero.'

'Bastion, this is Dragon Leader, wilco, passing angels eight.'

At least the raiders seemed to be heading for

somewhere other than Biggin Hill. He quartered the sky, realising that he felt more relaxed, calm even, with no hint of airsickness. Good, but the continual changes of mood were very wearing.

It was a beautiful morning. In the sunlight, the ground beneath them was a kaleidoscope of colours: more shades of green than it was possible to count, straw-coloured standing crops, red farmhouses and housing estates, and sandy yellow limestone churches and country houses. Even the deep blue of the sky was mirrored in the waters of the Thames Estuary, just visible to his left.

He took a few moments to admire Jack's Spitfire. From its black propeller spinner, along its camouflaged fuselage to its curving tail, it was a thing of beauty. Sitting atop, encased within the smooth lines of the curved canopy, the pilot, in Jack's case at least, looked at one with the machine.

It was said you didn't so much climb into a Spitfire as put it on. In his darker moments, that feeling of intimacy made it a little too cosy, but for now, with the sun streaming in, Alex felt fine, and immensely proud.

He widened his gaze to the other Spitfires climbing gracefully into the blue sky. Perhaps he could yet make others proud of him as well.

Sophie was watching the map with concern.

There were two raids, both of about 100 aircraft. The first, assigned to Dragon and some of the Hornchurch, North Weald and Debden squadrons, had seemed to be heading west over Kent, but when the counter had last been raked on after an update, it had veered north for the Thames Estuary. The second raid, about ten minutes behind the first, had crossed the coast further south and was also heading for the Estuary.

The Controller was climbing Dragon into the gap between them. She could only marvel at the judgement he was exercising. If he wasn't careful, he could leave them prey to one of the two sets of escorting fighters, maybe both. But he also had another squadron to worry about.

He spoke into his handset.

'Soho, this is Bastion, 100 plus bandits, passing abeam Ashford, angels two zero. Vector one six zero. Buster.'

'Bastion, this is Soho Leader, wilco, passing angels four.'

Sophie was most worried about Dragon and Alex, but she didn't envy Soho and Bunter either. They'd been scrambled from Gravesend and Squadron Leader Rice was vectoring them towards the second raid. To reach it, they'd have to fly under the first and its fighter screen, and Dragon, and they'd be looking into sun the whole way. Even at buster - full throttle - they'd be lucky to make 20,000 feet by the time they reached the bombers. Tactically, they were in a bind.

The counters for Dragon and the first raid were raked off the table. After a short pause, they were pushed back on

'Dragon, this is Bastion, bandits should now be in your twelve o'clock, approximately fifteen miles.'

'Bastion, this is Dragon Leader, roger, passing angels one two.'

The map fore-shortened distances, but looking at the counters, Alex seemed to be heading straight into a trap between 200 enemy aircraft, over 100 of them fighters. She was beginning to understand why some of the other WAAFs in the plotting room watched events unfolding with such trepidation.

'Dragon Leader, from Yellow 3.'

Alex recognised the broken English of the Pole, S to Z.

'Friendlies nine o'clock low, passing behind.'

He looked down to the left. It took a while to spot their camouflaged forms against the patchwork of fields, but 5,000 feet below, another squadron of Spitfires was about to pass behind.'

'Thank you, Yellow 3, Dragon Leader visual.'

There were 12 of them, four tight vics in line astern, moving at high speed. The sight brought a lump to Alex's throat. Did Dragon look half as magnificent?

'Okay chaps, very pretty I grant you, but get those bloody eyes moving again.'

Alex smiled. It was poor radio discipline, but also a timely reminder to look out for Snappers, rather than Spitfires.

'Dragon, this is Bastion, vector zero seven zero, bandits, eleven o'clock, ten miles.'

'Bastion, this is Dragon Leader, wilco, passing angels one five.'

The bandits were now a bit to the north of them, so they should be easier to see. Alex strained into the airspace just to the left of his Spitfire's long nose. It was another minute or more before the radio crackled.

'Dragon Leader, from Red 3, bandits, eleven o'clock, just above the horizon.'

Sophie looked from the map to Squadron Leader Rice. He and the other Controllers made light of the ability to get the squadrons into the right place at the right time.

'Oh, just a matter of using the Mark One Eyeball,' they said nonchalantly when asked. 'And then constructing a 3-D model in your head and directing the squadrons to where the bandits are going to be. Simple really.'

If pressed for more detail, they usually muttered about the TeeLar Method – which she'd subsequently found out meant, That Looks About Right. However they tried to explain the process, they always ended with, 'Simple really.'

Well, simple or not, this Controller had just manoeuvred Dragon into what looked like a perfect position above and behind the first raid.

A tinny voice issued from the speaker on the wall.

'Bastion, this is Dragon Leader. Tally-ho, tally-ho, one hundred plus bandits approaching Isle of Sheppey.'

On the far wall, a light toward the bottom of 646 Squadron's tote board illuminated the word, 'Engaged'.

'Dragon Leader, this is Bastion. Roger and good luck. Bastion, out.'

Sophie watched the Controller lean back and dab the sweat from his mottled skin with a handkerchief. Then, he leaned forward again, peering intently at the map.

'Soho, this is Bastion…

The CO had turned Dragon behind the enemy and formed them into line abreast. Alex went through his pre-combat routine, finishing by lowering his seat to gain maximum protection from the engine and rear seat armour, and to give as much headroom as possible. Even so, the top of his leather helmet was only a few inches below the curved perspex of the canopy.

He suddenly felt very lonely. Although Jack and Piers were close to his left, and the other nine Spitfires were spread out to his right, no-one else could help him control his fear, or this powerful machine. What happened in the next few minutes was down to his skill, or, judging by his performance to date, lack of it. It was all up to him.

'Don't black out this time,' he admonished.

The CO's voice prevented further self-criticism.

'Dragon, in we go. Good luck all.'

Alex eased the stick forward to dive down with the others. The enemy stretched into the distance, the core of bombers surrounded by groups of fighters. Miles ahead, black shapes manoeuvred over 5,000 feet of sky. Gouts of smoke and flame told of a mighty battle.

At the rear, the enemy fighters seemed to be focusing on the same action. For the moment. Dragon were closing fast.

Alex picked a bomber to the rear left, a Dornier, and had a last look round. All clear.

His heart was pounding so hard he fancied he could hear it over the roar of the Merlin engine. Tracer spat from the Spitfire on his right, S to Z anxious to exact revenge for the ravaging of his homeland. Perhaps too anxious. Alex waited.

The Dornier grew steadily.

'Wait, Alex, wait.'

A pinprick of light appeared just behind the canopy of the bomber. It was joined by others. They spread and elongated, racing towards him, then streaking past. His stomach constricted in panic. How could he escape?

From somewhere within, he found the strength not to duck, or pull away. But he had to retaliate. He pressed his thumb hard against the gun button, as if firing back was the only way to save himself.

To his surprise, debris flew off the bomber's fuselage and right wing.

'Got ya,' he shouted, panic giving way to euphoria as he continued firing.

Only when the Dornier grew alarmingly, did he realise he'd made another stupid mistake. His fixation on the target had led him too close to dive behind the bomber. He stopped firing and pulled. His vision dimmed. He felt sweaty and airsick. But he remained conscious and, to the best of his knowledge, undamaged.

A Spitfire passed so close above that it darkened the sky. His aircraft rocked in the slipstream. His thin veneer of control was cracking. Then, two more Spitfires appeared to his right, mirroring his own climb. The sight helped him regain some composure.

They were closing rapidly on a group of about 20 Messerschmitt 110s, behaving very strangely. Jack had told him how the supposedly invincible twin-engined fighters had taken to flying in defensive circles, like cowboys circling their wagons against marauding Red Indians. But weren't they meant to be defending their bombers, rather than themselves?

The thought that someone might be scared of him gave Alex a further boost. He relaxed, flexed his fingers and released his vice-like grip on throttle and stick.

They were nearing the circle of fighters. At a range of about 100 yards, with the black crosses beneath their wings and swastikas on their tailfins plainly visible, he fired at the first 110 crossing his path. Again, bits flew off, but he'd flashed beneath it and into the circle before he could see any further effects.

The air around him erupted with tracer. The nearest Spitfire streamed vapour and rolled right. Expecting to be hit at any moment, Alex rolled left and pulled over the top into a dive. Another 110 appeared below. He pressed the gun button, firing a long burst, more in hope than expectation.

Oblivious to the results of his shooting, he passed through the gap between two 110s into the tracer-free air below. His mind and body already craved rest, but it was not to be. The sight before him was incredible.

The ordered phalanx of bombers had fractured into a chaotic jumble of aircraft manoeuvring frantically to avoid the attentions of Spitfires and Hurricanes that wheeled and dived amongst them. They, in turn, were being assailed by dozens of Messerschmitt 109s.

Until this point, Alex had been only dimly aware of the noise in his earphones.

Now, the cries of warning and terror added immeasurably to the confusion of the scene. It was impossible to tell which agonised voices belonged to which flaming aircraft?

All too soon, he was diving into the mêlée himself. He picked out a Dornier being attacked by what he assumed to be one of his own squadron. Just as he was about to fire, a 109 weaved in behind the other Spitfire.

'Behind you, Snapper on your tail,' he shouted into the general hubbub, rolling and pulling in a frantic effort to engage the Messerschmitt.

Without knowing a name or a callsign, the best he could hope was that all who heard his message would react in some way. But the Spitfire flew straight on, firing at the Dornier.

'Snapper on your tail,' Alex shouted in desperation.

The 109 opened fire, and the Spitfire exploded in a ball of rapidly expanding orange flame and debris.

Tears of anger and frustration stung Alex's eyes. He pulled towards the Messerschmitt. But he'd forgotten how quickly things were moving. From looking down on the whole affair in plan view, he was now diving behind the Dornier and the fireball and onto the 109. It grew and grew, its pilot looking up at him in terror. Missing it's tailplane by inches, Alex plummeted past.

His heart was pounding, his body ached, and his head was so full of conflicting emotions he didn't know what to think.

He was meant to fire on them, not ram them!

But now he was diving at the ground again. With aching arms, he pulled the nose up, praying once more for a respite.

Just as he levelled and his pulse slowed, he spotted a lone Dornier about a mile ahead at a similar height. It was flying a steady course, seemingly unaware of the mayhem a couple of thousand feet above.

Making an instant decision, Alex pushed on the already open throttle. At about 1,000 yards range, he eased into a shallow dive, jinking to make sure the air around him was clear. It was, although the battle above was still raging fiercely.

Following Jack's advice, he closed to about 200 yards behind and a thousand feet below the bomber, and pulled up. The lower rear gunner immediately began to fire at him. This time, he found it easier to ignore the tracer.

Only when he was within about 100 yards did he

press his thumb onto the gun button. After firing a few rounds, his guns stopped.

'Damn'

He pressed again. Nothing.

On the three occasions he'd opened fire previously, he'd failed to control his emotions and wasted precious seconds of ammunition. Now, when he was coolly registering hits on a target, he had no rounds left. Another painful lesson. A fighter without ammunition was about as much use as an ash tray on a motorbike. He pulled away from the tracer arcing in on him.

Looking back, he watched a stream of black shapes tumble out of the Dornier.

Jack glanced anxiously at the Messerschmitts to his left. Even though some of the Spitfires and bombers had begun exchanging fire, they still failed to react.

He returned his attention to the Dornier to his front, and waited for the distance to close. At 100 yards, he fired a short burst, then, with more composure than on the last couple of occasions, pushed to pass beneath its twin tailplane.

'That's better, Jack.'

He was sure he'd hit it, but nothing dramatic had happened.

Alex hadn't appeared beneath the bombers, and Piers was turning hard left into the 109s, which had finally decided to join the action. They'd split into two groups of ten, one running in high, the other low.

Jack made a split-second decision to go with Piers and pulled hard left, grunting against the g. He rolled out head to head with the lower group. Flashes erupted from the lead German's nose and wings, and he returned fire. His opponent's windscreen turned black and Jack pulled up and right. The oil-splattered 109 flew straight on, passing ten feet below. Piers was also climbing, but he rolled left.

Jack decided to continue his right turn and set himself up for a beam attack on another Dornier. Above was a confusion of Spitfires, 109s and a defensive circle of 110s, but a line of dots setting out from his intended target narrowed his interest. Estimating the lay off, he raked the Dornier, feeling a burst of elation as his bullets ripped a swastika-emblazoned tail fin in two.

'Yes.'

He shot behind and beneath the damaged bomber.

Ahead, a Spitfire attacking a Dornier was latched onto by a 109. Before he could shout a warning, the Spitfire exploded.

Another Spitfire appeared, diving vertically. He flinched as it bore down on the 109, but, by some miracle, it passed just behind and plummeted out of sight.

Turning for the 109, he fired. Tracer flashed above him and he pulled hard right. An unidentified wingtip sped past. He picked another Dornier and fired a two second burst. Unsure whether he'd had any effect, he closed to within 50 yards and fired again, watching chunks fly off the left wing and engine cowling.

'Take that, you bastard.'

A hint of darkness in his peripheral vision. He pulled right. A 109. He fired and jinked left to pass down its right hand side. Another 109 to the left. Again he turned hard, grunting, vision dimming until he snapped wings level for a left rear quarter attack. He jabbed the gun button. Nothing. He jabbed again, just in case. But no, nothing.

Breathing heavily, he pulled hard right and dived out of the fight.

Yet again, Alex seemed to have lived a lifetime in an hour: the near miss with the Dornier, the Spitfire hit by withering fire from the circle of 110s, another Spitfire destroyed, while his own effort to engage its nemesis had almost ended in a collision. The images were so vivid they were bound to be added to his nightmares.

But as he taxyed in, what plagued him most was the memory of the bombs dropping from the Dornier. What havoc had they wreaked on the ground below?

For the first time he understood why the absolute priority was to prevent the bombers disgorging their deadly cargo. And he'd failed again.

Rather than remaining cool and professional, he'd fired on impulse, wasting precious ammunition in the heat of the moment. And because of that, innocent people on the ground were probably dead and maimed.

'Been getting into trouble again have we, sir?'

Wearily, Alex rolled off his helmet and draped it over the stick. 'I don't know, Sandy. Have I?'

The smiling engine fitter took his shoulder straps. 'Well you've picked up a few holes in your tail again, sir. It's becoming a bit of a habit.'

'I'll try and be more careful next time,' Alex said as he stepped from the cockpit.

'Yes, please do, sir. We're just getting used to you.'

Alex sensed a hint of seriousness behind the stocky Welshman's banter, and he was touched. He jumped from the wing and walked over to Mead, inspecting the jagged holes in the left tailplane, about half a dozen in total.

Probably from the 110s. Or maybe the Dorniers.

But the offending rounds could have come from anywhere in the mayhem up there.

'Anything wrong with her apart from these, sir?' Mead asked, pointing at the holes.

Jack had said that the groundcrew viewed battle damage as a badge of honour, and Alex could see what he meant from the expression on his rigger's face: part admonition for the damage caused, and the work that would be necessary to fix it, part pride at the visible evidence that his pilot had been in the thick of the action.

They were lifting his spirits again.

'No, she's a real beauty, Scouse. Will you be able to fix her?'

'No problem, sir. We'll have her patched up in no time, don't you worry.'

Alex placed his parachute on the wingtip and walked away. God, he was tired, and it was only just after 9.30 am.

As he exited the pen, he noticed the small groups of tradesmen waiting for their aircraft to return. He knew some were waiting in vain, and his own woes suddenly seemed small in comparison.

'Hold on, Alex.'

He turned to see Piers trotting towards him. His dark-haired friend looked sweaty and grubby, but also happy.

He's not putting it on, Alex thought, he really enjoys combat.

Piers stopped and took a few seconds to light a cigarette, taking a deep drag and sighing in appreciation as he breathed out a cloud of silver smoke.

'Did you manage to stay awake this time, old boy?'

They carried on walking, Alex looking down on his friend, eight inches below.

'Yes thank you, Piers. How about you?'

'Oh, you know. Had a little nap on the way there and back, but managed to stay awake for the main feature. Quite a show, wasn't it?'

'Yes, quite a show.' What a way to describe it, Alex thought. 'Quite a show.'

They came up to the Intelligence Officer just as Ginge Clough was walking away.

Piers gestured Alex forward. 'After you, old boy.'

Nick Hudson was in his usual pose, leaning against the blast wall of the pen nearest the dispersal hut, wearing a uniform and a cap that had seen better days.

In fact, he looked as if he'd seen better days himself. His complexion was sallow, and his wrinkles stood out in a world in which few others were older than their mid-twenties. He took his pipe from what looked like a handy niche in his teeth, and blew out a thin stream of smoke.

'Right, young man, anything to report today?'

He put the pipe back in his mouth, raised his clipboard and pen, and gave Alex his undivided attention.

'Well, on the first bounce, I'm sure I hit a Dornier on the upper fuselage and right wing.'

'Any effect?' the older man interrupted.

'A few bits flew off, but after that, I didn't see anything. Sorry.'

'All right. Carry on.'

Alex replayed the entire engagement in his head, trying to decide what would be of interest to the IntO. 'Then I hit a 110 in a group circling above the formation.' The man looked up. 'I saw bits fly off that as well, but nothing after that.'

Nick Hudson scribbled.

'Then I fired at another 110 on the way out of the circle, but I don't know if I hit it. The only other thing I fired at was a lone Dornier a couple of thousand feet below the main formation. I'm sure I was hitting it, but I ran out of ammunition.'

'Right. Did you see anyone else hitting anything?'

Unless damage or kills were corroborated, either by other pilots or the discovery of wreckage, you were very unlikely to receive credit for anything you claimed.

'Sorry, I didn't. But I did see two of ours get hit.'

The Intelligence Officer looked concerned. 'Go on?'

'Well, a Spit to my right got hit as we climbed into the 110s. It streamed vapour from the nose, and I didn't see what happened after that. But I'm afraid I did see another one buy it. He was chasing a Dornier when a Snapper crept up behind and fired. He exploded straight away. I'd tried to warn him, and then to get the Snapper off, but I was too late.'

'I think that must have been the one I saw, Nick,' Piers butted in. 'Alex is right, it just exploded. Then another Spit speared right past the Snapper. I thought they were going to collide.'

Alex decided to save that story for later. Nick Hudson wouldn't be interested.

The Intelligence Officer tapped the clipboard with the stem of his pipe. 'And I'm afraid it fits with what some of the others say.'

He looked up at the taxying aircraft and the groundcrew standing outside the pens. 'There's still a few more to come back though, so we'll keep our fingers crossed for the one streaming vapour at least.'

Alex asked, 'Has Jack Williams come through yet?'

'Yes, about five minutes ago. Now, unless you've got anything more to add, I'll deal with young Piers here.'

Alex moved to one side, but decided to wait for his friend.

He was embarrassed at inquiring after Jack, but the advice and support of his section leader had become tremendously important to him, perhaps too important. He didn't know how he'd cope if Jack bought it.

Piers finished his more animated report.

'Right, sounds as if you might get a probable out of that, maybe even a kill.'

Piers beamed.

'And you might get a couple of shared damaged, Alex, maybe even a shared kill if the evidence pops up. Remember to fill in your reports both of you.'

'All right,' they muttered, walking away like a couple of recalcitrant schoolboys.

'So that was you was it, sir?'

Jack gave Alex a friendly nudge as the three members of Blue Section walked out of the hut clutching mugs of coffee. 'You do know you're meant to shoot at them, not ram them. That's why they've given us machine guns and two thousand four hundred rounds of ammunition.'

'Oh! Why was I not told this before?' the young officer replied playfully.

Jack was glad Alex was able to joke about what must have been another truly terrifying experience. But he was worried by other developments.

The CO and S to Z had both failed to appear, and

they were certain at least one of them was dead. It was invidious to favour the survival of one over the other, but there was no doubt whose loss would have a greater effect on the Squadron.

Freddie Fowler was the senior flight commander, so he'd take over in the short term. Jack would rather have seen Muddy in the chair. His friend was much better suited to the role. But such decisions were way above his pay grade.

He stopped a short distance from the deck chairs and sank to the grass. 'Right then, let's see what we can learn from that last little lot?'

The two young officers sat down in front of him.

It was just before one o'clock and Sophie watched a black counter being pushed onto the map just off the French coast at Cap Gris Nez. The enemy formation had been designated Hostile 14, and it comprised 100 plus aircraft at 18,000 feet. An adjacent blue arrow pointed towards the English coast at Dungeness. There were no red counters on the map.

She turned towards Squadron Leader Rice. He was looking nervously between the clock, the map and the tote board, drumming the fingers of his mottled right hand on the desk. Every few seconds, he cast a glance at the phones, as if willing the 11 Group Controller to speak to him. He smiled at her, and she smiled back. There was sadness behind the marbled features. Hardly surprising though, was it? Poor man.

He turned away and she looked at the other men on the platform. They were equally pensive. On the map floor, the WAAFs were mostly standing, rakes at the ready. Some were looking back at the platform, others at the map. There was a background hum of female voices talking into headphones, locked in conversation with invisible, inaudible, characters.

Minutes passed. The black counter was raked off the table.

It was replaced with two. The formation had split over Dungeness.

One yellow arrow was pointing north east towards Dover or, more likely, the airfields along the coast: Lympne, Hawkinge and Manston. The other was pointing inland. There were any number of airfields in that direction, but the targets of the morning had been Rochester and Eastchurch.

A buzz of expectation rose from the platform and the floor, and Sophie turned to her flight sergeant. 'Here we go.'

But nothing happened. The hubbub died down, and most eyes turned back towards the platform.

Squadron Leader Rice tapped his fingers and looked at the phones.

The next two minutes dragged endlessly. Sophie signalled to one of her WAAFs. The young girl walked out of a door in the far corner of the room and returned a few seconds later to confirm that the phones were working.

The counters were raked off the map again, and when they were replaced, both raids were heading inland.

Even though it was the sound she'd been expecting for the last five minutes, Sophie jumped as the phone rang. The Sector Controller snatched it up and listened intently.

'Ralph, scramble Soho.'

The flight sergeant to his right picked up a phone.

Squadron Leader Rice listened for another few

seconds, put down the handpiece and immediately picked up another.

'Dragon, scramble, fifty plus bandits, angels one eight, vector one four zero.'

Jack didn't like the way things were developing.

Freddie's tic had developed into a full scale twitch as he'd briefed that he was their Acting CO. It hadn't inspired confidence. More; it had given Jack a deep sense of foreboding that was being borne out now.

They'd been scrambled far too late, and were climbing straight into the incoming raid, and almost into sun. The Controller had done his best, suggesting weaving to gain extra height. But Freddie had ignored him, doggedly maintaining heading. At this rate, they'd still be in the climb when they met the bandits. Tactical suicide.

Jack looked to his two wingmen. If anyone could cope, Piers could, but Alex was still too green to be put in this position.

The R/T crackled. 'Dragon, this is Bastion, bandits twelve o'clock, ten miles. Suggest orbit to gain height.'

Freddie Fowler's strained monotone was devoid of Gerry Palmer's warmth and humour. 'Dragon maintaining heading, passing angels one six.'

'Why maintain heading, you fucking dullard,' Jack shouted in frustration. 'You're going to kill us all.'

And then he saw them. Unable to keep the edginess out of his voice, he made his report. 'Dragon Leader, from Blue Leader, bandits twelve o'clock, slightly high.'

The enemy formation was smaller than many they'd encountered over the last few days, but infinitely more dangerous. If Dragon carried on as they were, the Snappers would be on them before they were anywhere near the bombers.

'Bastion, this is Dragon Leader. Tally-ho, tally-ho, fifty plus, angels one eight.'

'Dragon, this is Bastion. Roger. Good luck.'

'Because you'll bloody well need it,' Squadron Leader Rice snapped as he positively slammed the handset into its cradle.

Sophie had never seen him so angry, but he swept a hand down his face and his cool, professional, persona re-emerged.

'Soho, this is Bastion, bandits ten o'clock low, five miles. Buster, repeat, buster.'

Tracer ripped through the Spitfires to Jack's front. They took evasive action, but oh so slowly. That's what happened when you were caught in the climb!

Dark shapes against the sun. A wingtip swept over him. He pushed, desperate to accelerate, to gain energy. His engine coughed. The sky darkened as 20 plus Heinkels passed overhead. He rolled right to seek sanctuary beneath their bulky forms.

A white rod flashed past, followed by others. He may have evaded the fighters, but the Heinkel lower gunners had spotted him. His refuge suddenly seemed anything but safe.

The formation passed overhead, and he turned right to follow it. More tracer, this time from above and behind. A violent impact. The stick flew from his grasp. He was thrown against the right hand side of the cockpit.

Bruises on bruises!

The aircraft nose dropped and it rolled left. The stick was jammed in the front left hand corner of the cockpit. Jack levered himself forward, grabbed it and yanked it over to the right. Still the aircraft rolled left, only reacting to his control input when just short of the inverted.

He looked left. 'Dugger!'

He was rolling upright, but his entire left wingtip to a depth of about three feet had disappeared, leaving a jagged edge and a few severed wires whipping about in the airflow.

A 109 flashed in front of his nose. Tracer shot from over his left shoulder. Two more 109s. He pulled into their fire, rolling more crisply than he'd expected.

Well, at least he still had control, but for how long? And who knew what other damage he'd sustained, or how robust the remains of the left wing were?

The two Messerschmitts passed close overhead. If they turned back, he was dead. But they were suddenly enveloped in tracer. One belched smoke, rolled onto its back and fell away.

Two Spitfires appeared, diving at high speed. They turned to engage the remaining 109.

'Thank you, boys,' Jack shouted, as he rolled and dived away from the fight.

Alex heard shouts. Before he could react, his airframe shuddered and there was a stinging pain in his right wrist. He resisted the urge to let go of the stick, and pulled right, blinded by the sun.

His legs were cold and wet. Bullet wounds? Bloody stumps? Wincing in anticipation, he peered down. The limbs were there, but his trousers were soaked in dark liquid. He felt sick.

Raising his head, he looked out. His Spitfire was on its back, its nose dropping.

'Fly the fucking aircraft, Alex!'

He rolled upright. This time, it wasn't only his claustrophobia, the motion and the fear that were causing his nausea.

His nostrils were full of a cloying smell. Something was making him light headed, adding to his airsickness and indecision.

Opening the canopy, he gulped fresh air. After a few seconds, he steeled himself, and looked in again. His watch was missing and there was a tear in his flying glove from which a thin stream of blood flowed. The stain on his trousers was growing, like ink on blotting paper, and his lower legs and feet were soaking. But there was no pain?

Then, he placed the overpowering smell. Fuel!

An image of Crispy Rice flashed into his mind. Heart racing, he swivelled his head in a fearful search for the enemy. There were aircraft high above, but, as far as he could see, none near him. His pulse slowed, and he tried to reason.

What had happened? And what was he to do?

There was no way he could rejoin the fight, of that at least he was sure. He lowered the nose and dived on the reciprocal of the Squadron's climb heading.

What had happened?

Strange as it seemed, a shell must have entered the cockpit, taken his watch, scratched his hand and holed the lower fuel tank. All without exploding, thank God. But he was still in a pickle. He looked in at his fuel-drenched legs, and then out in another, less panicked search for enemy aircraft. Still clear.

But it wouldn't need another shell to ignite the fuel,

any spark would do.

Switch off the electrics then? No, that would generate sparks. And don't speak on the radios. So much for help from the Controller.

Another cruel picture of Crispy Rice, head and hands burning.

Perhaps he should take to his brolly? But he'd never parachuted before, and the aircraft was behaving for the present, so why risk it? He must still be losing fuel, but hopefully not so much that he'd run out before reaching Biggin Hill. Of course, there could be a bigger hole on the other side of the tank, but…

'Damn it. Come on, Alex.'

He decided to stay with the aircraft, but he wished he was wearing regulation flying gear. The heavy flying suit, gauntlets and goggles would have offered far more fire protection than his uniform.

He undid his seat harness and readied himself to jump at the first sign of smoke or flames.

Jack walked slowly along the line of largely empty pens.

He hadn't felt so dejected since his first few missions over Dunkirk, when they'd realised their heavy losses were partly due to their own stupidity in pursuing tactics devised in peacetime that were impractical in war. Since then, although he still believed they could have done more, they had learned lessons, and his morale had improved as he, Muddy and Binky had used their time at Pembrey to hone their tactics to minimise losses.

And now this.

How could they allow themselves to be led into such a disaster?

Nick Hudson's voice roused him. 'What's the matter, Jack?'

'Am I the first back?'

'Yes. Did you have a problem?'

'You could say that. Lost a wingtip. Probably to a Snapper. Lucky to get away at that though. I was rescued by the cavalry.'

The Intelligence Officer raised a mystified eyebrow.

'Another Spit squadron. They must have managed to get to height. Sorry, sir. Not being very coherent am I?'

'You're okay, Jack. Just take your time.'

'We were late getting off. Fifty plus, they said. It was always going to be difficult, but Freddie just kept climbing us straight ahead. Wouldn't take any help from the Controller. And we just followed him. The Snappers pounced out of the sun while we were still climbing.

'We should have left him to it, sir. Done our own thing. But we're all too bloody disciplined. Just followed him, like lambs to the slaughter. Bloody stupid. Thank God for the other squadron.'

'Any idea who they were?'

'No. Sorry. Just Spits, and not a minute too soon. For me anyway.'

'And for some of the others by the look of it.' Nick Hudson pointed.

Other aircraft were nearing the pens.

Jack recognised Alex's fitter and rigger running out. The Spitfire they were approaching turned away and stopped, but didn't shut down as expected. With the engine still running, an extremely tall pilot stepped out onto the wing. Only when he leaned back in did the propeller wind down amid clouds of smoke.

Alex stood in the fumes belching from the stub exhausts and rolled off his helmet.

He turned and walked uncomfortably down the wing. Sandyman and Mead were looking up at him. At first, their faces registered quizzical concern, but then they crumpled in disgust.

Their loyalty was obviously being tested by the stain darkening his trousers from crotch to boots, but he couldn't think of anything to say. As he neared them, their nostrils twitched. The penny finally seemed to drop, and they both looked relieved.

'Bloody hell, sir, you're not meant to bathe in it you know.'

'Thank you, Scouse. As you can see, I seem to have suffered a small fuel leak.'

The enforced levity was a welcome relief. The return to the airfield had tried his nerves to the limit. Every glint of sunlight on glass or metal had raised the spectre of fire, and set his heart racing.

'More than a small leak from the look of you, sir,' Sandyman joined in. 'And I wouldn't spend too long in those trousers if I was you.'

The engine fitter was right. It would be a shame to survive the attentions of the Luftwaffe, only to succumb to a stray spark from a Swan Vesta or Woodbine. But there was no way he was de-bagging and walking bare legged to the dispersal hut, whatever the fire risk. He'd just have to be careful until he reached the locker room.

Sandyman continued, 'I saw something as you taxyed in, sir, but I didn't think it would cause a fuel leak.' He signalled them to follow.

They walked round the tailplane to the right hand

side of the Spitfire. The engine fitter pointed towards the cockpit. Just beneath the canopy rail, where Alex's right armpit would have been, was a jagged hole.

'Seeing that, sir, I was relieved to see you get out in one piece.'

'Thank you, Sandy.'

Trying to maintain his air of studied nonchalance, Alex held up his right hand and pulled back his jacket sleeve. 'Took me flaming watch off though.'

Both airmen whistled at the bloody welt on his wrist where the strap had been ripped away.

Alex too was impressed. It was the first time he'd seen it himself. He removed his flying glove and inspected his hand with renewed interest. The fleshy part behind his little finger was crossed by an ugly graze. He shuddered at the thought of the damage the shell might have caused.

'I should get those seen to, sir,' Sandyman advised. 'Hundred octane's horrible stuff to get in cuts; we should know.'

'Thanks, Sandy, I'll do that.'

The cuts had been stinging since he'd first put his hand down to ease himself off his wet parachute pack for a few seconds. And perhaps it was his imagination, but his nether regions also felt sore.

'Now, if you'll excuse me, I'm going to change.'

'Take your time, sir,' Mead said pointing to the underside of the aircraft. 'This one's going nowhere but the hangar for a while.'

All the way back from the cockpit to the tailwheel, droplets of liquid were dribbling along the bottom skin and dripping onto the grass.

Jack couldn't help but laugh as the tall, blond young

man walked, stiff-legged, towards Nick Hudson.

'You look like Douglas Bader, young sir,' he shouted, having cast around for a more heroic description than the first that had come to mind.

'More like someone who's shat 'emselves,' shouted Ginge Clough, displaying no such squeamishness. Raucous laughter rose from the small group hovering near the Intelligence Officer.

'Very funny, ha ha,' Alex retorted.

It had been a very sober group until now, and Jack was grateful they'd found something to laugh at. Only six had returned so far, and Ginge, Birdy and Dusty Miller had all, like him, limped home with various degrees of damage.

'Phwoah, you don't smell too good either, sir,' Ginge continued, playing to the gallery again. 'You should try a different perfume.'

Alex flicked a V sign and stopped in front of the clipboard-wielding flight lieutenant. Jack couldn't hear what he was telling the older man, but, if he was anything like the rest of the group, it would be a tale of fighting for survival against a largely unseen enemy.

He watched the young officer hold up his forearm and hand, and Nick Hudson adopted a concerned expression, before speaking a few words. Alex nodded, turned away, and waddled towards Jack.

'I'm sorry, sir, but it does look funny.'

'Doesn't feel it, I can tell you. I think most of it's evaporated now, but half my skin seems to have gone with it.'

'What happened?'

Jack listened attentively while Alex related his story, and showed his wounds. He made to offer some advice, but the young man cut him short.

'I know. I'll get changed and try and get a lift to the medical centre straight away.'

Jack smiled as the young man walked towards the dispersal hut. Yet again, he thanked the German shell manufacturers for their shoddy workmanship. Turning back to the airfield, he was relieved to see Muddy emerge from a pen and walk wearily towards them. He had no doubt the Squadron would need Flight Commander B's leadership now, whether the CO and Acting CO were safe or not. His thoughts were interrupted by a shout.

'That's Freddie's aircraft.'

Ginge was pointing at a Spitfire at the end of its landing run, over half a mile away.

His Geordie companion's eyesight was legendary, but how he could be so positive at that distance was beyond Jack. Unusually, the aircraft didn't turn and taxy towards them, and even Jack could tell that the pilot looked worryingly immobile, stiff and upright.

An ambulance and a three-tonner from the pens raced across the grass and halted by the Spitfire. Two men jumped from the lorry and climbed straight onto the wings. They opened the canopy, leaned in and were enveloped in smoke as the propeller wound down.

The ambulance crew joined them, and together they helped, or more accurately, lifted the pilot from the cockpit. He was walked down the wing, where others helped him to the ground and into the back of the ambulance. The doors were shut and it drove off.

'Save me wringing his fuckin' neck,' Ginge growled.

Jack took a seat in Muddy's smoke-filled office.

Like the rest of them, his friend looked desperately tired, still trying to come to terms with the results of the last engagement.

Smithy, Boy and Tubby Granger were missing, and seven other aircraft had been damaged. Only Piers and Grizzly Houlahan had survived unscathed. Muddy himself had suffered an oil leak and been lucky to make it back.

'I've just had some good news from Ops for a change,' he said with a weary smile, placing his pipe in the ashtray. 'The CO's phoned in. Fished out of the Estuary by a passing ship about an hour ago, and he's in one piece. Says he might not be in 'til tomorrow, but he will be in.'

'That is good news,' Jack said with a feeling of genuine relief, dampened only by the implicit confirmation that S to Z had been in the Spitfire he, Alex and Piers had seen explode.

He'd known so little about his Polish colleague. They'd never exchanged anything beyond banter and shop talk. Did he have a wife and family? And if so, had they survived the invasion of their country, and did the Squadron have any way of getting in touch with them, or any other relatives? Once again, he was glad it wasn't his problem.

But they still had the rest of the day to get through. And who was going to lead them?

'Any more news on Freddie?'

'Not really. Flight Sergeant Patterson helped him out of the cockpit and into the ambulance. As far as they could tell, he was uninjured, but they couldn't get him to move under his own steam. Couldn't get him to talk either. Even his tic had gone.'

Although Jack was more sympathetic than Ginge,

he hoped they'd seen the back of the poor man. His brief stint in command had cost the Squadron dear.

'Do you think we'll see him again?'

'You can never be sure, but I doubt it. If he does pitch up, I'm going to have to speak to Group. Should have done it in the first place, or at least led a mutiny when he wasn't listening to the Controller. We all knew he wasn't up to it, didn't we?'

'Don't blame yourself, Muddy. It's not what we do, is it - mutiny?'

'No. I suppose not. But where do we go from here?'

As usual, Jack was flattered that Muddy had chosen him to talk things through. A few days ago, Binky would have been with them, and his absence emphasised the dire straits they were in. He decided to start on a positive note.

'Well, I don't think we need to worry too much about aircraft.'

'No. If the last few days are anything to go by, they'll make up the losses overnight. Until then, I've told Ops we don't have enough kites to launch more than a flight. Not that we've got the manpower to do much more than that anyway. That's what I wanted your help with. Could you run through who's come and gone since we talked on Friday night? I'll tick them off.'

Jack waited patiently while his friend picked up his pipe, re-lit it in a series of puffs that reduced the visibility in the room still further, then picked up a pencil, nodded and looked down at the pad in front of him.

'Well, the nineteen on Friday went up to twenty two for a short time on Saturday, with the new sergeants, Ellis and Thomson, and Alex. But then we lost

155

Thomson and Johnny Thwaite the same day, then Ellis on Monday and S to Z today. So, eighteen.'

Muddy was scoring through names. Jack waited for another nod before continuing.

'Binky's out of it, and now, another three are missing. Fourteen. We'll count Freddie out, and Olly Barratt won't be back 'till Monday at the earliest. Twelve.'

The rule of thumb of one day off in five was a joke, but you had to give people a break eventually. 'Chips and Pete went on 48s today, and Dunc is on compassionate. So, a possible nine tomorrow, if the CO gets back on time, and Alex turns out to be okay. In the meantime, we're down to seven.'

Muddy looked up. 'That's what I worked out, but I couldn't quite believe it. We've only been here just over a week.'

There was a knock on the door, and Birdy looked in.

'Smithy's okay. He's just rung the Adj. Took to his brolly over Sittingbourne and says he should be back tonight.'

'Thank goodness for that. Thanks, Birdy. And tell the boys the CO'll be back tomorrow as well.'

'Great. I'll tell them now.' He backed out.

The door had hardly shut when they heard a cheer, Ginge's voice clearly audible above the others.

Jack and Muddy looked at one another and smiled.

'A possible ten tomorrow then,' Jack added.

'And twelve by the afternoon,' Muddy continued, looking a bit sheepish. 'I hated doing it, but I asked George to try and get Chips and Pete back. I told him to leave Dunc.'

'Good. I think it's his parents' funeral tomorrow.'

'Birmingham, wasn't it?'

'Near enough. Castle Bromwich.'

'And I'm sorry, Jack, I meant to stand you down tomorrow, but…'

'Thanks for the thought anyway, Muddy.'

'And as if all this wasn't enough,' the flight commander's tone had lightened.

Jack raised an inquisitive eyebrow and waited for him to elaborate.

'We're going to have to grovel to 629. They saved our bacon today.'

'I know, but even so, I don't think I can stomach being nice to them.'

'I think you might have to. I bet they make it over for the dance.'

'Sorry, Muddy. I won't be there.'

'Not like you to miss the chance to drink beer and ogle pretty WAAFs, Jack.'

'I know, but I've still got to unpack and settle into me digs.'

'Bit of a battleaxe, is she?'

'You could say that, Muddy. You could say that.'

Kelvin Rice put the phone down.

The Group Controller had listened to Dragon's various woes without interruption. Then, he'd undertaken to give them a break, if he could, and to find them an experienced flight commander, although where from, and when, he wasn't sure.

The man at Group also expressed relief at the news of Gerry Parr's survival, and let slip that they'd probably have pulled the Squadron from the line if he'd been lost. As it was, they were barely a functioning unit until he returned.

He looked across at Sophie. What had he said to cause her such anguish?

It was five o'clock by the time Alex returned to the Squadron. He'd taken a bath in the Medical Centre, and his lower body was fine; just a few chafe marks from walking in trousers soaked in chemicals. His right wrist and hand had been dressed, a tad over-dramatically he thought, and he'd been given enough tubes of cream to keep him going for months.

The survival of the CO and Smithy was good news, but he now knew he'd watched S to Z die.

Or had he failed to save him?

Overly harsh perhaps, but it didn't stop him thinking it.

There was still no news of Boy and Tubby, but he was glad to see Piers and Grizzly, neither of whom had returned before he'd left.

On the way back, he'd dropped into Clothing Stores.

'They said I could have new socks,' he related to the backs of half a dozen deck chairs. 'But there was no way they'd give me a replacement watch.'

He continued in an officious voice. 'Watches are valuable and attractive items, sir. I'm afraid I can't replace it until you return the old one.'

Laughter rose from the deck chairs, and a Geordie voice piped up.

'Fuckin' storemen. Don't you just love 'em? And by the way, sir, you need another bath. I can still smell fuel.'

Alex sniffed. It wasn't just paranoia then! Or was it?

They'd been brought to cockpit standby at about 7.30pm. And now, they'd been sitting in their Spitfires awaiting the call to start engines for 30 minutes.

It had been the most nerve-jangling half hour of Alex's young life. Despite the proximity of his groundcrew and fellow pilots, he felt desperately lonely and fearful. Every crackle of the radio made him jump.

And why could he still smell fuel? He'd bathed till his skin wrinkled, put on clean clothes, even changed his headset, and still the stench was attacking his nostrils. He could taste it.

The radio crackled again and he started, his pulse quickening in anticipation. But the static died into silence. He clenched his right hand and manipulated his wrist. The bandages, such a potent reminder of his frailty, wouldn't be there tomorrow. They were just too restrictive and cumbersome.

Sandyman leaned against the right wingtip, waved, then put his hand to his mouth in a theatrical yawn. Alex smiled and waved back. To his other side, Mead laid his head against the left wing and feigned sleep. Alex smiled again, but then retreated into his shell.

He just didn't want to fly a third time. Not today. If he did, he knew his luck would run out.

A few pens along, Jack was also feeling tortured. He hated cockpit standby. Once he was strapped in, he wanted to be off.

He tapped impatiently on the side of the canopy arch and watched Brummie strolling around beyond the left wingtip, absentmindedly kicking at blades of grass. On the other side, his engine fitter, Stokes, leaned against the blast wall, basking in the last rays of the sinking sun. He looked as if he was having a pleasant daydream.

For once, Jack seemed unable to concoct a diverting fantasy himself.

He tended not to be plagued by memories of past combat, even events as dramatic as his recent parachuting experience, nor to dwell on the loss of friends. No, more often than not, when combat didn't intervene, he could lose himself in an erotic encounter with Gwen. This evening though, he found himself unable to conjure up any diverting images of his girlfriend.

But there was more. The enforced solitude was making him face up to thoughts he'd rather avoid. He still hadn't had the opportunity to finish with Gwen, so why had he told Caroline he didn't have a girlfriend? And why had he told Muddy that he had to go to his new digs to unpack, when it had taken him no more than five minutes the previous evening?

He leaned back and closed his eyes.

A front door opened into a brightly lit hall. Before him, stood a voluptuous young woman in a diaphanous nightgown. She turned…

His eyes flicked open.

Alex walked into the Sergeants' Mess bar with Piers and Olly. They'd been giving him a hard time all the way there.

'Stood down early and we still end up late. It's nearly half past nine for God's sake. All because you have to have another bloody bath. And how do you repay us for our loyalty? You turn up smelling like a Turkish brothel. We're risking our reputations just being seen with you.'

'Oh shut up,' Alex said in mock exasperation as they approached the bar. The bath with one bandaged hand had taken longer than intended, but he wasn't going to give in to their bullying. 'Do you want a beer or not?'

'Least you can do, old boy,' Piers said, winking at Olly.

The barman's nose twitched and Alex knew they were right. He had overdone the Gentlemen's Cologne. But it had to be better than fuel, didn't it?

The thought transported him back to the cockpit, just over an hour earlier.

'Dragon, this is Bastion.'

After over half an hour of inactivity, this was it, the call he'd been dreading.

'Stand down, I say again, stand down.'

The words had been as welcome as they'd been unexpected, and, when he heard the tone of Muddy's reply, he realised he hadn't been the only one to feel relieved.

'Bastion, this is Dragon Leader, wilco. Thank you.'

'You're welcome. Have a good night, Bastion out.'

Somehow, it had felt like a stay of execution.

He turned with their beers and Piers blew smoke over him.

'Watch it.'

'Just trying to camouflage the smell, old boy. You'll thank me in the long run. Now, where are all the WAAFs?'

The sound of music floated in from the next room, but most of the WAAFs seemed to be sitting at tables on the far side of the large bar. Opposite them, most of the men stood in boisterous groups, drinking beer. One of the groups comprised Muddy, Birdy, Ginge and

Dusty. And Smithy. Alex, Piers and Olly walked towards them.

Ginge's nose crinkled and Alex steeled himself.

'Well, young sir, nobody can say you smell of fuel now.'

They all laughed, and Ginge continued, 'Welcome to the Sergeants' Mess. Not quite the gin palace you're used to I know, but we like to call it home. Or we did, till we was made 'omeless by an uncaring system.'

'Hardly homeless from what I've heard, Ginge,' Muddy chipped in. 'Sounds like you landed on your feet. A merry widow in a large semi.'

'Merry, but ancient, unfortunately. But it is quite spacious I grant you. Not quite Sambrook Hall though, is it, sir?'

'Sambrook House actually. But okay, Ginge. I give in. You're a poor disadvantaged waif, now shut up and get the next round in.'

Ginge turned to Alex with a pitiful expression. 'See how I'm treated, young sir.' He scuttled off to the bar to a chorus of catcalls.

Alex looked around their smiling faces. He'd formed strong bonds over his months of flying training, but this was different.

No matter how soppy and melodramatic it sounded, he loved these men, even after only four days in their company, and he was prepared to do anything to earn their friendship and respect.

He wished Jack was there, and was just wondering how he was getting on with his unpacking, when Sophie walked in, surrounded by a group of WAAFs.

Jack was sitting in the front room of 5 Keston Avenue, listening to the sound of clinking china.

He was examining the wedding photograph again. The couple smiled out as if it was the happiest day of their lives, the start of a long and happy marriage. How could they know otherwise? Alfie looked a few years older than Caroline. A handsome chap though.

She came in with a tea tray, walked round and placed it on the low table. Part of him regretted concocting the story about unpacking. He'd have been much more at ease in the Sergeants' Mess bar. But, for some reason, he'd wanted to sit in this room again.

'Your husband looked very smart in his uniform,' he said, spouting the first thing that came into his head.

'Thank you. Alfie was very proud of it. And so was I.'

'Quite right too. I don't know where we'd be without the merchant fleet.'

The exchange provoked images of ships sinking off Dunkirk and in the Channel. Not a subject he wanted to raise with Caroline. She jumped in to save him.

'Sorry, Jack, I'm afraid I can't remember how many sugars you take.'

'Two please.'

He admired her as she spooned in his sugar, poured a little milk in both cups and poured the tea. She was free of make up, wearing a dark skirt and white blouse, and she looked beautiful. The vital statistics he'd imagined a couple of hours previously seemed very close to the mark. He felt himself colour as he remembered the daydream.

She handed him his cup and saucer, picked up her own and sat back in her armchair.

'I'm afraid I'm not very good at accents, Jack. Which part of Wales do you come from?'

'A little place called Barry.' He hoped he wasn't

blushing too noticeably.

'Oh yes. Near Cardiff, isn't it?'

She laughed at his look of exaggerated surprise.

'Well done. Not many people have heard of it.'

'Well, it's only because Alfie mentioned it. I'm not sure he'd sailed from there, but he'd certainly sailed out of Cardiff, and Newport. Are the docks as big as Cardiff's?'

'Not far off. Most of my friends work there, or on the ships. But there's an RAF base nearby, and it was aircraft that grabbed me.'

'Have you always been a pilot?'

'No, no. Always wanted to be. But I joined the RAF as an engineering apprentice when I was sixteen. Did two years training at Halton, near Aylesbury. But I was still interested in being a pilot, and we could apply just before we graduated, so that's what I did. I should have done three years on the ground before the final selections were made, but I was called forward early for some reason, and here I am.'

'I'm sure it wasn't quite that easy,' she laughed again.

'Well, selection and training took a bit of time, but I joined the Squadron – 646 - at Hornchurch in May last year, just before Dunkirk. We went to Pembrey in south west Wales in June, and came here just over a week ago.'

'I know. I work in the NAAFI shop.'

'Well I never,' Jack said, genuinely surprised this time.

'I started just before your squadron flew in. We don't see many pilots, but we get your groundcrew in all the time, so we hear some of what's going on.'

'I'm sorry, but I'm sure I'd have noticed you on the

NAAFI wagon.'

'Ah, that's a sore point. I'm not allowed out yet. Not experienced enough. Would you like another tea?'

'Yes please, Caroline.' He smiled and handed her his cup and saucer.

Alex was over the moon. Although she'd seemed surprised at first, Sophie now looked genuinely pleased to see him. They exchanged coy nods as she walked to the bar. He was just wondering what to do next, when 629 piled in and she disappeared in the crowd.

Most of the other squadron's pilots came over eventually, and they were forced to engage in good natured banter with their rescuers. Alex tried to play his part, but he found himself increasingly distracted.

Sophie was with a few of her WAAFs, but Bunter, the slightly podgy, red-faced chap who'd summoned her in the corridor a few nights previously, was standing in front of her, hemming her in, like an over-attentive sheepdog.

Every now and then, she looked over and they exchanged shy smiles, but Bunter always seemed to interpose himself between them again.

Alex was plagued by indecision. Even if Piers was right, and Sophie really liked him, he couldn't just go over and butt in, could he? He'd probably just dry up and make a fool of himself.

'Come on, Alex.'

'What?'

'Come on,' said Piers. 'I've just spotted Angela, and I'm going to introduce Olly to her friend. I'll introduce you to Bunter as well if you like?'

Alex looked across the room.

'Well come on then. Don't just stand there gawping

like a goldfish, or do I have to spell it out?'

Olly was laughing at Alex's obvious confusion.

Enunciating as if talking to a congenital idiot, Piers said, 'I'll introduce you to Bunter. And Bunter's talking to Sophie. And then you can talk to both of them. Okay?'

That was all very well, but what was he going to say? Before he could remonstrate, his two colleagues grabbed his elbows and marched him over. They only let go when they stopped in front of Sophie and her companion.

'Alex, meet Bunter Arbuthnott. Bunter, meet Alex Lowe.'

Alex watched Sophie put a hand to her mouth, suppressing a giggle. He felt dreadful.

'Hello, Bunter,' he said in as confident a voice as he could muster. 'I've heard a lot about you.'

Bunter sniffed. He looked at Piers and Olly, as if fearing some trick. Eventually, he turned to Alex. 'Hello Alex, pleased to meet you too, although I think we met this afternoon, when you and your squadron ran away.'

He guffawed loudly and looked at Sophie, waiting for an echo of laughter that never came.

'Bunter, you're such an arse,' Piers said contemptuously, before adding, 'excuse us,' and dragging Olly towards Angela and her pretty, dark-haired, friend.

The young women looked away as the two pilots approached.

Alex was wondering how to recoup the situation when Bunter's name was called. Muddy and a young pilot from 629 were beckoning him over.

Reluctantly, Bunter excused himself. 'Won't be a

minute, Soph', he said, and sloped off.

'Sorry about that, Alex. Piers is right, he is an…'

Alex feigned shock, but she curtailed the sentence and laughed. 'Well, he is, isn't he?'

'This is only the second time I've clapped eyes on him, but I have to say that he does come across as a bit of a plank.'

'Very politely put.'

She smiled briefly, before taking on a more serious expression. 'I'm actually quite relieved to see you looking so well. The last I heard, you were heading off to the Medical Centre.'

'Have you been checking up on me?' he asked in mock concern.

It was Sophie's turn to blush.

'Don't be mean. No, I heard Squadron Leader Rice going through the state of your Squadron with Group, and he mentioned you going to sick quarters.'

'Oh I see. Well to be truthful, these bandages make it all seem much worse than it is. Just a couple of cuts. And I've got the Station's entire supply of yellow cream to put on them.'

Sophie smiled again, her cheeks dimpling as she maintained eye contact.

Alex reddened under her gaze. 'Can I get you a drink?'

'Yes please, that would be lovely.'

Great, he thought, but he couldn't help noticing her nose twitch as he squeezed past and made for the bar.

'I should go back to my old trade after six years as a pilot,' Jack was explaining. 'But I can't imagine life without flying now.'

Caroline Spencer was leaning back, listening

intently to the handsome young Welshman talking passionately about flying. He reminded her of Alfie in some ways. He'd had a similar passion for seafaring. It was part of what had attracted her to him.

Jack was lost in his subject now, but not so lost that he couldn't admire Caroline, her face aglow in the flickering light of the fire.

'It's hard to explain, but there's such a feeling of freedom up there. Even when you're with eleven other aircraft, you're on your own really. None of them can help you control this incredibly powerful machine. It's all up to you.'

'Sounds terrifying,' Caroline interjected.

'I suppose it does to some people, perhaps most people. But not to me. It's the most liberating thing in the world.'

Like this conversation, he thought. He'd never spoken like this with Gwen. She would never have understood, or even been interested. But he could tell by the arch of her eyebrows, by her intensity, that Caroline was interested; and, somehow, he sensed that she also understood.

'And what about when you're fighting?' she asked.

'Well, I have to admit, that's bloody terrifying at times, if you'll pardon my French. But there's also an incredible feeling of control. It's me and my Spitfire against them.'

She suddenly looked tired, as if talk of combat had touched a raw nerve.

'Sorry, it's late, and I'm banging on.'

'No, it's fine. I'm really interested. I meet all these people in the shop, but I never really have the opportunity to talk about what they do.'

Well, she'd certainly had him talking. He seemed to

have related his life story pretty comprehensively, minus Gwen of course. But Caroline had given little away, and what she had revealed had only been gleaned by reading between the lines. For instance, he sensed that her parents hadn't really approved of her marriage, and that she wasn't prepared to go back to them. Hence the job in the NAAFI shop.

'But you're right. It is late, and I expect you've got to be up at four again. I'm not in until lunch time. I'll think of you up there, enjoying your freedom, while I'm trapped amongst the baked beans.'

Jack had no doubt he'd think of Caroline as well.

Chapter 5 – Thursday 29ᵗʰ August 1940

The CO was waiting at dispersal when Jack and the others arrived at 5.00am. He looked worse than he'd have had them believe, more strained, and with a nasty limp. But he made time for some light-hearted banter, before he and Muddy disappeared into his office. Jack found a chair and was soon oblivious to his surroundings. When he came to, Muddy was standing over him, smiling broadly.

'Aha. Welcome back. I thought you were never going to wake up.'

'Oh, hello, sir,' Jack stretched and yawned. 'What time is it?'

'Eight. Breakfast has just arrived. Grab yourself something and come for a chat.'

A few minutes later, Jack was sitting in Muddy's office with a bacon butty in his hand and a steaming mug of tea on the desk. Thankfully, the weather outside was still dank. It had already given them a few hours' respite, and it might give them a few more; it wasn't meant to clear up until after lunch.

Muddy drew on his pipe. 'How was the battle axe?'

'Sorr… Oh fine,' Jack answered. He'd have some explaining to do if Muddy ever saw Caroline. He changed the subject. 'Amazing what a few early nights without beer can do. I ought to try it more often. Don't suppose I will though.'

'Well, we had a good time in the Sergeants' Mess. Smithy turned up, we ate a bit of humble pie with 629, drank lots of beer and went back to Sambrook House. And then we drank more beer, as far as I can remember.'

He pulled a face that indicated he was still suffering

from the after-effects, then put his pipe in the ashtray. 'But, on with the war. We want you to lead B Flight.'

Jack held the sandwich short of his mouth.

'I know, but the CO and I think you're the best man for the job. Grizzly'll be nominated as flight commander, but we want you to lead in the air.'

Jack considered remonstrating: shouldn't it be an officer not an NCO? But since the demise of Binky and Freddie, he had more combat experience than anyone other than the CO and Muddy. And hell, he was proud to be given the opportunity, despite the ribbing he was about to get from Ginge and Dusty.

'Thanks, I accept your kind offer.'

Muddy smiled, looking relieved. 'Good.'

'But what about Blue Section?'

'I'm going to give it to Piers.'

'Another fine choice, if I may say so.'

'Thank you,' the flight commander said in mock gratitude, and they both laughed. 'We'll sort the detail out in a minute, but I'm afraid there's more bad news from yesterday.'

'Go on,' Jack said, preparing himself for the worst.

'Tubby bought it. Found him still in his kite, not far from where Smithy baled out. And Boy's in hospital.' Muddy's face took on an even more pained expression. 'He's lost a leg, I'm afraid.'

Jack felt a knot in his stomach. He put the remains of his sandwich on the desk. Death he could deal with, but the thought of the ridiculously youthful 19 year-old lying in hospital minus a leg made him feel sick. Just as with burns, he wasn't sure he could face losing a limb.

Douglas Bader was an example of what could be achieved with supreme determination, and arrogance, but Jack still leaned towards the negative. It might be better not to survive. How would Boy be coping?

'I know. Bloody, isn't it,' Muddy said, and Jack realised he must have let his horror show for a second.

'Yes. Bloody.'

The word seemed pathetically inadequate, but what else could you say? No time for moping though Muddy moved straight on, as Jack knew he would.

'I'm not sure whether the next snippet is good or bad,' he said, pausing in thought.

'Well, give us a clue then.'

'Freddie definitely isn't coming back. Don't know where he's gone, but he's not on the Station any more.'

'Either hospital or a training unit,' Jack said dispassionately. 'And my bet's on hospital.'

'I think you're probably right. But there is some good news.'

'About bloody time, Muddy.'

The young officer smiled. 'Chips and Pete should be back this afternoon. So there could be twelve of us by the time the weather picks up.'

'I guess we'll all be in the first team then?'

'Yes, we don't seem to have many reserves at the moment, do we? Now, let's run through who you'll have on your Flight.'

Outside the office, Alex leaned back and rubbed his face in his hands. He was suffering, partly from the aftermath of too much beer, but also from a bewildering cocktail of emotions.

Overnight, the desire to be with his parents in the warmth of his family home had reduced him almost to tears. It was only the presence of Olly, snoring softly a few feet away that had forced him to keep his composure.

And yet, leaving the Sergeants' Mess only a few hours previously, he'd been euphoric. He and Sophie had really seemed to hit it off. Even persistent interventions from Bunter hadn't ruined things. If anything, they'd helped, easing them through the awkward silences and blunting their embarrassment. He'd even managed to explain the strong whiff of Cologne. But Bunter had allowed them no time alone before the transport left.

Not that it seemed to matter much. There was no telling when, or if, they'd get the chance to meet again. Perhaps it was this uncertainty that had dragged him down.

In the harsh reality of another Kent morning, they seemed such a small, vulnerable, group. The CO and Smithy had returned, but S to Z, Tubby, Freddie and Boy had not. He couldn't help wondering how many would be missing tomorrow morning, and, inevitably, whether he'd be one of them, especially as he wouldn't be following Jack into combat. No doubt Piers would make a worthy successor, but it wouldn't be the same.

It was 10.30 and the intermittent phone calls had all been about relatively minor administrative matters. He longed to get away from the ringing, and the foul air of the dispersal hut; even with a reduced number of occupants, it was thick with tobacco smoke, beer breath and worse. But the weather was too cold and showery to decamp outside.

Playing with the lighter bandage Piers had grudgingly wrapped round his hand, he tried to forget his headache, and his fear, and think of Sophie.

Tired of reading and writing reports, Sophie walked

out of the office into the map room. The map displayed a few hostiles, single aircraft on reconnaissance missions, but there were no red counters. Group seemed to be holding back, waiting for the larger raids expected when the weather improved. So, apart from the few WAAFs raking the black counters, most of the girls were sitting in small groups, knitting or gossiping, or both.

She contemplated the change in her circumstances. She'd only been at Biggin Hill a month, but she'd met plenty of fighter pilots in that time. Nearly all had been charming, the sort of young men it would have been all too easy to swoon over. But, for some reason, she hadn't fallen for any of them. As romances blossomed around her, she'd begun to wonder whether there was something wrong with her. What was it that led her to maintain an emotional distance from the handsome young men that courted her attention? She certainly enjoyed their company.

Perhaps it was witnessing the agonies endured by the girls going out with pilots; their fear as their boyfriends flew into combat, their despair if they were killed or injured. But she didn't think she was being that rational. She just hadn't met the right person, until Alex.

She'd liked him from the moment she'd first met him in the corridor, sensing an inner strength and warmth behind the blushing modesty. But now, she realised why she'd been taking uncharacteristic notice of his squadron's fortunes. She'd fallen for him.

So, for the first time, she was feeling the anxiety she'd witnessed in others. And Squadron Leader Rice's features were an ever-present reminder of the dangers. She'd see his face every time Alex flew, and she'd have a front row seat if anything went wrong.

Jack settled back in an armchair. He looked at Gwen's handwriting on the envelope and sighed. He'd avoided writing to her because he was still determined to break up in person. And he'd been relieved not to receive anything from her either, until now.

He slit the seal, slipped out the letter and started to read.

Dear Jack, I am so sorry we parted the way we did. I have really enjoyed going out with you these last three years, - what? - *but I think it is time we stopped seeing one another.*

He hadn't expected this.

I still like you very much, but I could never be happy away from home, and while you are in the RAF, there is no way we can be together without me leaving Barry Island. I had hoped you would decide to settle here, but I think we both know that is never going to happen.

These thoughts have been building up for a while, and I wanted to tell you in person, but who knows when you will next be home. I just could not wait any longer. I hope you understand.

Please forgive me. Best wishes, Gwen.

He couldn't pretend it wasn't a bit of a blow that she'd been the one to take the initiative. But he'd been fretting endlessly about what he was going to say to her, and how: composing little speeches to deliver on the doorstep, or on the beach. Now, none of it mattered. It was in the open, and it was a tremendous relief. He could just reply. He could even pretend to be the injured party, feign shock and disappointment. He wouldn't of course, but he could.

A burden had been lifted, and he could move on with his life, if he was to be granted a life beyond the next few hours.

The weather had picked up as advertised and they'd been scrambled just after three o'clock. In the end, only ten aircraft had been available. Pete hadn't yet returned from his 48, and the CO had wisely decided to stay on the ground, leaving Muddy to lead. So every fit pilot available to the Squadron was airborne.

Alex was weaving at the back of the formation, to the right of his new section leader.

'Dragon, this is Bastion, fifty plus bandits approaching Hastings, angels one four. Vector one five zero.'

'Roger, Bastion, this is Dragon Leader, passing angels ten.'

Muddy sounded cool, in command. It was a welcome change after Freddie, and it helped steady Alex's nerves.

He looked across at Piers, who made a yawning motion. No other aircraft were yet in sight.

The plotting table had come alive. Sophie watched more and more counters being raked on to both the landward and seaward sides of the south coast.

Behind the smaller raids toward which Dragon and Soho were being vectored, a huge formation was advancing. An estimated 700 enemy aircraft. To meet them, a total of 13 squadrons had been launched so far. It might sound impressive, but they were hopelessly outnumbered.

Despite the likelihood of a head-on encounter, Alex

seemed to have left his fear and sickness 10,000 feet below. He was nervous, but in control. They'd climbed above the enemy and were ranged out in line abreast, he and Piers at the extreme left of the line.

The Controller was counting down the range, and Alex was peering into the distance to try and pick out the enemy formation.

He imagined the pinched features of Crispy Rice as the Controller gave his latest update. 'Dragon, this is Bastion, bandits twelve o'clock low, ten miles, maintain heading.'

At this closing speed, that meant little more than a minute. And Jack said the final 1,000 yards would take about three seconds.

'Wilco, Bastion, this is Dragon Leader, maintaining angels one six.'

Muddy's voice betrayed a hint of excitement, and Alex thought it must be quite something to be leading a squadron into combat for the first time. His next transmission was more openly exuberant.

'Bastion, this is Dragon Leader, tally-ho, tally-ho, fifty plus, slightly low, going in.'

The whole formation dipped into a gentle descent and Alex could finally see about 20 Heinkels, just below the horizon against the background of dark fields. Supporting formations of Messerschmitt 109s held station above and to either side.

'Roger, Dragon, this is Bastion. Good luck.'

The Heinkels were growing by the second. Alex took a last look round. All clear. This time, he knew they'd get a pop at them before the fighters could intervene. He picked the second Heinkel from the left and stroked his thumb over the gun button.

The bombers suddenly began bouncing around, as if

seeking an escape route. But, hemmed in by the shepherding fighters and the tightness of their own formation, they were trapped. With about ten seconds to go, they began to fire.

Alex ignored the tracer, feeling a moment's satisfaction that he'd suppressed the urge to retaliate. He forced himself to wait, then, at what he estimated to be 1,000 yards, he pressed the gun button. His Spitfire juddered. The bomber grew alarmingly. Its pilot raised his arms across his face. Alex pushed and streaked under it, frighteningly close.

He had no idea whether pilot or bomber had been hit. He was just grateful to have survived unscathed. His avoidance of a collision had owed as much to luck as judgement.

'Dragon, this is Bastion. Pancake. I say again, pancake. Six hundred plus bandits ten miles south, angels two zero.'

Sophie looked from the Controller to the map.

When tracked over land by the Observer Corps, the enormous formation had turned out to be made up entirely of Messerschmitt 109s and 110s. Fighter Command had been drawn into a very clever trap.

Kelvin Rice looked at Sophie as he repeated the recall message. What had happened to change her manner towards him? Gone was the sympathetic concern with which she'd once regarded him. All he saw now was fear.

She tried not to wrinkle her nose at the sight of his burned features. Please, Alex, come home safely.

A fighter pilot had to know when to run away. And, whereas Jack may have railed against a straight recall without explanation, the news of 600 plus bandits just to the south brooked no argument. He stood his Spitfire on its nose and dived for the deck.

'Well done, sir,' Mead shouted as Alex walked down the wing. 'You seem to have come back in one piece for a change.'

Only because they recalled us, Alex thought. But perhaps it did mark some kind of personal milestone.

'And not just me, Scouse. I think we've all made it.'

'First time in a while, sir.'

'Yes. Let's hope it's not the last, ay.'

'I'll drink to that, sir.'

'That's nothing to go by, sir,' a Welsh voice joined in. 'He'll drink to anything.'

'Give over, Sandy.'

Alex smiled and left the two of them performing their usual double act, bickering like a married couple.

Despite the brevity of the engagement, it hadn't been a total failure. They seemed to have damaged several bombers, the remainder heading south, jettisoning their bombs over open country. Jack was right. You didn't have to shoot them down to spoil their plans. In a welcome change, the Intelligence Officer was confronted by a noisy bunch of pilots in high spirits.

The euphoria didn't last long. All too soon, they were sitting, waiting to be called back into action, or stood down. It brought home to Alex why the evenings were so unpopular. Having lost friends throughout the day, you finally dared hope for your own survival. The waiting seemed particularly cruel.

Late in the evening, they were scrambled again. But it ended in another recall before they'd met the enemy.

Despite his fear and tiredness, Alex realised that the late scramble had benefits. With every flight, he was becoming more familiar with his aircraft, and with Squadron procedures. Heck, he was even becoming more confident at landing the thing. Most importantly though, with his weaving duties, he was beginning to feel useful, a part of the Squadron, rather than a costly passenger.

Much as he wanted to go to the Mess in the hope of bumping into Sophie, he decided to join the rest in his first visit to the pub.

Chapter 6 – Friday 30th August 1940

Alex sat up and watched Olly usher a pilot officer and two sergeants to the side of the Adjutant's desk. The pilot officer and one sergeant were about his age, the other in his early twenties, about the same age as a flight lieutenant who'd arrived with them, but been sent straight to the CO's office.

Alex watched him pass and guessed that the disparity in treatment was based on more than mere rank. The three now listening intently to George Evans wore clean, smartly pressed uniforms. The flight lieutenant's uniform was shabby, as if he'd been sleeping in it. But that wasn't what really marked him out.

The eyes and cheeks of those stood by the desk shone almost as brightly as the new wings on their chests; whereas, like Jack, Muddy and some of the others, the flight lieutenant's complexion was sallow, and he had the grey sockets and heavily bagged eyes of a 60 year old. And when he'd smiled at the Adj, there'd been no light in his eyes, and a jaw-clenching tightness to his cheekbones. Despite his comparative youth, Alex was sure he was an experienced fighter pilot, and probably their new flight commander, the replacement for Freddie.

He glanced across at Piers, slumbering in a chair opposite. His friend didn't look as bad as the flight lieutenant, but the greyness and bags were there. Alex tried to remember how he'd looked when he'd shaved several hours earlier. Was he already as crumpled and careworn as the pilots he'd seen in the bar on his first night? Perhaps he'd take an interest next time he passed a mirror.

The three new boys – he suddenly realised he'd lost that honour – followed Olly and George into the locker room. He looked around at the others, a few sitting up in silent contemplation, but most lying back, trying to rest. It was nearly nine o'clock and there was a bit more cloud than the previous evening, but not enough to deter the Luftwaffe.

Although welcome, the lack of activity felt a little sinister.

Sophie had drawn up the rosters for the next week and was watching the map again.

The previous evening had shaken them. When the large formation had first appeared, it had seemed fortuitous they already had squadrons airborne. But without the Observer Corps' warning, Dragon and the others could have been destroyed. As it was, it had been a close run thing.

The Luftwaffe had started the new day with variations on the same theme. The first force of 60 plus hostiles had turned out to be all Messerschmitt 109s, and the small formations harrying shipping in the Channel seemed designed to entice fighters into the air. So far, Group had resisted the temptation, and there were few red counters on the map.

But now, more waves of German aircraft were crossing the Channel, three thus far. The first comprised a small formation at 14 to 15,000 feet, and a much larger shadowing force at 20 to 25,000.

Sophie gave an involuntary shudder. She feared another trap. If, as expected, the smaller force was bombers, they'd have to be met before they reached their targets. And if the trailing force was fighters…?

The first of the black counters was approaching the

English coast.

A telephone on the platform rang. All eyes turned towards Squadron Leader Rice. After a brief, almost theatrical pause, he breathed in deeply and picked it up.

The CO had declared himself fit to fly and was leading the 11 serviceable aircraft climbing away from Biggin Hill.

'Bastion, this is Dragon Leader, Dragon airborne.'

Jack was in the middle of the formation, leading B Flight for the first time. They'd left Muddy on the ground to bring Sammy Samson up to speed. The new flight commander had come across from Tangmere, and those that knew of him were very glad to see him. He'd already earned a DFC, and couldn't be far off getting his own squadron, despite his tender years.

'Roger Dragon, this is Bastion, fifty plus bandits approaching Deal, angels one five. Vector one zero zero.'

'Bastion, this is Dragon Leader, wilco.'

Jack loved being in the centre of the Squadron. Against the greens and yellows of the countryside, and the deep blues and whites of the late morning sky, the Spitfires had a mythical quality, their sleek lines and role in protecting those below once again bringing a lump to his throat.

Most of them had had a vague feeling they were part of a great undertaking, but they'd rarely, if ever, discussed it openly, and the general public had always seemed pretty disinterested.

But since Mr Churchill had labelled them The Few just over a week ago, they'd all experienced a surge in self-awareness, and public support.

'Hardly bought a drink all night,' Pete had said on his premature return the previous evening. 'And I got the impression I could have gone home with half the women in the bar, if the Mrs hadn't been with me of course.'

Jack looked back and right at his balding, gap-toothed wingman. If Pete was being feted, there was hope for all of them.

But did he have a hope with Caroline, he wondered? He hadn't seen her the previous night because he hadn't left the pub until sometime after midnight. It had been a good night, as the headache testified, but he'd managed only about three hours fitful dozing before the alarm signalled the start of another day. He hoped she'd slept better, and that her shift would be quieter than his was shaping up to be.

He shook himself and took a good look round. Out to the rear right, beyond Pete's aircraft, Piers was leading Blue Section, Alex and Chips to either side of him, Alex weaving diligently, the sun glinting off his Spitfire's wings and canopy.

'Good lad, Alex, good lad.'

He continued his scan above and behind his own tailplane, past Smithy, and to the front. The sky to their right was already criss-crossed with vapour trails, the telltale sign of a battle raging towards Ashford.

'Dragon, this is Bastion, bandits maintaining angels one five, passing abeam Canterbury, maintain vector one zero zero.'

'Bastion, this is Dragon Leader, wilco. Passing angels ten.'

They were obviously bound for a different formation, one that didn't seem to have been engaged yet, if the absence of trails to their front was anything to go by.

Should be able to get above them, Jack thought. He looked over his shoulder at the lone aircraft weaving at the rear of the formation. If young Alex could stop them being bounced.

Alex felt like a mother hen trying to protect a fast moving brood of chicks. He also felt very vulnerable. He didn't want to end up like Johnny, disappearing from the back of the formation without anyone noticing.

'Shame about old Alex. Wonder if we'll ever know what happened to him?'

So, he was manoeuvring as much as he dared, trying to strike a balance between keeping a good lookout for the whole formation, and not being left behind. It wasn't easy when they were climbing away from him at nearly full throttle.

'Dragon, this is Bastion. Your bandits still angels one five, twenty five miles. Maintain vector one zero zero.'

Twenty five miles was far too far to see anything, but Alex looked anyway. His instructors had said the eye was best at spotting objects just off centre. So you scanned large areas, moving your eyes in small darting jerks until you spotted something, usually at the edge of your vision, then focussed in on it. Jack said Muddy practised with dots on his office wall. Alex had done the same in the dispersal hut, feeling vaguely stupid and praying no-one noticed. He hoped it paid dividends now.

'And be aware, further one hundred plus bandits, possibly Snappers, thirty miles, angels two five.'

One hundred plus! Now they really should be easy

to see when they were in range.

'Bastion, this is Dragon Leader, roger, passing angels one four.'

With the bulk of the fighters above and behind the bombers, a frontal attack seemed to offer the best hope of getting at them without being bounced. Even then, it probably wouldn't be long before the Snappers swooped in and they ended up in a free for all like the one taking place to their right.

The vapour trails toward Ashford were now so numerous they'd merged into an area of impenetrable cloud. Alex still fancied he could see individual dots though, some weaving on the peripheries, others falling, leaving darker, more sinister trails as they fell.

The sight darkened his mood, and he felt his fear and claustrophobia returning.

'Bastion, this is Dragon Leader, levelling angels one seven.'

'Roger, Dragon Leader, this is Bastion, bandits two zero miles, angels one five. Further bandits now confirmed as Snappers maintaining position above and behind.'

Feeling his mouth dry and his stomach tighten, Alex set his rpm to 2650, pressed the emergency boost override, switched the reflector sight on, set the gun button to fire and tightened his straps.

Lowering his seat would do nothing for his claustrophobia, but he gritted his teeth and lowered it a notch.

'Dragon Yellow and Green Sections, line abreast, line abreast go. Blue Section climb and provide top cover.'

What?

As Alex tried to come to terms with the unexpected

turn of events, Piers replied, sounding a little less confident than usual.

'Blue Leader, wilco.'

Sophie was walking among the girls when she heard Alex's section being told to climb. She tried not to let her anxiety show, but the Observer Corps had just confirmed that he was heading for over 100 Messerschmitt 109s.

The map was becoming saturated with counters, as more and more hostile formations set out across the Channel, and more and more squadrons were scrambled to meet them. Some of the raids seemed to be feints, while others were splitting up to further complicate life for the Controllers.

She willed herself to concentrate on the performance of her girls, under even more pressure than usual now. But she couldn't resist frequent glances at Dragon's red counter, or listening out for their transmissions amongst the increasing hubbub in the room.

Jack couldn't fault the CO's tactics. They had to try and ward off the high flying Snappers, but he didn't envy Piers the task. As he slid Green Section to the left, and Yellow Section completed the line on the right, he watched Blue Section climbing above them, Piers slightly ahead, Alex and Chips to either side of his tailplane. They looked brave, but lonely.

He felt for his erstwhile wingman, leading his friends into a situation they'd not experienced before. He'd just whispered a heartfelt 'good luck' when the Controller's voice drew him back to his own part in the unfolding drama.

'Dragon, this is Bastion, bandits angels one five, in your twelve o'clock one five miles.'

'Bastion, this is Dragon Leader, roger.'

Another transmission followed immediately. 'Dragon Blue Section, this is Bastion, your bandits angels two five, in your twelve o'clock, two zero miles.'

The Controller had picked up on Blue Section's new task, and was giving them individual help.

'Bastion, this is Blue Leader, roger.' Piers sounded more confident again. Good.

Peering ahead for the enemy, the time seemed to drag interminably, but less than a minute after the last transmission, Jack picked out an ominous dark patch in the sky above the horizon. It wasn't the bombers. They'd be lower down, their camouflage making them difficult to pick out in the haze. It must be the fighters.

'Bastion, this is Dragon Blue Leader, tally-ho tally-ho, one hundred plus Snappers.'

Jack squinted, but he still couldn't see more than a smudge. Piers's eyesight must be exceptional. And he sounded excited, rather than fearful, which would be a more normal reaction when leading three aircraft into a confrontation with 100.

'Roger Blue Leader, this is Bastion, good luck.'

Jack added his own, silent, 'you'll need it.'

'Dragon, this is Bastion, bandits twelve o'clock ten miles.'

He scanned the area around the horizon, easing the stick forward to follow the CO's Spitfire into a shallow dive.

'Bastion this is Dragon Leader, tally-ho tally-ho, fifty bandits, going in.'

'Dragon Leader, this is Bastion, roger and good

luck all.'

Jack was glad the CO could see the enemy, because he couldn't. What he could see though, was a small group of other aircraft out to their left.

'Dragon Leader, this is Green Leader, friendlies ten o'clock, slightly high.'

He was sure they were Hurricanes, and that they were heading for the same bandits. They looked as if they'd arrive just after their own frontal attack. Ideal timing.

'Roger, Green Leader, nice to have company.'

Well said, sir, although it still meant they were only about 20 against 50, 150 if you counted the Snappers above. They were bound to get involved before it was all over.

He spotted the bandits emerging from the grey just below the horizon line. There were about 20 twin-engined Heinkels and three groups of about a dozen 109s, one to either side and one just above and behind the bombers. The front line of Heinkels was six strong. Jack picked the one on his extreme left and wound the type's wingspan into his reflector sight.

Smithy's Spitfire was bobbing gently just to his left. They'd be going for the same target, so they'd have to keep an eye out for one another. Head-on collisions weren't the only danger!

The Hurricane formation had fallen slightly behind, but they too were diving in.

Dragon had closed to within a couple of miles before they received evidence they'd been spotted. The enemy front rank began to heave and lose shape, as if its members were searching for an escape from the two-pronged assault.

Then, the Snappers to the right of the bombers

pulled up to engage the Hurricanes. Jack's chosen Heinkel began to turn right into the space they'd vacated, followed a short time later by the aircraft inside it.

An orange flash lit the corner of his eye. He risked a quick glance to the right. A large fireball. No time to dwell on it. Tracer arced towards him. Their bomber was still turning away, unwisely presenting its unprotected underbelly. Smithy fired.

'One thousand yards, Jack.'

One second to aim. He pointed at the front of the bomber's lower fuselage.

One second to fire. He jabbed the gun button and his aircraft juddered, the guns hissed and the cordite inflamed his nostrils. A brief image of sparks on the target, though whether from him or Smithy, who knew.

One second to avoid a collision. He pushed forward and dived under the bomber.

Before his engine had fully recovered, or the dust settled, he pulled hard right, fighting the g to look back over his shoulder. A tangle of wreckage was falling from the front left of the formation. Two other bombers trailed smoke. Spitfires wheeled. Half a dozen Hurricanes were diving from over his left shoulder, tracer spitting from their wings.

More Hurricanes had engaged the right hand fighter screen. At least one aircraft from that mêlée spiralled down engulfed in smoke and flame.

The left and upper elements of the fighter screen were joining in. Time for only one more attack before they were on top of him. And as if all that wasn't enough, he heard an excited voice in his headset.

'Dragon, this is Blue Leader, fifty plus Snappers coming in.'

Alex was mesmerised by the massed ranks of fighters 5,000 feet above them. If they chose to dive down, it seemed impossible for their small section to survive.

But he didn't consider diving out of harm's way, not even for a moment. In the two Spitfires to his left, Piers and Chips stared upwards. His duty was to fight alongside them.

That didn't mean he wasn't scared. His mouth was dry and he felt sick, but he was getting used to that.

They'd levelled at 20,000 feet and were orbiting to try and gain speed - energy - for the forthcoming combat. And there would be combat, one way or another. Even if the massed formation didn't dive on them, they'd have to join the fight about to commence below.

He looked down and almost forgot his fear.

The eight remaining Spitfires of 646 Squadron were flying in perfect line abreast 20 yards apart. They were speeding towards a much larger formation of German aircraft that must surely outflank and engulf them. A force of nine Hurricanes was also bearing down from the northwest, but they wouldn't arrive in time to save his comrades.

Yet as he watched, it was the Germans that cracked. The right hand screen of fighters turned for the Hurricanes, and the first line of bombers started to heave and turn outwards. So frantic was their urge to escape that two bombers to the left of the formation touched wingtips. The inner aircraft rolled over on top of the outer, engulfing them both in a huge orange and black fireball. They seemed to hang there for several seconds, before falling slowly earthwards, locked in a deadly embrace that allowed neither crew any chance of escape.

Dragon pressed home its attack, maintaining its formation with parade ground precision, tracer flashing between the Spitfires and the remaining Heinkels. When they finally disappeared beneath the bombers, two more were smoking. The enemy formation had been broken. Alex was so proud he was moved almost to tears.

And then, the Hurricanes too entered the fray, diving into the frantically weaving bombers.

How would he ever be able to explain any of this to anyone who hadn't experienced it?

Piers's shout of 50 plus drew his eyes away and he looked up. The huge mass of Messerschmitts had split in two. Half were ploughing on towards south London. The other 50 or so were diving towards them.

'Blue Section, here we go chaps.'

Alex could hardly believe it, but there was laughter in Piers's voice. He looked across and his friend's eyes were also smiling. The sight failed to banish his anxiety, but it made it less keen.

The leading 109s were probably no more than 3,000 feet above now, with line upon line behind them. Alex pulled hard enough to ease away from Piers and Chips, but not so hard as to pull into the buffet. He eased the back pressure only when pointing head on at the mass of German fighters.

The rate of closure was phenomenal, and the leading phalanx began firing just as Alex pressed his own gun button. Tracer flashed all around his Spitfire. His response seemed puny in comparison. The Messerschmitts grew in his windscreen until the risk of collision became much more threatening than bullets or shells. Three 109s from the first line flashed past, one to either side and one just above his canopy.

Alex pushed, pulled and skidded to avoid the ranks of following aircraft, firing intermittently as targets arced in front of him. Whether he hit anything, he had no idea, but he certainly made some of them clear out of his way.

And then he was through, nose pointing high into the dark blue. No more than a few seconds had passed, but he was breathless, in a red-faced sweat. He couldn't quite believe he'd survived unscathed. But he was running out of energy fast, so he rolled left to 90 degrees of bank and pulled round into a steep dive, all the time looking for other aircraft.

There seemed to be no-one at his height, not even Piers or Chips. The vast majority of the Messerschmitts were about to join the confused jumble of aircraft whirling among the fog of vapour and smoke trails below. But several were pulling back up to engage them – him – to engage him.

Two pairs climbed to his right, and one to his left, but one pair, the black crosses standing out on their stubby square-tipped wings, was looping towards him. Condensation trails streamed back from their wingtips, giving an indication of the g they were enduring in their effort to pull over the top and engage him before he dived past. He was sure they'd be too late, but he also knew they'd then slot in behind him and fire at will. He had to do something imaginative.

Feeling his stomach tighten again, he pulled towards them, meeting the right hand 109 head on as it reached the inverted 200 yards ahead. The German must have frozen at the unexpected appearance of a Spitfire, because only Alex fired. He had no idea whether he hit anything, and the Messerschmitt passed ten feet beneath him, upside down at the top of its loop.

Alex rolled inverted and pulled into a steep dive, heading for the smoke cloud below.

Jack had been right. He'd had time to engage only one other bomber before the fighter screen intervened. The Heinkel was at the rear right of a section doggedly maintaining formation while others broke up around them. He approached it from the rear, ignoring the tracer from its lower dorsal gunner, and fired a two second burst that hit the right wing, causing a shower of debris.

Its right propeller was slowing and he was preparing to engage it again, when a pair of 109s dived from his rear left, firing as they came.

'Spoil sports.'

He wanted to turn towards them, but that would take him behind the remaining Heinkels, exposing him to the fire from several rear gunners. So he pulled up and right, grunting as the g dragged the blood from his brain and his vision dimmed. Tracer flashed past, but he didn't seem to be hit.

Continuing to pull, he spotted three Spitfires climbing towards an overwhelming force of 109s. And then they were gone, and he was looping over the top and diving back towards the mêlée.

The enemy formation had been split apart, and it should have been possible to attack lone bombers at will. But there were so many Snappers. And, no matter how brave the efforts of Piers, Alex and Chips, their numbers were bound to increase.

'You've got to try though, haven't you Jack?'

He rolled upright and dived back into the fight.

How Alex survived the next fifteen minutes was a total mystery to him. He was in a perpetual state of sweating disorientation bordering on panic, manoeuvring madly to avoid enemy fighters, pulling and pushing with arms that ached, and a brain that was almost continually drained of blood. The enemy seemed to be everywhere, and even when he spotted a friendly aircraft, it was invariably surrounded by several 109s.

When his ammunition finally ran out, he had not taken one coolly considered shot. Every jab of the gun button had been in reaction to a target that had flashed across his sights as he was attempting to escape yet another pair of 109s.

Yet survive he had, and as he dived for the comparative safety of the ground just north of Maidstone, he wondered how many others could say the same.

Approaching the airfield, it became apparent that at least some bombers had got through. Ugly pillars of black smoke rose, a few from the airfield, but most from Biggin Hill village and some of the countryside to the north. He thought of Sophie, but the Ops Block looked to be intact.

Sandyman and Mead seemed more agitated than usual, but the Welshman tried to maintain an air of normality as he took Alex's shoulder straps.

'You've picked up a few holes again, sir. I knew yesterday was too good to last.'

'Only a few, Sandy? I thought there'd be more.'

'That bad was it, sir?' The gap-toothed smile couldn't hide the tradesman's underlying nervousness.

'Well, let's just say it was pretty bloody busy up

there.' Alex climbed from the cockpit and looked around at the smoke rising in the distance. 'And down here by the look of it?'

'You could say that, sir. I don't think I'll ever get used to sitting in a shelter.'

The thought horrified Alex, and he had no trouble in sympathising. 'No. I'd hate it.'

Mead jogged up as Alex was stepping down from the wing. 'Where were you when we needed you, sir? This keeps happening when you're away.'

'I know, Scouse. I'm sorry.'

'Oh that's alright, sir. We'll be okay.' He pointed at the jagged holes in the Spitfire's tailfin. 'But you ought to take more care.'

'Thank you, Scouse, but I think I might have given as good as I got today.'

'Good for you, sir. You must be getting the hang of it then?'

'I hope so,' Alex said with heartfelt sincerity. 'Is she alright?'

'Yes, sir, just a flesh wound. We'll have her right as rain in no time.'

'Good.'

How quickly he'd learnt to say one thing, when his mind was screaming something totally different.

'Keston?' Jack repeated.

'Yeah, bloody Keston,' Brummie chimed again, missing the look of concern on his pilot's face. 'Pretty lousy bombing if yow ask me, Sarge, hitting a village that far away. What d'yow think?'

Jack turned away abruptly, shouting over to his engine fitter. 'Stokesy, she seemed to be running a bit hot. Have a look, will you?'

Without waiting for an answer, he walked away.

His rigger and fitter looked at one another and shrugged, then set to work turning the aircraft round.

Until that moment, Jack had felt fortunate to return to Biggin Hill in one piece. The enemy fighters seemed to have been omni-present, and given that none of them could spend much more than 20 minutes over southern England, they must have been coming over in waves. It would have been a minor miracle if all the raids had been split up as successfully as theirs. But he hadn't for a moment thought that Caroline might be in danger.

He looked at his watch. 12.30. Hadn't she said she started work at lunchtime?

His reaction to the word Keston had taken him by surprise. He'd frozen, sick to his stomach. And all for a woman he'd met only briefly. Twice!

Binky, Tubby, Boy, the countless others over Dunkirk, he'd dealt with their deaths and disfigurement with equanimity, with professional coldness. But the mere possibility of Caroline lying dead or injured in a pile of rubble had filled him with real dread.

He walked out of the pen and towards Nick Hudson. She was probably fine. And anyway, there was no way to find out, or do anything about it before stand down. He still had a job of work to do. He also had a feeling that this was going to be a very long and hard day. There'd be no room for distractions.

But, as he stopped in front of the Intelligence Officer, he couldn't totally clear the nagging concern, the fear, from his mind.

'Four?'

'Yes, four!' Olly confirmed, pleased that, for once, he'd had something to contribute to the conversation.

Piers whistled. 'Well good for the CO. He must have been really hacked off at being dropped in the Estuary the other day.'

The three of them were lounging on the grass outside the dispersal hut.

'Did you see what happened to Chips?' Alex asked.

Piers blew out a stream of cigarette smoke and flicked ash with his index finger. 'No. One minute he was out to my left, and the next he was gone. But I never saw you again either.'

'Nor me you. Saw plenty of Snappers though.'

They both laughed.

Olly looked on and prayed the doc would clear him to fly on Monday. As his friends gained in combat experience, it was becoming increasingly difficult to feel part of their little group. He had to join them in the air.

And he was getting fed up with playing nursemaid to all the newcomers. He looked across at the three latest arrivals, sitting together a few yards away. They'd already been in a state of shock as he'd bombarded them with kit and information. The real bombardment had just about finished them off. He hoped none would have to get airborne on their first day. It never seemed to end well for those that did.

The ringing of the bell cut across his thoughts.

'Dragon Squadron scramble, one hundred plus, Folkestone, angels fifteen, Dragon Squadron scramble.'

He sat up and watched his two friends running to join the others haring towards the Spitfire pens. No lunch for them then.

He rubbed his arm and shouted after them. 'Good luck, both. Good luck.'

Alex smiled and waved to Sandy and Scouse as they relinquished his wingtips and touched their forelocks in salute. They seemed to have perked up a bit. Perhaps the sunshine had banished memories of sitting in a dark shelter as bombs dropped around them. He shuddered at the thought. For once, his cockpit seemed light and spacious.

By some miracle of the maintenance system, they had 12 aircraft again.

Bouncing over the grass ahead of him, the CO was leading Red Section; the new flight commander, Yellow; Muddy, Green; and Jack was back in charge of Blue Section. Piers would assume weaving duties once they were airborne.

Alex welcomed the familiarity of a return to the position he'd started in only five days earlier. Fear and nausea still bubbled just beneath the surface, but he felt much more confident than he had on that first terrifying scramble. Although he'd yet to see any evidence of the success of his gunnery, he now knew he could meet and fire on the enemy without running away.

He'd also discovered he could fly into battle following someone other than Jack. The Welshman would always remain his hero, but he'd proved he could survive without him. Things changed so quickly, people disappeared so quickly, that you had to be flexible if you were to cope. Maybe he'd avoid falling to pieces if others he'd relied on to date also disappeared.

They turned into wind. He realised how morbid his

thoughts had become.

'Lighten up, Alex. It's a beautiful day.'

And it was. The few fluffy white cumulus clouds hung in a deep blue summer sky. Rather than sitting in a cockpit behind a Merlin engine, he should have been lying back, enjoying the song of the skylarks hovering above the tufted grass.

'Dragon, here we go.'

He opened the throttle to keep pace with Jack and Piers.

Sophie looked to the map. It was 1.15 pm. Seven of the RDF stations on the south east coast were down. They suspected a power line had been severed, but nobody really knew. The result was that they had no idea what was approaching their Sector from across the Channel. Only when formations appeared over the Observer Corps posts on the coast could they get an idea of their size, height and heading. And then, only if cloud didn't intervene, as it frequently did.

The hostile formation Dragon were rushing to intercept would be well over Kent before they or any other Fighter Command squadron could get anywhere near it. And all because 12 Group had not only failed to protect the airfields again, arriving late, or not at all, off chasing phantoms, but now they were needed, they were returning to refuel. The AOC would be livid. And so he should be.

He'd have been even angrier if he'd been standing where Sophie had been when the bombs started falling. It was no fun working through an air raid, even if most of the bombs seemed to miss the airfield. Next time, they might not be so lucky.

Angela stood up and raked another hostile

formation onto the map, just over the coast, about ten minutes behind the first. It was going to be a busy afternoon.

Jack thanked God that Freddie was no longer leading the Squadron. They'd been scrambled late again. Not that they could have been launched much earlier; they'd only been on the ground 45 minutes. But the bandits had already passed Ashford.

The difference this time was that the CO and Controller were working together, doing all they could to ensure they made height before they met the bombers. To that end, they'd climbed to the south before turning onto an intercept heading, and they'd done a few climbing turns since. It was still likely to be a head-on attack, unless the bombers changed course, but at least they were in with a fighting chance.

After take off, he'd tried to look over his shoulder towards Keston. But it was pointless. Not only could he not see the village, but smoke from any bombs had long since dispersed.

What time did a lunch shift start? Hopefully, early enough for Caroline to have been on base when Keston was hit. And she should still be in the NAAFI shop now.

So stop worrying.

He'd never been like this about Gwen, even when the South Wales coast was being bombed. In fact, he'd worried more about Caroline in two days than he had about Gwen in three years.

'Dragon, this is Bastion. Bandits in your twelve o'clock, one five miles, angels one six.'

'Bastion, this is Dragon Leader, roger, angels one eight.'

Crumbs. While he'd been daydreaming, they'd closed to within spitting distance and levelled at 18,000 feet.

'Time to snap out of it, Jack.'

He shook himself and looked around. Alex was sitting 50 yards to the right, and Piers was away to the left, still weaving diligently. The other three sections were bobbing gently to his front.

'Dragon, line abreast, line abreast, go.'

Finally concentrating on the job in hand, Jack slid Blue Section to the left of the line.

Alex found himself excited at the prospect of a head-on attack. Before his first, they'd been bounced, the second had been a complete blur, and this morning, they'd been split off as top cover. This time, he was in the line, and he was prepared.

During the climb, Crispy Rice had sounded uncharacteristically nervous, but he and the CO had eventually guided them into the ideal position. You could almost sense the Controller's relief at the tally-ho call a few seconds earlier.

Now, the CO's voice crackled again. 'Dragon, here we go. Good luck all.'

They were diving into about 30 Dornier bombers, supported by what looked like an equal number of Snappers in three formations, one to either side and one above. Small beer compared to the morning's odds.

The Dorniers had a smaller frontal cross-section than the Heinkels, but it was still an all-perspex nose, so the crews should be feeling just as vulnerable. Hopefully, they'd scatter as readily. Alex had a gut feeling that Biggin Hill was the target again.

He took a last look round as the bombers grew in his windscreen. Some of the Spitfires to his right opened fire, and the Dorniers repaid the compliment. They were bouncing about in agitation, but not as wildly as the Heinkels had, and none turned away.

Alex waited for 1,000 yards. It was like a game of chicken. They were closing at 600 miles per hour, frighteningly fast.

Unable to contain himself any longer, he jabbed the gun button, firing at the second Dornier in from his left. Bits of perspex flew off before he pushed frantically to avoid a collision.

'Ouch!'

His energetic push caused his head to hit the canopy – hard. But at least he'd avoided the bomber with plenty of room to spare this time, perhaps too much. Must have been more than 1,000 yards when he'd opened fire? One day he'd get it right; if he got the chance.

He eased out of the dive and looked to his left. The Messerschmitts were turning in, and Piers and Jack were rolling left towards them. On the spur of the moment, he decided to stick with the bombers and pulled up and right to put himself above and behind them. Rolling wings level, he picked one to the rear left of the formation and eased the stick forward to put its left wing root in the middle of his gunsight. Tracer rounds raced towards him from several rear upper guns, but he ignored them, determined to wait until he was within 200 yards before pressing home his attack.

Some of the upper group of Messerschmitts were diving down through the bombers to get at the Spitfires below. Others from the sides were turning back towards him. They seemed strangely distant for the time being.

'Plenty of time, Alex.'

But 200 yards came all too quickly. He fired, bracing against the juddering recoil. Bits flew off the Dornier. Proof he'd actually hit something.

'Yes.'

Before he could confirm the damage, he'd dived past into a scene that was becoming all too familiar, but no less frightening. The air was full of aircraft, some with colourful roundels, most with black crosses and swastikas, but all flying in different directions in every possible position of flight: right way up, upside down, climbing, diving and banking. Some, including two of the bombers, were trailing smoke, and his headset was full of shouted orders, warnings and cries of pain.

His new-found confidence evaporated. What to do next?

The bomber formation was breaking up, but its rear lower gunners were filling the air with tracer. He'd just picked another target when a cloud of vapour erupted from his engine cowling and enveloped his canopy in grey fog.

He could smell glycol and remembered Olly's story. But unlike Olly, he was in the middle of an angry nest of Messerschmitts. If his engine cut, he'd be a sitting duck, if he wasn't already. He couldn't see anything beyond the tight confines of his darkened cockpit. Fear was turning to panic.

Was his aircraft on fire, or just about to be fired on? He was reaching for the canopy handle when the fog cleared. The claustrophobic terror subsided and he looked around.

No sign of smoke or flames. And was that his name

among the other chatter? If it was, the message, if there'd ever been one, was lost. Pushing the nose into a steep dive, he prayed that his engine would keep going and that the fighters would be distracted by other targets.

The answer to both prayers came swiftly. With an ear-splitting graunch, his propeller slowed to a halt, and, over his right shoulder, a 109 was turning hard onto his tail, closing fast. He pushed the nose forward more forcefully, and the German aircraft followed suit. Alex imagined its pilot smiling as he cut the corner to ease his gunsight the last few degrees towards him.

The airspace below was clear. If he could just evade this one hunter, he might stand a chance. He looked back over his right shoulder, sweat seeping from his forehead and upper lip, the tang of fear in his mouth.

'Come on, come on,' he urged, rocking in his seat to encourage his damaged aircraft forward.

The Messerschmitt was lining up for a finishing shot, when suddenly, in his peripheral vision, Alex saw a flash of tracer.

Jack had followed Piers into the 109s to their left, firing on one, but with no discernible result. With his wingman lost to sight, he rolled right, pulling back towards the bombers.

He fired briefly on a straggling Dornier, before diving beneath the formation, which was starting to fragment. 109s were swooping in from all angles, but his eyes lit on a Spitfire. It looked so lonely, so heroic, diving into a hail of concentrated tracer from several bombers, and followed by a swarm of ravening hunters.

He should have been weaving and searching for

new targets, but he found himself unable to look away. It seemed impossible for the little fighter to pass unscathed through such withering fire. And sure enough, a plume of vapour suddenly erupted from its nose and engulfed the canopy.

Jack remembered the Messerschmitt a few days earlier. 'Get out of there.'

Most of the fighters turned away, but a pair closed on the damaged Spitfire, more scavengers now than hunters. Jack willed the pilot to bale out, but when the vapour cleared, he was still sitting, either incapacitated, or intent on staying with his aircraft, presumably unaware of the Messerschmitts chasing him down.

And then, whether from sixth sense, or some conscious analysis of the height and posture of the pilot, Jack knew who it was.

Pressing the transmit button, he shouted, 'Alex, get out of there!'

If the young officer heard, he misinterpreted the message. Instead of opening the canopy and jumping, he pushed the nose forward. He was trying to dive away, even though his propeller had just ground to a halt.

Ignoring the tracer and the other fighters, Jack pushed hard on the throttle and dived for the nearest of the chasing Messerschmitts. Its wingman was a few hundred yards back and to its left, ready to turn in and finish off the stricken Spitfire in the unlikely event that his leader failed. But they'd both become fixated on their prey. The wingman at least should have been more wary.

Jack was in a shallower dive, but closing fast from the right. He could have done with more time, but the lead 109 was bound to fire any second. Pointing about an aircraft's length ahead of it, he fired a short burst. The result was better than he could have hoped for. Its canopy shattered and it started to fall away.

The wingman woke up and turned in. Jack eased left, firing a brief burst as they flashed past one another, wingtips no more than a few yards apart.

He was sure the first Messerschmitt was out of it, but he hadn't bagged the second, and its pilot wouldn't be able to resist the wounded Spitfire. He rolled inverted and pulled into a dive, looking for Alex's aircraft against the patchwork of fields. It was the Messerschmitt he saw first, looping down in a near mirror image of his own manoeuvre. Assuming it would be heading for Alex, he scanned ahead of the German's flight path until he spotted a lonely dot.

Perhaps he should be staying with the bombers, but he couldn't help feeling he'd let Johnny Thwaite down. He wasn't going to lose another wingman without a fight.

He continued his dive, keeping tabs on Alex, but heading for the German. Having had more speed in the first place, the Messerschmitt was edging ahead, but Jack pulled hard to cut the corner. Any hope that this pilot would become fixated on his target was dashed when he turned away from Alex and pulled up.

The 109 streaked past and Jack pulled round to try and gain an advantage over his new adversary.

'Alex, get out of there!' blared from the wall speaker.

Kelvin Rice looked across to see Sophie blanch as if about to faint. He'd seen similar reactions many times before, usually when one of the girls heard a boyfriend in trouble, or worse. It was one of the reasons Sophie and her flight sergeant monitored them, ready to replace those unable to carry on.

In this case, the young officer was quick to recover her composure. Just as well, because the lack of RDF was making things very difficult. The Observer Corps were doing their best, but cloud cover meant some of the raids weren't appearing on the map until they were well inland. At least with the girls so busy, none of them seemed to have noticed their officer's moment of weakness. He could tell she was still shaken though, and the flight sergeant was watching her closely.

A tiny part of him hoped that Pilot Officer Lowe had met a sticky end, and that Sophie would turn to him for solace. But he knew it could never be. If the young man died, or was horribly maimed, his own shrivelled features would always come between them, providing an unwelcome reminder of the past.

The colour was just returning to her cheeks as another voice crackled from the speaker. He returned his attention to the map.

Alex would be eternally grateful to the pilot of the lone Spitfire. He hadn't seen it after it passed behind him, and, apart from two aircraft that had swooped towards him then disappeared, he'd seen no more potential threats.

High above, the main battle seemed to be continuing with undiminished ferocity. But down here, it was eerily quiet, although the stationary propeller emphasised that there were dangers beyond the enemy. He eased out of his dive.

Where was he?

Somewhere between Tunbridge Wells and Ashford, he guessed, and with too little height to reach any of the airfields he knew.

'Go west, young man.'

He put the sun just in front of his left shoulder. The Spitfire could glide. But it was not a high performance soaring machine, and he was descending fast. Time to see if he could get some of the assistance Crispy Rice had been so confident he could provide.

'Bastion, this is Dragon Blue Two.'

After a short pause, a weak reply crackled in his headset. 'Drag.......Two, thi......ion. Pas........age.'

'Bastion, this is Dragon Blue Two. Engine failure near Tunbridge, heading west, passing angels seven.'

'Ro......Blue   T............tion.........ead St.............'

It was hopeless.

'Bastion, this is Dragon Blue Two, you're broken unreadable. Attempting force landing. Dragon Blue Two out.'

The reply was nothing but static. Well, he'd get no assistance from that quarter, but at least they, and hopefully Sophie, would know he was alive – for the moment.

The wind was a light south westerly, so he was heading in a reasonable direction. Ahead was a large village. He wasn't sure whether he'd clear it with enough height to choose a landing area on the other side, and he was already over a group of large fields, so he decided to try one of those.

He entered a left hand spiral, feeling apprehensive but on more familiar ground than when in combat.

'Just like in training Alex.'

Of course, with practice force landings in training, he'd been able to open the throttle and climb away if it all went wrong. Not today. He looked around for the final time and thanked the unknown Spitfire pilot yet again.

The ground was rising to meet him as he completed his curving final approach to a large pasture field running towards the village. The trick was to skim over the front hedge, land and stop before the far hedge, not run into it, like Olly.

'Don't lower the gear Alex,' he nagged as his hand instinctively reached for the undercarriage handle. At least any onlookers wouldn't see him yo-yoing wildly. Small mercies. He debated whether to open the canopy and decided to keep it shut for added protection.

The front hedge raced towards him. He raised the nose to pass over it, then, as the speed washed off, raised it again and held the landing attitude. He could see nothing ahead of the long engine cowling, but the tufted green pasture was flashing by to either side.

The first contact, to the accompaniment of a light scraping sound, was satisfyingly smooth. But, as the aircraft settled into the turf, the ride became rougher. The mild scraping became a persistent grinding with intermittent loud bangs, and he was thrown from side to side. The far hedge was rushing up.

Alex was steeling himself for a crash, when there was a loud clang and the aircraft stopped abruptly. He banged his head hard on the instrument panel and felt himself rising, as if the Spitfire was pivoting tail up around its nose. Soon, he was hanging forward against his straps, terrified that the aircraft would tip over. After an agonising wait, it fell back, crashing onto its belly with another painful impact.

Apart from the low groans he emitted as he stretched his aching limbs, the only sound was the ticking of cooling components. It was strangely soothing after the last few hectic minutes. He felt like closing his eyes and staying where he was.

Fuel!

Fear overcame any lingering lethargy. Amidst more groaning, he opened the canopy, undid his seat harness and stepped onto the wing, taking his helmet with him. He walked unsteadily down to the turf and about ten yards beyond the right wingtip, then turned to survey the scene.

The Spitfire had stopped about 70 yards short of the far hedge, at the head of an increasingly wide and deep gouge in the turf. There was no sign of the obstacle that had finally brought it to a halt and, apart from some mud splatter and a few bullet holes in the engine cowling, it looked remarkably intact. You could even forget that it should have been sitting on an undercarriage.

He put a hand to his forehead. Ouch! No blood on his fingers, but it was quite a lump, and it hurt like hell. He touched it more gingerly and looked to the hedge, wondering whether the aircraft would have stopped if its nose hadn't dug in so dramatically.

A policeman was leaning on the far side of a five bar gate, watching him.

Jack lay back in a deckchair and closed his eyes. He was dog tired. It had already been a bloody day, and he sensed it was far from over.

A familiar voice chimed, 'Why the long face? As the jockey said to the racehorse.'

'And why are you so bloody happy?' Jack shot back in mock exasperation, reluctantly opening his eyes and sitting up.

'I have no idea,' the silhouetted figure said,

blocking the sun.

'But you look as if you've lost a tanner and found a threepenny bit. Come on, speak to Ginge.'

Sergeant Ginge Clough sank onto the grass. His freckled face was grimy, his prematurely thinning red hair plastered to his head. He looked desperately tired, but his pale blue eyes and thin red lips were smiling

Jack looked worried because he was. But what could he tell his Geordie friend?

The combat with the second 109 had been long and inconclusive, but when the German had finally broken away, he'd known its pilot would be more concerned about making it back to France than chasing disabled Spitfires. And yet he couldn't be sure that Alex hadn't been attacked by someone else, or met with any number of other misfortunes. He just hoped his young friend had managed to land somewhere and would be back later.

And there was still no word from Chips, missing after the first scramble, or Grizzly Houlahan, missing after the last one. The CO thought he'd seen a parachute, but he couldn't be sure.

'Me and Gwen have called it a day.'

Why he'd selected this topic to offer up he wasn't totally sure, but Ginge seemed to accept it as reason enough for his pained expression.

'Oh. Sorry to hear that, Jack. Sorry, but not totally surprised.'

'What d'you mean?'

'I could tell things were cooling off a bit over the last few weeks at Pembrey, and you haven't mentioned her once since we arrived here.'

That meant his friend had known before he'd realised himself. They'd been together too long. They sometimes felt like an old married couple.

'How did she take it?'

'Ah, now you'll like this. She wrote and broke up with me.'

It was a twist that could have been greeted with derisive laughter, but his friend seemed to be in an unusually sympathetic mood.

'Ow. I didn't see that one coming. Sorry.'

'Oh, it's all right. She just beat me to the draw. I'm just wondering what to write back.'

'I bet you are. Not easy, and for once I don't think I'd be much help. I've never had to write that sort of letter, thank God.'

Ginge was still going out with his childhood sweetheart.

'No, and I hope you never do.'

'So do I, mate. Anyway, I'll leave you to it then.'

He rose and started to walk away. Jack was just beginning to think there was something seriously wrong with his friend, when he threw the expected parting shot.

'But if you need a second opinion when you've written it, give it to me and I'll pin it on the notice board for suggestions.'

'Too kind. Now bugger off ya bald Geordie git.'

Jack sat back. He'd got away without mentioning his real concern. Although he'd convinced himself that Caroline had been on base when Keston was bombed, Biggin Hill had been the intended target. The Luftwaffe were bound to try again, and how safe would she be then?

Alex fell into step beside the policeman. He was used to looking down on people, but this man was a good inch taller, and of much bigger build, with a weathered complexion and a dark moustache. Alex guessed his age at about 30. He cut an imposing figure, and you could only imagine what villains thought as he bore down on them, his tall black helmet adding another eight inches to his height.

Apart from the rhythmic cadence of their footfalls on the metalled lane, and the creaking of the policeman's black pushbike, all was eerily silent. Where were the birds he'd imagined singing in the fields and hedgerows?

'I was just riding back to the village, when I heard a whoosh and you came shooting over the top of me. Almost fell off me bloody bike.'

'Sorry about that.'

'Oh, don't worry,' the policeman smiled across. 'Wouldn't have missed it for the world. Not every day you get to see a Spitfire close up, and meet the pilot. Not ideal for you though, I expect,' he said with another smile. 'And sorry to rush you along, but I don't like the look of that smoke.'

Alex had to agree. There was a sinister black cloud rising from the centre of the village.

'We might pass it on the way to the Station, but if not, I'll drop you there and you can ring for a car. Oh, and I'll get the local volunteers out to guard the plane. Hopefully, they'll get to it before it's been picked clean. I'm surprised we're not surrounded by kids already.' He frowned as he looked towards the village.

They carried on in silence. Alex put his hand to the bump above his right eye.

He'd declined the offer of a trip to the doctor. But he wasn't so sure now. It had grown to the size of an egg, and still seemed to be swelling, stretching the skin of his forehead.

After another hundred yards, they entered a narrow street of terraced houses. Again, all was eerily quiet. The smoke pillar was lost to view behind the buildings, but as they approached a junction with a wider road, a buzz of voices could be heard. They exchanged worried glances.

Turning the corner, the reason for the lack of activity to date became clear. About a hundred yards ahead, the road was full of what Alex thought must be the entire population of the village. They were standing in front of a demolished red brick building, from which the smoke was rising. A fire engine was just visible through the crowd, and uniformed figures were playing a hose into the rubble. There were no flames, and the plume of smoke was diminishing. A stretcher was being loaded into the back of an ambulance. Its bulky load was covered head to toe by a dark blanket.

'Bloody hell, they've hit the bank,' the policeman exclaimed.

As they made their way down the street, a few people turned and nudged those next to them. The hubbub subsided, although whether out of respect for the body on the stretcher, or because of their approach, Alex was unsure. He became uneasy.

'There's one of the bastards,' a male voice shouted from somewhere in the crowd.

This didn't tally with the enthusiastic greeting he'd been led to expect.

A group of five men emerged from the throng. Only one was actually rolling up his white shirt sleeves, but Alex could tell that, metaphorically, the others were doing the same, preparing themselves for some, as yet,

215

unspecified action. The rest of the crowd advanced slowly behind them, exchanging glances, and words that reached him as a low hum.

He felt the policeman's arm across his stomach and stopped. His companion took another step forward before he too halted.

'Now then, you lot. What's all this?'

'It's no good, George. You can't protect him,' the sleeve-roller challenged.

The policeman's voice rose in incredulity. 'Protect him. What d'you mean, protect him?'

The men stopped five yards away, and three others emerged from the crowd, one holding a shovel.

'Hand him over, George,' the ringleader growled menacingly. 'They've killed Mr Granger and Alice.'

The policeman bristled theatrically, wheeling his bike to form a flimsy barricade.

'Now just a minute, Arthur Manley,' he started in a voice Alex guessed was used to deter everything from small boys scrumping apples to real villainy.

Silence fell, and Alex could sense the crowd waiting to hear what the tall policeman would say next. After a thoughtful pause, he looked at Alex, then at the vigilantes, then back to Alex.

'Drop the parachute and take your life jacket off, lad.'

As far as they could tell, there were about 400 enemy aircraft over the south east.

They'd approached along the Thames Estuary and most had turned north and east, but a few seemed to be heading for the airfields and factories to the west.

It was 4.15, and looking at the number of red counters on the map, Sophie guessed that the whole of

11 Group was in the air again. 12 Group had also been called to provide support.

She looked at Squadron Leader Rice, sensing real tension beneath the marbled exterior. He was bearing great responsibility, but bearing it well.

Dragon were airborne for the third time. They'd mustered ten aircraft and had just tally-ho'd for a frontal attack on 20 plus Heinkels over Sheerness.

She was trying not to think of Alex. It was so embarrassing to have gone into a swoon earlier, even if only for the briefest of moments. After all, she was meant to be looking out for that sort of thing, not falling victim herself. It was unprofessional, and she'd have to apologise to the flight sergeant when their shift was over.

The trouble was, she wasn't sure it couldn't happen again. Her reaction hadn't been the result of a rational thought process. It had been instinctive. And her relief when she'd heard his voice on the radio a few minutes' later had been as uplifting as the earlier message had been devastating. She'd finally been forced to accept that she'd fallen head over heels for Alex Lowe.

Squadron Leader Rice had tried to vector him to Staplehurst, but they knew he hadn't heard their transmissions, and they had no idea how he'd fared since.

A hand appeared on her forearm. She looked into the eyes of the flight sergeant as the hand gave a gentle squeeze.

Alex tried to see things through the eyes of the villagers.

A massive battle rages overhead, the sky full of smoke trails and the distant sound of machine guns.

217

Suddenly, a bomb falls on the bank, killing the manager and one of the cashiers, and injuring several other friends and acquaintances. And then, around the corner, in the custody of the local bobby, comes a tall blond young man in blue/grey flying kit, the very picture of Hitler's Aryan ideal.

The heat had gone out of the situation as soon as they'd seen the wings on his chest. He'd gone from villain to hero in very short order, and had ended up telephoning Biggin Hill from the local pub. As far as he could tell, it had been opened in his honour, with Constable George Potter, not only turning a blind eye, but also joining in the festivities for a time.

But Alex remained disquieted. He doubted he'd ever been in real danger. Yes, there was a small chance that they'd have beaten him into unconsciousness before he'd opened his mouth, but otherwise, even without the help of the burly policeman, he was sure he could have talked his way out of the situation eventually. After all, there couldn't be many Germans with broad Shropshire accents!

But, he was also in no doubt that if he had been German, the men now raising glasses to him would have beaten him to death, despite George Potter's best efforts.

Perhaps his faith in the policeman was naïve, but somehow, he sensed that the man would have laid down his life to protect him, whatever his nationality.

So, although he was happy to share a drink with George, he was less keen to bask in the adoration of the others. And not just the ringleaders. The rest of the village had seemed only too willing to witness, if not openly encourage whatever vengeance was to be meted out. For that reason, he hadn't felt entirely comfortable since the policeman had made his excuses and left.

Was the malevolence peculiar to this village, or would the scene have played out in a similar way in any community in the country? It was a question he didn't want to dwell on for the present. Somehow, the answer threatened to undermine his faith in the justness of the cause for which he was fighting.

Jack caught a brief glimpse of something in his rear view mirror. His stomach constricted in fear as tracer raced past and jagged holes appeared in his right wing. He pulled hard right, wincing at the strain another dose of high g was putting on his body.

Unusually, he felt hot and disorientated, on the brink of nausea, and he fought to lift his head and look behind him. Nothing, but he kept pulling anyway, forcing his Spitfire into a tighter and tighter turn as the speed washed off. Finally convinced that no Messerschmitt could have kept up without pulling its wings off, he rolled upside down and arced into the dive he'd been contemplating as the shells smashed into his wing.

You rarely saw the aircraft that killed you, and he certainly hadn't seen that one. The numbing nausea was passing, but sweat trickled all over his body. His mouth was dry with the aftermath of his fear. And he was furious with himself. Without ammunition, he should have dived straight out of the battle, not sat around thinking about it.

'You were lucky that time, Jack.'

A few minutes earlier, three German aircraft had been less fortunate. The first, a Dornier, had rolled sharply away as his rounds smashed into its canopy during the head-on attack; he was sure he'd hit the pilot, but he hadn't been able to confirm it. The second and third, both 109s, were more definite, bagged by him and Piers within a few seconds of one another. He'd seen his target's engine stop, and the pilot had wasted no time in taking to his brolly. Piers's adversary had had no such opportunity, his aircraft exploding in a spectacular fireball.

He hadn't seen Piers since, and had spent the rest of his time avoiding 109s, firing at fleeting targets of opportunity. He was sure they were disrupting the raids, but there were so many of them today. The sky over the Thames Estuary had been full of the evidence of combat as they'd climbed and, as he dived away now, new vapour and smoke trails were forming as the old ones decayed.

His body ached and his mind craved sleep. How long before the cumulative affects of the last fortnight caught up with him and his luck ran out?

Alex was relieved when a blonde-haired young WAAF opened the door of the pub.

He'd drunk only sparingly, partly out of distaste for the company, but partly because he thought he might have to fly again when he returned to base. Those around him had been less abstemious, and most seemed to have settled down for the long haul.

The WAAF peered into the gloom, smiled and waved when she spotted him, then backed out. Feigning reluctance, Alex rose, picked up his kit, said his goodbyes and made for the door.

'You give them Gerries what for,' they drawled, staying in their seats. 'Give the bastards hell.'

He turned to acknowledge their cheers, smiling and

waving like the Prime Minister as he backed into the sunshine.

Outside, he found himself surrounded by a mob of children, and some of their mothers. The youngsters all seemed to be shouting at once, but he latched onto one question that was repeated again and again.

'What do you fly?'

A curly-haired ten year old with a grubby face raised his voice above the others.

'Fighters of course. Look at his top button.'

Alex reached for his tunic. The button had been undone since his second day in combat. The first hadn't merited it.

'What sort of fighters?' another, equally grubby boy asked.

'Spitfires,' Alex answered, looking down at the youngster, surprised at how proud the admission made him feel.

When he looked up again, the young WAAF driver was laughing. He blushed.

'Wow. What's it like up there?' the first youngster asked, pointing upwards. An expectant hush fell.

Alex was lost for words.

Down the street, men were throwing bricks and other debris into the shell of the bank. Most of the stonework had gone, and the front wall was no more than a couple of feet high, but the tall wooden counter had survived, stretching the width of the building, its dark pillars reaching for an upper floor that no longer existed. Would the bank be rebuilt around it, he wondered?

He raised his eyes to the sky. New battles were raging overhead. What could he say? Savage. Murderous. Terrifying. The young faces looked up at him.

'It's marvellous, absolutely marvellous,' he blurted. 'Every boy's dream. Now, if you'll excuse me, I've got to go.'

'To get back at the Gerries?' another young urchin piped up.

'Yes, probably,' Alex replied, his voice sounding more weary than he'd intended.

He put his parachute, Mae West and helmet in the back of the car and turned to open the front passenger door. A woman about the same age as his mother struck eye contact. She looked pained, close to tears.

'Good luck, son, good luck.'

Alex ducked into the car and laid his head against the window. After a few moments, he breathed deeply and turned to speak to his driver.

Jack looked down on Biggin Hill. Some of the tension bubbling within him eased. There were no fresh scars on the airfield, nor any pillars of smoke rising from buildings. A minor miracle given the number of bombers roaming over Kent.

Caroline should be safe. And given the time – it was nearly 5.15 – he couldn't believe the Luftwaffe wasn't running out of steam, for today at least. He certainly was.

'Just let me out of this bloody cockpit,' he shouted to no-one in particular.

When he taxyied in, Brummie and Stokesy ran out to meet him.

'Better make my peace with you two as well, hadn't I?'

There couldn't have been a greater contrast between his two groundcrew. Brummie, small and stout, was rolling over the grass in ungainly fashion, his brown hair long and tousled, a drill instructor's worst nightmare. Stokesy on the other hand, was tall and slim, his short black hair neatly Brylcreemed. Even in his dark blue overalls, he managed to look smart and elegant, moving with the grace of the champion ballroom dancer he'd been before the war had intervened.

Jack waved in answer to their smiles of welcome.

Safely back in the pen, he looked up as the taller man leaned over him. 'Sorry, Stokesy, I seem to have made a mess of another kite.'

The engine fitter took the straps in his long, slender fingers. 'You don't have to apologise to me, Sarge,' he said in his deep baritone, nodding at the jagged holes in the right wing. 'As long as the engine's okay?'

'Sweet as a nut.'

Jack lifted himself from the cockpit, stepped onto the left wing and stretched. His rigger appeared at the wing root and looked up expectantly.

'Afraid the right wing's full of holes, Brummie.'

'Oh well, Sarge, as long as it's only the right one, you're forgiven.'

Jack knew the forgiveness extended to his impatience after the previous sortie. 'Thanks. What's it been like down here?'

'We've been in the shelter a couple of times, but they seem to have passed us by for once, thank goodness.'

'But they've hit Kenley hard,' Stokesy added as he walked round the tailplane. 'And sorry to interrupt, Sarge.' He turned to his diminutive friend. 'Brummie, the armourers want to know whether to bother re-arming this one.'

Brummie looked at Jack. 'S'cuse me, Sarge, duty calls. I'll get a message to yow as well.'

When the message came, it was that his aircraft was unserviceable, and that there'd be no replacements until the morning. But, if Jack thought that meant he could take the rest of the day off, he was sadly mistaken. Smithy and Pete were to be rested. Oh well, ours is not to reason why... He decided not to finish the saying, even in his head.

Anyway, the rest of the news had mainly been good. Alex had landed in one piece and was on his way back, as was Chips Pye. And Grizzly had survived, although not unscathed. He'd taken to his brolly and broken his ankle on landing.

'Miracle it wasn't 'is fuckin' neck, great fat lump,' had been Ginge's considered opinion.

Jack wasn't quite as unsympathetic, but the large Canadian plummeting down under a parachute did make for an amusing image. It meant they were another pilot short though.

Only the lack of aircraft had spared the three new boys from a blooding on their first day. Sitting in a defensive circle on the grass, they tried to look disappointed, but their relief was all too evident.

Jack tried to remember what it had been like on his first day, waiting for the Squadron to return from operations over France. Like this trio, he'd seen pilots failing to come back. But, try as he might, he just couldn't remember how he'd felt. Too much had happened in the interim.

Perhaps he should go over and say hello before Olly took them to their respective Messes. But he'd only embarrass himself, and them. Better to wait for a more natural opportunity, even if it meant not meeting all of them before, as in the case of Sergeants Thomson and Ellis, some malign circumstance intervened. A sobering thought. Too sobering. He shivered. Anyway, they'd need another reshuffle after today, and he'd probably end up with one of them on his section.

He decided not to try and second guess the batting order for the morning, but to concentrate on more pleasant thoughts, hopefully leading to sleep.

They were just coming to the bottom of Westerham Hill when the driver uttered an inquisitive, 'Sir?' and pointed out to her right.

Alex put his hand on the dashboard and shifted in his seat - there was never enough leg room. He leaned forward and tilted his head to look up and right through the front windscreen.

Oh no!

About 1500 feet above, ten large aircraft were clearing the ridge, flying south in perfect formation.

He exchanged a worried glance with the young WAAF.

They were Junkers 88s, and their bomb doors were closing.

A siren was wailing. Jack sat up, eyes open, trying to place it. Then the ship's bell began its insistent ringing.

Before he could make any conscious decision, he was on his feet, running towards his replacement aircraft's pen, listening for the first hint of the enemy's strength and position.

Hopkins's voice sounded even more shrill and urgent than usual. 'Dragon scramble, ten Jay Yew 88s, ten miles north, one thousand feet, Dragon…'

Fuck. Inside ten miles. A maximum of three minutes. They'd be lucky to get airborne.

His joints were so stiff, he felt as if he was running through treacle. Why hadn't he sat outside his pen again? And why did it have to be the last one? Piers was ten yards ahead and receding fast. He thought of shouting and telling him to get airborne without him, but he hadn't got the breath.

Those groundcrew not required to see them off were running in the opposite direction, heading for the shelter behind the pens.

Brummie was there though, tin hat on, showing no sign of anything other than a determination to do his duty.

'Bugger off as soon as you see I'm moving,' Jack shouted breathlessly as he lifted his parachute off the tailplane.

'But, Sar...'

'Don't argue, Brummie, just do it.'

He doubted his rigger had any idea how close the bombers were. As he stepped onto the wing and into the slipstream from the propeller, he turned back and shouted again. 'And make sure Stokesy goes with you.'

'Okay, Sarge.'

Stokesy jumped out of the cockpit and he jumped in, grabbing his headset. Brummie shut the door and they passed him his straps. A few seconds later, he waved the chocks away and started edging forward. Brummie scuttled away, and Stokesy ran behind the tailplane. But he didn't reappear.

'Damn.' Jack looked around but could see no sign of the engine fitter. Too late to do anything, but it was another niggling worry.

Because of his poor showing in the 220 yards dash, most of the Squadron were weaving well ahead. Only Piers was waiting, his Spitfire rocking at low revs. As Jack exited his pen, the young man waved and slotted in behind. Before they'd gone ten yards, the other seven aircraft turned into line and accelerated towards take off.

The CO wasn't hanging around. Far too sensible for that.

Jack trundled another 50 yards before turning. They wouldn't be into wind, but it would have to do. Without waiting for Piers to stop alongside him, he opened the throttle. With a throaty growl, the Merlin engine drew him forward.

The rest of the Squadron were several hundred yards ahead now, the last one just getting airborne. Piers had dropped back, caught out by his section leader's impatience.

'Sorry, Piers.'

Jack's controls became more responsive and he eased the stick forward to raise his tailplane. Suddenly, a yellow flash to his front left.

He was blind. An enormous thump, followed by a loud report. His ears popped, then silence. He was airborne. Upside down! A primeval panic gripped.

Although he couldn't see or hear anything, he knew he was falling.

Piers saw the flash. Jack's Spitfire lifted and rolled to the right ahead of him. He put his arms up to shield his face, but his own aircraft shot sideways. After several seconds of jarring impacts encased in a blinding, choking, cloud, there was a final, violent, jolt.

He sat very still, listening. Ticking, the odd creak

227

from the airframe, and distant, muffled reports, but he was in one piece. More than that, apart from the grit in his eyes and mouth, he seemed unscathed. Shaken, but nothing more. He coughed and spat to clear his throat, wiped his eyes, unstrapped from his seat and parachute and stood up.

His aircraft was a mess, sitting on its belly, covered in earth, propeller blades bent back. The dense dust cloud was settling, and beyond it, smoke rose from several places along their take off track, and the dispersal area.

He turned. Jack's Spitfire was about 50 yards away. But it was upside down, tail towards him, a thin wisp of smoke rising from a crack in the bottom skin behind the engine.

Piers leapt from his cockpit and ran, closing the distance like an over-dressed Olympic sprinter.

Jack couldn't move. His limbs felt capable of movement, but he was wedged, trapped.

Without it offering any consolation, he registered that his blindness had become more yellow than black, and his deafness more ringing than silence. His sense of smell was unimpaired though, and he didn't like what he smelt: fuel and electrical burning. He struggled, expecting to feel flames playing over him at any moment.

Something brushed his shoulder. He flinched in panic and rocked, dropping and landing painfully on his head. His arms were now free, but before he could do anything, he was gripped under the armpits and pulled backwards like a rag doll.

His eyes picked out dark shapes against a blue background, and he could hear muffled sounds. He sensed the presence of another body and a voice urging him to his feet. With help, he rose unsteadily. Arm over an invisible support, he staggered forward, head down. He began to hear his own ragged breathing and could see a green blur of movement and what looked like legs.

His lungs were about to burst when he was lowered gently to the ground. He retched and coughed, his nose running and his eyes streaming. After several seconds of undignified heaving, his chest cleared and he breathed more easily, taking large gulps of air. He felt an arm across his shoulders.

Rolling over, he found that his vision was returning. Piers was leaning over him, breathing heavily, streaked with sweat and grime.

A muffled voice spoke. 'Sorry to rush you, Jack, but we had to get out of there.'

Jack looked back in the direction Piers indicated. A pall of orange and black was rising into the sky. He fancied he could hear it crackling and feel the heat on his cheeks.

'What happened?'

Piers sat back, reached into his jacket pocket, took out a cigarette and lit it, inhaling deeply and then blowing out a long stream of thin blue smoke in an audible sigh. He smiled broadly.

'Where shall I begin?'

The young pilot related the chain of events from the time the bomb fell just in front of them. The facts fitted the sensations Jack had experienced, and explained his temporary loss of sight and hearing.

'I think they were 88s, but aircraft recognition didn't seem that important at the time.' Piers pointed at his Spitfire, out to their left.

Jack whistled at the state of the wreck. 'Not a pretty sight.'

'That's what I thought. Anyway, I sat around for a bit, but it became apparent that you'd nodded off, so I thought I'd better wake you up.'

Jack looked at his own Spitfire. All bar the tailplane, the wingtips and the propeller spinner were still engulfed in smoke and flame.

'I'm glad you did. Thanks, Piers.'

He was confident the young officer would view the use of his first name as a sign of friendship, rather than insubordination. And he had good reason to offer his friendship. Piers had shown incredible bravery crawling under the upturned wing to drag him clear, all the time risking becoming trapped and burned himself. He wondered whether he'd have had the courage to do the same.

'Oh that's all right, old boy, any time.'

They both laughed nervously at even these understated displays of gratitude and humility.

After a few self-conscious moments, Piers pointed across the airfield to where several buildings were on fire. 'It looks as if the Station's taken quite a pounding.'

That explained why their little drama seemed to have gone unnoticed. The damage looked pretty extensive, and Jack tried to picture where the NAAFI shop was in relation to the pillars of smoke and flame.

'Jack?'

He sensed that it wasn't the first time Piers had called his name.

'Yes. Sorry, Piers, I was just wondering how much damage has been done over there.'

'Quite a bit by the look of it, but we haven't got

away scot free either.'

He pointed over his shoulder. A pall of smoke was rising from behind the pens.

'No,' Jack said, rising slowly to his feet, stretching and grimacing in pain. 'We'd better go and see if we can help, and explain that we've written off two kites.'

Alex could see smoke as soon as they reached the top of the ridge. Several grey columns rose, spreading outwards until they joined into a massive cloud hundreds of feet above the ground. He had little doubt what was at the base of the columns, and he thought of Sophie.

His driver, Penny, had been at Biggin Hill for several months, and she'd given him some useful gen on local pubs and restaurants.

But now they drove in silence, exchanging anxious glances as each turn in the road opened a new perspective. It seemed the Luftwaffe had found its target this time.

Confirmation came as they approached the Station gates.

Debris littered their path, much of it shards of glass. One of the pillars of smoke rose from somewhere behind the squat, one-storey Guardroom, its windows gaping darkly. They had little choice but to park outside the base and walk the final few yards, Alex towering over the young WAAF, his parachute and Mae West over his shoulder and his helmet in his hand.

As they passed through the large, wrought iron gates, there was a strong smell of gas. An ambulance drove behind the Guardroom, and a group of a dozen airmen ran in the same direction, harangued by a red-faced corporal. The NCO looked towards Alex and saluted, a bizarre action under the circumstances, but one that underlined the traditions and discipline of the Service he'd joined. He felt a flush of pride, but also embarrassment: without his hat, he couldn't repay the compliment.

Feeling the need to do something, but unsure what, he followed the group. Penny trotted after him. They emerged behind the Guardroom and stopped. Seventy yards ahead was a three-storey accommodation block, curtains flapping out of its smashed windows.

It was a shocking sight, but their attention was soon drawn to a commotion to their right.

Penny shouted, 'It's the WAAF shelter.'

Alex could see no structure, but, 50 yards away, about 20 young women were gathered.

Some walked around in a daze, a few sat or lay on the debris-strewn grass, but most were on their hands and knees, seemingly ripping at the ground. All were covered in dust, and some bore the signs of bloody injuries. Further to the right, next to a smoking pile of earth, sat the ambulance, its doors already closing.

The NCO halted his group next to the WAAFs. A few fell out to tend the more obviously wounded, but the majority dropped to the ground on all fours. Penny ran from his side and put her arms round a young woman bleeding from a head wound. Next to her, Angela was tending another blood-stained WAAF. Jolted into action, Alex jogged the last few yards.

Steps ran down into what had obviously been a slit trench, rather than one of the more sophisticated shelters dotted around the Station. From about the fourth step down it was full of soil and masonry where the walls had collapsed. The infill rose to just above ground level a few yards to his right, then fell away again towards another set of steps, just visible about 20 yards further on.

Sticking out of the soil by the nearer steps was a small white hand at the end of a slim, blue shirted arm. Just to its right was a hint of blonde hair. The kneeling figures were digging frantically with their bare hands. A soil-covered girl was being pulled, coughing and retching, from the far side of the trench.

Alex wondered whether, as an officer, he should stand back and direct things, but there was nothing to direct. He threw down his helmet, Mae West and parachute, fell to his knees next to a young airman, and started digging.

Sophie ran from the Mess. She hadn't had time to reach a shelter, so she'd stayed in her room, huddled under her tin hat and a table. One of the bombs had seemed very close, as if the building had been hit, but she'd stayed where she was until the silence was broken by voices rather than explosions.

Smoke and flame were rising from the area of the Workshops and the MT yard, and a stream of water was running down the road, but she was more worried about the smoke from the vicinity of the barrack blocks. She set off running towards the Guardroom. Halfway, she passed a bomb crater. Water was flowing from a jumble of broken pipes, and she put a hand over her nose and mouth at the smell of gas. As she distanced herself from the crater and the air became sweeter, an ambulance raced past.

A hundred yards ahead, outside the Airmens' Mess, she recognised the figure of the Station Warrant Officer. A tall, imposing figure with an immaculately groomed Kitchener moustache, he was standing ramrod straight with his pace-stick under his arm, as if on a parade, which in some ways he was. To his front, a squad of perhaps 100 airmen and WAAFs stood at attention in ranks of three.

Sophie found the sight of him reassuring, but also daunting. He scared the life out of her. She only ever spoke to him, or, more accurately, he only ever spoke to her when he wished to express extreme displeasure at the behaviour of one of her girls. She slowed her headlong progress to a brisk walk, and struggled to control her breathing as she covered the last 50 yards. An airman ran up to him. He dipped his head and listened, then raised his pace-stick and bellowed. A small group of airmen doubled away from the ranks.

She was about ten yards away when, as if some sixth sense had warned him of the approach of an officer, he turned and threw up a smart salute. She returned the salute, the action inducing a superficial air of calm authority that was far removed from her underlying feelings of fear and inadequacy.

'Good evening, ma'am.'

'Good evening, Mr Griffiths. Could you give me a quick run-down please?'

'Yes, ma'am. We've lost power, gas and water, and the telephones are down. Workshops and a hangar have been hit and most of the vehicles in the MT yard have been damaged. I'm hearing reports of casualties over at the flight line and I've sent what vehicles we have over there. An airmen's block's been hit,' – his voice softened – 'and I'm afraid they've hit the WAAF shelter, ma'am.'

After an involuntary intake of breath, and a vain attempt to look through the Guardroom, Sophie fought to regain her composure.

'I've sent as many as I can spare, ma'am.'

'Thank you, Mr Griffiths. I think I'd better go and join them.'

'Very well, ma'am.'

He saluted again, and she returned the compliment, before turning and running toward the Guardroom. Officers weren't meant to run, but perhaps he'd forgive her on this occasion.

What would she find, and how would she cope?

Alex lowered a young girl gently to the grass. She was covered in a thin coating of soil, but uninjured. Satisfied she was going to be okay, he looked up, straight into the eyes of Sophie.

He sprang up and ran towards her. She was likely to have been in the Officers' Mess, but he'd still looked at all the faces around him, just in case. And he hadn't known whether the Officers' Mess had escaped.

Sophie looked even more surprised and relieved to see him. She fell into his arms and they kissed. Remembering where they were, they eased apart, embarrassed at their public display of affection.

'I thought you might have…' her voice trailed off.

'And I thought you might have been here,' he took over, turning to look at the scene.

He pointed at the shelter. 'The masonry seems to have fallen in one big slab and wedged between the walls, so most of the girls were okay. Trapped and terrified, but not actually buried. Only those nearest the steps were covered, and some of them were pulled clear from inside as we were digging out here.

'There were some nasty crush injuries and a few weren't breathing when they came out, but most…most of them are okay. I'm afraid one's in a very bad way.' He pointed to a group about 20 yards away, gathered round a prone figure.

'I'd better go and see what I can do, hadn't I?'

She looked so vulnerable, he wanted to hold her to him and kiss her again, but that would have been bad form, so he contented himself with a squeeze of her hand.

'Yes, I suppose so. And I better report to the Squadron. Do you know if they were airborne?'

'No. I finished about an hour ago. I heard aircraft taking off as the bombs fell, though. And I'm sorry, Alex, but I've just heard there's some sort of flap on over there.'

Reluctantly, he let go of her hand, and, seemingly with equal reluctance, she moved away. He watched her for a couple of yards before turning, picking up his kit and heading for the airfield.

They still hadn't organized a date, but they had exchanged a kiss. Who'd have thought it, Alex Lowe had a girlfriend!

Jack and Piers headed for a gap in the pens through which a steady flow of men had been rushing. The thin wisps of smoke were dispersing with their approach, and they seemed to be the last to half walk, half jog between the blast walls. Nothing could have prepared them for the scene that greeted them.

The air raid shelter had received a direct hit. The entrance to their right had disappeared, replaced by a deep crater with a rim of earth and masonry. Where this butted the remains of the shelter before them, large concrete blocks and the covering grass banks had been heaved outward. Only the last few yards to their left looked untouched.

Masonry and rock were strewn over the area. But, amongst this lay the true source of the horror: a gruesome selection of barely recognisable body parts, bloodied feet, arms, a head, chunks of flesh and blood-soaked fragments of blue clothing.

Amongst this carnage, stepping around the entrails and puddles of blood, wandered the survivors. The Adjutant and Flight Sergeant Patterson were trying to generate activity, pointing and shouting directions, but most seemed in a daze, shambling aimlessly, or just standing or sitting around in silent resignation.

Jack winced. If a similar number of body parts was scattered all around the perimeter of the crater, the death toll must be very high. The shelter could hold nearly 100 people, although most of 629's groundcrew should have been at Gravesend. It was little consolation.

He spotted and walked towards Stokesy, sitting disconsolately on one of the earth banks at the back of the nearest pen.

Stopping in front of him, he inquired quietly, 'Brummie?'

The tall Lancastrian was studying his hands. He looked up, his eyes moist and lined with red.

'I didn't follow him straight away, Sarge. Don't know why, but I ran over to shift some ground equipment. Barely finished when the first bomb went off - just over the wall. I was only a couple of seconds, while the debris was falling. But when... this was it.' He gestured weakly around.

'No sign of Brummie, Sarge. Don't know whether he was in the shelter. Doesn't seem to matter though, does it? Inside, it...it's just mush. And outside....' His voice trailed off as he swept an arm over the scene.

Jack put his hand on his engine fitter's shoulder. 'Nothing you could have done, Stokesy. I swore when you didn't run after him, but if you had…' His voice also trailed off.

'I know, Sarge. I know. What happened to you anyway? What're you doing here?'

'Long story, Stokesy. Another time maybe.'

Vehicles were arriving and Flight Sergeant Patterson was still trying to rouse people from their introspection.

'Come on, you lot, let's clear this up. Leave the bloody bits for now, at least until the medics arrive, but let's get the rest back in the hole. We've got a squadron of aircraft to recover.' He looked quizzically at Jack.

'Sorry, Flight, there's at least one, maybe two kites written off on the airfield.'

'Corporal Jenkins.' The Flight Sergeant was straight onto the new problem. 'Take a few lads on one of those trucks and see what Sergeant Williams has done to his kite.'

'You won't find it hard to spot, Jenksy,' Jack shouted to the Corporal, 'It's upside down, next to the one with no undercarriage.'

He felt shamefaced at his levity, but the Flight Sergeant was right, they had a returning squadron, probably two, to prepare for. And did this horror change anything? Since Dunkirk, he'd known it was a vicious war, and this merely re-confirmed it. He doubted whether it would change the way he fought.

But what if Caroline had been caught up in something similar on the other side of the airfield?

He looked around for Piers and was delighted to see

him talking to an exceptionally tall, blond-haired, young pilot in a very grubby uniform.

Alex listened to Piers without really hearing what was said. He could see all too well what his friend was trying to explain. The WAAF shelter had been nothing like this, thank God.

He looked around for Sandyman and Mead. They might just be out of sight of course, but he feared not.

Images of the Welshman's young bride and the Liverpudlian's six-year old daughter came to mind. Please God, let his groundcrew be safe.

Pulling injured WAAFs from the dirt, he'd wondered what he'd have done if a German airman had been marched towards him? At the time, and unlike the villagers earlier in the day, he'd been sure he wouldn't have wanted to beat the man to death. But what about now? He still didn't think he could harm a helpless prisoner, but he might be more determined to destroy enemy aircraft next time he met them. If only he had the skill to do it.

'Young sir?'

Alex turned at the familiar voice. Jack was walking towards him, a broad smile beaming out of a face spattered with specks of black, some of which had been smudged into oily smears. He also had a nasty gash on the left side of his chin.

'Jack? What happened to you? Were you here?'

'No, thank goodness. If I had been… But you don't look so hot yourself.'

Alex rubbed the lump on his forehead and looked around. This was what he'd expected to see as he'd run towards the WAAF shelter, and he'd been fearful of displaying weakness at the sight of blood and gore.

Now, confronted with the reality of body parts littering the ground, he seemed strangely indifferent to the horror. Perhaps you could only take so much in one day before you became anaesthetised, or was it just fatigue dulling his senses?

Jack continued, 'Come on, let's get out of their hair. I don't think there's anything we can do here.'

Alex felt guilty at not mucking in as he had 15 minutes earlier.

But Jack was right. This was different. They turned and walked away, retracing their steps through the line of pens. Piers pointed at their wrecked Spitfires and explained why they were still on the ground. Jack's was pretty well burned out, just a blackened tailplane and an engine with wisps of smoke rising from it.

'Looks as if you're both lucky to be alive. Especially you, Jack.'

'Yes, although young Piers here has missed out a few important details.'

Jack retold the story, concentrating on the elements his rescuer had been too modest to mention.

By the time they reached the dispersal hut, they were in surprisingly high spirits.

'I'm just going to ring Ops and let them know what's happened,' Piers said, jogging up the steps.

'I don't think you will' Alex shouted after him. 'The phones were down a few minutes ago.'

'Oh well, I'll give it a go. I need the heads anyway.'

As Piers disappeared inside the hut, Alex and Jack walked clear of the shade of the building to sit on the grass in the evening sunshine.

'So, what happened to you, Alex?'

Alex was delighted at Jack's use of his first name. Feeling a fillip out of all proportion to the tiny gesture, he related the story of his engine failure and subsequent forced landing.

Jack listened intently, making only a few humorous interruptions, along the lines of: 'That'll teach you to be tall and blond.'

Alex was explaining what he'd encountered behind the Guardroom, when Piers rejoined them.

'The power's still off and there's no telephones, so the IntO's sent Hopkins to Ops. He might be a while though. He's had to walk. Anyway, carry on, Alex. I guess you know more about what's going on over there than any of us.'

Alex continued, letting Piers know that Angela was all right, but omitting mention of Sophie. He finished with what he'd been told by the driver of the vehicle he'd flagged down on the way to dispersal.

'As well as the telephones and power, he said they'd hit the gas and water mains. And as well as the WAAF block, they've damaged one of the airmen's barrack blocks, the Officers' and Sergeants' Messes, MT, uh...Stores, the Armoury and the NAAFI shop. He seemed really hacked off about that.'

He saw Jack stiffen.

'Are you alright, Jack?'

'Yes. A bit of a stinger.' He touched the gash on his chin. 'I'll just try and find some water.'

Piers joshed in his usual light-hearted way. 'Make sure you wash behind your ears. That oil gets everywhere.'

Jack managed a half-hearted smile, rose painfully to his feet and hobbled towards the hut.

Alex watched him go. 'He doesn't look well, does he?'

'Neither would you if you'd had the couple of days

he's had, although you very nearly have, haven't you?'

They both laughed.

'You know it was him who kept the 109s off you, don't you?'

'No. He never mentioned it.'

'Didn't think he would. But he told me as we walked back from our aborted take off. He said the first one was a lucky beam shot, but he never got a bead on the second.'

'I didn't even know there was a second one.'

'Well, there was, and he chased it around until it only had enough fuel to run home.'

'He's quite a chap, isn't he, Piers?'

'Yes he is, Alex. Quite a chap.'

'Sammy Samson's dead', Birdy blurted as he staggered into the hut.

They made him sit before he carried on. He looked dreadful, greeny-white, shaking with emotion. Jack and the others sat in the gloom and waited for him to compose himself.

'He must have taken one in the fuel tank. The cockpit was …It was awful. Just burst into flame. I hoped he'd copped one as well. But he hadn't. I could see him…trying… For fuck's sake, he only arrived at half eight this morning.

'And now this, this…' He gestured out of the door. 'Murdering bastards. How many have they killed out there?'

'We don't know yet, Birdy. The CO and Muddy should be back soon.'

It was Piers who'd piped up, with the soothing tone of a parent trying to calm a distraught toddler.

Jack smiled. His friend didn't know it, but he was

shaping into a fine leader. And Alex, although different in temperament, was cut from the same cloth. He'd been lucky to have them both in his section. That would all change tomorrow, and for good.

He looked around at who was left, Ginge, Dusty and Pete, all NCOs, Birdy, Piers and Alex, all relatively new. Without reinforcements, if Smithy was okay and Chips got back in one piece, they'd be down to 14, including the three new boys.

The CO and Muddy walked in. Jack and the others stirred as if to rise, but the CO waved them back into their chairs. The group maintained a respectful silence as the two men sat. The CO looked drained. He rubbed his face with his hands before looking up and speaking, making eye contact with each in turn.

'I'm afraid, there are about 30 of our chaps missing, plus a few from 629. We won't know how many until the rest of them get back from Gravesend. You wouldn't have known, but they're due to go north tomorrow, Acklington I think.'

'Rotten luck,' someone grunted from the gloom.

'I know. They lost two pilots as well. And if the raid had been this time tomorrow, they wouldn't even have been here.

'The Station Commander was out there just now. He said they hit a WAAF shelter over the other side as well. One dead.'

Jack looked to Alex, but his young friend chose not to interrupt, and the CO continued.

'He's confident that the holes on the airfield will be patched up by morning. And the GPO are already working on the telephone lines, so the Sector HQ should be up and running as well. Hornchurch has taken our sector for the moment. Oh, we're stood down by the way. Sorry, should have said that first.'

There was a collective sigh, and shoulders sagged in relief.

'They've also damaged the Messes, some barrack blocks and MT.'

And the NAAFI shop, Jack thought. Don't forget the NAAFI shop!

'So I'm afraid there's not much transport, and the NCOs will either have to make their own way to their digs, or wait for the wagon to come back after dropping off the officers.'

'Typical,' a Geordie voice whinged.

'Sorry, Sergeant Clough, just one of life's many iniquities. You'll cope.'

'Bloody well have to, won't I, sir?'

The CO laughed as he rose from his seat. 'And I'll make sure you won't have to walk in in the morning.'

This time, they all rose respectfully and moved aside as Squadron Leader Parr walked wearily past them and into his office.

Surely he's not going to start writing letters now, Jack thought?

He and Alex should really get their cuts and bruises seen to. But not tonight. The medics had greater priorities.

He heard his name called and looked at Muddy.

'Can we have a chat?'

'Certainly, sir.'

He followed the Flight Commander into his office.

Muddy and Jack went through the order of battle. The rest would be greeted with a few surprises when they rolled up in the morning. For a start, Smithy and Birdy were to be given 48 hour passes, so there would be only 12 of them, although how many aircraft they'd have, and who'd service them, would be anyone's guess.

And Jack was going to be a flight sergeant, and receive a Bar to the DFM he'd only just received for his flying over Dunkirk.

After the last week, he was pretty sure he was an 'ace' twice over, with ten kills to his name, but it wasn't something he or anyone else talked about. Shooting a line was frowned on almost as much as cowardice.

His promotion and his gallantry award should have been reasons for celebration, but not after the day they'd just had. Perhaps he'd feel differently in the morning, but he doubted it.

They were working by the light of a Tilly lamp by the time they called it a day. The others, bar the CO and George Evans, had all gone, and Muddy offered him a lift in his MG. Without giving the flight commander any indication of the depth and nature of his concern for his landlady, Jack persuaded him to take a detour via the NAAFI shop.

It was shut, and the sentry guarding the building had no idea whether anyone had been hurt in the explosion that had blown a large hole in the stock room wall. Jack tried to be rational, but he couldn't help feeling fearful. What would he find in Keston?

At least the houses were still there as they turned into the Avenue, and they looked to be intact. There was no light from Number 5, but that could just be the blackout. He steeled himself.

What would he do if she wasn't in? Come to think of it, what would he do if she was?

'Do you want me to wait, Jack?'

245

'No thanks, Muddy. I've got a key. See you in the morning.'

'Okay. Sleep tight.'

Jack saluted and his friend drove off to turn round at the end of the lane. He suddenly felt incredibly weary.

Not wanting to appear rude by just letting himself in, he knocked. To his relief, he heard movement. Caroline opened the door and he stepped briskly in, hearing it close behind him. He turned.

She looked stunning. Even more beautiful and desirable than in his daydreams. Was the flowered dress worn for him, or was it just wishful thinking? It showed off her figure to perfection. And she seemed to have applied a little make up – some lipstick at least. And was that a hint of perfume? But she was frowning.

'Jack, you look awful.'

Caroline, you look wonderful. Thank goodness you're safe. I love you.

'Jack? Are you all right?'

He wasn't. He felt light-headed and weak, close to a faint.

'Come in here and sit down.'

She helped him to the kitchen and sat him in a chair, then rummaged in a cupboard and busied herself at the sink. He felt hot and cold, nauseous. But even in this state, he couldn't help admiring her. She turned, pulled a chair close to his and started dabbing his forehead with a cool cloth.

Perhaps fortuitously, he really was speechless, trembling slightly as he leaned forward in his chair. Her presence, her scent; they were overpowering. She put the cloth down, squeezed some cotton wool in a bowl of steaming water and started to dab at his chin. He winced.

'Sorry Jack, but it's full of oil.'

He didn't doubt it. As expected, there'd been no water in the dispersal hut.

When she pulled the cotton wool away, it was stained red and black. She put the dirty piece to one side and picked up another.

Had she spent the day thinking of him? He couldn't think of anything to say that wouldn't sound insane unless she had been, and in a similar way. And how could he know that?

She used several more wads of cotton wool and he bore the pain more stoically. He also maintained his silence, enjoying her proximity as she tended him.

'There's another gash on your head Jack. I'm just going to have a prod.'

He lowered his head and she stood to lean over him. He felt the warmth of her body, imagined the sway of her breasts above his head. Her knee touched his and he fought to stave off the feelings of arousal that coursed through him. She placed a hand on his cheek and pressed against his head, revealing that there was a painful bruise as well as a gash in his hairline.

'Sorry.'

He wanted so much to reach out and put his arms round her waist, to pull her to him in a tight embrace. But it would be madness. Wouldn't it?

'There. I think they're a bit cleaner now.'

She sat down again, pushed the bowl away and looked at him earnestly with her big, dark eyes.

'How are you feeling?'

Completely knackered, but marvellous. If only I had the strength to take you in my arms and make mad passionate love to you.

'A bit better, thank you. I don't know what came

247

over me.'

'Have you had anything to eat?'

'No. But...'

'Well there's one reason then. And you've been up since four. I've got some bacon. Would you like a bacon sandwich?'

She was talking quickly, insistently, and he sensed that she too was on edge. Had she been waiting for him to arrive, and now that he had, was she, like him, too timid to do anything, too scared to reveal her true feelings? But what were her true feelings?

'It's nine o'clock, Caroline. I don't want to be a nuisance.'

'Rubbish. Bacon butty and a cup of tea then. I'd just boiled the kettle.' She jumped up, full of enthusiasm and energy. 'Or would you prefer beer?'

'No, tea would be fine,' he lied. Beer would have been better, but he didn't want to appear too demanding. He did want to make himself more presentable though. Heaven knows what he must look and smell like.

Before he'd thought it through, he asked, 'Do you mind if I freshen up?'

There was a moment's hesitation. 'No, of course not, Jack, you go ahead. There's plenty of hot water in the kettle. Use the sink there.'

'Thank you.'

She'd spared him the journey to the washstand in his room. There was no bathroom.

He rose unsteadily to his feet, feeling a fresh spell of giddiness that had him leaning against the table.

Perhaps sensing his weakness, Caroline carried the heavy kettle to the sink and poured in the steaming water.

'Thanks.'

She busied herself in the cupboards and around the cooker as he removed his jacket and undid his shirt. Should he take it off?

He turned and struck eye contact. 'Do you mind?'

Again, a small hesitation, and a less than emphatic shake of the head.

'No.'

He was going too far, but he desperately wanted to feel clean – cleaner. He took off his shirt, wincing as he stretched to pull off the sleeves.

A cloth and a cake of soap appeared on the wooden draining board at his right elbow, and she reached across to turn on the cold tap.

'Just in case you forgot,' she smiled apologetically.

He smiled his thanks, and felt her eyes on him as he tested the water and started to bathe.

'How did you get those cuts and bruises?'

'We were caught up in this evening's raid. Hit me and my wingman on the ground, just as we were taking off. He risked his life to pull me clear. I was lucky to get away with these.'

Although he'd decided to be more open than he had with Gwen, he chose not to tell her about the bloody aftermath of the raid. But when she asked about the older wounds, he told her about his parachuting escapade. And after he'd reluctantly re-buttoned his grubby shirt, and was eating his bacon sandwich and drinking tea, she sat opposite, watching him and telling him about her day.

She hadn't known about the raid on Keston, or the bombing of the NAAFI Shop, having been asked to work eight till five because someone was ill. So she'd been on base when the village was bombed, and had only heard the evening's raid in the distance. The little he was able to tell her about the Shop did nothing to put her mind at rest.

In the ensuing silence, he finished his sandwich and drained the last of his tea.

'You still look shaky, Jack.'

And you still look gorgeous, Caroline.

'I'm just dead tired. It's been a long day.'

'Come on, I'll see you up the stairs.'

He wasn't confident enough of his strength to turn the offer down. And it wasn't histrionics. He only just made it without her physical support. On reaching the landing, he clasped his bedroom door handle and turned.

'Good night, Caroline, and thank you.'

'Good night, Jack.' As if reacting to some sudden impulse, she put a hand on his arm and planted a kiss on his cheek. 'Sleep tight.'

He watched in stunned silence as she walked the few steps down the landing and entered her bedroom, closing the door behind her.

Caroline leaned back against the door. What was she doing?

Something she wouldn't have contemplated until three days ago. But he'd reawakened yearnings she'd thought lost with Alfie's death.

They'd married on a whim the day before he went back to sea. What with their shyness and the state he was in when they'd escaped the company of his shipmates, the marriage had barely been consummated. But the brief liaison had awakened feelings that made her impatient for his return. It was one of the reasons his death seemed so cruel. But she thought she'd accepted that a door had closed on that area of her life.

And then, Jack. The closeness as she'd tended his wounds. The sight of his sinewy body as he'd washed at the sink. His feral scent. His strength. His vulnerability.

It was madness. But was it wrong?

Chapter 7 - Saturday August 31st 1940

Jack crept out of his bedroom and turned to shut the door as quietly as possible. When he turned back, Caroline was on the landing dressed in a long dressing gown.

'I just wanted to see if you were alright.'

She looked sheepish, and he could tell that his health wasn't her only concern. He closed the distance between them quickly, looked into her eyes, giving her a brief opportunity to back away if she wanted, then leaned down to kiss her. His heart leapt as her lips parted in response.

He was amazed he'd had the nerve to act so decisively. But he'd had to kiss her before she apologised for the previous evening, and British reserve led them to talk themselves out of an encounter that he at least desired above all else.

Reluctantly, he pulled back.

'I'm sorry, Caroline, I really do have to go.'

'I know, Jack. Take care.'

He sensed her fear for him, but he feared for her also.

'I will. You too. See you tonight.'

He turned and walked briskly along the landing and down the stairs. As he let himself out into the cold morning air, he wondered if he'd just woken from an especially vivid daydream. Even the twitch of the blackout curtain as he ducked into the waiting car couldn't quite dispel the feeling that it was all too good to be true.

Alex gazed around the dispersal hut.

Most of the occupants looked completely done in

before the day had even started; although, lounging to either side of him, Jack and Piers seemed remarkably well, considering what they'd been through less than 12 hours previously.

Alex was sure he looked dreadful in comparison. His head was throbbing and he felt sick. When he'd eventually gone to bed after an impromptu Squadron wake, he'd tried to concentrate on Sophie and their kiss, but too many other, less pleasant, images from the day jostled for his attention. A scene from one of the most persistent nightmares was reawakened by the conversation taking place behind him.

'There wasn't one complete body. Not one. And some had just vanished, blown to smithereens.'

Alex grimaced. He feared Sandy and Scouse were among the dead. They'd certainly been missing from the clear up party.

The CO coughed, and the talking stopped.

'Good morning, chaps.'

Squadron Leader Gerry Parr looked as tired as the rest of them, and, from a little tic pulsing at the corner of his mouth, Alex sensed deep emotion bubbling just beneath the surface.

'Difficult to know where to start really, but I think I'll pass on the bleakest news first. The final death toll from the shelter is 38 or 39. The doubt is over whether one of 629's fitters has been sent on leave by an NCO who's on leave himself, if that makes sense.

'I've asked Flight Sergeant Patterson to read you the list when I've finished.'

He nodded over to where the NCO stood in the shadows, nervously clutching a sheet of paper.

'I hope knowing the names will make it easier for us to face those who've survived, and perhaps even stop us putting our size 14 aircrew boots in it. When you hear the list, many of you will realise that you're going to have to get used to new groundcrew. They've dragged tradesmen out of the hangars, and more will arrive from other squadrons during the day, but they're going to be a bit short handed for a while, so just be patient if things don't happen with their usual efficiency.'

The CO looked to the Flight Sergeant again, and he nodded his gratitude at the plea for forbearance.

'And I've just heard that a couple of 629 pilots will be joining us when the rest of them fly north. Flight Lieutenant Waters will give a run down of the batting order after the Flight Sergeant has finished, but I think we've got ten aircraft to start with, haven't we Flight?'

'Yes sir, nine at the moment, ten in about an hour.'

Ten. Alex couldn't help wondering what Muddy and Jack had come up with. Chips had turned up in one piece and fit to fly, but Smithy and Birdy hadn't been at breakfast. So there'd be at least one new section leader, and they already knew they needed a new flight commander, unless one of 629's was coming across. And at least one of the new boys was likely to be needed. They were still sitting together, trying to look relaxed, while wondering which was likely to be chosen.

He felt sorry for them, arriving at such a difficult time. He'd introduced himself briefly to the Pilot Officer, Harry Beaumont, but they hadn't chatted for long before he'd been dragged off by Piers and Olly. When he'd thought of the newcomer again, he'd disappeared, gone to bed if he had any sense.

The CO's voice interrupted his thoughts.

'As promised, the telephone lines are up and

running, so we're a Sector HQ again, and,' he pointed at the bare light bulbs shining above their heads, 'you've already discovered that the power's back on. Not sure about the gas?'

He looked to the Flight Sergeant.

'The cookhouse was open sir, and the NCOs got breakfast in the Sergeants' Mess.'

'Alright for some,' Geordie whinged.

'I'm sure they'll bring breakfast out to you as usual, Sergeant Clough.'

'If there's any transport, sir.'

For the first time, Alex sensed the CO getting miffed, but he maintained his cool.

'Well I'm sure the Adj will make sure you don't starve, won't you Adj?'

George Evans glowered at Ginge. 'If I have to march Sergeant Clough down to the cookhouse myself, sir.'

There was a ripple of muted laughter.

'Good. Nearly finished. There is some better news, although it may seem out of place this morning. Two of our number are incorrectly dressed. Sergeant Williams has been awarded his crown, and a bar to his DFM, and Pilot Officer White has been promoted Flying Officer and awarded the DFC.'

Alex beamed across at both of them. That explained why they'd looked so relatively chipper. The Distinguished Flying Cross. Wow. He'd sensed that Piers was good, and scoring steadily, but the DFC!

'Congratulations to both of them,' the CO smiled weakly, before adopting a sterner expression again.

'Now, looking at the weather forecast, I think we can expect another busy day. We've all seen what happens when the bombers get through…'

'Fuckin' 12 Group!'

'Yes, perhaps, but if we can get to the bombers first, we won't have to rely on AOC 12 Group to mind our backs, so let's give it our best shot. And finally, just remember to be patient with the groundcrew.

'Any questions?' He looked around the room to a chorus of silence. 'Good. Carry on.'

They stood up as he walked to his office, and Flight Sergeant Patterson stepped forward.

Alex looked at the two airmen going efficiently about their tasks in the half light. Even going up and talking to them seemed disloyal to the memories of Sandyman and Mead. But he now knew for certain that the two men he'd come to rely on for psychological as well as physical support were not coming back.

He swallowed hard and walked into the pen.

One of the airmen saw him coming. He was dark haired, of medium height and slim build, perhaps a couple of years older than Alex.

'Good morning, sir. Afraid we haven't finished the Daily yet.'

'Oh, don't worry. I'll set myself up around you. I'm Pilot Officer Lowe by the way.'

'Pleased to meet you, sir. Aircraftman Hayman, your new rigger, I think.' He had a fairly thick West Country accent. Somerset or Devon, Alex thought.

'And that's Jock, sir, Leading Aircraftman Lammerton.'

His new engine fitter, Alex presumed, as he was beetling away under the engine cowling.

'Right, well thank you, Hayman.' Alex blushed. He couldn't help feeling he was sounding pompous again. 'Like I say, I'll just set myself up, and have a chat with you and Lammerton later perhaps.'

Why was it so difficult to be natural across the rank boundaries?

He moved away to hang his parachute on the left wingtip, carrying on his train of thought. He wasn't so different from them. In fact, he probably had more in common with them than he had with most of the officers. He'd only been to Grammar School because of a scholarship, and if they were ex-Halton like Jack, they'd have passed the same School Certificate, or demonstrated the potential to pass it.

He sometimes felt stuck between two worlds. It had been the same at home. Living in a working class neighbourhood with working class parents and friends, but going to school with the Town's middle and upper crust. He still had friends in both groups, but felt that he belonged to neither.

The familiar whiff of the cockpit brought him back to reality. He leaned in, connected the oxygen and took several deep breaths. The gas eased his headache, but the smell of the mask exacerbated his nausea, and renewed memories of prowling Messerschmitts and crash landings. He completed his checks as quickly as possible and stood up again.

Hayman and Lammerton were standing in front of the tailplane as he stepped off the wing. He guessed the engine fitter was waiting to get at the cockpit. The air was already thick with the growl of other Merlins.

'Hello, Lammerton, I'm Pilot Officer Lowe.'

'Hello, sir,' the engine fitter said in an accent that Alex failed to place beyond Scottish.

They both stood and looked at him. He couldn't think of anything clever to say, and he blushed. 'I can see you're both busy now, so I won't interrupt, but I'm sure we'll meet again before the day's out.

'No doubt, sir,' Lammerton smiled.

'Well, see you later then.'

'We'll be ready, sir,' Hayman shouted after him.

Alex waved without turning. He wondered what they thought of him. They looked competent, and more enthusiastic than he'd have been in their shoes. They weren't Sandyman and Mead, but he'd get used to them.

Sophie watched the map filling with black counters. It wasn't even eight o'clock yet, and formations as large as these usually didn't appear for at least another two hours. She sighed. It was going to be another long day.

The feeling permeated the rest of the room. Kelvin Rice looked tense, anxiously eying the map, with the occasional word to his assistant and the Army officers to his left.

Some of the WAAFs bore the marks of the evening's raid, hands covered with dressings, and faces bearing angry welts. But they were here, and already busy, the telephonists talking into their headphones, the plotters listening and then standing to rake on new contacts, or update existing ones.

Sophie was immensely proud of them.

The phone link to Uxbridge gave its characteristic ring, and the Controller picked up the receiver and listened intently, before replacing it in its cradle.

He turned to the Flight Sergeant to his right. 'Bring Soho to standby John. I'll contact Dragon. You can tell them we're just waiting for a visual from the Observer Corps, and we'll speak to them in cockpit.'

They passed their messages to the squadron telephone clerks. All those not actively engaged in taking messages or moving counters had turned towards the platform, and Kelvin Rice. The Uxbridge line rang again. As he replaced the handset, he spoke to the room.

'The first three formations are all fighters, so there'll be a short delay before normal service is resumed.'

There was a slight easing of tension, but they could all see other plots following on behind, and more again over the French coast.

Kelvin looked at Sophie and tried to smile reassuringly. The unpleasant thoughts of yesterday were gone. He hoped her young man survived another day unscathed.

They'd been called to cockpit readiness at just after eight, and had been sitting there for no more than 15 minutes. Seemed like hours though. Jack looked at Stokesy. The poor man still appeared shell shocked, standing, ashen-faced, staring into space.

He could do with some leave, Jack thought. But couldn't they all?

He shifted in his seat, wincing at his various aches and pains.

His new rigger was standing by the left wingtip. New being the operative word. Baby faced and straight out of training.

Jack gave an encouraging smile and wave, both of which were returned, although the young man couldn't entirely conceal his underlying apprehension. Hardly surprising though, was it? Arriving on your first squadron was daunting enough, but arriving the day after nearly 40 had been killed, now that really was tough. Although, strangely enough, being one of tens of new faces probably made it easier, not that he'd dream of trying to express that thought to the young man.

He looked around the cockpit again. 'Come on, let's get on with it.'

Had she really kissed him? He reached up and ran his hand over the place on his chin brushed by her lips. And had he really kissed her back?

Please God, let me survive another day.

'Dragon, this is Bastion, Dragon scramble. Two hundred plus bandits approaching Sheppey, angels one five. Dragon scramble.'

Jack was in the middle of the formation, leading B Flight.

They were clawing frantically for height, the five Spitfires ahead of him silhouetted against the blue of the sky, the four behind projected onto a shifting background of sunlit fields and low white cumulus.

'Dragon, this is Bastion, bandits twelve o'clock, approximately twenty miles, maintaining angels one five.'

'Roger, Bastion, this is Dragon Leader, passing angels one two.'

Muddy was up front, sounding calm and in command.

There were battles raging away to the north, and they'd been heading that way themselves to start with. But they'd now been turned east to face a new threat. Jack was glad. Let 12 Group look after their own fucking airfields.

He knew such thoughts were stupid. The threat to Biggin Hill and the other 11 Group airfields could come from any direction, and Dragon's ten aircraft were tiny pieces in a much bigger picture. They had to go where they were told. It just made him feel better to be somewhere close, protecting Caroline.

Fifty plus the Controller had said. It was enough. Yesterday's devastation had been caused by no more than a dozen.

'Dragon, this is Bastion, bandits in your twelve o'clock, fifteen miles.'

'Roger Bastion, this is Dragon Leader, passing angels one four.'

He had two new wing men this time. Another tall blond officer, Harry Beaumont, and a young NCO, Sergeant Johnathan Charles: JC. He could see the fear in their eyes as they prepared for their first experience of combat, but there was little time for sympathy.

'Dragon Leader, this is Red 2,' – there was no mistaking the tension in Ginge's voice – 'bandits twelve o'clock, slightly low, and one o'clock, slightly high.'

Jack could see the higher formation just to the right of dead ahead: about 20 black silhouettes. They looked bigger than Snappers, maybe Dorniers or 110s?

'Roger, Red 2, thank you. Bastion this is Dragon Leader, tally-ho, tally-ho, two formations of approximately forty and twenty.'

'Dragon Leader, this is Bastion, roger and good luck.'

'Thank you, Bastion. B Flight Leader, this is Dragon Leader, stop right hand formation interfering please.'

'B Flight, wilco.'

The courtesy of the calls was almost comical, but it was better for the nerves than frantic shouts, especially for the new boys. As the five aircraft of A Flight levelled and pulled away, heading for the larger formation he could now see just below the horizon, Jack eased B Flight to the right, continuing the climb.

Their adversaries turned out to be Messerschmitt 110s. The twin-engined fighters held all the cards. They'd already succeeded in drawing half the Squadron away from the bombers, and now, with odds of four to one in their favour, excess height and the sun at their backs, they had B Flight at their mercy.

Jack was just deciding how best to position, when the lead 110s started to turn.

'Well I never. The stupid bastards.'

Why the 110s were wasting their tactical advantage and forming a defensive circle was beyond him, but he had to act before they realised their mistake. He levelled his Spitfire and accelerated into the gap between the 110s and the bombers.

'Dragon B Flight, line astern, line astern, go.'

The other four aircraft dropped back and, one by one, disappeared to tuck in behind him: JC, then Harry Beaumont, then Piers, with Alex bringing up the rear.

Despite their inexperience, they'd all be familiar with this attacking formation; it was one they practised in flying training. They were accelerating fast now.

'Blue Two. Keep an eye out for those 110s.'

'Blue Two, wilco.'

Alex sounded determined. Good lad.

Down to their left, A Flight had made their initial attack. The bomber formation, 20 or so Dorniers, was in the process of splitting up, even as a similar number of 109s was diving in. The air was full of wheeling machines and blossoms of smoke and flame.

Jack took a last look up to his right. The redundant but very welcome defensive circle was almost complete.

'Dragon B Flight, diving in.'

Making his control movements smooth enough for young JC and Harry to keep up, he rolled left into the inverted and pulled towards the combat below. He found himself spearing almost vertically down on a Dornier, pulled his gunsight ahead of it and fired. The airframe vibrated around him as the guns clattered and the bomber grew in his windscreen. Already sweating, he pulled hard to pass behind the target's right wing, buffeted by its slipstream and unsure whether he'd caused any damage.

He hoped the rest of his Flight were coping.

'What the...'

Alex rolled hard right and pulled to avoid Piers. It hadn't taken long for it all to go pear-shaped.

JC had rolled smoothly behind Jack and followed him into the dive. But, having rolled upside down, Harry just hung there, seemingly frozen into immobility.

As the Spitfire to his front rapidly ran out of airspeed, Piers, who was already inverted, pulled down and left. Alex had had to go right to avoid nibbling into his friend's tailplane with his propeller.

He had no idea what had happened to Harry, nor, for that matter, anyone else in his Flight. He found himself pointing down at about ten 109s, all diving into the mêlée, seemingly oblivious of him bearing down on them.

Oh well, it was an ill wind and all that. He decided to take advantage of the situation, picking a 109 to the rear of the formation and dragging his nose just in front of it. He was closing fast, but he held his fire.

Just as he was about to press the gun button, the German pilot looked up. Alex sensed the other man's horror.

'Too late, pal.'

He jabbed his thumb forward and the familiar clatter and judder assailed his senses. His rounds smashed into the glinting perspex of the Messerschmitt, and his adversary's face disappeared in a mist of red.

Alex was shaken. Sickened. But he retained enough control to avoid the German fighter as it rolled left.

Pulling hard round, he looked over his shoulder. The 109 was falling in a tightening spiral.

Shouldn't he feel triumphant? His first definite kill. And shouldn't he have been shouting for Sandy and Scouse as he'd hit the gun button? But he hadn't even thought of them until now, and there was nothing glorious about the cold-blooded act he'd just committed. He was hot and shaky, still feeling sick.

'Come on, pull yourself together, Alex.'

Some strength returned as he heard his own words. He looked around. The 110s were finally diving out of their circle, too late to prevent the bomber formation being broken up, but with time enough to exact retribution from those that had done it.

What should he do?

Against the backdrop of the English countryside, a confusing array of dark shapes weaved in imminent risk of collision, some engulfed in hellish balls of smoke and flame. His colleagues were being assailed by fire from the bombers and the far more numerous 109s, and they were about to be hit by the diving 110s.

Making up his mind, he rolled right and pulled hard, straining against the g to maintain his vision. As the

110s came into view, he rolled out and checked the nose to point at them, pressing his own gun button as tracer from the leading three spat towards him. With a closing speed of over 600 miles an hour, the large fighters grew alarmingly in his windscreen. But he had no intention of shying away.

At the last moment, the lead 110 heaved upward. Alex flinched as its oil-streaked underside and twin tail flashed inches above his canopy.

A few moments later, the encounter with the second line of Messerschmitts ended the same way. Before he met the third line, he ran out of ammunition, but he flew on regardless, barging through to the rear of the formation.

His clothing was soaked in sweat, and he could feel cold rivulets tickling down his face and body. He jabbed a thumb and forefinger into his eyes and slumped back, exhausted.

It was 9.15am.

By the time he'd gathered his composure and turned to see what was happening behind him, the sky was empty.

'Where were you working before this then?' Alex asked his new engine fitter.

'The hangars, sir,' the Scotsman answered.

'And did you know any of the men that were killed?'

'Yes, sir, I knew most of them.' He lowered his eyes as if seeing some of their faces. 'I only left 646 when we came here from Pembrey.'

'And I was on 629 until a few months ago,' Hayman added. 'So I knew most of their blokes.'

'And we all met in the NAAFI and cookhouse,

didn't we, Dev?'

The Englishman nodded.

'Well, I'm very sorry. It sometimes feels as if I've been here a lifetime, but I only arrived a week today, and I only really knew Sandy Sandyman and Scouse Mead.'

'They were great blokes, sir. I went to Sandy's wedding in that place nobody can pronounce, especially not a Scotsman.'

They all smiled, and Alex took advantage of the lighter tone. 'Well, don't ask me, I'm from Shropshire. But yes, they were great blokes. Anyway, I better get off to the IntO and file my report. Good to meet you both. See you later.'

They smiled their replies as Alex turned and walked away. He sighed. With due respect to their predecessors, he liked Jock and Dev, and he felt better for having taken the time to chat to them.

'Detling?'

'Yes, Detling,' Olly confirmed as he walked towards them, cradling his arm.

When Harry Beaumont had failed to turn up, they'd feared the worst. At least they now knew he was alive, even if he had landed at the wrong airfield.

Alex remembered how he'd felt after the spin on his first sortie, when he'd had no idea where he was, or how to get back to base. He'd have landed at any airfield appearing in front of him. Perhaps Harry had done just that.

'Good. I thought we'd all had it when he froze in front of me and Piers.'

'You thought we'd had it!' Piers snorted. 'It was me that almost chopped his tail off.'

Alex decided not to tell his friend how close he'd been to losing his own tailplane.

'Still no word on Ginge, though,' Olly continued.

Instinctively, the three of them looked at Jack, sitting alone, deep in thought. Alex wondered if he should go over, but it was early days. Ginge might ring in at any moment, having landed elsewhere, or baled out, or anything really. And Jack had other things to worry about, like his Flight.

'That leaves us a bit thin on the ground, doesn't it?'

'Aha. Would do old boy, but I've just heard that when 629 bugger off north in the next half hour or so, Bunter and Jet are coming across.'

'Poor bastards. Wonder what they've done to deserve that?' Piers enquired.

'Nothing. Volunteered, so the Adj says. Want to stay close to their 'young floozies' as he so delicately puts it.'

They both looked at Alex.

'Yes?' he said defensively, choosing to ignore their inference that Sophie was one of the floozies in question.

But she probably was. And after yesterday's kiss, Bunter could be risking his life for a lost cause.

Jack was angry. They'd been on a fruitless pursuit to the south, their quarry turning away before they were even close. And now it seemed that Biggin Hill was under attack again. To lose Ginge was bad enough. If he lost Caroline as well!

'Dragon, this is Bastion, bandits angels one two, heading south east, vector three four zero.'

'Bastion, this is Dragon Leader, wilco, maintaining angels one seven.'

'Too bloody late though, isn't it?' Jack fumed.

They'd be seeking revenge rather than protecting their battle-scarred base. At least they were ten again, and they had the advantage of height. Flying Officer Arbuthnott and Pilot Officer Black had brought their airframes with them. Black was to his left, in place of Harry, who had yet to return. Arbuthnott was in Dusty's Yellow Section. The CO was leading, and Piers and Alex were at the back.

Jack looked at Alex's Spitfire, weaving out to the right. Perhaps he'd be worrying about his new girlfriend.

It was mayhem in the Ops Room. Hostile plots were appearing all the time, with the larger formations splitting into smaller groups that jinked and feinted, making it almost impossible for the Group Controllers to decide what to attack, when, and with which squadrons.

And by the time they'd made their minds up and told the Sector Controllers, the defenders were always scrambling for height. And now the bombs were dropping again.

Sophie looked across at Kelvin Rice, sweating under his tin helmet and talking continuously into his handset.

The lights swayed and dust fell as the crump, crump of explosions advanced across the airfield. So far, they'd all stopped short, but surely it was only a matter of time. Just occasionally, one of the girls looked up at the heavy ceiling, but mainly, they just carried on, heedless of the danger. Sophie could only marvel at the courage of those who knew only too well what it was like to be buried alive.

The explosions stopped, but they'd done so several times before, only to start again, and always closer than ever. This time, however, the near silence continued. Shoulders began to uncurl, and necks stretch. It was strange how they all seemed to hunch as the bombs dropped, as if making themselves a few inches shorter could reduce the risk of being hit.

She looked at Kelvin Rice as his back straightened. He smiled reassuringly and she listened to his words.

'Roger Dragon, this is Bastion, good luck.'

Jack now accepted that the bombing of Biggin Hill, and especially the shelter, was changing him. Previously, he'd been content to disable German aircraft to prevent their crews returning to France. Even seeing his fellow pilots killed and injured had failed to change that philosophy. But now, he wanted to kill.

The grisly deaths of Brummie and the other groundcrew, the potential for the same to happen to Caroline, these were somehow different. They made him angry, and, as he looked at the smoke in the distance, fearful.

How dare these bastards drop bombs on Kent?

And somehow, even though they were flying in machines yards apart, he sensed that many of the others had undergone a similar change of heart. There was an added urgency, a hatred that hadn't been there before. And, once again, these emotions were intermingled with a fierce pride at the sight of the Spitfires diving alongside him, sunlight glinting off curved metal and glass, pilot's faces set in grim determination.

The CO had ignored the screen of 110s this time.

No doubt they'd have to cope with them later, but for now he was concentrating on the Heinkels. Their upper gunners were already firing, sending streams of tracer towards the diving Spitfires. Jack ignored it, and sensed no wavering in the line. As usual, others fired before him, but he concentrated on his target, the nose of the nearest twin engined bomber.

The Heinkel grew and grew until he could see scared faces. Only then did he fire, feeling none of his usual concern for the effect his bullets might be having inside the aircraft. The perspex canopy shattered into glistening shards that seemed to hang, rotating slowly, until the airflow tugged them backward at high speed. He intercepted the shimmering shower behind the bomber's tail, flew through it and began to pull out of the dive, tensing his stomach muscles and grunting to avoid blacking out as his weight increased to about six times normal.

Finally, with the nose above the horizon and his arm muscles burning, he slackened the pull, breathing deeply as the blood returned to his brain and his vision cleared.

Three bombers were falling from the formation. He thought he might be responsible for one of them, although he might never know for sure. Two others were trailing smoke from engines. That still seemed to leave about 40 intact though. Once again, the 110s seemed reluctant to intervene, and the Spitfires were being left to their own devices.

The bombers were far from defenceless however. As if to emphasise the point, beads of tracer began to arc towards him. Picking a Heinkel on the right hand edge of the formation, he climbed towards it, taking fire from several lower gunners.

He'd lost energy pulling out of the dive, and the climb into the gunfire seemed endless. It took all his resolve not to duck as the tracer raced towards him and flashed past, but he gritted his teeth.

At about 300 yards, he felt a jolt through the control column.

'Shit!'

But there was no dramatic follow up. Shortly afterwards the fire of all but his prey moved onto other targets and he pressed his own gun button, invigorated by the loud clatter and the smell of cordite. He was disquieted by the change in his personality. Gone were the jokey asides and shouts as he entered combat, to be replaced by a grim silence he was not sure he liked.

His rounds hit home, and chunks of debris flew off the engine cowling on the right wing. He kept firing. The return fire from the lower gunner ceased, the right engine began to smoke and the right wing dropped.

'Dragon, 110s coming in.'

He recognised Piers's voice but ignored its message, intent on finishing off the bomber.

Banking left, he flashed beneath its tail and climbed above it, reversing the turn to look down on its unblemished left side. At no more than 100 yards, sight of the black crosses on wings and fuselage, and the swastika on the tailfin, reignited his anger.

He rolled towards the bomber, placed his gunsight over the canopy and fired a long burst. Again, he knew his rounds were hitting home as chunks of perspex and metal lifted into the air. Rolling right to pass behind, he had every intention of continuing to hound his quarry, when tracer flashed over his right wing.

'Bugger.'

He smashed the stick to the right and pulled. A

large shape passed behind and another barrelled down on him from about 50 yards to his right. The Messerschmitt 110 screamed a few feet above his canopy, darkening the sky as it passed. He pulled hard right again, this time passing down the left hand side of another 110. Rolling out, the sky was clear.

'Idiot.'

He should have listened to Piers. He'd become fixated on his target and broken all his own rules. This new hatred was a dangerous development. If it didn't dissipate naturally, he'd have to learn to overcome it. How easy that would be depended on what was happening on the ground.

Smoke was rising over Biggin Hill.

Sophie removed her tin helmet. Most enemy formations seemed to be heading home.

Others were forming up over France, but their Sector seemed remarkably quiet for the moment.

Squadron Leader Rice was taking advantage of the respite to speak to the Room. 'The airfield's been heavily cratered. Too bad to be used for the moment I'm afraid. 629 got away for Acklington, but craters will need to be filled in if their replacements are going to land later this afternoon.'

Sophie was relieved that Bunter was away safely. Not only did he and the rest of them deserve their rest, but it would make things easier. He could have made life difficult for Alex.

And what about Alex?

The Controller continued. '646 have been diverted to Croydon, but,' and he looked across at her with his dark, sad, eyes, 'at least one tried to land here during the raid, and crashed. He's being taken to Bromley hospital.'

Sophie prayed it wasn't Alex.

'Most of the technical buildings seemed to have been spared this time, but the quarters and the Officers' Mess have been hit again. Now, I suggest we take advantage of this lull and get some lunch brought in. Carry on.'

He nodded at an airman by the door. The young man went out.

Sophie was wondering where she might spend the night if the Mess proved uninhabitable, when she noticed the Controller gesturing to her. She walked over.

He looked at her, his marbled face deadpan, but his eyes full of sympathy. 'Sorry to spring the news of the crash on you like that, Sophie. I'll let you know as soon as I have a name.'

'Thank you, sir.' She smiled weakly and walked away.

Once again, despite his best intentions, Kelvin Rice couldn't help thinking what might be if the injured pilot turned out to be Alex Lowe.

Alex looked around. Croydon was a state.

It had been attacked at about the same time as Biggin Hill and some of the craters on the airfield were still smoking, although they'd managed to find a landing run threading through them. But it was the terminal building that made the greatest impression. The pristine white, art deco façade he remembered from pre-War magazines was grubby and heavily pockmarked. It looked a far cry from its heyday as the home of Imperial Airways.

'Know any good plasterers?' Piers ventured as they

lounged on the grass nearby.

Out on the airfield, the resident groundcrew were doing their best, tending the visiting Spitfires as well as their own Hurricane Squadron. The latter had landed at about the same time, but had suffered several casualties, including their CO.

For once, 646 had landed without loss.

'Your kite looked a bit of a mess, Jack,' Alex shouted over.

'Not as bad as the Heinkel,' the Welshman batted back.

Despite his smile, Alex thought his friend looked strained, weighed down by some invisible concern. Ginge, he suspected.

The CO walked out of the terminal building and strode towards them. They turned to face him and he stopped a few yards away.

'The airfield's unusable at the moment, I'm afraid. But the whole Station's working on it and we should be able to get back later this afternoon.

'There is one casualty though. It took a bit of working out, because they thought it was one of us, but,' - he glanced towards the new sergeant pilot, JC - 'I can only think it must be Pilot Officer Beaumont, trying to get back in from Debden. Anyway, I'm afraid he crashed. In a bad way by all accounts.' He looked at JC again. 'They've taken him to Bromley.'

'Any news of the rest of the Station, sir?'

'Yes, although I don't know how complete it is, Flight Sergeant Williams. They've hit some of the quarters and the Officers' Mess again, but the phone lines and the like are okay this time, so we'll still be controlled by Bastion. And by the way, I spoke to the Squadron. Sergeant Clough has phoned in. Seems he landed in a dung heap outside Maidstone.'

Speaking over the general laughter, he continued, 'He's okay, and says he'll be back this afternoon.'

'Even more full of shit, no doubt,' Dusty Miller shouted to more laughter.

'No comment, Sergeant Miller,' the CO smiled. 'Anyway, let's try and get a few minute's rest before the next adventure. Same batting order, section leaders.' He struck eye contact with each in turn and, when there were no questions, walked on and settled himself into a wicker chair.

Alex could tell Jack was pleased about Ginge, but his features still belied some other anxiety. At least Sophie should be okay. Unless something had disrupted her routine, she should have been nowhere near the Officers' Mess.

'Worried about Sophie, Alex?'

Alex looked round. Bunter had lowered his large frame to squat next to him.

'Yes, I am a bit,' he said conversationally.

The newcomer leaned in until his round red face was very close. The smell of stale sweat was almost overpowering, but it was his expression that caught Alex unawares. It had hardened into a mask of malevolence.

'Well don't be,' he spat.

Before Alex could reply, the former 629 pilot heaved himself up and walked back to sit with Jet Black.

Alex felt himself flush. He was taken aback. Even if he'd wanted to shout after the disagreeable fellow, he had no idea what to say. Bunter couldn't know about the kiss outside the WAAF block, although he now wondered if it would make any difference if he did.

Perhaps not. Anyway, as far as he was concerned, Sophie had made her choice, and Bunter would just have to lump it.

'Alright, Alex?' Piers asked.

'Yes. Just Bunter being an arse.'

'Nothing new there then,' his friend snorted.

Alex woke with a start.

'…Dragon scramble.'

He sprang to his feet in a state of total confusion. He had no idea where he was, or what had preceded the few words he'd heard, but he automatically set off in the same direction as the other blue clad figures. After a few paces, his eyes adjusted to the blinding light and he began to take in his surroundings.

Croydon. Saturday afternoon or evening.

Piers and Jack were just ahead, and other familiar figures were panting all around him. He glanced over his shoulder. Bunter was puffing along at the back, already red-faced and sweating. Their aircraft were in the open and he jinked left behind a pair of heels to run up to his Spitfire, throwing a grateful nod at the unfamiliar rigger manning the starter trolley. Another stranger jumped out of the cockpit as he walked up the wing into the propeller wash, and both helped him strap in.

What a way to earn a living. He was about to fly one of the most advanced fighting machines ever devised, yet he was barely awake and had no idea where he was going. What would his parents say?

He turned on the oxygen and took a couple of deep breaths. His head began to clear.

Three fifteen. He must have slept for an hour at least, but he wasn't sure whether he felt better or worse. No nightmares though. In fact, no recollection of anything after the exchange with Bunter.

Other aircraft began to edge forward. He waited until Piers passed, then waved away the chocks, released the brakes and opened the throttle a growl, easing the power back again as the Spitfire began to rock over the grass. At least the cockpit was more familiar now. And, in a major breakthrough, he felt no hint of nausea – yet. He completed the pre-take off checks with more confidence than at any time to date, and used the extra time to take in what was going on around him.

It was a beautiful summer's afternoon; another skylark day. The Squadron was turning into line, the CO leading his vic, then Dusty's pair, Jack's vic, and finally, he and Piers.

Very egalitarian. Two sections led by officers and two by NCOs. Until his arrival, he would have expected officers to have led them all, but this squadron seemed to be a meritocracy, in the air at least. Bunter and Jet would have to prove themselves before they were considered for leadership of Jack and Dusty's sections.

Despite his success on the last sortie, Alex suspected he would always be a foot soldier, toiling in the shadow of the knights of the air, like Muddy and Jack, and now Piers. Not that he was complaining. Even to be a part of this enterprise was a privilege he could not have contemplated a month ago. If he could prevent his fear getting the better of him and make a worthwhile contribution, that would be enough.

He gave a thumbs-up to Piers and waited. In his peripheral vision, he could see the other sections easing forward, but he didn't advance his throttle until his own section leader started to move. The growl of the Merlin engine rose in volume as he pushed the throttle to match Piers's speed. He enjoyed a last whiff of exhaust fumes before they dissipated in the quickening airflow.

Again, in his peripheral vision, he saw Jack's section skip into the air just before Piers's mainwheels left the ground and the rumbling of his own mainwheels on the grass ceased.

Swapping hands, he began to pump up the undercarriage, gaining mild satisfaction from the fact that his porpoising movements were no more eccentric than his Section leader's. Now if only he could become as successful in combat, he'd really know he'd made it. But one thing at a time.

'Bastion, this is Dragon Leader, Dragon airborne.'

'Roger, Dragon, two hundred plus bandits approaching Sheerness, angels one four, vector zero eight zero.'

Two hundred plus. Where were they all coming from?

'Bastion, this is Dragon Leader, wilco.'

Croydon was a much tighter airfield than Biggin Hill, red brick housing estates encroaching all the way up to the boundary. The tiled roofs were so close, Alex felt like lifting his feet as they cleared the fence and climbed away.

They turned left onto a heading of 080 degrees and he eased out to begin his weaving duties.

Jack looked down on Biggin Hill as they passed to the north, climbing through 3,000 feet. The CO had failed to put his mind at rest.

Columns of smoke rose above the heat haze, but he

was too far away to see from which buildings. Hopefully, Caroline was okay. And their groundcrew. They were probably thankful they didn't have a shelter to go to. He wasn't sure he could have gone into one after last night.

Good to hear about Ginge though, and somehow pleasing that he hadn't come out of his latest scrape smelling of roses. Jack smiled, and felt his tension easing a little. His anger also seemed to have subsided – for the time being anyway, but he sensed that it would be more easily ignited from now on.

The sky down to Alex's left was full of smoke trails. He hadn't yet attacked a formation being hit by other squadrons. It should be easier, shouldn't it?

They were up sun in loose echelon, the CO leading with the next aircraft sitting slightly back 20 yards to his right, and so on, all the way down to Alex at the end of the line. When not keeping an eye on the eight aircraft bobbing gently between him and the CO, he was looking around for enemy fighters, and watching the heated combat 5,000 feet below. The black shapes grew all the time: diving and climbing, rolling and looping.

Fear still stalked, but there was no nausea yet. Another sign of progress perhaps.

The CO's voice rang out. 'Dragon, follow me, follow me, go.'

On the word 'go', he rolled left into a dive.

One by one the other Spitfires followed, the effect rippling down the line towards Alex. It was a magnificent sight and, as the last few aircraft presented their undersides, he held his breath as if he was about to plunge into water. As soon as Piers's aircraft commenced its roll, he banged the stick to the left and followed, ending up diving just to the right and behind his Section Leader.

The dark shapes resolved into a constantly changing cloud of Heinkel and Dornier bombers, single and twin-engined Messerschmitt fighters, and Spitfires and Hurricanes. Tracer flashed between them all and it was almost impossible to tell who was the attacker and who the attacked. Most of the fighters seemed to fit into both categories, firing to their fronts while simultaneously being engaged from behind. Several aircraft were on fire.

It seemed madness to dive into such a confusion of whirling metal. But, like the others, he resolved to do just that, and still his usual sickness held off.

Then, he spotted a Heinkel detaching itself from the mêlée, turning away and descending, like a burglar creeping from a house on tiptoe.

'Oh no you don't.'

He eased right to follow it towards a layer of cloud drifting inland from the Estuary. The bomber was accelerating, but Alex was going faster and he began to overhaul it, approaching from above and to its right. Could he catch it before the cloud swallowed it?

The range closed and tracer from the Heinkel's upper gun fizzed towards him. With the sanctuary of the cloud layer nearing, the urge to return fire was almost overwhelming.

'Patience, Alex, patience.'

Then, to his left, a stream of tracer raced towards the bomber. It was coming from a Hurricane, a few hundred yards away, in a similar dive.

'Good job it wasn't a Messerschmitt, Alex.'

Chastened, he completed a belated lookout scan. All

clear save the Hurricane, which was dropping back, and the Heinkel, which was nearing the cloud layer.

With a few seconds to spare, the bomber finally filled the reflector sight and Alex fired, stopping only when it disappeared into cloud. He entered the grey mist himself, unable to see the bomber, or the Hurricane. Fearful of a collision, he eased right, hoping the layer wasn't too thick. It was weeks since he'd done any instrument flying, and he hadn't checked his instruments before entering the layer. And even if he could regain straight and level flight in this clag, he didn't fancy bumbling around with at least a Hurricane and a Heinkel doing the same.

He'd hardly finished these trains of thought when he re-emerged into clear air. Eight thousand feet. Couldn't have been more than a couple of thousand feet thick, thank goodness.

For once, he seemed to know where he was. The Estuary and Sheppey were to his left, with Whitstable to the front, and Margate and the North Foreland just visible in the distance. The likelihood of rejoining the battle above cloud was slim. He decided to stooge around and see if the Heinkel reappeared.

'If you were driving a bomber and you'd lost all your mates, where would you head?'

Staying about a thousand feet beneath the thin layer of altostratus, Alex turned south east. No sickness. No fear really. More like excitement.

About a mile away, the Hurricane fell from the base of the cloud and pulled from its dive. It was hard to believe the Heinkel wouldn't do the same at some point, unless it had set off in a totally unexpected direction. Alex considered this for a few moments, but decided to stick with his gut instinct and continue towards France. The Hurricane pilot obviously decided to do the same, and started weaving about half a mile to the right.

Even though he had no idea who the other man was, or where he was from, Alex felt a strange bond between them. They shared a common goal, both in the bigger drama, and in the small scene they were playing out now.

'There!'

A momentary darkening in the cloud just to the right, about half a mile ahead. Alex weaved so as not to overtake whatever it was too quickly, if it was anything at all.

Again a darkening, like the bottom of a great grey whale. He was sure it was the Heinkel.

And then it appeared, sinking slowly from the protective layer, its tailfin still half in cloud, a small trail of smoke or vapour flowing back from the left engine.

That shouldn't stop him maintaining height, Alex thought. And yet, it continued slowly to descend.

The bomber banked towards him slightly. The right hand propeller was stationary.

'Ahh. Now that's different.'

So it couldn't maintain height, but would it be able to reach France? He couldn't take that chance, could he? Well, could he?

Was the Hurricane pilot agonising in the same way? Whether he was or not, he'd arrived at the same decision, because as Alex pushed on full throttle, the other fighter also accelerated markedly.

The Heinkel continued to drift down and Alex dived to maximise his speed. A trail of tracer set out towards him from the lower gun. His stomach constricted in fear, but, after a few seconds, the yellow beads hosed off towards the Hurricane. He didn't envy the gunner, nor did he wish the Hurricane pilot harm, but he was happy to see the hot metal being directed at someone else.

At about 300 yards behind and 1,000 feet below, he eased out of his shallow dive and pulled up. The gunner transferred his attention again, but Alex ignored the fire and concentrated on putting the Heinkel's left wing root in the centre of his reflector sight. The tracer swapped sides intermittently as he closed.

At 200 yards, he pressed the gun button and held it for about three seconds, fighting to maintain aim as his aircraft shuddered. He turned away to the left, anxious at presenting his belly to the Heinkel, but judging it safer than sliding under the bomber and risking a collision with his colleague.

He was sure he'd scored hits, and he strained to look over his shoulder as he continued his turn. The Hurricane was performing a similar manoeuvre. Would they need to attack again? He for one hoped not.

Rolling out of the turn, he could see the bomber was in a bad way. The smoke from the left engine was streaked with yellow flame, and the nose had dropped further. Surely it was incapable of reaching France now?

But it's still flying, Alex.

Despite the havoc he'd seen such machines wreak, he couldn't help thinking there was something unsavoury about the two of them stalking the limping hulk. It wasn't an animal to be put out of its misery. It contained young men. Young men not unlike him, he suspected, and they'd be fighting for survival.

This wasn't about the bomber now. It was about him. Was he prepared to finish off this aircraft, and its occupants, even though he knew it had no chance of reaching safety?

You're being too sentimental, Alex.

He closed on the Heinkel, his thumb quivering above the gun button. Whether or not he was having a similar anguished debate, the Hurricane pilot was mirroring his actions.

But, as they approached the bomber, a crewman appeared, falling from the bottom hatch. Alex throttled back and watched. A parachute opened, rapidly disappearing behind him. Then, with a lurch, the bomber's nose dropped and it entered a steep dive. Alex lowered his Spitfire's nose to follow.

Another man emerged, seeming to fall alongside the burning wreckage. Again a parachute opened and, this time, it seemed to shoot swiftly upwards.

They were passing 5,000 feet.

That's it. If anyone's alive, how are they even going to make it to the hatch?

To his surprise, another crewman appeared in the airflow, a parachute already deploying behind him. But the billowing silk snagged, and he was left flailing on the end of several yards of parachute silk and rigging lines. He began struggling, legs kicking, arms outstretched as if trying to pull back along the parachute lines to regain the stricken bomber.

Levelling at 3,000 feet, Alex watched the aircraft drag its unwilling victim into the ground. It was another horrifying death that would haunt his dreams.

After what seemed an age, he shivered and drew his eyes away from the fireball to look around. He'd have been a sitting duck to any marauding Messerschmitt, but he was too drained to care. Apart from the Hurricane sitting out to his right, the sky was clear.

He banked towards the other aircraft, closed the gap and eased his Spitfire alongside. For some reason, he expected the other pilot to exhibit a similar feeling of world-weary resignation at what they'd just witnessed. But how wrong could you be?

Even if he'd missed the smiling eyes, the fist raised and punched repeatedly into the roof of the canopy could not be misinterpreted. His fellow pilot was as pleased as punch.

Try as he might, Alex couldn't share the other's enthusiasm. Okay, they'd downed an enemy bomber and prevented it returning to cause more death and destruction, but he couldn't delight in their enemy's fate. Thankfully, he was spared the need to provide a response. The other pilot waved and dropped his right wing, presenting his oil-streaked belly in plan view, before breaking away to head north-west.

Alex sighed. Ashford was to his right. He lowered the nose and started a gentle descent into the west. The sun was bright in the sky and the fields formed a shining tapestry of green and gold. Heads looked up at the lone Spitfire, and workers in the fields waved, but the pilot was oblivious to his surroundings, lost in thought.

Jack was relieved. He hadn't been able to get to the NAAFI Shop himself, but one of the groundcrew had confirmed that it hadn't suffered further damage. And Ginge had bounded up, larger than life and twice as ugly. He hadn't actually landed in a dung heap, but close enough to make for a good story.

The Station had worked miracles on the airfield. Apparently, everyone had joined in, officers and men. Even the Station Commander had rolled up his sleeves to set an example. There were still craters to be avoided, and red flags marking unexploded bombs, but they'd managed to land without incident, as had 637 Squadron, 629's replacements.

Looking around now, his fellow pilots appeared totally knackered. Three scrambles and still only 4.30pm. And just as Ginge was back, Pete was missing. Someone had seen him bale out, but they had no idea whether he was okay or not. And Chips' aircraft was bound for the hangar, so they were down to eight.

The CO had decided to rest Chips, Ginge and JC. Ginge had protested, but JC had been unable to hide his relief. He'd survived his first day.

Alex looked tired and thoughtful. He was sitting with Piers and Olly, but not joining in their usual playful banter. Jack was wondering whether to go over, when Muddy beckoned him to the hut.

No doubt he wanted to discuss tactics, or tomorrow's batting order, but Jack wanted to speak to him as well. During the first scramble, he'd seen Alex single-handedly take on a formation of about twenty 110s. If anything had taken guts, that had, and he was determined his Flight Commander should hear about it.

Before he reached the hut, Hopkins appeared at the window and the bell began to ring.

Sophie had rarely felt so vulnerable.

All the 11 Group squadrons were at least 50 miles to the east, 12 Group were nowhere to be seen, and a hostile plot had just been raked on five miles from the airfield.

She listened to the young WAAF briefing the evening shift Controller.

'Group say they're approaching Westerham along the Ashford Redhill railway line, sir.'

It was the same time they'd hit the previous evening. They might carry on towards Kenley or Croydon this time, but then again…

Squadron Leader Frankland stroked his thin black moustache. He thanked the WAAF, spoke quietly to the man on his left, then faced front and cleared his throat.

'Tin hats everyone, please. And those not on essential duty, take cover.'

Sophie put on her helmet. As the sirens began to wail, she thought of her day shift girls. Did they have a shelter to go to, and would they dare go in if they did? She was grateful her relief had been delayed planning the morning's funerals. It felt safer in the Ops Room than the Mess.

The evening shift donned their helmets and resumed their tasks. Sophie smiled as it became apparent that none intended to leave. The Controller adjusted his own helmet, cast his eyes over the room, and, presumably having failed to spot anyone looking surplus to requirements, turned his attention to the map.

She flinched as she felt a distant tremor. It was closely followed by another, then another. For a few seconds, they held to a regular beat, but then became more chaotic, all the time increasing in intensity. Dust began to fall from the ceiling. The building shuddered and the explosions became audible, the volume increasing incessantly as the dust falls turned into a steady shower.

The CO had bought it.

Jack knew, because he'd seen Squadron Leader Gerry Parr's final moments. It had shaken him more than anything over the last four months.

He'd bottled it up until he and Muddy were sitting in an office off the booking hall at Croydon. Now, the story was pouring out.

'It burst into flame almost straight away. I could see him struggling to open the canopy, but he couldn't seem to budge it. He...he was on fire, but somehow he managed to get out. He even managed to pull his chute, but when it deployed, the silk caught light. I could see he was alive, kicking, patting the flames on his body. But the parachute was burning, and he knew it. After a few seconds, it candled and he just dropped away. Ten thousand feet, Muddy. Ten thousand feet.'

'Poor bastard.'

A contemplative silence fell. Muddy re-lit his pipe.

Jack leaned back and pushed a thumb and finger into his eyes. And what about Caroline? Biggin had been on fire again. They'd known something was wrong when Kenley piped up and diverted them back to Croydon. They'd seen the smoke as they'd passed abeam. She should have been on her way home, but how could he be sure?

He heard movement and looked across to see Muddy holding the phone to his ear.

'Still nothing. I think we're here for the night, Jack.'

'Fuck!'

The violence of the outburst startled his friend.

'Sorry, Muddy. I'm just worried about Biggin. And I fancied a night in my own bed.' He winced at how petty it sounded.

'I know what you mean, Jack. But I don't think we'll make it back tonight. By the time Group stand us down, we'll be stuck, even if the airfield's up and running again. Mind you, any bed would do at the moment. After beer that is.'

They both smiled at that.

'Is there a bar here then?' Jack asked.

'I bloody well hope so. It's called the Airport Hotel, isn't it?'

After a further short silence, Jack struck a more serious note. 'Do you think they'll pull us out of the line?'

The Flight Commander leaned back and sucked on his pipe. 'Don't know. Not sure they can afford to.'

Alex sipped his beer. Muddy had spoken to Group, but he still couldn't get through to Biggin. Hopefully, it was just the phone lines. He pictured Sophie and longed to see her again, to kiss her again.

'Penny for your thoughts?'

Alex looked at Piers. 'Oh, this and that.'

'A tall dark haired this and that no doubt.'

Alex blushed.

Chapter 8 – Sunday 1st September 1940

The explosions creep closer and closer. The girls flinch at each new blast, turning their eyes anxiously to the ceiling, coughing and waving at the dust in the air. The room shakes and the counters bounce off the map. The roof

The Station Commander walked in and Sophie shook herself free of the vivid flashback.

The Ops Block had been hit by one of the last bombs to fall, but the Ops Room itself had been spared. Overnight, the place had been cleaned up and the GPO engineers had restored the telephone lines. Apart from her memory of the scene, it was as if nothing had happened.

They were used to the Station Commander's presence. He visited at least a couple of times a day, but they hadn't expected to see him before the funerals later in the morning. As he walked round the edge of the platform in his best uniform, he looked especially tall and imposing. Those sitting stood up, and those standing snapped to attention.

'Thank you, everyone,' he said in his warm baritone, waving them back into their seats. 'Carry on.'

He stopped in front of the Controller.

'May I, Kelvin?'

'Certainly, sir.'

Turning to face them, he took off his hat, placed it under his left arm and smoothed his brylcreemed hair. In a familiar affectation, he coughed and patted his tunic pocket with his right hand. Sophie knew it held the pipe that was usually clamped between his teeth.

'I'm afraid I don't have much time, but I thought I'd pop in, see how things were and give you a bit of an update. Firstly though, I'm very impressed with the way this place looks after last night. Well done to all concerned. Pass my thanks to the other shift would you please, Squadron Leader Rice?'

The Controller nodded. 'Wilco, sir.'

'As to the Station. Still a bit of a mess I'm afraid. As well as this building, they hit a couple of hangars, and the armoury again. No fatalities this time, thank goodness, but quite a few injuries.'

He hesitated slightly before continuing. 'I know this morning is a very sad time for many of you, but I also know it will make you all the more determined to see things through.'

Behind the strong words, Sophie sensed vulnerability. The man looked drawn. But was it surprising? It must be terrible to see your Station in such a state, and to lose so many personnel. No hint of it in his parting shot though.

'And don't you worry, we'll have the rest of the airfield back on its feet in no time. So, chins up everyone, and let's do all we can to make sure the Hun doesn't have it all his own way. Now, sorry to be in such a rush, but carry on.'

As those in the body of the room returned to their duties, he turned to face Kelvin Rice and put his hat on the platform.

'Sorry to hear about Gerry Parr, Kelvin.'

Sophie looked away, but unashamedly strained to catch the conversation.

'Thank you, sir. He was a fine man, and a good squadron commander.'

'Yes, amongst the best. A great loss. Have you spoken to Muddy yet?'

'Yes, sir. I think he's relieved they're not bringing

an outsider in for the moment.'

Sophie wasn't sure what the reference to Muddy meant. Before she could think further on it, the Controller coughed, as if about to ask something sensitive. 'They're not being pulled from the line then, sir?'

The Station Commander didn't seem to mind the question. 'Group would like to, but I'm afraid they can't at the moment. If Gerry had bought it earlier, I think they'd have sent them north instead of 629, but they won't try and swap them over now. The new pilots will help, especially Arbuthnott and Black.'

Neither heard Sophie's sharp intake of breath, nor saw her look of surprise.

'Yes, sir, Muddy was pleased about them. And Sergeant Atkins re-appeared last night. A few cuts and bruises, but alright apart from that. They'll have another three aircraft as well, when they get back. Group are leaving them at Croydon for the time being.'

'Just as well. There are still a few unexploded bombs to deal with. Should be clear by the time they've flown their first sortie though.'

He turned to look at the map. 'Anything brewing yet?'

'No, remarkably quiet at the moment, sir.'

'Good. Too much to hope that it'll stay like that, I suppose?'

'I think you're probably right, sir.'

Jack wasn't complaining at the slow start. And despite the disappointment at not spending the night in Keston Avenue, the Airport Hotel had proved a comfortable resting place. He'd had his first proper bath since moving out of the Sergeants' Mess, then a few beers to say farewell to the old CO, and a relatively good night's sleep.

Now he sat in the office off the booking hall again with his new CO. They'd locked themselves away as soon as they'd prepped their aircraft, but hadn't been able to do much until Group had deigned to speak to them at about 7.00am. And the final pieces hadn't fallen into place until the Biggin Controller had piped up at eight.

Jack was delighted for Muddy, but, after the losses they'd suffered, he was less sure about the decision to leave them in the line. Not that he wanted out, but there was a real dearth of experience. Pete Atkins was back at base, and the two from 629 were a boon; and two of the other replacements, a Fleet Air Arm and a bomber pilot, wouldn't be complete novices; but even so…

'I think you should be radical, sir.'

The change from Muddy to sir was a necessary outcome of his friend's promotion. It caused no anguish on either side.

'How so, Jack?'

'I'd go for Piers.'

'He's only been on the Squadron for about three weeks.'

'Yes, sir, but he's already one of the best in combat, and he gives as good as he gets on the ground. They'd follow him. I know they would. I would.'

'But what about Bunter?'

'Don't know, sir. And I suspect you don't either. He may be all right in the air, but all he's done on the ground so far is put everyone's noses out of joint. You might be turning your back on a complete star, but he could just as easily be a complete dud. We know Piers is a solid bet.'

'You're sure you're not his dad?'

'Very funny, sir. Look, if Bunter proves himself, you can give him A Flight in a few days…if you don't use Smithy or Birdy?'

Jack was fishing. He didn't know why the two young officers had been given 48s at such short notice.

'Oh, very clever, Jack. Now, not a word to anyone. Birdy's not coming back. I hope he's already heading for an OTU post.'

'He did look pretty strung out on Friday night.'

'Yes. Couldn't risk him coming back. But Smithy just needed a break. I'm sure he'll be alright, but I'd rather just leave him with Yellow Section for now. We'll consider him again in a few days.'

He paused and took a contemplative draw on his pipe.

'Okay. Piers becomes Flight Commander B, but I'd like you to lead A flight in the air for the time being, and the Squadron if I stay on the ground for some reason.'

Jack hoped he didn't look too stunned. It wasn't unheard of for NCOs to lead squadrons in extremis, but Jack was surprised to be considered worthy of the honour, and proud.

'Of course, sir, if you're sure.'

'Who else would I trust with my new Squadron?'

They both smiled self-consciously.

'Now, who are we going to give Blue Section to if you're up front?'

'Well, we haven't mentioned Chips yet,' Jack said.

'No. Nice chap, Chips.' Muddy smiled, but didn't seek to elaborate as he took another draw on his pipe.

Pilot Officer Chips Pye was a bit of a joke between

them. He was their quietest pilot. They thought he'd probably been commissioned because he looked and sounded the part, and because he'd been on Oxford University Air Squadron at the start of the war. But he was ineffectual on the ground. It would be unfair to say the same in the air, but he'd made no real impact in his two months with them. Having said that, he'd never run away either. He was solid and dependable, like Pete and Ginge, and many of the others that had come and gone. But they always discussed Chips when they looked at leadership positions, and always with the same form of words.

'Yes. Nice chap, Chips,' Jack replied, before continuing more seriously. 'I think it should be Dusty, sir, again until we know where we stand with Bunter.'

'What about your other son, Alex?'

'Ha, ha, again, sir. Although, I think you could probably do worse. But he's been through a hell of a lot in a very short time. I think he'd benefit from a tad longer as an Indian before we make him a Chief.'

'Okay, let's just bear him in mind for the moment. But I tell you what, Bunter'll be really hacked off if we overlook him a second time.'

Sophie could tell the lull was over. It was just gone 10.00am and black counters were being raked over the Channel.

Squadron Leader Rice was looking impassively at the map. His injuries still made his mood hard to judge. Unexpectedly, he looked across.

'Time for your next lesson, if you like?'

'Yes please, sir.'

During some of their quieter moments, he'd been giving her little insights into the mysteries of controlling. It was a welcome diversion from her more mundane supervisory and admin duties. She walked to the front of the platform.

'Right. You saw yesterday how they split over the coast, and then again further inland.'

She nodded.

'Well, the only way to get at them before they split would be to mount standing patrols near the coast. But we haven't got the aircraft, or the pilots, plus, half the contacts out there are probably feints, like Hostile 05 there.'

He pointed at a black counter just off the coast near Deal.

'They've been flying in circles for nearly ten minutes now, and I bet they're all 109s. If we went after them, they'd lead us such a merry dance we'd run out of fuel before the bombers arrived. Not to mention losing valuable pilots in the oggin. I was one of the lucky ones.' He pointed at his face and smiled.

Sophie chose not to react, and he continued.

'Anyway, that's why the AOC decreed we meet them over land. So, to get to the point, that's also why we're relying on the Observer Corps so heavily, and why we're launching so late. I know it makes life difficult for us in here, but it's positively lethal for the squadrons. Being bounced in the climb is no fun. Ask your boyfriend.'

It was the first time anyone else had acknowledged that she had a boyfriend. She blushed and wasn't sure what to say. The Controller also looked embarrassed, although she wasn't sure how she'd picked that up from a face that couldn't be any redder to start with. She decided to return them to safer ground.

'What about Hostile 07 then, sir, is that a feint?'

'Well, I can't be sure, but I think it's probably a real raid, say about 50 bombers and three times as many fighters.'

'But we've still got to wait for them to coast in and split up before Group call you.'

'Correct, Sophie. When can you start?'

They exchanged nervous smiles. Not for the first time, Sophie admired his courage and resilience in the face of such horrific injuries. After a few moments, his smile faded and his face hardened with determination.

'Not long now, Sophie. Not long.'

Alex liked flying in a pair. It was so much easier to keep an eye out for one another than in a vic. And it was much more manoeuvrable. Piers's Spitfire hung in the haze, and he sensed the other five, bobbing around in his peripheral vision. It would be nice to see a return to full strength though.

Jack said they usually spent at least half their time flying patrols as sections or flights. Well not in the week since he'd joined. Squadron scrambles had been the norm, and he'd become used to seeing at least nine other aircraft ahead of him, often 11. Six seemed a bit thin. And the loss of the CO had shaken him. He'd seemed so professional, so confident, someone to rely on in a rapidly changing world.

But his death, and the manner of it, proved that no-one was invulnerable. He shivered.

'Dragon, this is Bastion. Fifty plus bandits approaching Ashford, angels one six, vector one zero zero.'

'Bastion, this is Dragon Leader, wilco.'

Muddy was a fitting replacement though. If anyone could steady the ship, he could. Alex needed all the steadying he could get. The episode with the Heinkel had unsettled him. His nightmares had included one in which he was lashed to the back of a flaming bomber, plummeting earthwards, like Ahab strapped to his whale.

He felt much less confident than at the start of the previous sortie. His sickness had returned, and fear bubbled in his stomach. He'd been to the toilet several times before the call to scramble, and he still felt delicate, his sphincter twitching in a disquieting way.

The one positive had been a snatched conversation with Sophie. They'd agreed to try and meet in the Mess that evening. But his joy at the prospect had been short-lived. Turning away from the telephone, he'd spotted Bunter sitting apart from the others on the far side of the booking hall. The sight had darkened his mood. He'd have to confront him at some point, but not yet.

They rolled out of the turn and he eased away from Piers to begin his weaving duties. It was another beautiful day of hazy sunshine, and the scattered low stratus was burning off rapidly. He tried to work out what sort of attack they were likely to make, but he wasn't sure of the distance to Ashford, or how quickly the Squadron would climb. He'd just have to cope with whatever came up.

Passing 4,000 feet, they emerged from the grey haze into clear blue sky, the crisp horizon line broken only by the startlingly white tops of small cumulus clouds. It was beautiful, and his spirits rose until another radio call intervened.

'Dragon, this is Bastion, height passing?'

'Bastion, this is Dragon Leader, passing angels four.'

'Roger, Dragon Leader.' Alex caught a hint of concern in Crispy Rice's voice. 'Suggest orbit.'

They must be closing too fast, and Crispy was trying to prevent them being caught in the climb. He'd tried to do the same when Freddie was leading, and been ignored. No need to worry this time though.

'Bastion, this is Dragon Leader, thank you, turning left.'

Piers followed the other two sections into the turn, and Alex applied a fistful of throttle to try and stay close. Being on the outside rear of the formation, he needed more power than anyone else to hold station. If he dropped back now, he might never catch up, making him easy prey for any free hunters.

His eyes darted between key features on Piers's Spitfire to assess his position.

Where he spotted himself drifting away from the ideal, he used combinations of stick and throttle to slot back in, constantly striving to match his friend's bank and speed. It took supreme concentration and, in other circumstances, he'd have been enjoying himself immensely. Formation flying was the sport of kings. But today, it was also a matter of life and death. Sweat prickled on his forehead.

They rolled out of the turn and Alex heaved a tremendous sigh of relief, breathing deeply for what seemed the first time in several minutes.

'Bastion, this is Dragon Leader, rolling out passing angels eight.'

'Dragon Leader, this is Bastion, bandits passing Maidstone, angels one six, maintain vector one zero zero.'

'Bastion, this is Dragon Leader, wilco.'

Perhaps he was just getting more used to voices on

the radio, but he could sense the mutual respect between these two, Squadron Commander and Controller. He was as safe in their hands as in anyone else's. But how safe was that?

'Blue Two!'

He'd drifted off again. He gave Piers an apologetic thumbs up and eased out, scanning the sky diligently for the first time in goodness knows how long. He was so tired.

Jack had also drifted off, but into a much more pleasant reverie.

He was lying in bed with Caroline, running a hand down her bare stomach.

His arm was dark and tanned against her smooth, white, skin. The contrast somehow added to the eroticism. He stroked gently into her pubic hair. Her breath caught. Her eyes were pleading, her lips pouting.

The daydream was certainly more enjoyable than yesterday's anger, but probably just as dangerous. Reluctantly, he shook himself free and looked about.

Muddy was leading, with Dusty and Bunter to either side. Jack was behind them with Jet on his right wing, and Piers and Alex were at the rear. The sky was a brilliant blue.

Between them, Muddy and the Controller had done their best, but he doubted they'd get above the bandits this time. His money was on a frontal attack from a similar height...

'Dragon, line abreast, line abreast, go.'

He smiled. Muddy had obviously reached the same conclusion. He eased himself and Jet to the left of Dusty and watched Piers and Alex climbing into position to the right of Bunter.

There was something going on between the new man and Alex. He'd seen aggressive looks from the former 629 pilot that definitely didn't fit on their Squadron. Whatever it was, it needed resolving, but it was a battle his young friend would probably have to fight on his own.

Alex lowered his seat and took a deep breath. He'd never felt more like running away. All he had to do was dip his right wing and head for home. But he couldn't do it. To be precise, he was too scared to do it. Ironic really. More scared of confronting his own weakness than the enemy.

Would it always be like that, or did fear of combat eventually win out? He hoped he never had to find out.

The enemy formation was a long dark smudge on the horizon. He swallowed and steeled himself for the attack. Why this regression? He felt worse than at any time since his first mission.

'Bastion, this is Dragon Leader, tally-ho, tally-ho. Going in.'

'Dragon Leader, this is Bastion, roger and good luck. Bastion out.'

Was it fatigue? What with nightmares and homesickness, he didn't seem to have slept for a week.

The smudge turned into discrete shapes, dozens of them: small black circles with slim lines projecting from either side. Another few seconds and he could differentiate between the bombers and the fighters. Dorniers and 109s, about 50 in all. He picked a bomber and watched it grow, slowly at first, then more quickly. His thumb stroked over the gun button.

Tracer flashed ahead of Bunter. It was returned

tenfold. He held his fire. He'd committed himself too early last time. Now, he waited while the Dornier grew, and grew. The crew were clearly visible before he pressed the gun button and the bomber's canopy shattered. He pushed the stick forward. After a hesitation during which the Dornier rushed on, his Spitfire began its dive.

Too late.

A bone-rattling impact. A bent propeller blade. The whoosh and tug of air. Massive vibration. Bombers passing overhead in freeze-frame bursts of movement.

He grimaced in pain, unable to turn his head.

But, instead of panic, he suddenly felt a strange sense of detachment.

Everything developed an unnatural, other-worldly quality. He was floating above the cockpit. It was quiet, peaceful, like wallowing in a hot bath. Four feet below, in the remains of his Spitfire, his body sat, hands on throttle and stick.

Somewhere in his mind, he sensed conflict, but outwardly, there was no surprise or alarm. All remained calm.

He watched with detached disinterest as his hands slowly and deliberately unclipped his oxygen and RT and began undoing the seat harness.

In an instant, he was awake. His Spitfire fell away and he tumbled behind it, the silence and warmth banished again by the buffeting airflow. He reached across for his parachute D-ring and pulled.

There was a sharp tug.

'Ouch.'

His neck hurt like hell, enough to take his mind off the start of his first parachute descent. And there were other distractions.

Out to the right, towards the docks, fierce fires were raging, dense pillars of dark smoke reaching into the sky. Closer to hand, a ferocious aerial battle continued, the few remaining Spitfires surrounded by Snappers, the bulk of the bombers streaming away. He was just thanking God it was all taking place above him, when, about a mile away, a single engined aircraft pulled out of a dive and flew towards him.

He squinted. A Messerschmitt!

His bowels grumbled. He'd heard of pilots being shot while floating down under their parachutes. No-one knew if the stories were true, but right now the threat seemed all too real.

Instinctively, he wriggled in his harness.

Fool, Alex. What good's that going to do?

He flopped back into the straps, resigned to his fate. The German fighter grew menacingly. Five hundred yards. Four. In range. He flinched.

With an ear-shattering roar, it passed overhead.

He blew out in relief and opened his eyes.

Then the slipstream hit. He started to rock violently.

Yelping at the pain in his neck, he looked up. The silk canopy flapped, its edges billowing, spilling so much air that he experienced a series of nauseating drops.

Several times, the canopy threatened to collapse, leaving him to plummet to his death, 10,000 feet below. With every drop, his stomach leapt into his mouth. But slowly, the silk regained its smooth, circular, shape. The oscillations and rate of descent steadied.

His heart still pounded though, and bile rose into his throat. He swallowed and grimaced, feeling uncharacteristically sorry for himself. How much more of this could he take?

But, as he drifted down and no other aircraft came near him, he began to feel more composed. Once again, he realised how lucky he was to be alive. And apart from the sore neck and a headache, he seemed to be in one piece. By the time he'd reached 5,000 feet or so, he was quite enjoying himself, floating gently towards the haze layer and the fields below.

Another adventure to add to those he already knew no-one at home would believe.

Sophie walked out of the admin office. She could hear the air raid sirens clearly. The girls had paused, waiting to see if they heralded an actual raid, or a false alarm.

Beneath their tin hats, some of the young faces betrayed concern. But what would you expect? Half of them had been buried alive two nights previously, and bombed again last night. Why at least some weren't running for the door was beyond her.

Dust motes began to dance in the beams of the overhead lights. She tensed, and then felt the first tremors. As before, they started with a regular beat, slowly increasing in intensity until they became more chaotic and incessant. The bombs seemed to be falling much farther away than on the last two nights, so distant she wasn't sure whether she was hearing explosions, or imagining them.

The sound of voices drew her back to the room. The waiting over, the girls had returned to their duties.

She looked at the clock. Just after noon. She hoped the bombs weren't falling near the cemetery.

Jack stood in front of Nick Hudson. The Intelligence

Officer looked even more gaunt than he had only 24 hours previously.

'We got amongst them all right, sir, but there just weren't enough of us. Once we'd made the first pass, the fighters dived in and most of the bombers carried straight on. Even if we'd all got one on the first pass, that's only seven, and there were another ten or so at least.'

'Well, I reckon there were about 15 in the raid.'

Jack looked around. The Station was a state. Much worse than it had been when they'd left the previous afternoon. Only one hangar looked to be intact, and many of the other buildings were visibly damaged.

'Anybody hurt?'

'Not over here, Jack. Some over the other side I think.'

He prayed that Caroline wasn't among them.

'Anything else to report?'

How could he find out if she was all right, and what could he do if she wasn't?

'Jack?'

'Sorry, sir. Miles away. Well, I hit my Dornier, but I've no idea what happened to him, and I'm sure I hit two Snappers later on, but I don't know what happened to them either. They were all over us.'

'Okay, Jack, I'll take your combat report later. Go and get some rest.'

'Fat chance,' Jack tutted as he turned to walk away. 'But thanks for the thought.'

Outside the dispersal hut, Piers and Olly were in earnest conversation. He noticed that Olly had removed his sling.

'Ready for the fray then, young sir?'

'I think so, Jack.'

305

Something in the officer's tone made him stop. He turned towards them. Their faces were etched with bad news.

'Jack?'

His heart sank. 'Yes, sir.'

'It's Alex.'

Bugger. Another good friend.

'What happened?'

Piers took over. 'I think he must have collided with a Dornier. I saw his kite going down with the back end missing. Didn't see a parachute I'm afraid, although I didn't watch for long. Sorry, Jack.'

'Thank you.' He knew he should say more, but...what? The two young officers were hurting as much as he was, perhaps more. But it was bad form to linger on such matters. Life had to go on. He sighed.

'Is the CO back yet?'

'Yes. Walked in just before I got to Nick. You're the last one back, except for Alex that is.'

'Thanks.' He walked on, still unable to think of anything constructive to say. It seemed hard, but there was no point in standing round chewing endlessly over what might or might not have happened, or mourning in public, and perhaps prematurely. If it came to the worst, he'd find time to drink to another short-lived friendship.

On entering the hut, he could see several familiar faces, and some new ones, but he went straight up to Hopkins at the desk.

'Is the CO alone, Chris?'

'Yes, Flight. He said he wanted to see you when you got back.'

Jack put on his forage cap, knocked, heard an unintelligible grunt, but walked in anyway and saluted.

Muddy had never had a tidy desk, but the volume of paperwork had doubled overnight. He was in danger of disappearing behind it.

'Ah, Jack. Sorry to hear about Alex.'

'Thanks, sir. I'm not going to write him off yet though. You never know.'

'No, you certainly don't. Look, sorry to get straight down to business.'

'That's okay, sir. Go ahead.'

'I've got to go and see the Station Commander, so if I'm not back, I'd like you to lead the next shout.'

'Blimey!' He hadn't expected the call to come so soon.

'I know. But you'll be fine. We're down to nine aircraft, so it's not much more than a big flight anyway.'

They looked at one another and laughed, the CO leaning back and stroking his moustache.

'I don't know about you, Jack, but I sometimes wonder if all this is really happening. If I'm going to wake up in a classroom back at Cranwell.'

'I know what you mean, sir, but we'd better pretend its real for now, hadn't we?'

'Yes, I suppose so. Look, I've got to go in about ten minutes, so I'll have to leave you to work out your own batting order. And send Piers in will you? I'm going to dub him OC B Flight.'

Nearing the ground, Alex knew he was fortunate to be floating down over relatively flat farm land, and with little wind to complicate matters. But even so, his scant knowledge of parachute landings was a worry. His neck was painful enough without doing something akin to jumping off a ten foot wall.

He was descending into the corner of a large grass field, close to a picture postcard thatched cottage. The smoke rising vertically from its chimney had alerted him to the calm conditions, but he couldn't help wondering who had a fire lit on such a lovely warm day. All too soon, he landed, or rather, crashed, in a crumpled heap. He lay, winded, and let the parachute canopy settle over him.

It formed a pleasant cocoon, warm and safe. He was tempted to stay there.

When he finally decided to release the harness and get up, he wished he hadn't. He was trapped in a tangle of fabric and cords, from which he spent several undignified minutes trying to extricate himself, sweating profusely and swearing uncharacteristically every time his neck twinged, which was every few seconds.

Emerging into the light, he squinted up. A figure stood over him.

'Would you like a cup of tea, young man?'

Aware of the language he'd just been using in the mistaken belief he was alone, he blushed the reddest of blushes.

The little old lady trotted off towards her garden gate. Alex rose and followed her, bearing his pain in stoic silence.

It was 12.30. The first raid was heading back across the Channel, and Sophie and Kelvin Rice were watching the next forming up over the French coast. It was a pattern that had been repeated for days now, and there seemed no end in sight.

646 had landed back at Biggin Hill. She hoped they were all okay, and wondered if they knew they'd soon

be airborne again. They could probably guess. How they must be praying for bad weather.

The Station Commander had dropped in after the funeral. During the raid, he'd ordered the civilians to the shelters, and then the padre and the military mourners had carried on with the service. No peace, even in death.

Despite all the recent setbacks, Jack's overwhelming emotion was pride. He was leading the Squadron into battle.

Ginge and Bunter were on his wings, their Spitfires bobbing gently as they climbed. And behind him, Piers was leading the two vics of B Flight for the first time. As he'd left the CO's office to give them his news, the young man's pleasure had been all too evident. Jack guessed he'd still be wearing a wide smile.

Bunter, on the other hand, had been unable to mask his disappointment. But it was early days. He still had time to prove himself, and attrition was working in his favour. Sadly, it seemed as if Alex was out of the running.

'Dragon Leader, this is Bastion, one hundred plus bandits passing Folkestone, angels one five, vector one one zero.'

For the merest instant, Jack waited for someone else to answer, but he recovered quickly.

'Bastion, this is Dragon Leader, wilco, passing angels eight.'

Hopefully, no-one else had noticed the hesitation. What to do now though?

Sitting at the rear of the formation, he'd always found it remarkably easy to decide what tactics the CO should be using. And on landing, he'd been more than happy to join his fellow NCO pilots in dissecting their leader's performance. He was sure the junior officers did the same. Gerry Parr had rarely given cause for serious complaint, and Muddy had started well. But how would his contemporaries judge him?

They'd have time to climb above the enemy bombers, but should he go for a head on attack, or climb to the south and dive from the sun?

What would Ginge and Dusty, Piers and Bunter be thinking? It was much easier being an armchair critic.

'Dragon Leader, this is Bastion. Your bandits now fifty plus, just north of Ashford, angels one five. Vector one zero zero.'

The hostiles had split again, their targets turning onto a more northerly heading. That did it. He was going to climb and come out of the sun.

'Bastion, this is Dragon Leader, wilco, passing angels one three.'

Alex replaced the telephone handset in its cradle, ducked through the low doorway into the front room and sat in an armchair. He was finding the situation increasingly surreal. If he'd gone to stores and asked for a little old lady, he'd have been issued with the woman opposite him, or something very similar. And she was acting as if he was a distant nephew who'd just called in for a pre-arranged visit.

It had its advantages. The best china was out, and he was tucking into a large slice of Victoria sponge. And he now knew why the fire was lit. The stone cottage was cool and dark, almost damp. As well as providing warmth, the crackling logs cheered the place up.

The old lady sat back in a creaking carver, patted the grey bun on the back of her head and asked,

'Where do you come from, Alexander?'

He was sure he'd said his name was Alex.

'Ludlow in Shropshire.'

'Oh, a lovely little town. Do they still have the May Fair?'

He was amazed. Most people hadn't heard of Shropshire, let alone Ludlow.

'Yes, although, having said that, I'm not sure they'd have held it this year, what with the war and everything.'

'Oh, I hope they did.' Her eyes sparkled and her thin lips creased into a smile as if re-living some pleasant memory. 'Such a shame if they didn't. It brought the whole town to life, don't you think?'

'Yes it did.'

'Do they still have…?'

Before long he was chatting to her as if he *was* a long lost nephew.

Jack cursed as the last rounds rattled from his guns. He'd fought from just north of Ashford almost to Gravesend. The opening gambit had worked well, for him at least. He'd hit two Dorniers before the 109s and 110s had joined the party. Since then, he'd fired on and even hit a few fighters, and, as far as he could tell, he'd avoided being hit himself. He hoped the others had been as lucky.

At first, he'd been aware of the rest of the Squadron around him, but now, there were no friendly aircraft in sight, only Snappers wheeling about in search of the unwary. Without ammunition, it was time to dive away. But he found himself unusually reluctant to seek safety.

Even as a section leader, he'd worried about his

wingmen. But somehow, this was different. He was getting an inkling of what it was to be a squadron commander. Somewhere up here, the men he'd led into battle were fighting for their lives. To leave without them felt like a betrayal.

'Got to go, Jack.'

Sighing, he took a last look around, then rolled onto his back and pulled into an arcing dive towards Biggin Hill.

Alex folded himself into another car driven by a pretty young WAAF. It was becoming a habit, one he was keen to break.

The old lady stood in her doorway and waved. She'd been marvellous company, but he was glad to be out of the claustrophobic cottage. He hated to think what it was like on a cold February night.

The woman's sister had married a Ludlovian, and she'd visited the town several times, so they'd had something in common to chat about. Her husband had died five years ago, and he sensed she was very lonely. He really should make time to visit again and thank her properly for her hospitality.

Wincing, he forced himself to turn and give a final wave. Then, he smiled blushingly at the driver and they started off down the long dirt track.

Sophie had heard that Alex was all right. It had come as a shock, because she hadn't heard he was missing in the first place. But hopefully, it meant he was out of the battle for the rest of the day.

A third wave of bandits had coasted in, and this time they'd splintered into even more raids than usual. One was heading for Biggin Hill.

Dragon had spent only 45 minutes on the ground before the next scramble. But this time they were climbing in the overhead, preparing to protect their own airfield for once.

'Bastion, this is Dragon Leader, passing angels one five.'

'Roger, Dragon Leader, this is Bastion, vector one zero zero. Thirty bandits, same height, approximately fifteen miles.'

'Bastion, this is Dragon Leader, wilco.'

Muddy rolled them onto a heading just south of 100 degrees and continued their climb.

Jack smiled. It was nearly 3.30pm and they had the advantage of the sun again. Ahead of him, Muddy had Ginge and Bunter on his wings, while Piers was leading the former Bomber Command and Fleet Air Arm pilots, already nicknamed Bomber and the Admiral respectively. He was leading JC, the young sergeant pilot blooded the day before.

JC's contemporary and two others that had joined since were being given some hasty schooling by Dusty. It would have to be ground-based though. Like all those arriving in the last week or so, they were unlikely to get even one training flight before being thrown into combat; there just weren't enough airframes.

JC looked steady enough, sitting out to the right, although his head was a bit too steady.

Jack gave his usual gentle nudge. 'Blue Two.'

The youngster's head jerked into motion, and an apologetic thumbs-up appeared. They all had to learn. Unfortunately, some never got the chance.

There were vapour trails far to the north and east.

The airspace around them still seemed clear, but he wasn't surprised when a Geordie voice piped up.

'Dragon Leader, from Red 3, bandits eleven o'clock slightly low.'

'Thank you, Red 3, visual. Bastion, this is Dragon Leader, tally-ho, tally-ho, thirty bandits angels one five. Going in.'

'Dragon Leader, this is Bastion. Roger and good luck. Bastion out'

'Dragon, echelon right, echelon right, go.'

Jack stared down as he drifted himself and JC to the right of the Admiral. Then he spotted them. About ten Dorniers, with ten Messerschmitt 109s to either side.

'Dragon, here we go, good luck all.'

With that, Muddy rolled left and dived. One by one, in quick succession, they followed, Jack rolling out just to the right and behind the Admiral with JC to his right. They were diving straight out of the sun and none of the fighters reacted, even when several of the leading Spitfires spat tracer at the lead bombers.

Jack had fired and dived past his first bomber before he saw the Snappers rolling towards them. He pulled out of the dive and into a right hand turn, his vision greying as the g forced him into his seat, sweat prickling his skin. It had been a text book attack, and when he rolled out of the turn, he could see it had had a devastating effect on the bombers. Several trailed smoke and their formation was scattering.

'That's it. Bugger off you bastards.'

It was unusual to have such a palpable sense of achievement, but this formation was not going to mount a concerted attack on Biggin Hill, or any other target. They'd been broken. Now all Dragon had to do was stop them re-grouping, or attacking targets individually, or getting home to fight another day. Oh, and evade the fighters, or engage them if it became unavoidable.

'Which is a racing certainty, Jack.'

109s were approaching from both sides. He took a last look at JC before concentrating on the closest Dornier, a swastika glowering from the nearer of its twin tail fins. It was already being attacked from the right beam by a climbing Spitfire, and Jack rolled left and then right to position for an attack from the rear.

Even before he pressed his own gun button, smoke belched from the bomber's right engine.

The other Spitfire turned left towards him, its belly passing startlingly close to his right wingtip, its pilot clearly oblivious to the potential catastrophe.

No time for further fear or analysis, Jack concentrated on his target, now banking right and descending. Its rear gunner began firing. Jack ignored the tracer and placed the gunner in the centre of the reflector sight. He fired from no more than 100 yards. The inbound tracer ceased and shards of perspex burst into the airflow.

He rolled hard left, sensing the bomber was no longer under control. To his left, two 109s dived in. The nearest fired and Jack felt the thud of impacts behind him. He pulled towards the 109s but they sped past before he could bring his guns to bear.

What was the damage? Run or stay? His aircraft seemed to be flying as advertised.

'Let's give it another go, Jack.'

He pulled through the fluffy white top of a cumulus cloud. When he emerged, the sky was empty.
Unbelievably, not an aircraft was to be seen.

Looking down, he identified Sevenoaks and began

to spiral earthwards, keeping an eye out for the enemy fighters that must still be out there somewhere.

Alex and his driver were just approaching Sevenoaks.

'What the...'

Wincing, he hunched his shoulders as a shower of small, dark objects clattered noisily onto the car.

The young WAAF also ducked. As the vehicle slowed, he tried to work out what was happening. He focused on a small bronze object bouncing off the road.

'Don't worry, Gertie. They're just empty shell cases. Must be a fight overhead.'

The metal continued to fall on the road and, more alarmingly, the roof and bonnet of the car.

His explanation seemed to cut no ice with Gertie. The poor girl still looked as if she thought they were being strafed. Until this moment, Alex hadn't considered what happened to the empty cases ejected from beneath his Spitfire's wings. Well, now he knew.

By the time they came to a halt, the impacts had stopped, much to Gertie's relief. She seemed fine, but declined to leave the car. Alex's neck had seized, and he extricated himself with difficulty, hearing her giggle as he leaned backwards over the roof. It was the only way he could look up at the sky.

Thousands of feet above, a battle was raging, the first he'd witnessed at relatively close quarters from the ground. Some of the larger aircraft were leaving ominous smoke trails. The majority were turning, high-tailing it for home he hoped, and preferably before they'd dropped their bombs. But all around them, smaller silhouettes wheeled, forming a confusing ball of combat. He squinted, trying to distinguish the

RAF fighters from their Luftwaffe counterparts, his ears full of the rise and fall of engine notes, and the distant rat-a-tat-tat of machine gun and cannon fire.

When he'd seen vapour trails from the train a week ago, he'd found it impossible to imagine what it was like to be among them. Now, he knew only too well. His face contorted into a grimace.

Thank goodness Gertie had stayed in the car.

The combat drifted away beyond the town, but Alex held grimly to his position, fighting to control his emotions, and his features.

'Bloody hell, Flight, what you been up to?'

'And a jolly good afternoon to you as well, Stokesy.'

'Well sorry, Flight, but your back end's one hell of a mess.'

'I thought it might be. Where's my new rigger?'

Stokesy looked across to the young man on the other wing. He'd been there all along, had even taken one of Jack's harness straps, but the engine fitter kept the little playlet going.

'Flight Sergeant Williams, may I introduce Leading Aircraftman Smith, better known as Smudger.'

Jack smiled up and offered his hand to the sandy-haired young man. 'Hello, Leading Aircraftman Smudger Smith, pleased to meet you.'

'Pleased to meet you as well, Flight.'

The youngster looked considerably more relaxed than he had an hour or so earlier, and Jack decided to spend a little longer keeping it that way. He stood up and stepped out of the cockpit.

'To be an LAC at your age, you must be an ex-apprentice, Smudger?'

'Yes, Flight.'

The words were defensive. Jack knew why. Some resented the accelerated promotion afforded apprentices who did well in their training.

'Don't look so sheepish about it, so was I. I only left Halton four years ago myself.'

That brought a beaming smile to the young man's face.

Stokesy shouted from the ground. 'Okay you two. I recognise a budding romance when I see one, but there is a war on you know.'

Jack and Stokesy had been together since Jack had joined the Squadron, and the engine fitter knew how close to the wind he could sail.

Jack jumped down from the wing and gave the older man a friendly nudge. 'Okay, Dad.'

LAC Smith walked round the tailplane to join them.

Jack pointed at the jagged holes in the tailfin and tailplane. 'Well, over to you Smudger. What d'you think?'

'Don't think you'll be flying this one again today, Flight. Tomorrow perhaps.'

'Oh well. Can't be helped. Now, much as I've enjoyed our little chat, I think I better go and report to the IntO. See you later.'

With a cheery wave, Jack walked away.

Despite the hours of work with which they'd just been presented, his two groundcrew smiled as he left.

The medical officer put the little torch down and stood back. 'Not everyone can say they've survived being hit on the head by a Dornier.'

Alex poked a finger through the jagged hole in his leather flying helmet and gave it a twirl.

The doctor shook his head. Pilots!

'I don't think the concussion will give you any more problems, but the stiff neck will last a few days at least. I'm going to put you off until Wednesday.'

Alex wondered whether he should remonstrate, but there didn't seem much point. To look anywhere other than straight ahead, he had to turn his entire upper body.

It was bad enough on the ground, but it would be impossible in the air.

'Wear this brace, and come back and see me if it's not right by then. And don't worry about the out of body experience. You'd be amazed how many similar stories I hear.'

'Really?'

'Yes. Really. Up until the last few weeks, I was getting one or two a month. I don't suppose they ever blabbed about it in the bar, but they found it worrying enough to speak to me. It generally seems to happen in quieter moments, especially at night, which is why I think yours was the result of the bang on the head. Remarkably similar though, the feeling of looking down on yourself from just above the cockpit, or out on the wing. Usually ends when something like a radio call brings you back to reality. I'd like to do a study on it when things quieten down. I'll look you up.'

Alex ignored the unspoken, *if you're still alive*.

'All right, Doc. It's a deal.'

Sophie was working late, covering for her relief, tidying up loose ends after the funeral. She didn't mind. It gave her the chance to meet some of the girls on the evening shift, and she always hated leaving the Ops Room when it was busy.

Most of the counters on the map were hostile. Group were holding the squadrons on the ground because the overland plots all seemed to be fighter sweeps. They were relying on the Observer Corps to spot the next wave of bombers coasting in. It was a risky strategy, especially as late evening cloud was making observation difficult. But they had to husband the dwindling number of aircraft and pilots.

She hoped that at least one pilot would be back in time for their date.

'Well you're no bloody use to us here, are you lad?'

Alex thought the Adj was being a bit unkind. Olly had made quite a niche for himself looking after the new boys, and he was sure he could do the same. But a 48 hour pass was like gold dust, and he'd raise more than a few eyebrows if he turned it down.

The older man preened his Walrus moustache and leaned across his desk. When he spoke again, it was in a kindly tone that excluded the rest of the room.

'Look, young Alex, you've had a hard week. A baptism of fire. And believe me, I don't say that lightly. You deserve a rest. Take it.'

They'd just exchanged more words than at any time since the older man had guided him through the arrival admin. In the interim, he'd heard about George's service in The Great War, and the image of a silly old duffer had been banished forever. He was touched by the concern for his well-being.

The Adj leaned back and resumed his public persona. 'Now bugger off and stop cluttering my office.'

He referred to the end of the dispersal hut as his office and habitually scowled at those walking through it, even though everyone had to do so at least twice a day, to and from the locker room, more if they bagged one of the camp beds behind the desk.

Alex smiled. 'Thanks, Adj.' Then, so as not to break the old man's cover, he backed away as if he'd been given a flea in his ear.

Two days leave, but what to do with them?

Jack was finally trying to write to Gwen. It should have been easy. 'Thank you for your letter. Goodbye.' But it wasn't. She deserved better. Only his heart wasn't in it and the page stayed stubbornly blank.

A shadow fell across the paper.

'Hello, Jack.'

He squinted up at a tall silhouette, framed by the evening sun. The figure squatted down with an expression like a schoolboy approaching a teacher with a poor excuse for not handing in his homework.

'Hello, Alex. Welcome back.' Jack noticed the neck brace, and began to guess the reason for the sheepish look. 'Another pleasant afternoon driving through Kent?'

'Not bad thanks. I seem to be making a bit of a habit of it though.'

'There are worse things, Alex.'

'I know.'

Jack let the silence lie between them.

'I'm afraid I forgot your advice about machine guns. Tried to ram another Jerry. Only this time I succeeded.'

'We guessed as much. Piers saw what was left of your kite, but he didn't see you take to your brolly, so we weren't sure what to think.'

'Well, here I am, but I'm afraid the Doc's put me

off for a couple of days.' The words were accompanied by an apologetic look.

'Good for you. Don't look so sheepish. You've earned it, with or without a stiff neck. Make the most of it. Get home for a few days. Who knows when you'll get another chance?'

The words seemed to help the young man resolve some inner debate.

He settled stiffly onto the grass, wincing as he did so, but looking and sounding much more positive.

'You're right. I think I will try and get home, even if I will have to start back almost as soon as I get there.'

'That's the trouble with 48s. But it's better than nothing, and it'll get you away from this madhouse for a while.'

Jack wouldn't have minded some time off himself, but the way things were going, it seemed unlikely.

Alex stretched out, grimacing again. 'What's been happening while I've been away?'

Glad of the distraction, Jack put his pen and paper to one side. He began to relay the day's events.

'Well, as you can probably tell, the Station was hit again. Made a real mess, but no mass casualties this time. Chips was missing, but we've just heard that he should be back tonight. Oh, and you need to congratulate Piers again. He's a flight commander now.'

No-one spotted the dust motes beginning their rhythmic dance. But, a few seconds later, Sophie felt the tremors. Looking around, she could see that others had also noticed.

'Tin hats, everyone.' Squadron Leader Frankland

shouted, putting his helmet on.

The air raid sirens began a belated wail.

'And Sergeant, tell Group what's going on. They may be able to rustle something up.'

A WAAF sitting at the switchboard talked urgently into her mouthpiece.

You could hear explosions now, a crump, crump, getting louder and louder.

The building began to shudder. The dust falls intensified and the lights began to sway.

The Station Commander walked into the room. Those who saw him were half out of their seats before he waved them down. Calm and unruffled, right hand firmly clasped on the bowl of his pipe, he turned toward the Controller.

'No warning, sir,' the Squadron Leader began, raising his voice just enough to be heard above the explosions. 'No idea how many or at what height. 'Fraid Dragon are on the ground, and the rest are out to the east.'

'Thank you, Roger. 12 Group?'

'Don't know, sir. We've told Uxbridge.'

The Station Commander looked to the switchboard and shouted above the din. 'Tell them again would you please, Sergeant.'

Sophie noticed some of the girls adjusting their headsets and tapping their microphones.

A WAAF corporal shouted to the platform, 'Station phone lines are down again, sir.'

The building rocked violently. Sophie fell against her table. A loud crack. A fissure opened across the ceiling.

She heard the Controller's voice above the din. 'Right. Everyone out.'

Some of the WAAFs hesitated, looking towards her. 'Now! Get moving!' she shouted.

There was a rush for the door. The noise rose to a crescendo and the visibility reduced to a few yards. The dust stung Sophie's eyes. She watched the last few WAAFs filing past.

Finally, the Controller held his arm out to usher her and the Station Commander before him.

Last to leave the bridge, she smiled.

She was almost at the door, following the Station Commander's large frame, when, for some reason, she looked back. The dust cleared momentarily. Still huddled over their posts on the switchboard, were the sergeant and corporal. Her shout was lost in the noise.

Brushing past the Controller, she grabbed them by the arms and pulled. To her amazement, they were still reluctant to abandon their positions. Another loud crack. Debris falling. Sophie felt a stinging blow to her forehead. She gave another tug. The two WAAFs relented and moved ahead of her.

The little drama had played out before the Controller had been able to react. He stood open-mouthed as they rushed past. Coughing on the dust, Sophie stepped into the corridor.

A yellow flash. Darkness.

Bombs straddled the area around the pens.

Jack watched Muddy dash out of the hut, man of action as always. But even he was forced to the ground, diving down where Jack and Alex were already huddled, hands over their heads, willing the impacts to come no closer.

After a tumultuous period when the ground shook and earth showered down around them, the explosions moved away across the airfield. A few moments later, they stopped as suddenly as they'd started.

So that was what it was like to be bombed. Jack preferred being airborne. He raised his head. Plumes of black smoke rose from the two farthest pens.

Not the groundcrew again?

Muddy looked at him.

Jack read his mind. 'They'll be long gone before we get airborne, sir.'

The bombers had made their approach above an extensive layer of medium cloud, and were now using it to mask their getaway.

'Fuck.' The new CO vented his anger and frustration. 'Alex, go and ask Piers to get in touch with Ops would you? Jack, let's go and see what the damage is?'

Jack stood up and followed Muddy towards the pens.

When Alex entered the hut, Piers was already tapping the cradle of one phone, while Hopkins was trying to get through on another. The rest were standing, still slightly stooped, as if ready to throw themselves down at the first sign of another blast. They'd just gained an uncomfortable insight into what the Station personnel had been putting up with over the last week.

Even the most resilient of characters, like Dusty and Ginge, looked shaken.

'Nothing,' Piers declared, smashing the phone down. 'Hopkins, go to Ops and find out what's going on. The rest of you, let's go and help the CO.'

Impressed at his friend's decisiveness, Alex turned and followed Piers back through the door.

Jack had feared the worst, but the physical cost was remarkably light, mainly superficial wounds for those unable to find cover behind either the blast walls or a large piece of ground equipment.

Of course, the mental cost was harder to judge. Some looked as if their nerves were stretched to breaking point.

They'd lost two more aircraft, one blown to pieces and one damaged beyond immediate repair by the shrapnel from a close blast.

He turned to see Piers and the others setting out from the hut at a brisk trot.

'Well, if they're coming to say get airborne, sir, we'll have to draw lots.'

'Pathetic, isn't it? We couldn't even put up a flight.'

Flight Sergeant Patterson walked over, stopped in front of Muddy and saluted.

'Harper and Stone are on their way to sick bay, sir. Should be alright, I think.'

'Thanks, Flight. Difficult I know, but any idea for the morning?'

'Well, I should be able to give you another two by then, sir, but the rest'll be up to the Civilian Repair boys.'

'Okay, thank you. And I'll let you know as soon as we're stood down.'

'Thank you, sir.' The Flight Sergeant saluted and walked away again.

Piers and the others puffed up.

'Anything from Ops?'

'Nothing from anybody, sir,' Piers answered, breathing heavily.

'Right.' Muddy raised his voice so the stragglers could hear. 'Everything's okay here. A couple of minor injuries and a couple of kites written off.'

He waited a few seconds for the message to sink in. The last person came to a halt and they all stood, red-faced and panting, looking at the Squadron Commander.

'Okay then, let's go and find out what's going on.'

He walked briskly through the group and back towards the dispersal hut.

Jack smiled as they turned and tried to keep up, Ginge muttering a string of expletives.

Ten minutes later, Hopkins returned from Ops. They'd been stood down.

They made quite a pair, Alex with a neck brace and a lump the size of a small apple on his forehead, and Sophie with a jagged gash on a slightly smaller lump in a similar place. And they both made the connection immediately, pointing and laughing as they walked towards one another.

There had to be less painful ways to break the ice. They embraced briefly and kissed, easing apart before anyone walked into Reception and caught them.

'You first,' Alex said, pointing again at Sophie's wound.

Jack's mind was a whirl of indecision. What was he going to do, dive in, sweep Caroline off her feet and into bed, or take a less direct route through tea and biscuits, hoping to end up with the same result? He'd been mulling over the problem since he'd left the house the day before, and he was no closer to a decision now than he had been then.

The door opened.

Alex reached across the white linen tablecloth to take Sophie's hand, admiring the way her eyes shone in the candlelight. Their table was in the corner of a dining room that was slowly emptying. It had been remarkably busy for a Sunday night, with several uniforms, but no-one they recognised from Biggin Hill.

'I was so worried when I heard they'd actually hit the Ops Room.'

'I don't mind admitting I was frightened,' Sophie said, a momentary cloud dimming her sparkle.

The final blast had blown the heavy Ops Room door shut, just as Squadron Leader Frankland was closing it. It broke his arm, and the rest of them had been thrown against the wall of the corridor, but there'd been no other serious damage beyond the stem of the Station Commander's pipe, about which he'd been furious.

The memory lightened her mood again. 'I could have killed the sergeant and corporal for making me go back in. And just to add insult to injury, I'm probably going to have to write them up for some sort of award!'

Alex smiled. She was especially beautiful when she laughed.

It had been a marvellous night, so good he'd seriously considered changing his plans and spending his 48 at Biggin. But Sophie insisted he visit his parents. Who knew when he'd get another chance, and she'd be working anyway. They'd made tentative arrangements to meet on his return on Tuesday evening.

'Right, you booked the table and drove, so I'm going to pay,' he said.

'Thank you. You're an officer and a gentleman.'

He hoped so. They came from such different backgrounds. It had been a lovely meal, but the restaurant was much plusher than anything he'd have attempted to book. He hoped he hadn't made a fool of himself.

Caroline eased away from Jack and closed the door. She turned back and they fell into another passionate kiss. He was already aroused. After what he hoped was a respectable pause, he moved his hands up from her waist. Caroline's response was immediate, and so different from Gwen's that he lost all fear of a similar rejection.

She started undoing his jacket buttons. Almost unable to believe his good fortune, he followed her lead. They giggled, hands clashing as he unbuttoned and slid off her blouse and she removed his jacket. He stood back, his eyes taking in her radiant face, the pale skin of her neck and shoulders, the hint of bosom brimming the low neck of her slip. They leaned into another kiss.

After another pause, he found the warm, smooth, skin under her slip.

She started to undo his shirt buttons and he slid his hands up, up, eyes closing as he reached her breasts, cupping and stroking them, teasing at the hardening nipples. She nibbled at his lower lip.

He was already in ecstasy, tiredness and pain forgotten.

'Shall we go upstairs?'

He doubted his ability to communicate in anything other than caveman grunts, but he managed a breathy, 'Yes, please.'

Laughing, she turned and led the way.

After hopping to remove his shoes, he followed, sliding his braces from his shoulders and removing his shirt and vest as he climbed the stairs and crossed the landing.

In her bedroom, she turned and lifted the top over her head. He drank in the sight of her breasts, then stepped forward and leaned down to kiss and caress them. She played her fingers through his hair. Encouraged, he slid a hand over the front of her skirt. His heart leapt at her reaction to his touch.

He rose into another embrace, delighting in the warmth of her body against his chest. His hands moved to the clasp of her skirt as she tried to locate the fastening of his trousers. After a few fumbling seconds, they giggled again, and moved apart to remove their own lower garments.

When she straightened, he was awestruck at her naked beauty. He wanted to rush ahead, but also to draw out each new experience, to cement the images and sensations in his mind.

Eventually, he moved towards her. His skin tingled as if tiny sparks were jumping between them. And when they finally caressed, he was almost overcome with the pure joy of a moment he'd feared he may not live to savour.

Slowly, she manoeuvred him onto the bed and he leaned over her. Their kisses became more passionate and he relived his daydream, easing a hand down her stomach. Unsure how to proceed, he felt a rush of relief as her legs eased apart. In sharp contrast to Gwen's 'that's enough of that', she sighed encouragingly.

He stroked, and her sighs became more ardent. She held his gaze until her eyes closed and her head arched back, her mouth emitting little groans of enjoyment. He looked down, revelling in the sight of her breasts rising and falling, the sounds of passion elicited by every touch of his fingers.

Like Caroline, he was becoming evermore aroused, and he moved closer to nestle against her. She looked at him, her words confirming the message in her eyes.

'Yes, Jack. Yes.'

He rose over her. Her flesh yielded and the sensation of tingling pleasure was more delicious than anything he had ever experienced. Caroline's enthusiastic reaction completed his ecstasy, and they gazed contentedly into one another's eyes.

All too soon, his excitement mounted.

'Caroline?'

'It's alright, Jack. It's alright.'

He increased his pace to a groaning finale of utter contentment.

Chapter 9 – Monday 2nd September 1940

Jack shivered and pulled the blanket up round his shoulders. He was finding it especially hard to shut out the assorted grunts and snores filling the hut this morning, and he couldn't get comfortable. Sighing, he eased himself up and looked around at the other bodies fidgeting in the gloom. What he wouldn't give to be back in bed with Caroline. He smiled at the thought of his departure from the house.

He'd woken to the sound of a strange alarm, immediately realising where he was and feeling acutely embarrassed. He must have fallen asleep very soon after their lovemaking. He wasn't altogether surprised, but it hadn't been very chivalrous.

Before he worked out how to locate the alarm, its harsh ringing stopped and a bedside light clicked on.

Caroline raised herself on one elbow, the bedclothes maintaining her modesty. She looked sleepy and tousled, but beautiful.

'Sorry, Caroline. I don't know what came over me. It's unforgivable.'

'What, the lovemaking or the sleeping?' she teased.

Relieved at her light-hearted response, he leaned over and kissed her.

'I set the alarm for four o'clock. I hope that's all right?'

The fear that he'd overslept was also banished. 'Spot on. Thank you.'

Bashful under her smiling gaze, he'd gathered his socks, pants and trousers and, blowing another kiss, had let himself out of the bedroom to find the rest of his clothes, scattered on the stairs and around the hall.

And now, here he was again, waiting for the

inevitable call to action. Ignoring the light starting to filter through the windows, he closed his eyes and tried to transport himself back into Caroline's bedroom.

Sophie looked at the lines of carefully labelled dark wood drawers covering the whole of one wall and smiled.

What a way to fight a war. She wondered if the squadrons knew they were about to be controlled from the back room of a chemist's shop! Probably better if they didn't.

Even above the general hubbub, she could hear a little bell tinkling as the shop door opened and closed for the stream of people helping to prepare the Standby Ops Room. Boxes were being delivered and unpacked, furniture moved and coils of wire unwound.

The telephone engineers had worked miracles. They were connected to Uxbridge and the dispersals at Biggin, Gravesend and Croydon. And they had a map table of sorts, some tote boards and even a small platform upon which the Controller and his staff were sitting behind a large kitchen table. Sophie and the Flight Sergeant were positioned just to the right of the platform, behind a smaller table.

The little bell rang again, and Sophie made eye contact with Squadron Leader Rice. They rolled their eyes and tutted, breaking into conspiratorial smiles. These disappeared as the Station Commander walked into the room.

My, how the man could get about.

He waved people down as he walked towards the platform. 'May I again, Kelvin?'

'Certainly, sir.'

He turned and coughed, waiting for them all to

settle. 'Now, you'll all have heard about the Ops Room, and probably from someone who was there.'

He smiled down at Sophie.

'I think we were lucky to escape as lightly as we did. A few injuries,' - he patted his jacket pocket – 'but nothing too serious, I'm glad to say.

'But I'm afraid it'll be quite a while before the Ops Block is up and running again, if at all. In the meantime, we're going to start preparing somewhere a little…' He paused as if searching for the right words. The shop bell rang again and his eyes lit up. 'A little less public. Anyway, I'm sure the Controllers will keep you abreast of developments.

'Finally, I know this set-up is less than ideal, but I also know you'll do your best to make it work. Righto, carry on.'

The girls returned to their duties, and he turned towards the Controller and leaned forward. This time, Sophie was so close she couldn't avoid hearing their conversation, even if she'd wanted to.

'How's it going, Kelvin?'

'Alright, sir. It's a bit less palatial, but it'll certainly do for now.'

'Good.' He glanced back towards the map. 'And how are things shaping up?'

'Not well, sir. There are already two plots crossing the Channel.'

'And what about the squadrons?'

'79 and 637 aren't in bad shape, sir, but 646 are struggling for airframes. Two more were delivered last night, but that still only gives them nine.'

'Pilots?'

'Numbers are okay, sir; they'll have 16 if young Barratt passes muster, but they're so inexperienced.

Muddy's just made Piers White a flight commander. Good hand by all accounts, but he's only been on the Squadron about three weeks. Flight Sergeant Williams is leading the other flight, and the Squadron if Muddy stays on the ground. Group are trying to find them another experienced flight commander…'

'Yes I know, but from my last chat with the AOC, all the squadrons are in a similar state, so it's not going to be easy. I spoke to Muddy yesterday and he's sure he can cope as long as he keeps hold of some of the more experienced hands. If not… Well, we'll have to cross that bridge when we come to it, won't we?'

'Yes, sir.'

'Okay, Kelvin, I'll get out of your hair. It's going to be strange not being able to walk down the corridor and nip in. A bit of peace for you though, ay? You don't have to answer that. Give me a ring if you want some top cover; otherwise, I'll drop in later.'

They all stood as the Station Commander walked out with a cheery wave.

646 had fallen on hard times, but at least Alex was out of it for a few days. He'd looked very tired and lonely as she'd driven away from Sambrook House.

Alex woke after his lie in. He hadn't felt as relaxed for days. For once, he'd been able to sleep beyond 4.00am, and his nightmares had been banished by more pleasant memories. Sophie was a beautiful, wonderful, girl, and they'd shared a long kiss before saying goodnight.

As her shielded tail lights had disappeared down the drive, the only concern had been that he might bump into Bunter on his way to bed, but the silly oaf hadn't been about; just as well, because he hadn't felt up to anything physical. Between the neck brace and the lump on his head, he still didn't.

Sighing contentedly, he decided to sneak another ten minutes before searching for breakfast and catching his transport to Bromley.

Sophie watched black counters being raked around the map. As expected, the two hostile plots had split over the coast, and there were at least four separate raids setting out over Kent and the Thames Estuary. There could be more; the weather was making things difficult for the Observer Corps again.

The makeshift Ops Room was so cosy that Squadron Leader Rice could lean over to speak to her, so she was getting even more insights than normal.

'Group's decided to keep Dragon and a few other squadrons back to defend the airfields. The trouble is we don't know which airfields the Hun's targeting.'

'Or even where some of the raids are,' she added.

'Yes,' he smiled. 'We do seem to have lost some of them.'

When Alex was airborne, she sometimes found it difficult to look at the Controller's mottled features without fear, revulsion even. But today, with Alex safely on the ground, she had no such feelings.

He looked at the map and his expression became more serious. 'They'll have to put Dragon up soon, even if only to patrol, otherwise they'll never get to height.'

Sophie followed his gaze. Never mind the missing raids. One of those being plotted seemed to be heading straight for Biggin.

Jack smiled and shook his head.

'My how the mighty are fallen.'

One day you were leading the Squadron, the next you were arse-end Charlie again. Not that he was grumbling. Muddy was up front, with Ginge and Bunter on his wings. He'd decided to put Smithy straight back into the fray, so the Australian was leading the second vic with Dunc and Pete to either side, while JC was to the left beyond Piers.

Jack eased back and admired the eight Spitfires ahead of him. They were climbing in the overhead. Perhaps the AOC had given up on 12 Group.

Below, Biggin Hill was standing out like a green island in a bubbling sea of early morning mist and fog. It made the Station look very vulnerable.

'Dragon, this is Bastion. Fifty plus bandits, approximately twenty five miles, angels one six, vector zero seven zero.'

'Bastion, this is Dragon Leader. Wilco, passing angels one three.'

It would be close, but they should get to height before they met. Above the almost uniform layer coating the ground, it was a lovely day. The sky was blue and the sun was glinting off roundels and canopies. Not for the first time, Jack pondered the contrast between the beauty around him now, and the bloody mayhem into which they were heading. He seemed particularly attuned to such contradictions today.

Was it because of last night?

Perhaps. His will to survive had certainly been given new focus. Having lived long enough to enjoy the rapture of lovemaking, he desperately wanted to repeat the experience.

Would it change his attitude to combat?

That was more difficult to answer, but he sensed he was about to find out.

Perhaps it was the dark wood and low ceiling of the new Ops Room, but Sophie had never known things seem so chaotic. As the weather improved, more and more reports were coming in, and more and more plots were being raked onto the map, some of them appearing very near their likely targets to the north and south of the Estuary. The girls all seemed to be talking at once. It was becoming difficult to think.

'Quiet!'

The voice was loud and emphatic. Everyone stopped and turned to the platform.

Perhaps the face was a little redder than usual, but it was as hard as ever to gauge the underlying emotions. The speaker on the wall crackled, and some disembodied voices leaked from telephone handsets and headsets. Otherwise, there was silence.

'Thank you.' The voice was calm and even. 'I know we're all packed in very tightly, but please keep your voices down. Carry on please.'

The WAAFs returned to their interrupted conversations, but now speaking at much reduced volume. Sophie realised that the Controller's timely intervention had stopped the Room's descent into something approaching hysteria.

He looked across at her, shaking his head and smiling. She smiled back as he raised a handset to his thin lips.

'Dragon, this is Bastion, bandits should be in your twelve o'clock approximately ten miles.'

'Dragon Leader, from Red 3, bandits eleven o'clock,

slightly low.'

Jack sneaked a quick glance, but could see nothing. Muddy was obviously having similar trouble.

'Roger, Red 3, looking. Dragon, line abreast, line abreast, go.'

Jack continued to quarter the sky as he followed Piers to the right of the line. He still couldn't see anything below the horizon, but he did spot a hazy dark mass above it, just to the right of the nose. He was about to report the new contact when Muddy piped up.

'Bastion, this is Dragon Leader. Tally-ho, tally-ho, fifty plus bandits, going in.'

'Dragon Leader, this is Bastion. Roger and good luck. Bastion out.'

Jack could see their bandits now. About 20 Dorniers with an escort of about 30 Messerschmitt 110s, half 1,000 feet above the bombers.

'Green Leader, this is Dragon Leader. Occupy the higher fighters please.'

'Green Leader, wilco.'

Jack and JC followed Piers as he eased to the right and levelled. The rest of Dragon accelerated towards a frontal attack on the bombers, trading their 1,000 foot height advantage for speed.

When Jack looked to the far hazy mass again, it had coalesced into a large force of 109s three thousand feet above.

'Dragon Leader, from Green Two, Snappers right two o'clock, angels two zero.'

'Roger, Green Two.'

The presence of the 109s didn't change the plan, only the odds when they joined the party. The range to the 110s was falling fast and the vague hope that they'd form a defensive circle faded as several began firing.

Jack ignored the tracer and waited. One thousand yards. One second to aim. He held a 110 in the centre of his reflector sight. One second to fire. His airframe juddered as the rounds set off. And one second to avoid a collision. He pushed as the 110 grew alarmingly, its guns still firing but somehow missing him.

As the dust settled, he caught a brief glimpse of the bombers a thousand feet below. A couple in the first line were smoking, but the rest of the formation was intact, ploughing on.

A line of tracer speared over his canopy. He pulled up and right into a brief and inconclusive head-on encounter. Continuing the turn, he rolled out on the tail of a third 110. He was in the ideal position, below and behind, and it was flying in a straight line.

'Your funeral, Butt.'

Jack hit the gun button and watched his ammunition spark off the fighter's exposed underbelly.

It rolled right. Out of control? He didn't have time to find out.

Tracer flashed past and he pulled left into another tight turn, breathing hard, sweating and straining to maintain his vision. Only when he was convinced he'd shaken off his assailant did he straighten and look for another target. But more tracer arced in from the right. He pulled towards that as well. It came from a pair of yellow-nosed 109s.

They were the first of many. He ended up in a frantic fight for survival against overwhelming numbers of the agile singe-engined fighters. His personal battles took him far to the south east towards Dungeness.

In hindsight, perhaps they were trying to shake him off as they headed for home. But that wasn't the way it felt. He endured a constant stream of fleeting encounters, manoeuvring hard to avoid collisions and firing at targets of opportunity as they flashed past - a wing, a tailplane, a canopy.

Eventually, his ammunition spent, he dived for the ground, where the mist was clearing fast in the early morning sun. He was surprised to see the coast and prayed he had enough fuel to make Biggin Hill.

There had been no thoughts of Caroline in the heat of battle, but there were now. Last night's encounter had also been fleeting, and he longed for a more measured exploration of her beauty.

Sophie knew Dragon had hit the raid approaching Biggin, but the bombers had still managed to find the airfield. They'd felt the tremors, even in the village, although subsequent reports indicated that damage was slight.

The Standby Ops Room was relatively quiet.

For once, as the few remaining marauders were chased across the south east coast, there didn't seem to be any more raids forming up over the Channel.

Sophie watched Kelvin Rice lean back and dab a handkerchief down his face. He deserved a rest. It was just after 9.30am and she wondered how Dragon had fared.

Jack could see a few wisps of smoke rising. It didn't look as bad as other days, but that depended on what had been hit.

'Just a few more holes in the airfield, Flight,' Stokesy assured him as he took a strap.

'I hope you're right, Stokesy. We could do with some luck for a change.'

'Perhaps they're running out of bombs, Flight,' the young rigger joined in.

'Perhaps, Smudger, but they're not running out of bombers, I can tell you.'

'Shame,' Stokesy took over again, running a hand over his neatly brushed hair. 'How's the kite?'

'Fine, although it must have been running on fumes.'

'Yes. We were getting a bit worried, weren't we, Smudger?'

The airframe fitter nodded.

Jack climbed out of the cockpit. 'Anyway, don't be surprised if it sucks the bowser dry. See you later.'

He jumped off the wing, hung his parachute on the tailplane and walked out of the pen. He was feeling in a surprisingly good mood. If he'd been the sort of person who whistled, he might have chirruped a tune as he walked towards the Intelligence Officer.

A lone pilot was walking away from Nick Hudson. It looked like Piers.

Jack didn't rush. He couldn't. He still ached. 'Hello, sir. Am I the last?'

The IntO took the pipe from his mouth. 'Apart from Dunc Mason, yes.'

'Oh. Hard to believe he's still airborne. I was on the vapours.'

'I know. I was just about to shut up shop when you taxyed in. But now you are here, do you actually have anything to report? My tea'll be going cold.'

'Well, I hit two 110s in the initial engagement. Not sure about the first, but I'm pretty sure I did the second some damage. Spent the rest of the time performing aerial ballet with a succession of single-engined partners. We danced all the way to the coast, but I have no idea whether I stepped on any of their toes.'

'Thanks, Jack. Very poetic, but you might like to put a different form of words in your report.'

Approaching Victoria, the fog cleared. Alex saw vapour trails out to the east. He imagined himself up there, frightened, disorientated and nauseous, fighting to remain conscious as the g mounted, to remain alive as the Messerschmitts swooped. Sweat prickled his upper lip, and his hand seemed to develop a tiny tremor.

He shuddered and looked around the packed carriage. His fellow travellers, nearly all male businessmen above military age, had their faces buried in newspapers. No-one seemed to have spotted his discomfort.

With time in hand, he walked past the entrance to the Underground. He took out a map and set out on foot for Paddington, via Buckingham Palace, Apsley House and Hyde Park. Despite the prevalence of sandbags and soldiers, the capital still seemed a thousand miles from the war, and he enjoyed his sightseeing.

Passing the Serpentine, he spotted more distant vapour trails. This time, he imagined Sophie in the Ops Room, hearing shouts from the speakers. Was she listening to Dragon? Were Muddy, Jack and Piers in the thick of it as usual, and had Olly been cleared by the docs? He hoped his roommate had found the silk scarf draped over his locker.

Despite the irrationality of it, he still felt guilty at deserting them, and hoped they all survived during his absence.

Later, with Reading disappearing behind him, he looked at his reflection in the carriage window, just as he had over a week ago. Even he could see it was a different person looking back at him. For a start, the top button of his tunic was unashamedly undone. He was very definitely a fighter pilot now. But the short time he'd held that status had taken its toll. Neck brace notwithstanding, it was a very tired and careworn face that stared back at him.

What would his parents think? And what could he tell them? What could he tell anybody? It was bad enough trying to explain things to Sophie, and she was as close to the action as anyone. And should he tell them about Sophie?

The mid-morning lull was a surprise, but no-one was complaining. Certainly not Jack.

He lay back in the deckchair, hands behind his head, basking in the heat of the late morning sun. He also seemed to be basking in a feeling of general well-being and optimism that could, he was sure, be down to only one thing: Caroline.

He was glad he'd taken time to admire her standing naked at the foot of the bed. That image had already fed numerous daydreams. He ached to be with her again.

There had been some professional distractions as well. Dunc had run out of fuel, but he'd managed to glide into Detling and was now back with them, humbly accepting well-aimed banter from Ginge. Bunter had attempted to join in, but his intervention had been heavy handed and over-familiar for a new boy. It had done little to improve his standing as a future section leader.

According to Dunc, Detling was in a similar state to Biggin, although their groundcrew seemed much twitchier. It brought home how well their own had coped after all they'd been through. They'd already fixed two kites damaged in the first scramble, and received and prepped another, so they were up to ten.

And Olly was going to get back in the saddle, flying in a pair with Piers. His face had lit up at the news, but later, Jack had noticed a more worried expression. Eventually, the young officer had excused himself and walked through into the locker room, his face turning from ashen to green. Jack felt for him.

He was also to lead a pair again, with JC on his wing. He and the young sergeant pilot had just had their first proper chat.

JC was a classic example of the diverse characters that now made up a fighter squadron, about as far from the stereotype as you could get.

Small and so thin he appeared undernourished, he had sharp features and hooded grey eyes under a mat of dark hair. He hardly looked the part, especially when compared with the likes of Olly, blond hair and blue eyes, old school colours round his neck.

'I was a clerk in an office in Leeds,' JC had told him when they stopped talking tactics. 'Left school at 14, but the chap in the recruiting office didn't seem too worried about education. When I took all the tests, I ended up being selected for pilot. Nobody was more surprised than me, except perhaps me mam and dad.'

'Must have done well in training though?'

'Yea. Just took to it, I suppose.'

On closer inspection, Jack decided the young man was wiry rather than undernourished. Must be, if he was successfully hauling a Spitfire around.

He glanced down beside his chair. The top sheet of the writing pad glared back at him. 'Dear Gwen,' and nothing more. Must do it. But not now. He closed his eyes.

'After this morning,' Kelvin Rice was telling Sophie, 'Group say they're going to try and catch the formations before they break up over the coast. I'm not sure I agree.'

'Too risky?' Sophie offered.

'Yes. Holding back didn't work this morning, but that was because the fog stopped the Observer Corps tracking the raids. I don't think they'll have the same trouble this afternoon. But Group are too worried that Gerry'll hit the aircraft factories again.'

Sophie could see why. They were struggling to replace aircraft as it was. If the factories were hit... Well, it didn't bear thinking about.

The shop bell tinkled, but neither noticed as they concentrated on the map. A hostile plot had been stationary over the French coast for several colour changes. Angela raked it towards her again. After a few seconds, she pushed it back on, over water now, its blue arrow pointing towards Dover.

'Here they come.' The Controller leaned back, looking tense, excited. He stretched out his arms, rhythmically clenching and opening his claw-like hands, then clapping and rubbing them together in a washing motion, leaning forward as if preparing for some physical activity.

Sophie looked from him to the black counter. A vital piece of information was missing. 'No estimate of how many yet, sir?'

'Probably too early for the RDF operators to take a stab, but I wouldn't mind betting it's in the hundreds.'

He clapped and washed again. 'Not long now.'

Jack was slipping the strap from Caroline's shoulder when the bell rang and Hopkins began shouting.

'Dragon squadron scramble, bandits approaching Dover, angels one four, vector one one zero, Dragon squadron scramble.'

The strident voice faded as Jack closed the distance to his pen, breathing heavily and wincing at the pain in his muscles and joints. They weren't climbing in the overhead this time by the sound of it.

As he reached for his parachute, the Merlin engine started, great gouts of grey smoke streaming back in the slipstream.

The smell cleared away the final vestiges of sleepiness. He fastened the parachute, watching Smudger remove the starter plug and pull the trolley away. By the time he was ready to step onto the wing, the youngster was already running round the wingtip towards him.

He reached the cockpit, Stokesy climbed out onto the right wing and he stepped through the small door, sat and accepted the straps, nodding at the usual pat on the back of the head from his engine fitter. By the time he'd sorted out his headset and wriggled to get comfortable, both his groundcrew were looking up at him, holding the ropes that ran to the chocks.

Jack watched other Spitfires disappearing behind his engine cowling. His aircraft rocked at low revs and he breathed in the heady cocktail of exhaust fumes and cockpit smells – rubber, leather, oils, sweat.

Seeing Piers and Olly passing, he waved his hands

in front of his face and opened the throttle a growl. The groundcrew pulled the chocks out, threw them clear and grasped the wingtips. He released the brakes and they walked with him. As he exited the pen, he waved them away with a smile, before waving at JC, waiting patiently for him to pass. The young man waved and smiled back.

Over his shoulder, Stokesy and Smudger stood together, waving cheerily, presumably at JC. What a friendly bunch they all were.

Muddy was already turning the Squadron into wind. Jack completed his checks. 'Radiator shutter open, hood open, harness tight and locked.'

He turned into wind behind Piers and Olly, and watched JC stop alongside his right tailplane and give a thumbs-up.

A couple of seconds later, fumes belched from the exhausts of Muddy's section and they started moving. He flexed his hands around throttle and stick.

'Here we go.'

Alex was sitting in the café on Newport station, a small, wood-panelled room with half a dozen tables and a wooden counter in one corner. He'd just eaten a sandwich and was contemplating a cup of tea when one appeared on the patterned tablecloth in front of him.

Feeling clumsy and stupid, he turned his whole upper body to see an attractive older woman – perhaps in her early thirties - smiling down at him. He hadn't noticed her before, but he'd been miles away.

'I've been dying to buy one of you a drink all summer. Sorry it's only tea. May I?'

Wincing again, Alex stood. Blushing, he indicated

the seat opposite him. 'Please do.'

'Sorry to be so forward,' the woman apologised again in standard BBC English. 'But I said to mother, if ever I see one of those boys, I'm going to buy him a drink.'

She wore a light dusting of make up and was smartly dressed in a dark green coat and matching hat. Where did she live to see 'boys' such as him? Probably not Newport.

'Well, thank you, but I'm not sure I deserve it.'

'If you're a fighter pilot, and I think you are,' she said looking at his top button, 'you deserve it.'

Alex blushed more deeply. 'Well, yes, I am a fighter pilot.'

'I knew it. We overlook Dover. See you all the time, a few little dots flying towards hundreds of Germans.' She looked at his neck brace. 'It's a miracle any of you come out alive.'

'Well, it can be quite exciting at times.'

'Look, I can see I've embarrassed you, but I just wanted to show my gratitude.' She looked up at the large clock on the wall and started to rise. 'Sorry, I've got to go now.'

Still intrigued, but also relieved, Alex stood. 'Not at all.' He held out his hand. 'Nice to meet you.'

She took his hand and looked at him with motherly concern. 'Good luck, young man.'

He was getting used to such looks. 'Thank you. And for the tea.'

She gave a shy little wave and disappeared through the door carrying a small case.

Alex sat back, trying to ignore the looks of the other customers. Discounting the drinks bought by the people who'd tried to lynch him, which hardly seemed to count, it was his first experience of the spontaneous generosity that others had talked about. It sparked a strange mixture of emotions: humility, but also pride and a sense of privilege that he was one of the small band engaged in the battle his benefactor had witnessed.

Inevitably, it also re-kindled thoughts of combat, and concern for his friends.

How could they miss over 200 bombers? From the chatter on the radios, and the vapour trails in the distance, combat was raging all around them. But, after 55 minutes of vectoring and re-vectoring, they'd seen nothing.

Jack looked at the Spitfires glinting in the sunlight ahead of him. Oh well, at least they were returning as a squadron, something that was becoming increasingly rare.

Sophie had rarely seen Kelvin Rice more frustrated. As he'd predicted, Dragon had failed to reach the hostile formation before it split. And in the frantic period since, he'd been unable to direct the Squadron onto any of the more than 400 enemy aircraft over south east England.

Now, at 2.15, just as another wave of bombers was approaching the coast, Dragon had to return for fuel. They wouldn't be on the ground long.

The hills around Abergavenny looked much less threatening than ten days previously. In the interim, Alex had displayed many weaknesses, but his major concern at the time, cowardice, was not one of them – so far.

The kindness of the woman in Newport had also lightened his mood. He'd noticed admiring glances from other passengers since. And his guilt had eased. The train journey had emphasised how stupid it would have been to fly with his neck as it was. Every jolt of the carriage made him wince, so pulling 6g in a Spitfire would have been impossible.

Jack listened to the shouts and watched the groundcrew working on his Spitfire.

The engine fitters were refuelling and replenishing the oil; the riggers topping up the oxygen and hydraulics systems and checking the airframe; and the armourers were mucking in, having discovered they weren't needed in their primary trade: no-one had fired a shot on the last sortie.

He sniffed. Fuel and hydraulic oil. At times like this, he sometimes pined for the old days as a tradesman. But such thoughts rarely lasted long. His new life was in the cockpit. He couldn't really picture himself as an airframe fitter again.

His stomach rumbled. As soon as he got the nod from Stokesy, he'd be back in the cockpit, another lunch missed.

The train exited the tunnel and pulled into Ludlow station. Alex was one of the few passengers to alight, and there was no reception committee. He'd thought he might be able to get a message to his dad in the shop, but hadn't managed it, so his visit would be a surprise.

The sight of the tower of St Lawrence's and the battlements of the castle brought a lump to his throat. Home. He suddenly realised he hadn't expected to see it again.

Swallowing hard, he turned away, picked up his light canvas bag and crossed the footbridge onto the path to Gravel Hill.

Jack gritted his teeth. His opponent was flying with great tenacity and skill, constantly evading a scoring chance.

'Come on, just a bit m...'

And again, the 109 jinked away.

'Damn you!'

He pulled into another gut-wrenching turn, matching his opponent's eccentric use of rudder as closely as he could. His chest heaved and sweat prickled his body. This was the longest dogfight he'd fought for days and his arms ached. But, while they were pulling positive g, he'd always have the upper hand.

The 109 juddered, the slots on its leading edges opening as it approached the stall. Jack too was on the pre-stall buffet, but turning more quickly.

Just as the German fighter inched into his sights, it pushed and ruddered into a dive. Fearing his engine would cut if he attempted the same, Jack rolled and pulled, losing ground in the process.

'Shit!'

There were no other aircraft in sight. He decided to dive after the 109. Unless there was a dramatic reversal of fortunes, he sensed he was striving for another victory, while his opponent was fighting for his very survival.

'Don't get complacent, Jack.'

He set his jaw and pressed his left hand against the throttle until his palm ached.

Slowly, the distance closed to 1,000 yards. The coast passed 5,000 feet below, the white-flecked grey of the Channel opening up ahead of him.

'The Shit Canal' the Germans were reputed to call it, and with good reason. It had claimed many of their number, low on fuel or too damaged to make land on the other side.

But it had claimed many Fighter Command pilots as well, especially during the battles over Dunkirk in May and early June, and over the convoys in July.

Jack knew he should turn back, but also that he wouldn't. Three thousand feet and 800 yards. Perhaps the German pilot had assumed he would. It was he who seemed to have become complacent. He'd stopped manoeuvring.

They edged below 2,000 feet and the white caps became more prominent. Five hundred yards and still Jack held his fire. He'd be poorly placed if he met enemy fighters now, and he had so much more to live for than even a few days ago. But he was not to be deflected.

Fifteen hundred feet and 400 yards.

Was this ethical?

The answer was the same as every other time he'd asked the question. It was the Germans who'd invaded half of Europe and crossed the Channel to drop their bombs. Whether the other pilot was a rabid Nazi or merely an obedient Luftwaffe officer, in doing his duty, he was the aggressor. He had to be stopped. That he was being stalked to within sight of safety by an unseen enemy didn't change the fundamental issue.

The 109 levelled at 1,000 feet and Jack dived closer to the choppy water before pulling up and closing to within 100 yards. He could see the oil streaks running along the Messerschmitt's grey underbelly, the black crosses on the wings and the foreshortened swastikas on the sides of the tailplane.

His conscience rebutted a final plea for mercy and he pressed the gun button.

Smoke belched from the 109's engine cowling and it turned right. Expecting such a manoeuvre, Jack followed and kept firing. The German's turn developed into a tight descending spiral.

Jack levelled and watched him splash into the sea five miles short of the French coast. During his one orbit, the wings and tailplane bobbed to the surface, but the fuselage and cockpit remained buried beneath the waves.

He started a shallow climb, heading for the white cliffs some twenty odd miles away.

Duty done, but no whoop of triumph.

The door opened. His mother's face crumpled. After a few moments, she regained some of her composure, and the greeting became the embarrassing mixture of smiles and tears for which Alex had been steeling himself. But he couldn't forget the expression of shock and fear on her face when she'd first seen him.

Did he look that bad?

And as he sat in the kitchen awaiting the inevitable cup of tea, her frequent hugs and kisses made him uncomfortable. His reaction surprised him. After a week of homesickness, the reality was proving too cosy, too intimate, his mother's love and concern too much to bear. He already needed to escape.

'I'll go and surprise dad in a minute.'

He'd also developed an overwhelming urge to re-visit some of his childhood haunts, to look on his home town with eyes that had neglected its beauty for too long. It would have to be that afternoon. He wouldn't have time in the morning.

As he drank his tea, he looked into his mother's watery eyes and sensed the yearning for him to be her little boy again. And although he knew it added to her fear and pain, he batted away her concerns for his safety with the cold language of the crewroom.

'Don't worry, Mum. It's a piece of cake.'

She clearly didn't believe him, but he felt compelled to carry on in the same vein.

'Just a bit of a strain. No, it's the only time I've been in any real danger. And the Gerries are just about beaten anyway.'

It was a line that would work with his father. He tended to shy away from bad news, so he'd be only too happy to accept his son's reassurances. But his mother could see straight through the flim-flam. Always could.

Cold-heartedly rejecting her attempts to accompany him into town, he left her standing, a forlorn and shrunken figure on the doorstep.

He felt dreadful.

Jack guessed he was the last to approach Nick Hudson again.

'You're making a habit of this, my lad.'

Jack smiled. It was a long time since anyone had called him a lad. He was only 22, but most of the time he felt like a city father. There were just four people significantly older than him on the Squadron now – Dusty and Dunc, and the newly arrived Bomber Bailey and Admiral Turner – and none of them were beyond their mid-20s.

The IntO looked disapproving as Jack told him of his chase over the Channel.

'Just you be careful, Jack.'

On the way to the dispersal hut, he met Olly, sitting alone on the grass, head down, deep in thought.

'Alright, young sir?'

Olly looked up as if waking from a dream. 'Yes, I'm fine thanks, Jack. It's Piers. He hasn't come back yet.'

Not likely to now, Jack thought. He'd been on the vapours again.

'Oh well. It's a bit early to write him off yet.'

After a short silence, he decided to change tack. 'How was it?'

'Not too bad thanks.'

The strain etched on the young man's face didn't quite match the words, but Jack had seen worse.

Then his mood seemed to lighten. 'I'm flying as your number three next.'

'Good. Welcome aboard. I'll just go and check inside, then I'll get JC and we'll have a chat.'

The young officer seemed in a better frame of mind as he walked away. But it was bad news about Piers. If he didn't return, they'd have to find another flight commander.

Alex's father looked up, his face breaking into a beaming smile.

'Son. Good to see you.'

He walked from behind the cheese counter wiping his hands on his apron. As he approached Alex, his face showed the first hint of concern.

'Nothing wrong, is there?'

Apart from the battered face and the neck brace you

356

mean? It was as if his father feared a more sinister reason for the sudden return: cowardice, or some other failure to make the grade.

'No, just a cricked neck. They've put me off flying for a couple of days, so I thought I'd come home.'

The smile returned. 'Oh, that's alright then. Good to see you.'

He clapped Alex on the back and, radiating pride, turned to beam at his fellow shop assistants.

Angela looked deathly pale. Sophie hadn't heard the message that had caused her such distress, but she'd seen the young girl stagger as if from a physical blow, her face cracking in anguish. Had she looked the same when she'd heard about Alex?

It must be Piers White. She hoped he'd be alright. It would be horrible for Alex to return to bad news about his friend.

Whitcliffe was one of Alex's favourite spots. On the hill opposite, Ludlow was laid out in the afternoon sun: the castle above the curving River Teme, the mediaeval walls, Dinham House, the tower of St Lawrence's Parish Church and the other buildings stretching to the dome of the Catholic Church that dominated the top of the town.

He seemed to have spent most of his childhood within 500 yards of this very spot, exploring the Cromwellian Trenches, rolling down the dingle and collecting fossils from the limestone cliffs above the river and the Bread Walk. It had been a good time, largely free of conflict and worry.

The same could not be said of his new life. But, despite the constant fear and danger, he wouldn't want to be anywhere other than 646 Squadron, fighting alongside Muddy, Piers, Olly and Jack. Although it was complete madness, he ached to be with them.

He looked down at his shaking hands and screwed his eyes.

The Ops Room was tense. A formation had crossed the North Foreland and split to the north and south of the Estuary. Group were holding the Squadrons back this time, but they were expecting the call to action any moment.

The telephone rang and Sophie looked to the Controller.

Kelvin Rice picked up the phone with an emphatic, 'Here goes.'

But, when he put the handset down, rather than pass instructions to the others on the makeshift platform, he looked into the room and smiled, signalling someone to approach him.

Angela moved from her post, looking nervous. Perhaps she was less adept than Sophie at reading the Controller's facial expressions. The newly grafted skin could make it difficult. The pretty blonde stopped in front him, still looking pensive. He leaned over and spoke quietly to her. She grasped the edge of the table.

For a moment, Sophie thought it was she who'd misinterpreted the Controller's emotions, but when Angela turned and walked towards her, her face broke into a relieved smile. And as she rounded the map, she was greeted with more smiles and pats on the back. It was very difficult to keep secrets.

Kelvin Rice leaned towards Sophie. 'Young White. Crash landed in a field near Otford. Bit of a bump on the head, but otherwise all right. Lucky chap.' He looked towards Angela. 'In more ways than one.'

Sophie felt the pain behind the words.

The telephone rang again.

On the way to pick up his dad from work, Alex dropped into Toddington's, the Town's premier gentlemens' outfitter. He'd been in with his mother many times before, first, when he was 11, to be fitted with his Grammar School uniform, and thereafter, whenever he'd grown out of items, or the uniform requirements had changed with age.

He'd always dreaded it.

Toddington's staff could smell money, or the lack of it, at 20 paces, and say 'sir' and 'madam' with complete insincerity, much like the drill instructors he'd met since. His mother's relative poverty had been all too obvious, and he'd known they were being sneered at during their visits, but he'd lacked the confidence to challenge the affront. It was one of the many reasons for his constant feelings of inadequacy in social situations.

So, it was with a mixture of trepidation and curiosity that he opened the door and entered. The distinctive ring of the bell; the sight of the large wooden drawers lining every wall; the glass topped counters displaying gloves and ties; the even more distinctive smell, a cocktail of wood, leather and mothballs; all had the affect of taking him straight back to those earlier humiliations.

But as soon as he spotted the first shop assistant, he sensed that things had changed.

'Good evening, sir. How may we help you?'

No whiff of insincerity. The man was positively fawning, like Uriah Heep in a school production of

David Copperfield.

'I'd like to look at some silk scarves, please.'

'Certainly, sir, if you'd like to come this way.'

Bobbing humbly, the man shuffled ahead, looking back every few paces to check that he was being followed, dipping his head each time and smiling again. He led Alex round a corner and down some steps, glided behind a counter and flourished an arm across a display of scarves beneath the glass.

'I can find some more if sir is looking for a particular colour or pattern.'

'I don't suppose you've got any in Ludlow Grammar School colours?'

'Sorry, no, but we have some that are equally colourful.' He reached down behind the counter.

'No, no. It's alright thank you. In that case, I'll just take a plain white one.'

The man reached in and held a white silk scarf in his hands for Alex to inspect.

'That will be fine, thank you.'

He had a picture of Olly, smiling, his blue and white scarf blowing in the wind. He'd have loved to have returned with something more garish, but not just for the sake of it.

Jack tried to find a reason for hope, but there was none. Olly was dead.

They'd just smashed through the first line of Dorniers, when the Spitfire to his left, Olly's Spitfire, burst into flame. The fuel tank and cockpit were ablaze, the canopy shut.

Jack flew alongside the fireball, oblivious of the combat around him, until tracer flashed across his canopy and he was forced to pull away. But even with the aircraft out of sight, his mind tortured itself with images of the young officer struggling to release his canopy as the flames burned his flesh.

Such had been the intensity of the fire that he hadn't actually witnessed those final moments, as he had the old CO's, but he was just as affected – even more so.

Olly Barrett had seemed the epitome of British youth, physically handsome, mentally tough enough to overcome his fear, but gentle and selfless in support of others.

Why him?

The rest of the combat was a blur. Jack pushed and pulled, fired and was fired upon, but his mind was elsewhere. When his ammunition ran out, he rolled inverted and dived for the ground. Ahead of him, the sun was an orange ball sinking towards a western horizon tinged with gold. It failed to register on his numbed senses.

Squadron Leader Rice had refused to leave until Dragon had landed. Now, he and his relief were deep in discussion. Sophie picked up her bag and turned to go. Looking back, she returned his wave and walked into the shop. It was like walking into a different world.

In the Ops Room, the light was harsh, the pace frenetic. Here, much of the shop was in shadow, and there seemed little reason to hurry anything. The chemist was serving an elderly woman, and the two shop girls were leaning against the dark drawers chatting.

Sophie realised she was drawn more to the light than the shadow. How would she cope when all this was over?

It could be horrible, like the last two nights, but it was also exciting, life-affirming.

She loved being at the centre of things, seeing the battle unfolding, the thrusts and counter-thrusts. The losses were terrible, and her feelings for Alex had added a new anxiety, but, more than anything now, she feared a return to university, and the mundane existence that was likely to follow.

Sighing, she opened the shop door. The cheery tinkle of the bell and the bright evening sunshine precipitated a lightening of mood. She took a piece of paper from her pocket. The Section Officer had spent the day organizing billets in local homes for them all. She looked at the address and wondered what kind of welcome she'd find at 'The Gables'.

Alex met his father as the shop was closing. They walked home together, crossing the Bull Ring and strolling through Tower Street, up Galdeford and into Gravel Hill. He tried to paint a more realistic picture than he had for his mum. But, whereas she would have been interested in every little snippet he had to offer, no matter how painful to her, his father was less willing to engage.

After listening to Alex's attempts to explain Squadron life, he brought the conversation onto more familiar ground, spending the rest of the walk telling his son about the difficulty of getting tea and sugar for the shop, and rifles and ammunition for his local volunteer unit.

He'd been the same during Alex's flying training, nodding politely at his son's stories and explanations, but not really grasping what he was trying to convey. How much more difficult then to understand what it was like flying a modern fighter into combat?

Alex felt deflated, but tried not to show it. His life was so different from anything in his father's experience. And the man had sacrificed so much to put him where he was now. It would be churlish to sink into resentment at his inability to understand. Whatever the few hours at home might provide, it was not going to be an opportunity to talk through his fears.

The door opened and he could see his mother had regained some of her composure. She still looked on him with concern, but there would be no more tears, not for the moment anyway.

Jack sat back and closed his eyes. Smithy had seen two Spitfires spiralling down. The first had been Olly's, but Pete Atkins was also missing. The omens weren't good. Smithy had watched the second aircraft for a long time, willing the pilot to get out, but his pleas had been in vain.

Much as Jack would mourn Pete's passing when confirmation came, it was thoughts of young Olly that forced themselves to the fore. He could see him on the grass with Piers and Alex, laughing and joking: the Three Musketeers.

Such friendships were doomed from the outset. He looked at Muddy and Ginge. Didn't stop you entering into them though.

He woke to the touch of a hand on his knee and the sound of his name. The sun had dipped below the horizon.

'Sorry, sir. Must have dropped off.'

'That's alright, Jack.' Muddy looked awful. 'We've just been stood down. Can we have a quick chat about tomorrow?'

Jack shivered, raised himself painfully from the deckchair, and followed his commanding officer into the hut. Already sitting there was Piers, looking none the worse for wear, apart from a small scratch on his forehead. The sight raised Jack's spirits a little.

'Where are the bandages?' he challenged.

'Sorry to disappoint,' the young man retorted, blowing a stream of smoke to join the rest of the blue fug obscuring Muddy's office ceiling. 'The Doc wouldn't even give me a plaster.'

'So you can't pretend you're not fit to fly,' Muddy joined in, chewing on his pipe. 'Clever chaps, these docs.'

Despite the light-hearted tone, his relief was clear. The loss of another flight commander could have been the end of 646 as a fighting force. They'd been teetering on the brink for days.

'So, with the obvious exceptions,' the tone and meaning were serious now – no Pete and no Olly - 'and depending on how many kites we have, I think we'll go with a similar batting order tomorrow.'

'Including Chips?' Jack asked.

'Yes, including Chips. I just wanted to give him a rest. He's taken to his brolly twice in the last few days, and I thought he deserved it.'

Muddy could have said the same or similar about several other squadron members. It was difficult to rest people when the pressure was so intense and experienced pilots were in such short supply.

'And finally, I think we should all go to the Sergeants' Mess for a beer.'

Jack was deathly tired, and keen to be with Caroline. But he couldn't miss Pete and Olly's' wake.

'Bloody good idea, sir. Can I have a lift?'

Reluctantly, Alex had agreed to visit the pub with his father. He wasn't looking forward to it. What he really wanted was a good night's sleep.

Before they set out, they sat with his mother in the cosy kitchen. He'd been telling them about Sambrook House, and then his name was being called.

He was still in the kitchen. His parents were looking down on him with expressions somewhere between sympathy and horror. He'd obviously woken from one of his nightmares.

His dad finally seemed to understand. With very few words, they helped him to bed.

As he closed his eyes for the second time, Alex thought of his friends.

Jack ran a hand down his face. Concentrating hard, he made a second attempt to put the key in the lock.

He was much later than he'd intended. Partly down to Muddy and Ginge, but he'd been a willing victim once they'd started drinking. He'd forgotten how important it was to wind down together, to salute fallen comrades. Anyway, he doubted very much whether Caroline would still be up.

'Jack?'

'Caroline!'

The light flicked on as he stepped into the tiny hall. She was holding a full length silk dressing gown around her, looking concerned.

'I heard the gate. Are you all right?'

'Yes, fine.' He shut the door. 'I've just been for a drink with the Squadron. Sorry.'

'No need to be sorry, Jack.'

He felt a surge of relief. He'd feared he might

encounter a different welcome. Whether she'd be as understanding when she found out how regular an occurrence this was, he'd have to see. If they stayed together that was. If?

'I was just worried that something had happened.'

'No, I'm fine. We lost a couple of chaps, and…well.'

'Sorry. Would you like a cup of tea?'

'Yes please.'

'Come on.' The tone was deeply sympathetic. 'Let's get your jacket off.'

He undid the buttons and she slipped it from his shoulders and hung it on a hook. They stood looking at one another.

She smiled. 'Come on.'

Taking his hand as if he were a wayward child, she led him into the kitchen.

Chapter 10 – Tuesday 3rd September 1940

Jack opened the door to escape the oppressive fug in the dispersal hut.

'Bugger!'

What had happened to one fine day and a week of rain? It was the seventh beautiful morning on the trot. Not a cloud in the sky, although there was meant to be mist on the lower ground.

He took a mouthful of tea and grimaced. The sooner the NAAFI wagon arrived with breakfast the better. Only toast could scrape the fur off his teeth and mouth. He leaned against the doorpost and grimaced again as a beery reflux rose in his throat.

What had Caroline had to put up with?

From years of living in dormitories, he knew he was a loud mouth breather – the fallout from his broken nose – but also, with drink taken, a terrible snorer. He'd offered, albeit half-heartedly, to sleep in his own room, but she' refused to hear of it. She must have had a horrid night, but had shown not a hint of disapproval as he'd let himself out again.

How had their relationship developed as it had in such a short space of time? He'd been with Gwen for three years, and there'd been almost nothing beyond passionate kisses. But with Caroline. After three days…!

No point in trying to analyse it. Just enjoy it while it lasted. But how long would that be?

He looked up at the clear blue sky, sighed, and walked out onto the dewy grass.

Sophie watched the familiar early morning plot over the Pas de Calais.

'An hour later than yesterday, sir,' she said, trying to sound cheery.

'I suppose so,' Kelvin Rice replied. 'Thankful for small mercies and all that.'

He didn't look very thankful, she thought. But then a mischievous smile crossed his lips.

'What'll it be today then, Assistant Section Officer Preston-Wright? Airfields or factories?'

'Both, Squadron Leader Rice,' she replied playfully.

'Come on, you can't have it all ways.'

'Why not?'

'Well alright then. You're probably right anyway.'

She sensed a disapproving huff from the Flight Sergeant next to her.

The older woman looked away and Kelvin Rice made what Sophie guessed was meant to be a glum face. She giggled silently behind her hand. After another brief conspiratorial look, they returned to their own thoughts.

The Gables was a large detached house in a leafy avenue, and she'd been given a spacious bedroom overlooking a lovely back garden. She even had her own bathroom, an unexpected and welcome luxury. The couple, a bank manager and his wife, had been very friendly, inviting her to join them for supper, and in the sitting room later, where they'd swapped brief life histories before settling back to read and listen to the wireless. And they'd invited her to take breakfast with them.

She'd been made to feel very welcome. The major uncertainty of course, was the length of her stay, and, although they hadn't asked, she'd apologised for not being able to provide an answer.

At least as long as the raids on the Station lasted, she guessed. In the meantime, she'd fallen on her feet with a childless couple who seemed only too keen to treat her like a family friend, a daughter even.

'Here we go, everybody.'

Squadron Leader Rice's voice drew her eyes to the map. The black counter was setting out across the Channel.

They had ten kites. Where the engineers kept pulling them from was beyond Jack, but he wasn't complaining.

Much to Dunc's disgust, he was being left on the ground to look after the new boys again.

'I'm a bloody fighter pilot not a nursemaid,' he muttered as he walked away from a smiling Muddy.

Jack watched for another couple of seconds before looking down at the writing pad.

'*Dear Gwen,*

'*Thank you for your letter, which I received last Thursday. Sorry for the delay in replying, but things have been very busy here. Although I was sad when I read it, I am glad you chose to write rather than wait for us to see one another face to face. I have no idea when I will next be home.*

'*I agree that things had been building for some time, but I had not realised how much until our last night together. As you say, I want to stay in the RAF, and I know you would not be happy away from your friends and family. That seems to leave us with no way out.*

'*Thank you for a wonderful three years, and I hope we can still be friends. I also wish you and your family every good fortune in the future.*

'Best wishes, Jack.'

It wasn't a very clever letter, but it had been hanging over him for so long that he just needed to send something. It would have to do.

'Group are betting this is the one with the bombers,' Kelvin Rice announced, putting the phone back in its cradle.

The Observer Corps had confirmed that several earlier formations had comprised all Messerschmitt 109s. They'd been ignored, and all eyes were now on the plot of 150 plus approaching Margate.

'Hopefully, by the time we set off, the 109s will be short on fuel and heading for home.'

Sophie nodded sagely. It all made perfect sense sitting in the warm looking at counters on a map. But she wondered how clever any of their guesses would seem if your life depended on them.

Angela leaned over and raked the counter back towards her. She and the WAAF next to her both fiddled with plaques, then raked on a counter each. The formation had split, one remnant heading west along the south coast of the Estuary, the other along the north.

Airfields or factories?

Tired and hung over as he was, Jack could not but admire the beauty of the scene beneath him. The countryside was almost entirely covered by a sea of swirling mist, the surface broken only by dotted islands of variegated green and the odd tall chimney and mast.

To his front, another scene of beauty, eight shapely machines of gleaming metal and perspex: Piers's pair, and Smithy and Muddy's vics, hanging in the deep blue sky. And slightly low and back to his right, JC's Spitfire was caught in profile, its sleek lines and vibrant colours framed by the background of brilliant white.

All the aircraft were in constant motion, inching up and down, forward and back, their pilots striving to maintain a steady position in the formation.

'Dragon, this is Bastion, eighty plus bandits passing Whitstable, angels one five. Vector zero eight zero.'

The interruption shattered any illusion of a quiet morning's formation practice.

'Bastion, this is Dragon leader. Wilco, passing angels ten.'

Reluctantly, Jack drew his eyes away from the mist and the Spitfires, and recommenced scanning the sky for the enemy.

'Back to the real world.'

Alex's mother pottered about the kitchen, wiping down surfaces and sneaking concerned glances at him as he ate his toast. No assurance he could give would convince her he was as safe as he'd tried to make out. And his overwhelming fatigue had been only too apparent. They hadn't even bothered to wake him when his father went to work. In fact, his mother had left him in bed so long it would be a rush to make his train.

The only thing that might cheer her up was to tell her about Sophie. But, for some reason, he decided to keep that to himself.

At least his neck felt easier, but even that seemed to add to his mother's anxiety.

'Are you sure? Shouldn't you give it another day or

two? Why don't you give them a ring?'

He knew she was trying to protect him, but he had to get away, to get back. For once, he hadn't been plagued with nightmares, but he felt that the longer he stayed in these cosy surroundings, the harder it would be to face combat again. Better to return straight away. And he wanted to get back, to Olly, Piers and Jack, and to Sophie.

'I'll just go and tidy up, Mum.'

'All right, son. But put that brace back on!'

Jack looked down to his left at the large enemy formation heading away from them across the Medway to the north of Gillingham. The dark shapes stood out against the milky backdrop of the fast dispersing mist: about 25 Dorniers escorted by about forty 110s and twenty 109s. The fighters seemed to be at the same height as the bombers, so they'd probably get only one clear run. Better make it count.

Muddy had put them in the ideal place, above and behind in line abreast, ready to dive out of the sun.

'Dragon, here we go. Priority to the bombers, and good luck.'

Jack eased the stick forward to follow Chips and the other aircraft strung out to his left. To his right, JC followed him. It was very tempting to go for the fighters spread out to the sides rather than the bombers, packed tightly in the centre. It would certainly be safer.

'Bombers, Jack.'

He picked a Dornier to the rear right, wound the wingspan into the reflector sight and hoped that Chips and JC had picked different targets.

After a few seconds, they were diving steeply, the distance closing fast as their speed rose through 420 miles an hour. He took a quick look around. JC was tucked in nicely, no intruders were diving on them and the escorting fighters were maintaining heading. They were, as yet, unseen.

He tensed. The bombers really were close together. He worked out an escape plan and hoped they wouldn't all aim for the same gap. No time to compare notes.

Five hundred yards. Chips began to fire and fire was returned.

Four hundred and fifty miles an hour and 250 yards. Aiming off, Jack pressed the gun button. The Dornier flew into his stream of tracer and he pushed to pass behind its tailplane.

A bright flash drew his eyes to the left. A Spitfire was burying itself in the upper fuselage of a bomber. He grimaced as fighter and bomber merged completely, before bursting into a shower of tumbling wreckage. Two days ago, Alex had been lucky. Chips had not shared the same good fortune.

Would he ever stop witnessing the deaths of close friends and comrades?

'No time for this, Jack.'

Beyond the falling debris, a few other bombers were smoking, and at least one was dropping from the formation. The enemy fighters were reacting, noses and wings dropping as they dived in.

He pulled, grunting as the g piled on and his vision dimmed. Pointing skywards, he eased the pressure on the stick. As his sight was restored, all hope of an unopposed second attack was crushed. There were just too many fighters.

'Oh well.'

He picked a 110 and eased left to attack it head on.

They both fired, rushing towards one another at over 600 miles an hour. He felt no impacts and passed so close above the Messerschmitt that his belly must almost have scraped its canopy.

Tracer arced in from his left. He pulled towards it, his arms already aching and sweat forming on his brow. Head on to an inverted 109. Or was he inverted? He fired. Again, no impacts and they passed, canopy to canopy, about five feet apart.

'There must be easier ways.'

He pulled left and down in an attempt to gain more energy.

An unidentified wingtip narrowly missed his canopy and another 109 appeared to his right. He reversed his turn, reaching the buffet far too quickly. Tracer flashed past, as did the Messerschmitt. It was going too fast to come back at him.

More Spitfires had arrived and the air was full of machines, most of them fighters.

'Damn!'

The bombers were carrying on their merry way and he was in no position to follow.

His mother insisted on accompanying Alex to the station, and he had to abandon thoughts of rushing to see his father on the way.

In stark contrast to their stroll through the town just 11 days earlier, there were no stops to chat with friends and acquaintances. Perhaps his neck brace, the lurid, greeny-yellow lump on his forehead and his sunken grey eyes were too intimidating for small talk. But everyone they passed nodded sadly at his mother, seeming to share her pain.

When they parted on the platform, she remained

determinedly strong and dry-eyed, wearing an expression he hadn't seen before. He found it disconcerting, infinitely more worrying than her earlier tears. He understood those.

Close to tears himself as the train pulled away, he waved at the receding figure standing stiffly on the platform. And then, it came to him.

She didn't expect to see him again.

Jack had just reconciled himself to a series of fleeting engagements, when low to his left he spotted a Messerschmitt 109 stalking a Spitfire.

Without hesitation, he rolled inverted and pulled. The 109 was 1,000 feet below, closing fast on its unsuspecting prey from about 700 yards. But, as so often happened, its pilot seemed totally fixated on his target, head forward, urging his aircraft to close the gap more swiftly.

Jack arced down, easing his reflector sight through the Spitfire from nose to tail, and towards the Messerschmitt.

'Just a bit longer.'

He pressed the gun button. The German pilot, racing into a hail of glowing metal, looked up.

'Too late, Butt.'

Tracer and 109 converged. Large chunks flew off the Messerschmitt's engine cowling and its canopy shattered. As Jack passed behind, there was an orange flash. He checked his dive, rolled right, pulled, grunting against the g, and looked up. A flaming meteorite was hurtling through the sky, two dark rectangles tumbling away to either side.

He watched for a few seconds, then weaved and looked around to see if he himself was being stalked.

Nothing, not even the other Spitfire. But ominous pillars of smoke rose from the direction of Tilbury and the docks. They seemed to be getting closer to London all the time.

He suddenly felt incredibly weary. How much longer could he keep this up? And how much longer would his luck hold out?

The black plots were heading for the coast, still harried by a sprinkling of red counters, representing the few squadrons with fuel and ammunition remaining. 646 weren't among them; they were approaching Biggin, while 637 had already landed at Croydon. 79 were on their way back to Hawkinge.

Sophie watched Kelvin Rice put his head in his hands. Everyone on the platform looked desperately tired. And around the room, the girls were no longer gossiping or knitting in the quieter moments, but sitting back and closing their eyes. The air raids didn't help of course. They'd just suffered another; short-lived, thank goodness, but you didn't know that when the sirens sounded and the tremors began.

The pilots may be bearing the biggest burden, but she couldn't help thinking that they were all beginning to run out of steam.

And it was only just after 10.00am.

Jack finished his landing run, and turned right towards dispersal. It was hard to tell, but he wasn't sure there weren't a few more craters scarring the grass.

'Bloody hell!'

The Spitfire 100 yards to his left had suddenly pitched forward, leaving only its rear fuselage and tailplane visible, pointing up at 45 degrees.

They sat outside, listening to the sounds escaping the CO's office. The words were impossible to catch, but not the meaning.

'Serves the cocky bastard right,' Ginge ventured unsympathetically.

'Couldn't have happened to a nicer chap,' Dunc added, smoothing his sandy moustache.

Jack looked around. Twenty yards away, the new boys sat, staring at the ground. The prospect of combat was bad enough, but the danger of taxying into a crater suddenly seemed infinitely worse. They cringed at every new blast from the hut.

By contrast, the old hands sat around giggling like a gaggle of schoolchildren. But Jack knew their reaction had as much to do with relief as malevolence. Bunter deserved every syllable of the first rate bollocking from Muddy. After all, he'd denied them the use of another priceless aircraft. But they were all so knackered that, in truth, it could have been any of them.

The door opened and, red in the face, Bunter stepped out. Without looking towards them, he turned to walk along the front of the hut.

'Give my regards to the Station Commander, sir.'

Bunter turned and flicked the V sign at Ginge, then carried on towards his car.

Jack felt genuinely sorry for the young officer, setting off for his second interview without tea. He was doing well in the air, but this certainly hadn't strengthened his claim for elevation within the Squadron hierarchy.

Muddy stepped out.

Jack could tell the old lags viewed him with added

respect. The bollocking had marked the final step in his transition from flight commander to CO. But the new boys looked on him with fear. His friend wouldn't welcome that development, but, in the long run, it might not do him or them any harm.

At least they'd all be bloody careful how they taxyed for a while.

Alex had removed the neck brace. When he studied his reflection, he didn't think he looked that bad. Certainly better than he had on the journey to Ludlow. Thirteen solid hours of sleep had done him the world of good - physically.

Mentally, he wasn't so sure. He'd discussed none of the issues that plagued him: the pressures of combat, the loss of friends, or even the advisability of undertaking a relationship in such dangerous times. And, although he was trying not to dwell on it, his mother's demeanour on parting was causing him serious disquiet.

Was her fear just the natural concern of a mother, or was there more to it? After all, he'd already had premonitions of his own death, one as recently as yesterday, when sitting on Whitcliffe overlooking the town.

Was it totally irrational that she should have the same feeling?

He didn't want to think about it. Jack suspected his friend Binky's frame of mind had contributed to his downfall. Yet here he was, falling into the same trap. Ugh!

He needed to get back to his friends.

Muddy had asked Jack to lead the Squadron again.

On his right wing, flying for the first time, he had the sergeant who'd arrived with JC and Harry Beaumont five days previously. After so long on the ground, and seeing so many pilots fail to return, Sergeant Woody Woodham had every right to be nervous. But so far, he was doing fine.

And it looked like being one of the rare occasions in the last few weeks when they'd fail to meet the enemy. The first formation they'd been vectored towards had turned tail and headed back out to sea, and it sounded as if their second group of bandits was doing the same. Unless they bumped into a force of free hunters, they could land without firing a single shot in anger. Should please the armourers at least.

'Dragon, this is Bastion. Pancake. I say again, pancake.'

Good. If they could see the enemy off without risking the loss of pilots and aircraft, so much the better. This was turning into a real battle of attrition, and it was hard to see how they could win if the pressure on their airfields was maintained.

'Roger, Bastion. This is Dragon Leader. Coming home.'

'Group say there aren't any suitable replacements at the moment.'

Sophie knew this was one conversation to which she should not be privy. But, with her proximity to the platform, the Station Commander's pathetic attempt at a lowered voice and her own interest in the subject matter, it was impossible not to eavesdrop.

'That's frightening enough on its own, sir, but what with Olly Barratt and Sergeant Atkins yesterday, and Chips today, there won't be any of them left soon.'

Sophie gasped. She didn't know who Atkins or Chips were, but Olly. She pictured the handsome young pilot with striking blue eyes at the Sergeants' Mess dance, marching Alex over, and then laughing at Piers's baiting of Bunter.

She looked across the map at the dark haired young WAAF next to Angela. She'd have to make discrete inquiries to find out whether Betty and Olly had hit it off that night, like Angela and Piers. But even if they hadn't, she knew at least one person who'd be devastated at news of the young man's death. And how was he going to find out?

When she drifted back to the conversation, the Station Commander was talking.

'…so not even a flight commander?'

'No sir, none of them available either. By my reckoning, they're down to thirteen today. They could have sixteen tomorrow, if…'

'Yes, I know.' The Station Commander lowered his voice even more, looking briefly to either side. Sophie stared earnestly at a piece of paper. 'If they make it through today with no more losses. At least that idiot Arbuthnott didn't damage himself. I think he'll be a little less high and mighty for a while though.'

The Station Commander and Controller exchanged knowing smiles, and Sophie pondered another mystery.

Jack looked at Bunter. The young officer was sitting 20 yards from the rest with a face like thunder, throwing bits of grass at the ground like bolts of lightning.

What that idiot needs now, Jack thought, is a pep talk. If his sense of injustice was allowed to fester, he'd become a resentful loner, a liability to himself and the Squadron. Had it been almost anyone else, he'd have done it himself, but a character like Bunter would be more likely to heed advice from a fellow officer.

He looked across at Smithy and nodded in Bunter's direction, but the young Australian merely raised his eyes, tutted and gave a dismissive wave of the hand.

Feeling an increasing sense of urgency, Jack established eye contact with Piers. The reaction could not have been more different. There was an immediate understanding akin to telepathy. Piers nodded, raised himself from the grass and, with a mighty intake of breath, set off towards Bunter.

Sophie couldn't help smiling. Even Bunter would find it hard to talk up taxying into a bomb crater.

For once, they'd had lunch on time. It was eaten in haste, as if each mouthful would be the last before a call to scramble. And the air of disbelief continued as they returned their empty pudding dishes, filled mugs of tea and settled back into their chairs, or stretched out on the grass.

Jack was just closing his eyes when he heard his name called.

Aircraftman Hopkins ran up.

'Flight Sergeant Williams. The CO would like to see you.'

'Thanks, Chris. Any ideas?'

'Sorry, Flight. Just asked me to ask you to join him.'

Jack smiled as he raised himself from the deckchair. Another of those very polite orders.

'Ah, come in, Jack.'

Although Muddy's new office was bigger than his old one, it was no less cluttered. Most of the extra space was taken up by paperwork, much of it piled on the floor around the walls and to either side of the enormous desk.

Jack guessed his friend had stayed on the ground to try and clear some of it. But it was hard to believe he'd made much of a dent. What he had produced was three letters. The crisp white envelopes sat in a small oasis towards the front of the desk.

'Olly, Chips and Pete,' Muddy said. 'And I've just heard I'm going to have to write another one.'

Jack felt his stomach flip. 'Binky?'

'No, Harry Beaumont.'

Jack hoped he didn't look too relieved. Then he felt awful as he tried to recall who Harry Beaumont was.

'Died in Bromley Hospital this morning. Never woke up.'

Saturday, he thought. It was Saturday. He was the wingman the CO had told them about after they'd landed at Croydon.

'How's Bunter?'

Jack was having trouble keeping up.

'I saw you set Piers on him.'

'He didn't take much setting.'

'No. I could see,' Muddy smiled. 'Good choice as a flight commander, even if I do say so myself.' He laughed ironically, acknowledging Jack's wisdom in recommending his protégé. 'But did he get through?'

'I'm pretty sure he did. Bunter's back in the group anyway. Not sure they'll ever like him, but at least they're talking to him, and he seems a bit less full of himself, for a while anyway.'

'Good. We still might need him in an exec position if things carry on as they are. That's why I've called you in. Seems we're not going to get anyone parachuted in for a while. I'd welcome your view on who should take A Flight.'

Alex settled back in his seat and closed his eyes as the train puffed out of Newport station. No danger of missing his next stop. Hopefully, he'd be able to sleep. But not long after he'd closed his eyes, he found himself trapped in the close confines of a Spitfire cockpit, spinning earthwards. He started into wakefulness, sweating and feeling sick.

Slowly, the world stopped spinning. Feeling wretched, he leaned his head against the window, staring sightlessly at the sunlight playing on the Bristol Channel.

Once again, the bandits had turned about and set off for home.

But this time, Dragon had been launched earlier. The chase was on.

About 5 miles ahead and 3,000 feet below, dozens of dark shapes were passing Ashford bound for the coast.

Should catch them around Folkestone, Jack thought. Then they'd show them, unless Muddy obeyed the AOC's stricture not to operate over the Channel. He doubted it. The protection offered by enemy fighters was rarely as tenacious on the way home as on the way in. It was as if the pilots had a heightened sense of self preservation. Human nature he supposed. But it meant they had a real chance of giving the bombers a bloody nose.

'Eighty plus' the Controller had said, and that looked about right. A group of 25 Dorniers were slowly being left behind by the 30 smallest members of their escort. The remaining fighters, about 25 Messerschmitt 110s, were staying with their charges, perhaps feeling more sympathy with their twin-engined colleagues. It suited Jack. He'd rather face the 110s than the 109s.

They had nine aircraft in three vics: Muddy, Ginge and Bunter leading, with Smithy, Bomber and The Admiral to the right, and Piers with JC and Jack to the left. Jack was on the extreme left.

Apparently, somewhere out to the south, another friendly squadron was also in the chase, but they couldn't see them yet.

A picture of Caroline suddenly sprang into Jack's mind. She was naked, standing at the top of the small flight of stairs, beckoning him from where he stood in the hall. Pleasant as the image was, he knew he had to shut it out, especially if he ever wanted to experience it in reality. And he did, more than anything else he'd ever wanted in his life.

They were probably travelling 120 miles an hour faster than their prey, and they were closing fast. The 109s were already over the coast, still easing ahead. Even the 110s were starting to pull away. Perhaps they'd seen the Spitfires and decided to live to fight another day. You could only imagine what the bomber crews must be thinking as their escorts deserted them.

The coast and the Dorniers were just disappearing beneath them when Muddy broke the silence.

'Dragon, here we go.'

He lowered his aircraft's nose and the others followed suit, joining his dive upon the fleeing enemy.

'Watch for the fighters doubling back, and good luck.'

Wise words Muddy. And who was to say the 109s running ahead were the only ones about. Jack looked around. Sure enough, out to the right, beyond Piers and Muddy, another formation of aircraft was diving down. But these weren't hostiles. It was another squadron of Spitfires.

'Dragon Leader, from Blue 3. Friendlies right two o'clock two miles, diving in.'

'Roger, Blue 3.'

The other squadron looked to be about ten strong. Jack swallowed. He hadn't felt such tearful pride for days now, since before the shelter bombing. Now, it seemed more intense than ever. Someone else was obviously feeling the same.

'Bloody marvellous.'

And it was. Rarely did they get to attack in such numbers, or with such a clear tactical advantage. But there were still dangers, not least complacency.

'Steady, Dragon, steady.'

Muddy must be a bloody mind reader.

Both formations were closing on the bombers and their escorts showed no sign of returning. Jack looked over his left shoulder and quartered the sky. All clear.

Ahead, the bombers were growing fast. He eased away from Piers, placed the Dornier on the extreme left in the centre of his reflector sight, and poised his thumb over the gun button. Tracer shot ahead of several aircraft in both Spitfire squadrons, but return fire was directed mostly at the other outfit.

Mostly.

'Bugger!'

It had been too good to be true. The rear upper

gunner of his chosen Dornier began firing at him. He ignored the tightening in his stomach and the urge to duck, and waited for the distance to close.

He was just about to fire, when sparks flashed on the engine cowling and canopy arch by his left temple. The engine note changed, and a drastic deceleration forced him forward in his straps.

Instinctively, he pulled left, away from the immediate danger. As he did so, the whole airframe began to vibrate. It wasn't the pre-stall buffet. He hadn't pulled that hard. It was the damaged engine. It was juddering so violently he feared the aircraft would break apart. It was hard to keep his head still and he couldn't focus on the instruments.

He throttled back and the vibration eased a little. He was over the sea. Not by far, but far enough to get his feet wet if he had to jump over the side.

'Come on, old girl.'

He concentrated on the altimeter as it bounced around in front of him. Passing 12,000 feet in a gentle descent. He'd make land if the aircraft held together, but he'd be hard pressed to make Biggin.

'Must be 65 miles.'

He focused on the Vertical Speed Indicator.

Sixty five miles at one thousand feet a minute.

'Bugger!' Five miles short.

If he survived, he wanted to spend the night with Caroline, not at some out of the way landing site, or in another farmhouse, pleasant as it had been the last time.

He edged the throttle forward. The vibration became bone-jarring.

'All right, all right.' He throttled back again.

Eleven and a half thousand feet and still shy of the

coast. He looked at the engine instruments. The oil pressure was dropping and the temperature rising, and he seemed to be using more fuel than his low revs warranted.

'Great!'

He tightened his parachute straps.

For once, there were no further raids forming up over the French coast. Those that had just tried to repeat their morning successes had turned back and were being chased across the Channel by several squadrons, Dragon among them.

Kelvin Rice was chewing his lip.

Debating whether to recall them, Sophie wondered? The red counters were further across the Channel than she'd seen them for weeks now.

'Bastion, this is Dragon Blue 3.' The voice from the wall speaker sounded strained. More than that, broken, as if the speaker was chopping his hand across his vocal chords.

'Dragon Blue 3, this is Bastion, go ahead.'

'Bastion, Blue 3, rough running over Folkestone, approaching ten thousand feet, request vectors for base.'

'Roger, Blue 3, this is Bastion, vector three zero zero. But be advised, you have airfield in your two o'clock, range three miles.'

The Controller was giving the pilot the option of going into Hawkinge. From where Sophie was sitting, it seemed more sensible than heading for Biggin.

'Roger Bastion, vector three zero zero.'

There was no mistaking the steely determination. The pilot was going to try and make it home.

She looked toward Kelvin Rice and smiled at what

would have been raised eyebrows, if he'd had any.

Jack pulled the engine cut-out and leaned back as the propeller wound down and exhaust fumes filled the cockpit.

'Well done, Blue 3. Welcome home.'

'Thank you, Bastion. Blue 3 out.'

The Controller had been very patient, giving vectors to every airfield he'd passed. There'd been no doubt he'd wanted Jack to make use of his directions on every occasion. And he'd been right.

Jack had pushed his luck. More than that, his dogged determination to reach base had been poor airmanship. He'd risked himself and his aircraft. His rationale that they needed the aircraft at base wouldn't stand up to scrutiny. The engine must be a write-off.

'Stop beating yourself up, Jack.'

Selfish and foolish it may have been, but here he was.

The sound of a bell ended his reverie. He looked round to see a fire-truck, an ambulance and a lorry-load of groundcrew bouncing over the grass towards him. After undoing his straps and the cockpit door, he stood, stepped out onto the left wing and raised his arms.

'See, I'm fine.'

Whether fine or not, they'd dragged him off to the Docs. And to be truthful, he did feel pretty lousy.

It had been a toss up whether the engine would rattle itself to death, seize for lack of oil or run out of fuel. The tension had been draining, but it was the vibration that had taken the greatest toll, especially when he'd opened the throttle to reduce his rate of descent. His hands were numb, and a tingling sensation ran up his arms to his shoulders. He felt as if he'd been using a road drill non-stop for the last hour.

Feeling was returning slowly, but the Doc had taken him off flying for the rest of the day.

Alex decided to walk. This time, he opted to take in Oxford Street, Piccadilly Circus and Trafalgar Square. Apart from the prevalence of uniforms, life seemed so normal, and there were no trails visible in the late afternoon sky. Whitehall was more sobering. All the government buildings were heavily sandbagged, especially in Downing Street, but Big Ben and the Houses of Parliament stood defiant. And Victoria Street offered another taste of near normality.

By the time he reached Victoria, his mind was a swirl of contradictory emotions: excitement at the prospect of meeting Sophie and his friends, concern at how they'd fared during his absence, and re-awakened fear at the thought of strapping into an aircraft in the morning. It was very wearing.

He wasn't meeting Sophie until eight, so he decided to find somewhere to eat before catching the train to Bromley.

The Squadron had returned while Jack was at the Medical Centre. He was relieved to find that he'd been the only casualty.

'I don't know, first time we get a good pop at the bombers, and you get a fit of the jitters and run for home.'

'Crawl for home more like,' he fended off Ginge's banter. 'And it was a fit of the judders, not the jitters. You should try flying with half your spark plugs missing.'

'As opposed to half your marbles, you mean.'

Jack threw a cushion. His friend caught it and placed it behind his head. 'Thanks.'

The morale of most of those involved in the last engagement was high. They'd claimed three definite kills and five damaged. The two newcomers yet to fly, a short dark-haired pilot officer and a tall blond-haired sergeant, sat to one side, still looking pensive. Perhaps it was cruel to leave them on the ground, but would it be less cruel to fly them?

Their time would come soon enough.

Sophie couldn't remember another evening in the last two weeks when she'd left with no black counters on the plotting table. Was the Luftwaffe running out of steam? It would be marvellous if they were, but it was probably wishful thinking. After all, it was only one quiet evening.

And if there was a respite, it had come too late for Olly Barrett. Betty had rather fallen for him, but they'd only spent that one night together at the dance. The young WAAF had hoped to see him again this Wednesday, but...

There'd been a couple of other surprises, neither of them very welcome. First, there'd been another air raid, but it had left only a few holes on the airfield and no casualties. They hadn't even felt the tremors. Second, she'd had a telephone call from Bunter. He'd sounded very down and asked to meet her. She'd felt incredibly mean making her excuses, but it was no good giving him false hope.

The Controller was busy with his handover again, and they exchanged a brief wave as Sophie walked out of the Ops Room and into the shop. The chemist, brandishing a small brown bottle, was speaking in hushed tones to another old lady. The pair gave her a disapproving look, before turning their backs and lowering their voices even further. It didn't help Sophie's frame of mind.

Walking briskly past, she emerged into the sunlight and tried to think of something more positive. Squadron Leader Rice had said Dragon had given the bombers a real pasting. Perhaps the incessant pressure really was getting to the Germans. She hoped so.

'I don't care, Jack, you haven't had a day off since we came here.'

Jack considered countering 'neither have you', but thought better of it.

'I don't want to see you tomorrow, until the dance in the Sergeants' Mess that is.' Muddy smiled and Jack shrugged in surrender.

He was completely knackered.

'Now, Piers, what are we going to do with Alex?'

Chapter 11–Wednesday 4th September 1940

Jack woke. The room was still dark, but he knew it was morning. Only a full night's sleep could have left him so rested. He moved, grimaced and let out a small groan.

'Jack?'

'Sorry Caroline. Just a bit stiff.'

'Turn over. I'll give you a massage.'

A warm hand encouraged him onto his front. The bedclothes lifted back and he felt bare legs straddle his buttocks.

Some time, he feared he'd wake up from this marvellous dream. But not yet. Please God, not yet.

The previous evening, Alex had felt terrible. If he'd stayed at Biggin instead of swanning off to Shropshire, Sophie would have been spared the ordeal of breaking the news about Olly. Bunter's misfortune had brought a brief smile to his face, but even that was more than countered by the bad news about Chips and Pete Atkins, again, delivered by Sophie.

It had all made him rather poor company. And then, when she'd dropped him at Sambrook House, he'd met Bomber and been told of Olly's final moments. That night, surrounded by his friend's possessions, sleep had proved impossible. To escape the ghosts, he'd arranged to move in with Piers, also on his own now that Chips was gone.

This morning, sitting in the hut amongst the snoring bodies, he felt sick. But his nausea wasn't caused by images of death; it was the thought of strapping into that cockpit again. The small, dark space, the smell. It had been all he could do to set the aircraft up at first light. He was sure Lammerton and Hayman had noticed.

'Welcome back, sir.'

'Thanks, Jock. I'd say good to be back, but I'm not sure you'd believe me.'

'Oh, we'd believe anything you said, sir, wouldn't we, Dev?'

'Yes, Jock. Nice scarf by the way, sir. Very bright.'

He'd had to smile at that.

'Yes. I suppose it is a bit too clean.'

The double act had raised his spirits for a while. But now, waiting for the big black phone to ring, he was struggling to control his fear. And to cap it all, Jack wasn't about, and Bunter was still prowling. Sooner or later, he'd have to confront that issue, but not now.

Sophie was worried about Alex. It wasn't only his reaction to the deaths of his friends. That was understandable. No, she sensed something different from the youthful apprehension she'd noticed on first meeting. He seemed more fearful, his eyes less bright.

And Kelvin Rice was worried about Sophie. She was quieter, more distracted. She hadn't engaged in the playful chatter that so annoyed her flight sergeant. Boyfriend trouble? He hoped not. Or did he?

She suddenly seemed to snap out of whatever it was, looked at him and smiled.

'Things are hotting up,' he ventured.

'Yes, sir. An hour late again, but this looks like it.'

'Yes, and I hate to admit it, but you were right yesterday.'

Sophie looked at him quizzically.

'Airfields *and* factories.'

'Oh?'

'Yes. North Weald had a real pasting and they hit a factory at Brooklands. Same again today I expect.'

They both turned their attention to the map.

There were two main thrusts of attack. The first into the Estuary, the second between Dover and Folkestone.

They'd just turned back towards one another when the telephone rang.

Alex, red-faced and puffing, ran into the pen just as the engine started.

He retrieved his parachute and looked up at Lammerton, sitting in the cockpit. The fumes were clearing, the Spitfire rocking gently. Nodding at Hayman, he set his jaw and stepped forward.

Lammerton jumped out as he clambered up the wing into the slipstream. He'd been dreading this moment, but now it came to it, with the eyes of his groundcrew upon him, it was easier to step into the confined space than hang back. Yet again, the fear of failure had proved stronger than claustrophobia and fear of combat.

Jack made a small gap in the blackout and a sliver of daylight shone in. It striped Caroline's pale back as she eased out of bed, and played on the curves of hip and breast as she put on her dressing gown.

'Tea?' she asked cheerily, tying the cord.

He hadn't totally blanked out thoughts of the Squadron. And he still felt guilty at his lie in, especially as he was sure he'd just heard the sound of engines at full throttle.

But the last hour had reinforced that there was so much to live for. If his number came up tomorrow, or the next day, so be it. But today, he had to live life to the full.

'Yes please. I'll keep the bed warm, shall I?'

Alex had done his job, spotting the 109s. But they were in deep trouble. The yellow-nosed fighters, about 20 of them, were diving out of the sun from about 5,000 feet above.

As they all manoeuvred madly following Muddy's call to break, he doubted whether half the Squadron would have seen anything. They'd been caught in the climb and they'd just have to make the best of it. At least they had the first team out, minus Jack of course.

Alex broke right, pulling just hard enough to avoid the buffet. But now, should he lower the nose to gain energy, or climb into the enemy and risk stalling? Either way, he was a sitting duck. He decided to dive. Remembering Jack's advice, he also jinked madly, throwing the controls around and using as much rudder as he dared without flicking into a spin.

In seconds, he could hear his breath rasping and feel the sweat on his skin. He looked round, wincing at the pain in his neck. Tracer filled the air. He reversed his roll to the left and pulled, feeling his stomach cramp and his vision dim. A dark shape flashed behind, followed by another, much closer on his left.

He rolled to what he hoped was upright and eased the pull.

As his sight returned, he saw an aircraft spiralling down a few hundred yards ahead, smoke and flames trailing behind. It was a Spitfire.

No more tracer, but several other aircraft at a similar height, all Spitfires. One was smoking. The Messerschmitts were way below, but some were already zooming up towards them. He'd been in a section with Dusty and Dunc, but any hope of re-forming and setting out for the original bandits was gone.

'Bastion, Dragon bounced by twenty Snappers, angels one four, out.'

'Roger, Dragon, Bastion standing by.'

Alex wasn't sure why the 109s hadn't high-tailed it after their first pass, but there was no time to consider the matter. They were approaching his height again.

Was he about to enter his first dogfight?

His sphincter twitched and his palms felt sweaty against his thin flying gloves. He swallowed hard.

'Come on, Alex!'

His voice helped galvanise him. He picked a 109 flying inverted at the top of its looping climb and jinked to fall in behind. But then, 500 yards in his 10 o'clock, he saw another 109 roll off the top behind a Spitfire. Forgetting his initial target he pulled hard left and shouted.

'On your tail.'

He was turning as fast as he could, but he was going to be too late. The Spitfire passed abeam.

'Bunter, Snapper on your tail. Do something, Bunter.'

Bunter's Spitfire rolled.

The Messerschmitt followed and Alex shot behind having never been in a position to fire. He looked back but both aircraft had disappeared.

Tracer flashed over his right wing and he pulled towards it. Straining against the g, he looked over his shoulder. A 109, turning and shooting, its tracer passing menacingly close. His neck and arms already ached, but he pulled until the first hint of buffet through the stick, then eased the pressure. Running on cobbles.

Jack's phrase.

He looked back, fearing his neck was about to seize.

The 109 was still there, but its wing slots were opening, its nose dropping as it stalled. Alex was flying a tighter circle, pulling ahead. If another Snapper targeted him, he was dead. But if he stopped pulling, he was dead anyway, so he maintained the back pressure, sweat pouring from him.

Slowly, he advanced to the point where he and the German were opposite one another, both turning at the maximum rate their machines and their skill allowed. Alex didn't quite believe it, but he seemed to be flying more skilfully. He imagined the worry on the pale face looking 'up' at him across the circle.

He wasn't sure how much more his neck and arms could take, but he grunted and held on. In his effort to escape, his adversary was still pulling too hard, his aircraft slowing and losing ground every time it stalled.

Alex maintained the pressure. Any moment, he expected the German to reverse his turn, or to dive, but he pressed on, doggedly pursuing a failing policy.

Finally, Alex inched his reflector sight over the tailplane of the Messerschmitt and onto the thin fuselage ahead of it. Tensing in expectation of the noise and juddering, he pressed the gun button.

The 109's tail detached. It hung in the air while the rest of the aircraft cart-wheeled away. It was still hanging there as he shot past.

After what had seemed like several minutes of cat and mouse, the end had been startlingly quick. Groaning in relief this time, Alex eased the back pressure and flexed his limbs. He fancied he could feel his neck graunching as he swivelled his head gingerly to look around. Nothing. The sky was empty.

He'd won his first dogfight. But there was no feeling of triumph, and any slight sense of achievement was buried beneath utter weariness.

Why had she fallen for a pilot?

She was sure the voice from the speaker had been Alex's. The warning had been for Bunter, but what had happened since? How had they fared against 20 Snappers?

She looked across at the Controller. His appearance re-awakened old fears. Please no.

'Sir?'

'You heard, Alex. Don't look so stunned. I want you to take Yellow Section.'

Alex had heard. But hearing a second time made it no easier to comprehend.

'Look.' The CO leaned back and put his pipe down. 'I admit that if Smithy was around, you'd have had to wait a bit longer, but he's not.'

Smithy's had been the aircraft trailing smoke. He hadn't returned. Neither had Jet. He'd been the one in the fiery spiralling dive.

Muddy continued. 'Whether you've realised it or not, you've been making a very good impression, Alex. You're ready for this, and no-one will begrudge you a section lead.'

Despite his CO's words, Alex didn't feel ready, and he could think of at least one person who wouldn't be best pleased.

'Now go and find Bailey and Turner and give them

the benefit of your superior ability and experience.'

He leaned forward and took up his pipe, making it evident that the 'quick chat' was at an end.

Alex saluted. 'Thank you, sir.'

He still sounded hesitant, Muddy thought, and his elevation was a bit earlier than planned, but he'd just have to get on with it. Without looking up, he said, 'Good. Send in Piers, would you?'

Jack put his mug on the kitchen table. Discounting the night Caroline had tended his wounds, and the two nights of unthinking passion, this was the first domestic situation they'd been in since his arrival at 5 Keston Avenue. He felt strangely ill at ease.

Would they be as compatible out of bed as they seemed to be in it?

Caroline looked as if she might share the same concern. 'More toast?'

'No thanks, I'm totally satisfied. Inside and out.'

Caroline blushed, but returned his smile.

He decided to persevere with being more open.

'It seems strange being together during daylight.' Clumsily put, but he hoped she knew what he meant.

'Yes. I was just thinking something similar. I've really enjoyed the last two nights, but we haven't exactly done much talking, have we?'

She blushed again.

He rose, walked to where she stood next to the stove and took her hand. 'No, but I want to put that right.'

'And me, Jack.'

They joined in a tender embrace.

If the Luftwaffe allowed, he sensed he could find happiness with this woman.

'Don't worry, Alex, I know I'm older and uglier than you, but I'm more than happy to bow to your greater experience at this lark.'

Some lark, Alex thought, but he was grateful for Lieutenant James Turner RN's support.

'And I'm sure Bomber feels the same.'

The tall, moustachioed, former bomber pilot nodded his agreement. 'Apart from the uglier bit that is.' He smiled, before adopting a more serious, almost pleading, expression. 'Look, Alex, everything's been a complete blur to me so far. I'll take any advice I can get.'

It's still a blur to me, Alex thought. But, having been put in this position of trust, he had to give it his all. At least his personal fears and phobias seemed to have been sidelined for the moment.

'Okay, I'm not sure what Smithy used to tell you, but once we're in contact, don't worry about trying to stick to me or any of that rubbish. You can't fly in close formation and look out for the enemy, and I'll be making it as difficult as possible for anyone to follow me anyway.

'So concentrate on your own targets, and your own survival. And while I think of it...'

Alex began handing down some of the wisdom Jack had passed on to him.

Caroline waved as Jack drove out of the avenue in the pretty green sports car. A net curtain twitched on the other side of the road.

If only they knew the half of it. She really was a fallen woman. She'd thought about it endlessly, and she could only hope that Alfie would understand. She didn't love him any less. She'd just been unable to help herself when Jack came on the scene. And she was sure Jack understood, that he didn't think any less of her for the ease with which she'd slipped into his embrace. She certainly hoped not.

Wrapping her cardigan around her at a sudden chill, she turned and walked back into the house.

Alex looked to either side. Were those two Spitfires following *him*? He could still barely believe it, or suppress his pride. The fears of the morning had been replaced with an overwhelming sense of responsibility for the two older men following him into battle.

Only Muddy, Ginge and Bunter were ahead of him, their aircraft clawing for height. Three hundred plus coasting in between Dover and Beachy Head, the Controller had said. At least they'd have plenty of time to get above them – if they weren't bounced again. The memory set him to quartering the sky.

Bomber was staring straight ahead.

'Yellow Three?'

The mild admonition had an immediate effect, and the tall pilot's head began moving again.

This was just too bizarre.

They'd had longer on the ground than expected, and he'd passed on as much knowledge as he could. And yet, when the scramble call came just before one, he knew he wouldn't have covered the circumstances they'd encounter in the air. Sod's Law. But more than that. Even when they faced a similar enemy formation, at a similar height and position, the combat always developed in an unexpected way. You just couldn't cover everything.

He looked at Bunter's aircraft bobbing 50 yards

ahead of him. They hadn't had their encounter yet. Perhaps the other man was avoiding him. He certainly hadn't been thanked for his warning earlier in the day. It was a worry, but not one to be concerned with now.

'Dragon, this is Bastion, your bandits, fifty plus, ten miles north of Hastings, angels one six, vector one one zero.'

'Bastion, this is Dragon Leader, wilco, passing angels ten.'

Sophie had heard Alex was safe, but it was still a relief to hear his voice, no matter how briefly. Was he leading a section? She felt a flush of pride. Irrational perhaps, but nonetheless real for that.

The unusually wide enemy formation had crossed the Channel and split into five elements, all heading in different directions. There was a smaller formation approaching the coast further to the west, but she was watching Hostile 23. Squadron Leader Rice was directing Dragon towards its 50 aircraft. They seemed to be heading for the Medway, or maybe the Isle of Sheppey.

Caroline's work had absolved Jack of the guilt of leaving her behind. This was one journey he had to make on his own. He already felt guilty enough for seeing the visit as an ordeal, but it was hard to think of it as anything else.

When he'd outlined his intentions the previous evening, Muddy had forced the car on him, said Chips had bequeathed it to the Squadron as a runabout. Some runabout! The Riley was a definite cut above the previous bangers they'd inherited. A beautiful car and a delight to drive.

Sighing, he resolved not to think of what might confront him at his destination, but to enjoy the journey. Driving down Westerham Hill, the beautiful Kent countryside was laid out before him. But it wasn't long before his eyes drifted up from the green fields and hedges to the sky, searching as if he was airborne. The weather was glorious, hardly a cloud in the sky, but to the south and east, at the limits of his vision, he fancied he could see signs of combat: a barely visible jumble of thin white lines.

The pristine blue ahead had suddenly erupted into a rash of grey and white threads. Those responsible were too distant to be seen, but Alex had no doubt that several squadrons were already in combat. And Dragon were about to add their own trails to the chaotic mix.

Below them were 20 Heinkels and about thirty 109s. On the call into line abreast, Alex slid Yellow section to the right of Muddy's Red. Piers had moved Green Section to the left of the line, and Dusty's Blue Section were now tucked in to Alex's right.

He wondered briefly how the new pilot officer next to Piers was feeling, and admonished himself for not even knowing the young man's name. The fact that he'd been away for two days hardly seemed sufficient excuse.

The fear that had threatened to unhinge him only a few hours previously had not re-surfaced – yet. He looked to either side at his two charges. They gave determined thumbs-ups in return to his barely perceptible nod.

'Good lads.'

He smiled. His 'lads' were much older and better

versed in the ways of their respective Services than him. And yet, here they were, being led into battle by a 19 year old that had joined the Squadron only a week earlier.

Would this be the defining period of his life? Was it all to be anti-climax from here? Muddy's voice broke in.

'Dragon, in we go lads. Watch out for Snappers.'

Alex eased the stick forward to follow his squadron commander into the dive. Bomber and the Admiral followed him, as did the rest of the formation.

Now, hold your nerve lads. Don't do a Chips.

Best he remembered that himself. He picked a Heinkel to the rear centre of the formation and had a last look round for enemy fighters. All clear, and the 109s in the escort seemed oblivious of their approach.

Bunter fired. Alex resisted the urge to follow suit and was glad to see Bomber and The Admiral show the same restraint. The enemy gunners took advantage of the warning though. Fiery rods of tracer raced past and the enemy fighters reacted, turning towards the bombers.

'Blast you, Bunter.'

The 109s would still be too late to catch their first pass. The Heinkel grew in his reflector sight.

'Wait, Alex, wait. Now!'

He jabbed his thumb down and his Spitfire shuddered as his rounds sped towards the upper fuselage of the Heinkel. Rolling right, he pulled to pass behind it, relieved to see The Admiral perform a similar manoeuvre.

After a short pause, he rolled left, pulled and looked up, wincing at the pain in his neck. He must have hit the bomber, but he saw no evidence before his vision dimmed with the onset of g. As his Spitfire's nose came above the horizon, he eased the pull and looked for his wingmen. Failing to spot either among the jumble of aircraft hurtling about beneath the bomber stream, he picked another Heinkel toward the front of the formation.

Tracer arced over his cockpit. He turned right towards it. Something flashed beneath him.

'The bombers, Alex.'

Reversing his turn again, he picked another Heinkel. And again, a stream of tracer distracted him. Two 109s were arcing in from the left. Gritting his teeth, he turned towards them, firing as the leader transited his gunsight. A dark shape passed above. Rolling out, he looked right to see another 109, firing as it came. He pulled up and tried to barrel roll onto its tail. But, somewhere over the top, with his vision dimming, he became disorientated.

In an instant, the sense of control he'd revelled in since Muddy made him a section leader evaporated. He was upside down, and falling. The cold sweat of fear and airsickness returned.

Tracer. He rolled. The aircraft seemed to wallow and his stomach rose into his mouth as if he'd gone over a humpback bridge.

After what seemed an age, he was right way up, but still in a cold sweat. How could things disintegrate so quickly?

He seemed to have fallen out of the battle and to be on his own again. No, he wasn't. Tracer! From behind.

Fighting down the sickness, he slammed the stick to the right and pulled. The pain in his neck was intense, but he fought the g to look round. A 109, further back than the one in the morning, but no less deadly if he couldn't evade it.

He was in a bind. If he kept turning, the Messerschmitt could turn inside, keeping him in upper plan view, an easy target. If he ran away, he'd still be a target. But perhaps a less inviting one if he could maintain his distance.

Ignoring the pain in his neck, he reversed the turn and pulled, rolling out when the German disappeared behind his tail. Then, he began to jink wildly, pushing on the throttle and urging his aircraft forward.

Every few seconds, he spotted the 109 in his rear view mirror. Tracer flashed past to one side or the other, never far away. The wild manoeuvring worsened his airsickness and his mood darkened. He felt as if he was moving in treacle, and his body ached.

What was the point? It was only a matter of time before the German nailed him. Why not just lie back and let it happen? He began to relax.

'Fuck that, Alex!'

He rolled hard right, reversed to the left, kept rolling until he was inverted and pulled into a dive, jinking with renewed vigour.

'Follow that, you bastard. Sorry, Mum.'

The Queen Victoria Hospital, East Grinstead, was a clean cut, low rise, red-brick building, unimpressive but for the architect's final flourish: a striking square tower. It could have been a modern factory or university building, until you stepped inside.

Jack's nose crinkled. He hated the smell. It reminded him of a childhood visit to his dad, crushed in an accident on the docks a week earlier. He'd had a fleeting glimpse of a grey face above crisp white sheets, a skeletal caricature of the rounded features he remembered. His dad had died the same night, and he'd vowed never to enter a hospital again, a promise he'd kept until the broken nose several years later.

So, what exactly was he doing here?

A young woman behind a desk smiled at him. She looked well used to witnessing similar internal debates.

'May I help you, Flight Sergeant?'

No going back now.

'Thank you. I was looking for Flying Officer Binkman.'

'Welcome back, sir.'

Hayman's cheeriness fed Alex's positive mood.

'Thank you, Dev. It's good to be back.'

He wondered how many pilots succumbed to the torpor that had threatened to overcome him. For a while, it had seemed easier to give in to the Messerschmitt than to keep on struggling. It was as if the mental and physical stresses of combat had become too much to bear.

He wasn't sure how he'd snapped out of it, but he felt immeasurably stronger for having done so.

'You've picked up a bit of damage to the left wingtip, sir.'

There were a few jagged holes Alex had failed to see from the cockpit.

'Nothing much though, are they, Dev?'

The airframe fitter looked surprised.

'I know, sir, but pretty frightening anyway, I should think.'

Alex hadn't even noticed the impacts. They could have happened any time before he'd dived away. The 109 hadn't bothered him for long after that, perhaps discouraged by his adversary's renewed vigour, or, less flatteringly, just short on fuel. Either way, he'd left Alex to return alone, buoyed by his narrow escape.

'Yes, it was a bit hairy for a while, but here I am. You'll have to do at least one more turnaround for me, I'm afraid.'

'Always a pleasure, sir,' a Scottish voice took over. 'And there's a fair bit of oil on the underside. Any indications in the cockpit?'

'No. All seemed fine, Jock. I spent a fair bit of time upside down though.'

'Och, that could be it then, sir. I'll have a wee look anyway.'

'Okay, Jock. Thanks. I expect I'll see you two again sooner rather than later.'

'Take your time, sir. We're in no hurry.'

'Nor me, but then, it's not up to me, is it? See you later.'

Alex waved and walked out of the pen.

'Jack.'

The thin, reedy, voice came from the small room to which the nurse had escorted him.

'Binky,' Jack replied, trying not to convey his shock. Buying time, he turned away to look at the young woman.

'Thank you, nurse.'

'That's alright, Flight Sergeant. No more than ten minutes, I'm afraid.'

He watched her walk away for a few seconds, then turned to his friend. Or what he assumed was his friend. There wasn't much to go on. Bloodshot eyes peered from a swathe of bandages that disappeared beneath a hospital gown. The hands were also wrapped in dressings.

'You look like a Mummy,' Jack said in as light a tone as he could manage.

'Better than getting sunburnt, old boy.' The thin voice was still cut glass. 'What, no chocolate?'

'Sorry. Didn't know whether you were allowed solids, and I know you're allergic to flowers.'

He wished he could keep the banter going, but the horrible reality was too intrusive.

'How're things?' he asked tentatively.

'Oh, could be worse they say. I have no idea.'

Jack fought to keep his composure as his friend continued in a tremulous voice, beginning to crack with emotion.

'Because, well you see, I haven't seen what I look like yet.'

'Don't worry, Binky, old boy.'

Jack looked round for the source of the confident baritone voice. A tall man in a hospital gown stood in operatic pose, arms outstretched.

'Perhaps you'll end up as handsome as me.'

The man's face was cadaverous, a patchwork of multicoloured blotches, minus some of the more usual features, such as a nose. And the flourishing arms ended in claw-like hands.

Jack was relieved at the interruption, but shocked at the appearance of the newcomer. He'd seen burns victims, most stations had at least one, but they were always further along the road to recovery. This man must be at a very early stage in the reconstruction process. Alarmingly so. Some of his skin was hanging off, as if it had failed to take.

'Jack, this is Chas Palmer. He comes in to *cheer me up* on occasion.'

'Hello, Jack, pleased to meet you. Excuse if I don't

shake hands. Can't spare the skin.'

The new pilot officer was missing. No-one had seen what had happened to him, unless Piers had, and he'd been taken straight to the medical centre with a bullet graze to the forehead. It was another serious blow to the Squadron. And to Alex. What he would do if he lost another room mate, he wasn't sure.

And the one piece of good news had a depressing caveat. Smithy had been found alive, hanging from the side of a barn by his parachute rigging lines. But the cheeky young Australian had suffered severe burns to his face and hands.

And finally, incredibly, if B Flight were scrambled before Piers returned, Muddy had asked Alex to lead it.

What was going on?

Jack was overcome, adrift in a sea of conflicting emotions. So much so that he was forced to stop in East Grinstead before driving further.

He sat in the corner of a tea room wondering what Binky might look like under all those bandages. It was hard to believe he'd be any less nightmarish than Chas, or any of the other patients he'd seen as he'd left the hospital. He'd been unable to look at them for long, cursing himself for his cowardice, even as he averted his eyes.

Would he react the same if he saw Binky with his dressings removed? And wouldn't it be kinder not to put either of them in that position?

Their friendship had been forged in the heat of an intense experience they'd shared daily, hourly. The fact that so few others knew what it was like to fly a

Spitfire, let alone fight in one, had strengthened the bond immeasurably.

Now, his friend was caught up in a new and horrific world, one from which Jack, thankfully, was excluded, and that he could never hope to understand.

Wasn't it inevitable that he'd find new friends among his fellow burns victims? And wasn't it equally inevitable that he'd feel uncomfortable in the company of old comrades?

Perhaps it would have been better if Chas had granted them a little more time alone, allowed them to break down, as would surely have been the case. Then, he'd have gained a better idea of Binky's true feelings. But he was sure the intervention had been planned, and to the second. It was probably based on corporate experience of many such hospital visits. They were protecting their own.

And it had been slickly done. Chas had eaten up the remainder of the ten minutes with clever banter in which he and Binky had been willing participants.

He stared into his empty cup. Binky's parting words still haunted him.

'Stay safe.'

The words were simple enough, expressing Binky's fear for the safety of his old friends. Had that been all there was to it, Jack could have convinced himself that the torch of friendship had been handed on to Chas and his fellow patients; that he could walk away with a clear conscience, duty fulfilled with that one visit.

But the tone had been more ambiguous. He still wasn't sure whether it had conveyed a plea for them to stay in touch, or the opposite. Stay away. It was so difficult to interpret meaning when all you could see were two watery eyes.

Standing at the small oak counter waiting to pay, Jack caught sight of his reflection in a mirrored wall behind shelves of glasses. He tried to imagine what it would be like, seeing a disfigured face you didn't recognise looking back at you. His efforts were interrupted by the waitress. As he handed over the price of a cup of tea and a small tip, she gave a coquettish smile.

Probably more taken with the wings on his chest than his looks – he'd always been self-conscious about his broken nose. But would she give the same smile if he looked like Chas, or whatever Binky looked like under those bandages?

He wasn't sure he could find the courage to visit his friend again, or whether he'd want him to.

Alex spotted Bunter sitting a short distance from the others. On impulse, he decided to clear things up there and then, while Piers wasn't around to intervene and inflame matters.

'Right, Bunter, is there something you want to say to me?'

The stockier man rolled himself upright and Alex tensed, ready for a charge. But when Bunter finally raised his head and spoke, he looked almost sheepish.

'How about, thank you and sorry.'

Alex's mouth opened in surprise.

'Yes, you heard.' The chubby face looked away as if its owner was searching for the right words. After a few moments, he turned back. 'Thank you for the warning this morning, and sorry for being such an arse about everything, especially Sophie.'

Alex felt himself colour. 'Well, thank you.'

'It's just that she was a link to home.' The words

started to tumble out. 'You know what it's like when you arrive; not knowing anybody. It was nice to see a familiar face. And it is a very pretty face, you have to admit. At first, I just used her friendship to impress my new squadron. But then… Well, let's just say I took it a bit far. Got a bit possessive. Sorry.'

Alex finally realised that Bunter, like him, was lost, and scared. He'd been hiding it behind a boorish exterior that he'd overplayed. Perhaps the episode with the crater, and the various little chats he'd received had led to a change of heart. Whatever it was, Alex was mightily relieved. He'd been dreading this confrontation, convinced it would end in fisticuffs, not his strong suit.

He held out his hand. 'Apology accepted.'

The two men smiled and clasped hands. A wolf whistle emanated from the group of chairs outside the hut.

They both turned and shouted, 'Piss off, Ginge.'

Sophie had known it was too good to be true. There was to be no second evening of peace and quiet. The hostile plot hadn't appeared until it was quite close to the coast, and there was still no estimate of numbers.

'Low level again, Sophie.' There was a look of stern determination in the Controller's dark eyes. 'Only this one isn't going to sneak through.'

Earlier, a formation of Messerschmitt 110s had taken advantage of the chaos in the upper airspace to attack an RDF station. They'd also had some success against aircraft factories again, although they'd hit only one airfield.

'Not long now, and we'll know where they're heading.'

They both jumped as the telephone rang.

Alex had never even been involved in a flight scramble before. Now, here he was leading one. He looked at the vast, uninterrupted, expanse of blue sky ahead of him. Who'd have thought it? Certainly not him. Being made a section leader had been surprise enough. But a flight! It was only a standing patrol over base, but even so.

And he'd spoken on the radios more in the last five minutes than in the preceding ten days. He couldn't help wondering if Sophie was still on shift. He hoped so, and that she recognised his voice and felt proud of him. His earlier fear had still not resurfaced, only anxiety not to let down those he was leading.

What Dunc Mason, sitting out to his left thought, he could only guess. He was so much more experienced, but he'd seemed perfectly content as Alex had briefed him. Dusty, leading Blue Section at the rear, had an even greater claim to lead the Flight, but he too had been very supportive.

They were climbing fast.

He composed his next message in his head before speaking.

'Bastion, this is Dragon B Flight, passing angels ten.'

Now, how exactly did you lead a flight attack?

'Roger, Dragon Leader, call passing angels one five.'

'Bastion, this is Dragon B Flight, wilco.'

Kelvin Rice hadn't recognised the slightly tremulous voice, but someone else had. The look of surprise on Sophie's face at the first few radio exchanges had left him in no doubt who was speaking.

She still looked amazed every time she heard him.

And it was pretty remarkable. Her beau couldn't have been on the Squadron much more than a week, and here he was leading a flight. Without being unkind to him, or doubting his ability, it showed the dire straits they were in.

He understood the reluctance to introduce new squadrons to the front line - their losses were horrendous - but Dragon were also losing pilots at an alarming rate. And not just the new boys. The more experienced were also falling fast. He couldn't believe the Squadron hadn't been relieved, and he didn't envy Muddy trying to hold it all together.

He looked to the map.

The 20 Messerschmitt 110s were still tracking towards Biggin, but the Tangmere and Hawkinge squadrons were very close now. Hopefully, the fighter bombers would be turned back before Sophie's young man had to do anything dramatic.

He looked at her nervously chewing her lip.

'Bastion, this is Dragon B Flight, passing angels one five.'

Jack sat in the kitchen of 5 Keston Avenue, drinking more tea.

It had been a very sobering afternoon. Not quite the relaxing time that Muddy had intended, but he was glad he'd made the effort. It was a weight off his mind, until he had to decide whether to make a repeat visit. But that was for the future. For now, he had to get on with his own life, the horizons of which had been expanded immeasurably by Caroline.

It wasn't just the sex, although that was pretty amazing. He'd fallen for her the moment she'd opened the door just over a week ago. She wasn't only beautiful and engaging, but also vulnerable and intriguing. He still knew so little about her.

He wasn't usually one for praying, but if there was anyone up there, please grant him the time to find out more. Inevitably, thoughts of his own survival made him think of the Squadron. What sort of day had they had? Since seeing the hint of vapour trails around lunchtime, he'd spotted no other signs of activity.

Muddy leaned against the doorpost and watched B Flight taxying back. He heaved a deep sigh. Thank goodness they'd returned without loss. Otherwise, it had been another bloody day.

Jet and the new boy still missing, and Smithy badly burned. Without replacements, 646 Squadron was slowly withering.

It wasn't just about numbers. If the Squadron was to have a future as a fighting force, it had to retain a core of strong and experienced pilots around which to rebuild. Dusty, Dunc and Bunter were okay, and Alex was developing apace, but they weren't enough on their own to pull the Squadron through.

And he was beginning to doubt his own stamina. So much so that if B Flight had taken casualties, and Piers had been laid off by the Docs, he'd been resigned to asking Group to take them from the line. The safe return of both B Flight and Piers had delayed that conversation, for the moment at least.

'Sir?'

Muddy turned to see George Evans smile benignly from beneath his walrus moustache. 'Here's a tea, sir, and I've done those returns that were on your desk.'

'Thank you, Adj. I meant to get round to them.

Sorry.'

'No need to be sorry, sir. You've got enough on your plate without meaningless paperwork. If…if there's anything else I can take off you, just push it my way.'

The young squadron commander knew that natural reserve meant this was as close as they'd ever get to a heart to heart, but he appreciated the older man's efforts.

'Thank you, George. I'll bear it in mind.'

He watched the Adjutant walking slowly through the gloomy hut towards his desk, head bowed as if in sorrowful thought.

Having fought in 'the war to end all wars', it must be immensely sad to see men dying in such numbers again, even if the cause seemed so undeniably just.

He looked out at the small group sitting in the evening sunshine.

'Piers?'

The dark-haired young officer sprang from his chair and walked briskly towards the hut.

'The Station Commander?'

Alex, sitting amongst the others outside the hut, watched the CO and the Adjutant walking across the grass towards them in animated conversation. He smiled at the sight of the Adj, five inches shorter and many more wide, rolling over the grass at the side of the slim young squadron leader. He strained to catch the stouter man's answer.

'Yes, the Station Commander, sir. Says it's got to go.'

'And he's going to do it?'

'That's what they said, sir.'

'Right.' The CO stopped in front of them, stroked his moustache, looked at the Adj with a 'you better not be pulling my leg' expression, then pointed across the airfield. 'See that hangar over there?'

They all looked at what was, although largely an empty shell, the only substantial building remaining.

'Well, the Station Commander's going to blow it up. I know. Not something you hear every day, but there it is. He thinks that trying to knock it down is the only thing that keeps the Hun coming back, so he's going to do it for them and hope they call it a day. Might work, might not, but I suppose it's worth a try.'

'He might have a few forms to fill in when Group find out, sir.'

'Yes, Ginge, I think he might. Anyway, fifteen minutes time. If we're still on the ground, keep me a seat, will you?'

And with that he turned and walked back to the hut.

Whatever next?

Jack picked Caroline up from the NAAFI shop at 8pm and, on the spur of the moment, decided to take her to the Sergeants' Mess dance. What he hadn't reckoned on was that she'd insist on going home first to 'freshen up'. So it was over an hour later than planned when they walked through the door, giving him ample time to consider the folly of his decision.

There was quite a crowd. Alex with what he assumed was the young lady he'd spoken of, Piers and his young lady, and Muddy and some of the boys. They all looked at Caroline in surprise and he feared the worst, especially when he saw Ginge. He gave his friend his strongest 'you dare' look and walked nervously towards them.

'Sir, may I introduce Mrs Caroline Spencer?'

'Muddy Waters, Mrs Spencer, how do you do?'

'How do you do, Squadron Leader, and please call me Caroline.'

She was obviously much more used to this sort of thing than he was, Jack thought.

'Only if you call me Muddy. Now, can I get you a drink?'

A long series of introductions followed, with Ginge mugging outrageously every time Caroline looked away.

She was bound to catch him sooner or later, if she hadn't already, and what she must make of them all, he shuddered to think. He'd known he'd be in trouble for not mentioning Caroline before, but they didn't know the half of it.

Alex's girlfriend, Sophie, or Ma'am to him, was a delight. They made a handsome couple, both tall and fresh-faced, but still touchingly nervous in one another's company, wary of making too public a display of affection, especially in front of Sophie's WAAFs. Piers, of course, had no such inhibitions. He and his young lady made no secret of the fact they were enjoying one another's company immensely. And why not?

It was about half an hour before Jack felt confident enough to leave Caroline chatting to Alex and Sophie. He and Muddy found space to talk.

'I'm afraid we lost Jet Black today, Jack. It was confirmed just before I left the office. And Smithy was badly burned.'

Jack winced.

'Sorry. How was Binky?'

'Pretty awful, sir. I've no idea what he looks like

because he's still swathed in bandages. But looking at some of the others… Well, I think it'll be a long time before we see him out of hospital. And now Smithy. Is everyone else all right? We seem a bit thin on the ground.'

'The new pilot officer that joined on Sunday is missing. Oh, and your second protégé led B Flight on a patrol this afternoon.'

'Alex?'

'Yes, Alex. Dusty said he did well, and I had a brief chat with the Controller. He said the same. No combat, but he got them out and back okay.'

Jack now had an explanation for the increased confidence he'd noticed earlier. Alex looked up and smiled at them.

'And what's this about the Station Commander blowing up a hangar?'

'Ah, you heard about that.'

'Caroline told me when I picked her up, but I heard the bang at Keston. Thought there must have been another raid, only closer to the village.'

'Well, let's just say the Old Man didn't skimp on the explosive. I'm sure you'll hear more about it tomorrow. More seriously though, no replacements in the pipeline and we're down to thirteen. Eight kites tonight, but with repairs and deliveries we might have a dozen by the morning. You'll still be leading if I'm on the ground for any reason, but I plan to fly first thing, so I've pencilled you in as Green Two behind Piers to start with. Any questions?'

They both smiled before Jack took up the offer.

'Yes. Why's Bunter looking so chipper?'

He and Ginge were sharing a joke, and there was none of the hostile body language Jack had grown to expect when the big lad was about.

'Another long story for the morning, Jack, but let's just say there's been a change of heart. So now, where did you find the delightful Mrs Spencer? And what's your landlady going to say about her?'

Jack swallowed. 'Can I get you a beer, sir?'

Chapter 12 – Thursday 5th September 1940

It was amazing what even one day's rest could do. Perhaps he still looked like death, but Jack didn't feel like it for once.

Not many of the others would be feeling as good. Especially not Muddy and Piers. They were the only old stagers that hadn't yet had a day off. And it showed. Their faces were drawn, their complexions sallow, eyes sunk deep into dark grey sockets, and with bags as wrinkled as scrotums.

The weather was no help. Although there'd been a hint of autumn in the air at 5.30, it had developed into another beautiful summer morning. Still, they'd just had that rare luxury, an uninterrupted breakfast. Most had decided to stay out on the grass.

Ginge took a swig of tea. 'I'm buggered if I can think of a single funny thing to say about your landlady, Jack. She's absolutely fuckin' lovely. Don't want to do a swap, do you?'

Jack was relieved. He'd feared Ginge would launch into a routine about merry widows, or ask how he was paying the rent. He rarely got tetchy with his outrageous friend, but he was feeling very protective of Caroline.

'Yes, she was delightful, Jack,' Alex joined in. 'Sophie really liked her. So did I.' He blushed.

'Thank you, sir. We thought Sophie was very nice as well.'

'Hark at you pair,' Ginge scoffed. 'You'll be off to tea at the Ritz next. In fact, if I can persuade me landlady to put her teeth in, we'll come too. What d'ya think?'

Jack looked at Alex.

They both jumped up and made a dash at Ginge, knocking him backwards off his chair. To the surprise and amusement of the new Squadron members, Dusty, Dunc and Piers joined in. A few minutes later, Ginge's trousers were flying from the Squadron flagpole.

The Station Commander's arrival in the temporary Ops Room was greeted with an immediate, reverent, hush.

He waved those that had risen back to their seats and said his usual, 'Carry on.' But, this time, the silence persisted, and all eyes followed him as he walked towards Kelvin Rice.

He knew they were looking for any outward sign that he'd lost his marbles. Perhaps he had. Group certainly seemed to think so!

'Don't worry, everyone, I haven't come to blow the place up.'

There was nervous laughter and he smiled at Sophie.

On reaching the Controller's table, he turned to look at the map. It was 9.15 and the black counters were only just leaving the French coast.

'They're late this morning, Kelvin.'

'Yes sir. Must have overslept.'

'May I?'

'Of course, sir. I think we've got a few minutes before it hots up.'

He cleared his throat and put his right hand in his tunic pocket. 'Firstly, I'd like to apologise to anyone who didn't get the message about me demolishing the hangar.

'A bit louder than I'd expected, and it must have come as a nasty shock, but I judged it had to be done.'

It had certainly been a talking point in The Gables.

Mr and Mrs Howley had been incredulous when Sophie told them what had made their china rattle.

'However, as I say, I don't envisage going on a bombing spree, so any other explosions will be the real thing, as it were. And secondly, I thought I'd let you know that the new Ops Room is coming along well. Don't know exactly how much longer it'll take, but, rest assured, everyone's working as fast as they can.'

Sophie had been given advanced warning that it was to be in Towerfields, the big house at Keston Mark. She was already working on a transport plot for when it opened.

The shop bell rang. The Station Commander smiled and nodded toward the sound.

'I'm sure most of you can't wait to get out of here.'

Turning his back on the resulting laughter, he leant on the Controller's table.

'If we can survive today without damage, I think we might get 637 back from Croydon, Kelvin. Should make things a bit easier for you, ay?'

'Yes it would rather, sir.'

'How are 646?'

'Well, they've got twelve kites again, but still only thirteen pilots I'm afraid.'

'So my little chat with the AOC didn't produce the sort of miracle the engineers seem able to pull off?'

'Fraid not, sir.'

'Oh well, I'm seeing Muddy later this morning. Hopefully they won't have lost any more by then.'

The brutally frank words caused Sophie an involuntary shudder. It had been such an enjoyable evening in the Sergeants' Mess. But, as the first hostile plot was raked closer to the English coast, and another appeared behind it, she realised it was impossible to know whether any of the young men she'd seen laughing and joking were going to survive, including Alex.

Ginge had just regained his trousers, if not his sense of humour, when the call to scramble came. The memory of him hopping into them in a red-faced sweat was still making Alex chuckle.

They were passing 15,000 feet, and the Geordie, probably still swearing, bobbed 50 yards to the left of the CO's tailplane, Bunter occupying the mirror image position on the right. Alex, leading Yellow Section, was slightly back and to the right of Bunter, with Piers's Green Section, including Jack, over his left shoulder beyond Bomber. Dusty's Blue Section was in the rear, JC performing the weaving duties again.

He spotted movement in Bunter's cockpit and smiled, returning his new friend's wave. The previous evening, Sophie's face had fallen as he'd walked towards them, but it hadn't taken her long to realise that a change had taken place.

They were after 50 bandits, last reported passing the Isle of Sheppey. Were they heading for Biggin again, or Kenley, or Croydon, or all of them? Who knew? Whatever the target, they had to try and stop them, or at least blunt the attack.

'Dragon, this is Bastion, bandits twelve o'clock, approximately twenty miles, angels one five, maintain vector zero eight zero.'

'Bastion, this is Dragon Leader, roger, levelling angels one seven. Dragon line abreast, line abreast, go.'

Alex opened the throttle and led Bomber and the Admiral forward into line abreast alongside Muddy's vic. Further to the left, Piers was bringing Jack and Woody Woodham forward, and, over his right shoulder, Dusty was leading his vic up to slot in to the right of the Admiral.

For the first time that day, Alex felt dry mouthed. He shifted in his seat. The last head-on attack hadn't ended well for him. Had he been in his usual position at the end of the line, he could have fired and dived early, giving the bombers a wide berth. But he was in the thick of it now, leading a section. He had to set an example.

He swallowed and his right hand clenched and unclenched on the stick.

'Dragon Leader, from Red 3, bandits one o'clock low.'

His sphincter twitched and sweat prickled on his forehead and palms.

'Thank you, Red 3, I see them. Bastion, this is Dragon Leader, tally-ho, tally-ho, fifty plus.'

'Dragon Leader, this is Bastion. Roger and good luck'

Alex eased the stick forward and right to follow the CO into the dive. He spotted the enemy just to the right of the nose. About 20 Junkers 88s and thirty 109s. They were closing fast. He looked to his wingmen. They were staring ahead, but holding steady.

Don't leave it too late this time, Alex.

The leading bombers started to bounce about. They'd been spotted. Tracer shot towards them and Bunter replied immediately. Alex picked a bomber and tried to ignore the stream of bullets. His stomach tightened as the bomber grew.

Not too early, but not too late.

'Now.'

He fired. His Spitfire juddered. Push. No response. The nose of the Junkers bore down on him. After what seemed an age, the Spitfire dived. Dust flew up around his head and the engine coughed. The Junkers passed overhead. He pulled to restore positive g, and breathed.

Too close again, surely. Would he ever get it right?

The bomber formation was heaving, but not broken. Beneath the stream, the outer Spitfires were already being chased by fighters. Alex thought he might have time for one more go at a bomber. He rolled and pulled up into the tracer criss-crossing the sky. A Spitfire flashed in front of him.

'Use your eyes, Alex.'

Belatedly, he looked around, wincing as his neck twinged. Picking another Junkers, he closed. The lower gun spat tracer. Bulbs of molten metal flashed to either side of his head. Sweating freely, he waited until 200 yards, then pressed the gun button.

Sparks raced along the bomber's belly. When they reached the gunner's dorsal gondola, they turned to shards of blood red perspex. Alex winced and pulled away.

Tracer arced in from the right and he pulled harder, firing at a shape to his front.

'Stupid.'

What had he just shot at? It was all so confusing. And he was becoming feverish with the motion. Just a short respite. Please.

Flashes to his left. Roll and pull. A 109. He fired. It passed. More weaving and jinking, his head spinning. Always another 109 to fire on or avoid.

He caught a final glimpse of the bomber formation, riven with ragged holes, but still flying inland on its westerly heading.

Jack had to weave around fresh craters to reach dispersal. Didn't seem to be too much damage though. Not that there was much left to damage. As he was pushed back into the pen, he was shocked at the sight of his engine fitter. He'd never seen him look so ashen, so scared.

'Alright, Stokesy?' he ventured as the older man took his straps.

'Fine thanks, Jack.' The deep voice was unusually soft and flat. 'You?'

'Yes, I'm fine. We obviously didn't stop the bombers?'

'No. I don't think anything's ever going to stop them.'

Before Jack could remonstrate, the engine fitter had turned and set off down the wing. He looked to his young rigger and raised his eyebrows.

Smudger stooped down next to the open door. 'Don't know, Flight. I think it's the last raid. A few of the others are the same; after the other night and everything. But Stokesy's usu…'

Jack raised a hand as Stokesy rounded the tailplane. He lifted himself from the cockpit and followed Smudger down the wing.

'The engine seems fine, Stokesy.'

'Good.'

The delivery was still deadpan, with no attempt at humour.

'Okay. See you later then.'

Stokesy carried on walking. 'Okay, Flight.'

Jack had to go. 'Keep an eye on him,' he whispered to Smudger, before hanging his parachute over the tailplane and walking out of the pen.

He thought back to the shelter, and then the bombing on Sunday night. That had been only one stick of bombs, but it had scared the life out of him. Stokesy had faced similar every day since. The man needed a rest. He vowed to have a quiet word with the flight sergeant, if he could find the time.

The Observer Corps were reporting small formations all over Kent and the Estuary. At one point, Sophie had counted 20 hostile plots on the map. At least most seemed to be heading back across the Channel now.

But they'd lost contact with the Station. Hopefully, it was just the phone lines again, because there had to be a limit to how much it could take. And the Squadrons. It didn't matter how safe the Ops Room was if they had no aircraft to control.

'Right, sir.'

She turned in time to see the Controller put down the telephone.

He looked across at her. 'Group say Dragon have landed, so we must have at least one usable strip. The trouble is, until they get in touch, I don't know how many pilots they have left.'

He hadn't meant to cause Sophie pain, but could see that he had.

Muddy was at a meeting with the Station Commander and Jack was standing in the hut doorway, surveying 'his Squadron'.

After the free-for-all they'd just been in, it was a minor miracle they'd all returned, and with all their aircraft in one piece. Good news for a change, although he wasn't sure Sergeant Pete Peters would agree. The tall, blond-haired young man had looked decidedly nervous since finding out that he'd be flying on the next sortie. Luckily, he'd been airborne on the flight scramble with Alex the day before, so he wasn't a complete novice.

Jack admonished himself. Since when had one sortie counted as preparation for combat? Until a few weeks ago, newcomers would have flown five or six training sorties, maybe more, before they were deemed fit to go on even a standing patrol. But they'd had over 20 pilots then. Now, the only qualification needed to enter battle was a pair of wings on your chest.

The young sergeant was sitting with Piers, who was using both hands to explain some point. The other member of Green Section, Sergeant Woody Woodham, was looking up no less attentively. Even he hadn't flown more than half a dozen times.

Funny, they were all sitting in their sections. Dusty and Dunc were both giving JC the benefit of their experience, while a few yards away, Alex was attempting to do the same with Bomber and The Admiral. Those three would be important when the Squadron had a chance to rebuild.

And more bizarrely still, there were Ginge and Bunter, lounging on the grass, chatting away like old friends. Jack smiled.

Ginge had always been wary of striking up relationships with officers. He seemed to see fraternization as some form of treachery. 'Come the revolution,' was one of his favourite sayings, and he often took the mick out of Jack for his class blindness. Now, there he was laughing and joking with someone who had a silver spoon and a plum in his mouth.

The phone rang. The lines had obviously been fixed. He glanced back towards the Ops Desk. Seeing the look on Hopkins' face, he set off, racing across the grass, the others rising to follow.

'Roger, Bastion, Dragon passing angels one five.'

Jack was leading the squadron toward a formation of 200 plus making up the Estuary at 20,000 feet. They hadn't encountered an enemy flying this high since Dunkirk, but, thanks to the early launch, they should have time to get above them, and take advantage of the sun.

Intriguing though, this change of tactics. Bombing accuracy would be impossible from such a height, unless of course they were going for a target so large that precision wasn't a problem.

He looked back at the Spitfires strung out behind him. Some of the pilots were about to fly higher than they'd ever been, and he hadn't thought to brief them on such an eventuality. He bet none of the section leaders had either.

Passing 18,000 feet, Alex checked his oxygen. Without it, he'd be unconscious in a few minutes.

He'd only been this high a couple of times before, and then only briefly in the run up to an attack, when he'd been concentrating on the enemy.

Now, still in the climb, he found that he had time to look around. It was a beautiful day, still hardly any clouds, and those there were looked like tiny cauliflowers thousands of feet below them.

The whole of southern England was laid out like a map. To the right of the nose, Kent and the south coast, all the way from Beachy Head, through Dungeness, to the North Foreland; to the left, the Estuary, Essex and East Anglia; and over his left shoulder, behind the wing, the snaking loops of the Thames leading into the heart of London.

'Dragon, this is Bastion, bandits maintaining heading and angels, turn left vector zero two zero.'

Alex updated his mental plot. It seemed the bandits were still heading straight up the Estuary towards London, while Dragon were turning north with the sun at their backs to intercept them. He hoped other squadrons were out there somewhere. Even by their usual standards, 12 against 200 seemed a bit steep.

'Bastion, this is Dragon Leader, wilco, passing angels twenty.'

He found Jack's confident Welsh voice reassuring. But here they were again, being led into battle by an NCO. Not that anyone would question the wisdom of it, and certainly not if they knew the NCO in question.

He and Sophie had really enjoyed Jack and Caroline's company. They'd chatted for much of the night and spent the last half hour on the dance floor gliding past one another, or gliding in Jack's case and clumping in his. Sophie had been very understanding, and, as she'd said, he did seem to be getting the hang of it towards the end.

Even now, sitting in a cold cockpit – it was noticeably colder at this height - he blushed at how his body had embarrassed him during the final slow dance. But, rather than pull away as she might have done, Sophie had held him close and put her head against his shoulder. It had been all he could do to maintain his composure as they brushed together to the rhythm of the music. But they'd been surrounded by her WAAFs, and she'd been Queen Bee again, so they hadn't had opportunity for more than a peck on parting.

Perhaps they'd have more luck on Friday night.

Ginge didn't know how close to the mark he'd been with the quip about the Ritz. The four of them had arranged to meet and drive into London at cease flying. He was looking forward to it, not least because he hoped he and Sophie would have more time, and privacy, at the end of the night. Nothing too outrageous probably, but anything would be more outrageous than his experience in that field to date.

'Dragon, this is Bastion, bandits two o'clock, approximately ten miles, turn left vector three six zero.'

'Bastion, this is Dragon Leader, wilco, passing angels two three.'

Alex shifted in his seat and shook out his limbs. Time to concentrate on the job in hand.

It really was cold. His fingers and toes were quite numb, and traces of silver fern were creeping over the canopy. If they were going to spend more time up here in the future, he'd have to dig out some more clothing, maybe even a flying suit.

'Dragon, line abreast, line abreast, go.'

Jack's canopy was beginning to show the first signs of icing. To his left, Piers was bringing Green Section up; while Alex was easing Yellow Section in beyond Bunter; and Dusty's Blue Section were closing up further to the right beyond the Admiral.

The reduced rate of climb at this height was very noticeable, but he was determined to gain 25,000 feet before levelling. A few miles ahead, low to the right of the nose, was a long dark smudge. He hadn't reported it yet, but he had no doubt it was the enemy, in a formation that ran back for several miles along the Estuary to the north of Sheppey. To the rear, trails in the sky indicated that other squadrons were already engaged.

'Good.'

'Dragon Leader, from Red 3, bandits one o'clock low.'

'Roger, Red 3. Bastion, this is Dragon Leader, tally-ho, tally-ho, two hundred plus, angels twenty.'

'Dragon Leader, this is Bastion, roger and good luck.'

They'd just reached 25,000 feet with the sun at their backs. The smudge had coalesced into a huge phalanx of black shapes, row upon row in perfect formation for two thirds of its length, the final third more chaotic. There, gaps had appeared and some of the bombers were turning aside, surrounded by smaller shapes.

'Let's see if we can do the same at the front,' Jack whispered to himself, before transmitting to the rest of the Squadron.

'Dragon, diving in. Good luck all and watch out for Snappers.'

The exhaled breath escaping Alex's oxygen mask was forming a fine mist. When it touched the canopy, it froze, slowly encasing him in a silver cocoon that filtered the sunlight and heightened his claustrophobia. More pressingly though, the Spitfires to left and right had become no more than dark shapes, glimpsed through glittering crystals. And the bombers had disappeared altogether.

He hoped his friends were maintaining their distance. The last thing he needed was a wingtip strike, or a propeller nibbling his tailplane. He leaned forward and rubbed at the ice with the back of a gloved hand, only stopping when he'd cleared an area big enough to see the Spitfires to his left, and the enemy formation to his front.

His hands were freezing. He could hardly feel the controls or the gun button under his thumb. And thin tendrils were already creeping across the areas he'd cleared.

'Damn!'

He leaned forward to rub again. Life was difficult enough without this. His airy glass office had turned into a dark cell, and he didn't like the change.

To the front, the Junkers 88s were growing fast. As usual, Bunter blasted off at about 1,000 yards. And again, as usual, his fire elicited a response. Because of the ice, most of the returning tracer was invisible, that is, until eerie balls of light suddenly shot past overhead and to either side. The enemy fighters were also lost behind the frosted glass. What were they up to?

Fighting the urge to panic, Alex pulled the reflector sight ahead of the nearest 88. Three hundred yards. He fired a short burst.

The twin engined bomber grew, and he rolled crisply to pass close behind it, sensing that he'd left it undamaged.

Despite the cold, he was sweating and his breath felt and looked like steam. It filled the cockpit, causing more condensation and ice on the canopy.

He pulled to level and reached out to wipe again. Large, black, shapes moved slowly overhead, and small glowing bulbs flashed past. It was surreal. He was sitting in a sealed box surrounded by huge aircraft and tiny bullets, none of which he could really see, and any of which could snuff out his misty breath in an instant.

The next five minutes seemed endless. In the brief

435

periods when he managed to clear enough of the canopy to see anything, he fired at assorted bombers and fighters, and pulled and jinked to avoid others that sped past or threatened to latch onto his tail. In the interim, he prayed that the other dark shadows and bright lights would miss him. He had no idea whether they belonged to friend or foe, but knew they could all be equally deadly.

As he dived away, ammunition spent, he felt reduced in stature, no longer the confident section leader, just a frightened novice. And, in truth, that was exactly what he was. No-one led a section ten days out of training unless there was no alternative. This engagement had reminded him that he'd no more than scratched the surface of what it was to be a fighter pilot.

He still knew nothing of operations at very low and high levels, of reconnaissance or escort duties, of flying and fighting in bad weather. He'd learnt less than pilots like Jack and Muddy had forgotten.

The last half hour had been an education, and a very frightening one, but there were so many other lessons to learn. Could he take any more in?

'Come on, Alex. Snap out of it.'

He was descending through 15,000 feet and, if anything, the ice was worse, forming again as soon as he cleared it. He was as sore from wiping as from pulling g. It was 10,000 feet before it really began to melt and he was able to attack the whole canopy, leaving a smeared mess that distorted everything.

Jack wiped away the last of the condensation and looked up. The dark trails drifting in the air were testament to the ferocity of the fighting, and he wondered how many of those he'd led into battle had survived unscathed.

They'd damaged, if not destroyed, several bombers. But there'd been too many for them to stop – about 70 all told - and he was crestfallen to see so many continuing towards their targets. Away to the north was a clue to the identity of at least one of those.

A thickening pall of smoke rose from the direction of the oil tanks at Thames Haven. Certainly a big enough target to be plastered from 20,000 feet, and one posing few navigational problems in good weather, especially once the first fires were lit.

All the effort, the loss of life, was beginning to seem futile. No matter how many fighters they threw up, and no matter how many bombers they destroyed, they just kept coming, and seemingly with no reduction in number, or in their desire to lay waste to the peaceful countryside beneath them.

Despite the sacrifices, they seemed to be losing the battle.

Sophie looked at the map. Dragon were returning, but they wouldn't be on the ground long. Even as the remnants of the last wave were being harried towards the southeast, another was leaving the French coast. Those squadrons still engaged would be on the ground refuelling when it hit, so Dragon were bound to be called upon.

She was trying to be cool and detached, but when Alex was in combat, she found herself permanently fearful, listening for his name or voice to issue from the speaker. It couldn't keep on like this every time he flew, could it? She hoped not.

At least she now knew beyond doubt that he loved

her. And that he desired her. She'd felt that as they'd danced, and had held him close as he became embarrassed and made to pull away. If only he knew how much she shared his longing. But how far either of them was prepared to go at this stage was a different matter. They'd have to see.

'Bloody hell, sir,' Dev Hayman said as he took Alex's straps. 'What have you done to my canopy?'

'Sorry, Dev. First time I've had to deal with ice. Hope I haven't scratched it.'

A clear canopy could be the difference between life and death. The good riggers spent hours removing every blemish so their pilot wouldn't miss an approaching enemy behind a spot or scratch.

'I'm sure you won't have damaged it, sir,' Dev said with a smile. 'But remind me to give you a chamois next time.'

The rigger was already polishing madly as Alex stepped off the wing.

He was used to the groundcrew descending on his aircraft straight after shut down, but there seemed a special urgency today. The fuel bowser was already parking alongside and the armourers were all over and under the wings.

He turned to his engine fitter. 'What's going on, Jock?'

'Don't know, sir. We was just told to turn you round, 'and make it snappy''. He imitated Flight Sergeant Patterson's stentorian tones.

Alex smiled as an armourer removed his forage cap and fed it up inside the wing to feed the first rounds into the breeches. No wonder they always had the scruffiest headgear.

'Oh well, best I rush off for a tea then.'

'Aye, best you do, sir. And dinner.'

Alex walked out of the pen. Another bolted lunch, if they were lucky.

Jack walked away from Nick Hudson. Muddy was waiting for him outside the hut.

'Welcome back, Jack. Can I have my Squadron again, please?'

'Certainly, sir. I think I've looked after it reasonably well.'

'Yes. I counted you all back.'

'Bloody miracle, sir. Two hundred plus, and up at 20,000. How was your meeting?'

Muddy led Jack a short way from those lowering themselves into the chairs or onto the grass.

'Not bad. Should get a new flight commander and at least a couple of other replacements on Sunday.'

'So we're staying around till Sunday?'

'Fraid so, Jack. I don't think they've got much alternative. Don't tell the others about the flight commander. Just in case. And I think we might be off again sooner rather than later. Happy being demoted to Yellow 2 again?'

Jack nodded.

'Good. Try and get some lunch.'

Jack walked towards the metal pans laid out on a trestle table. He watched the CO intercept Piers as he left the Intelligence Officer. Beyond them, the new sergeant, Pete, was walking unsteadily along the line of pens. He stopped to lean against one of the blast walls. Jack was just wondering whether to walk over when a tall, blond, pilot jogged up and put an arm over the young man's shoulder.

It was only a week or so since he'd done the same for Alex. Seemed a lifetime ago.

After chatting to his fellow pilot, giving his report to Nick Hudson and grabbing a hasty lunch, Alex had been walking towards Jack when the bell rang. He hadn't heard what Hopkins was shouting at the time, but he now knew they were bound for 100 plus at 16,000 feet over south east Kent.

Two kites were unserviceable, so only ten of them were airborne, the CO and Alex's vics, and B Flight flying as two pairs: Piers and Jack, and Dusty and Dunc. The sky to the north was still darkened by the smoke rising from Thames Haven, while to the south and east, it was full of vapour and smoke trails, some old and decaying, blown into wispy mare's tales, others crisp and new, writing messages of duty and death.

It was a sobering sight, but, despite that, Alex found his mood lighter than an hour previously, buoyed by his groundcrew, a hot lunch, and by his chat with Sergeant Peters, a young man suffering after his first experience of combat, much as he himself had a week earlier. And they weren't heading to heights where ice would be a problem again. What could possibly go wrong?

An expanding blossom of orange flame and black smoke in the distance answered the rhetorical question. And then the Controller's voice brought with it a graphic image of one possible aftermath of the approaching combat.

'Dragon, this is Bastion, bandits twelve o'clock, approximately twenty miles, maintaining angels one six.'

'Roger Bastion, Dragon passing angels one three.'

And thoughts of Crispy led to thoughts of Sophie, sitting in a makeshift ops room he still found hard to visualise, despite her amusing descriptions. They wouldn't be seeing one another that night, and he was missing her already. So much could happen before the next evening.

How fickle were his moods. Once more, he felt optimism and confidence giving way to fear and doubt.

'Dragon, line abreast, line abreast, go.'

Another frontal attack. The metallic taste was suddenly there, and his guts were churning. He forced a smile into his eyes and looked to Bomber and the Admiral, easing the throttle forward to bring them abreast Ginge, Muddy and Bunter.

Could he get it right this time?

He licked his lips with a tongue that suddenly seemed as dry as sandpaper.

'Come on, Alex. Pull yourself together.'

Once again, the loud admonition seemed to draw him back from the brink of panic. Saliva began to flow and he swallowed hard, attempting to rid his mouth of the taste of fear.

Relegation to humble wingman had given Jack plenty of time for thought. And he'd allowed himself a pleasant review of the previous night.

He and Caroline had been a little tipsy, and the final dance had kindled a passion not totally doused by the chilly drive back to Keston. As soon as they stepped into the hall and closed the door, his cold hands slid into the warmth beneath her unbuttoned coat. They swayed together as they had on the dance floor.

Her dress fell away with remarkable ease and he

caressed her through the thin material of her slip. By some magic, his clothes were also disappearing and he stroked his hand over her stomach.

They'd made love against the coats in the hall, their passion exploding in an ecstatic embrace that fulfilled all its earlier promise. But his mind drew him to the bedroom, where they'd made love for the second time. He tried to recall the sight, the touch, the smell of her naked body.

A distant flash of colour.

'Dragon, this is Bastion, bandits twelve o'clock, approximately twenty miles, maintaining angels one six.'

So much to live for.

'Time to concentrate, Jack.'

Out in his left 10 o'clock, about five miles away, another Squadron of Spitfires was climbing above the horizon.

Alex was back in control. The fear was still there, bubbling beneath the surface, but spectra of fractured sunlight playing on his instrument panel had sparked a memory of the last school play he'd watched.

That day in the mediaeval hall, the sunlight had shone through leaded windows and formed similar patterns on the names of Old Ludlovians killed in previous conflicts. He and his friends in the Upper VIth had sensed they would soon be involved in another war, and Shakespeare's words had seemed so moving, so appropriate.

'We few, we happy few, we band of brothers.'

Now, they elicited an even keener sense of pride and camaraderie.

To his right bobbed the Admiral, Dusty and Dunc;

to his left, Bomber, Bunter, the CO, Ginge and, finally, Piers and Jack, the clean lines of their Spitfires glinting in the full glare of the sun. In his mind's eye, he could also see the faces of those they'd lost; people he'd known only fleetingly, like S to Z, Tubby, Harry Beaumont, Sammy Samson and Sergeants Ellis and Atkins; and some he'd come to know better, like Chips, Smithy, the old CO, Sandy and Scouse; and finally, his roommate and confidant, Olly.

He heard Jack's call and looked out to see another squadron of Spitfires approaching from the left. The sight elicited a surge of such pride that his whole body tingled.

Cry God for Harry, England and Saint George.

He flexed his fingers and tightened his grip on the stick, readying his thumb over the gun button. Some of the escorting 109s peeled off to attack the other squadron. Meanwhile, the bombers began the characteristic bounce that betrayed their discomfort at the approaching onslaught.

One mile. He felt his stomach tighten and the sweat began to prickle. The outermost Heinkels were beginning to turn away and a few lines of tracer appeared from those bouncing nearer the centre. Bunter and some of the others returned fire. Alex forced himself to wait until he could clearly see two crew members through the perspex nose. Only then did he press his thumb down.

His rounds smashed straight into the bomber, sending shards of perspex into the air. As he pushed, he saw the two bodies fall back, hit either by his bullets or the shrapnel of their shattered canopy. Better judgement this time. He levelled and looked around.

High to his left, some of the other squadron were

mixing it with the 109s, while the rest were about to crash into the right flank of the enemy formation, from which a bomber was already falling in flames. Lower down, Dragon's Spitfires were weaving in all directions, while way to his front, smoke and vapour trails told of another fierce battle. To his right, the air was clearer for the moment, just a couple of Spitfires and a few 109s diving into the fray. Above, the bombers were streaming by, their lower gunners beginning to fire.

Alex rolled right and pulled, arcing round to sit 1,000 feet behind and beneath a bomber to the middle left of the formation. He pushed on the throttle and climbed straight into the stream of tracer issuing from the lower gun gondola.

The fire seemed startlingly accurate and he flinched as the bright rods streaked above his canopy.

A little judder. Were those impacts? No other evidence of damage, so he carried on.

Ahead, several bombers were descending, streaming smoke, as the second squadron drove through them. To either side, the 109s were encroaching, but he held his nerve and waited until he was within two football pitch lengths before firing. He fought to keep the reflector sight centred against the juddering recoil, and kept the button pressed. His rounds raked the underside of the bomber. As he continued to close, he eased right and fired a burst at the right wing. Black smoke erupted from the engine nacelle and the bomber rolled towards him.

'What the?'

Caught out by its sudden deceleration, he rolled right and pulled, his left wingtip narrowly missing the bomber as he dived away. Head on to a 109. They both fired, the German turning right as Alex did the same, passing one another belly to belly no more than ten yards apart. Breathing heavily, he rolled left and pulled round, trying to stay with the bombers.

More gaps had been ripped in the formation and the remaining Heinkels were turning south. Through the sweat and aching limbs, Alex felt a burst of elation.

'Yes'

He'd never know for sure, but he'd felt all along that their base had been the intended target. This time, they'd turned them away.

He picked another bomber and raised the Spitfire's nose to climb towards it.

'Snapper on your tail, Alex, Snapper on your tail.'

On the extreme left of the line, Jack couldn't believe his luck. The other squadron had drawn off most of the fighter cover, and his chosen Heinkel was turning out of the protective formation, exposing its belly.

'Bad choice, Butty.'

He waited until about 800 yards and fired, keeping his thumb on the gun button until the twitch of his sphincter told him it was time to dive. He was sure he'd scored hits.

Aware of the Spitfires to his right, he jinked left, seeing the bulk of the other squadron pass behind. He then rolled hard right and pulled back towards the bombers, grunting against the g. Rolling out, he pulled up to attack a Heinkel from the rear right quarter.

The air directly beneath the bomber stream was criss-crossed with a seemingly impenetrable network of tracer, but he ignored the flashes and closed to within 200 yards before firing. He could almost feel the rounds thudding into the bomber's lower fuselage and wing root. Satisfied he'd at least damaged it, he pushed and rolled left to stay beneath the stream.

More gaps had appeared. They could break this raid altogether if they kept up the pressure. While he looked for another target, he spotted a Spitfire climbing into the tracer.

Is that what they all did? Seemed madness.

A 109 appeared from behind a Heinkel, turning hard to get on the Spitfire's tail. Jack was torn. He wanted to stay with the bombers, and the German pilot may overshoot, but something made him ease left to keep the two fighters in sight.

The German rolled out perfectly lined up, using the energy from his dive to close steadily on the Spitfire. Jack suddenly knew who the pilot was.

'Snapper on your tail, Alex, Snapper on your tail.'

The Spitfire turned sharply left, but the 109 turned inside it, partially exposing its belly. Jack knew it was his only chance. The range wasn't ideal, nor the deflection, but he pressed the gun button and prayed.

'Shit!'

He'd missed. But the German hadn't, his tracer raking Alex's rear fuselage and tail.

Alex's Spitfire continued turning, pulling into a dive. The 109 followed.

'He's still with you, Alex.'

Alex was diving away and the 109 was arcing over the top to chase him down.

Jack wrestled with another dilemma. Should he take time to get on the tail of the 109, or cut the corner and try another risky deflection shot?

He rolled upside down and pulled his reflector sight ahead of the Messerschmitt. The German disappeared beneath his Spitfire's nose.

'Fuck!'

He already felt like a circus sharpshooter trying to blast a cigarette from a horse-rider's mouth. Now, a hood had been thrown over his eyes.

But he could still see Alex. He imagined the German's flight path.

'Now.'

He pressed the gun button. All too soon, his ammunition was spent. He jinked right and left to pull over the top. Alex was diving away, but the Messerschmitt was still following.

'Pull right, Alex!'

Alex turned. The 109 flew straight on. Jack dived after it, but it didn't deviate. Perhaps he really had hit the pilot. Luck or divine intervention, who knew?

Certainly not him. Body aching after even such a brief combat, he looked around.

A lone Spitfire sat 2,000 feet above in a shallow descent into the west. Using the energy from his dive, Jack pulled into a zooming climb, checking his ascent to sit two wingspans from the other aircraft. Its canopy was open, its pilot leaning back, motionless. Its tailplane and rear fuselage were peppered with holes.

Kelvin Rice watched Sophie's face crumple in horror. Subconsciously, even he must have been listening for that name among the babble issuing from the wall speaker.

But this time she appeared to regain her composure quickly, as if she'd been preparing herself for just such a circumstance.

'He's still with you, Alex,' the speaker blared.

She bit her lip, her eyes narrowing slightly, but continuing to scan the room, giving at least the impression of carrying on as if nothing untoward had happened. The flight sergeant looked at him and nodded 'she's all right'. He turned back to the map, knowing it wasn't true.

'Knightsbridge, this is Bastion...'

Alex started, his heart racing.

'Idiot!'

The other aircraft was a Spitfire, but it might not have been. Its pilot removed his oxygen mask and waved.

Jack.

He'd recognised the warning voice but, feeling the impacts, had thought he was hearing it for the last time. It seemed his friend had saved him yet again.

He waved back, then tried to assess the state of his aircraft.

All seemed well, apart from the rudder and elevators, which were sluggish, but still functioning. He decided to stay with the aircraft, hoping the back end would take him home, and stand up to a landing.

Jack obviously felt he could make it. He was signalling him to follow. Only too glad to do so, Alex gave a thumbs-up and eased the throttle back to slot into wide echelon abeam the other Spitfire's right tailplane.

Absolved of the need to navigate, he looked around. The sky was etched with vapour trails, and the smoke still rose in a dense pall from Thames Haven. There were no aircraft other than Jack's. It hung before him, a thing of grace and beauty. He knew he was stretching the Shakespearean analogies to the limit, but he couldn't help thinking of Jack as a fellow knight, his charger carrying him from the field.

Were they knights? Perhaps they were as close as you could get in modern warfare.

Beneath their aircraft, the countryside of southern England looked as beautiful as ever.

What a crazy way to spend a summer afternoon! Never in his wildest fantasies could he have envisaged all this as he'd sat in the school hall in the spring of 1939.

Alex made his landing as gentle as possible. Even so, on touchdown, he sensed all was not well. The landing run was bumpier than usual, and shorter. But otherwise, after some of the things that had happened to him, it was a bit of an anticlimax.

He shut the engine down, undid his harnesses and stood up. There was no reason to suspect fire, but no point in hanging about either, so he stepped out of the cockpit, walked down the wing and jumped to the grass. As he'd guessed, the tailwheel had collapsed. It could have been much worse. The rear fuselage was peppered with jagged holes.

A truck had set out from the pens, and Jack's Spitfire was sitting about 50 yards away, rocking gently at low revs. His friend beckoned him. Alex found himself strangely reluctant to leave his damaged aircraft before the groundcrew arrived. But, after a short internal debate, he dismissed the analogy of a captain deserting his sinking ship, and ran over. He climbed up and sat on the wing root, holding on to the canopy rail as the Spitfire set off across the grass.

Sophie had never felt so relieved. Tears stung her eyes, but she tried not to let the emotion into her voice.

'Alex?'

'Don't sound so surprised. Who did you think it was?'

She daren't speak.

'I thought I'd ring just in case you'd heard anything on the R/T.'

'No,' she lied, struggling to keep her voice neutral.

'Oh. That's all right then.' He sounded worried now, a hint of doubt in his voice.

But she didn't trust herself to respond more freely, or she'd end up blubbing, which would be bad form in the middle of the Ops Room. She already sensed eyes on her.

'Right then. I'll let you get back to work.' His disappointment was evident.

It was too much. Hang it if people heard. 'Alex?'

'Yes.' It was a verbal flinch, as if he was expecting bad news.

'I love you.'

'I love you too, Sophie.' His relief was so obvious it brought a smile to her lips. 'See you tomorrow night then.' She pictured him blushing.

'Yes. See you then. Be careful.'

She put the phone down. Most people looked away, but the flight sergeant put a sympathetic hand on her arm again, and the Controller gave her an encouraging smile.

Over the next hour, Jack and Alex fended off banter from everyone who'd witnessed or been told about their unconventional arrival at dispersal. Ginge had been particularly vociferous.

'Mark my words. They'll be getting married next.'

Only the threat of another de-bagging made him retreat into watchful silence.

The Squadron was in relatively high spirits. On the debit side, Dunc had had to take to his brolly, but he'd waved to Dusty as he'd drifted down, so they had no doubt he'd turn up eventually. And several kites had been damaged, but given the odds, things could have been much worse.

The only other excitement was the arrival, in the early evening, of a Hurricane piloted by a man in a white flying suit and helmet. As soon as he saw the helmet, Jack rushed into the hut to tell Muddy.

Air Vice-Marshal Keith Park was the Air Officer Commanding 11 Group, renowned for getting airborne to see at first hand what things were like for his squadrons, and for dropping in on them unexpectedly.

He was rumoured to have flown over the Dunkirk beaches on numerous occasions, and had surprised 646 with a flying visit at around that time.

While Muddy looked for his hat, George Evans rushed out to meet the visitor and Jack stepped back into the fresh air. The Air Marshal jumped from the wing and returned the Adjutant's salute without breaking stride. Jack smiled as they neared the hut, George puffing along several paces adrift. The AOC returned the salutes of those who'd found their hats, again without breaking stride.

'Good evening, Flight Sergeant Williams.'

'Good evening, sir.'

Jack was astonished. He'd been only one of several pilots the Air Marshal had been introduced to that evening, some three months ago. It was an impressive feat of memory, and he could see from the expressions of those about him that the Old Man's recognition had raised his stock considerably.

Muddy emerged, only to have to retrace his steps as

the AOC continued his determined progress into the building. They heard the office door shut and looked at one another.

Muddy saluted as the Hurricane taxyed away. He turned and walked back to them.

'Three weeks leave, sir?'

'Sorry, Ginge. Not yet, although I got the impression he'd have done just that if he could.'

Alex hadn't gained quite the same impression. He'd had a few seconds of eye contact during the AOC's little speech of encouragement, and he hadn't exactly found it a kindly gaze, more steely and determined.

The words had been pretty steely as well, as the CO was just reiterating.

'But you heard what he said. We've got to keep at them or we'll have nowhere to operate from. So, I'm afraid I can't offer much hope of a rest yet. Let's just pray for an early stack tonight, and I'll buy the first round.'

'I'll drink to that, sir.'

Muddy smiled at Ginge, but avoided the obvious reply and turned instead to Piers and Jack.

'Can I see you two in my office for a minute, please.'

Alex watched them go. He felt a bit cheerier. He'd survived another brush with catastrophe, and had had a heart-warming conversation with Sophie. And, despite the uncompromising message, the AOC's visit had been the first indication that someone above the Station Commander's pay grade was vaguely interested in what they were doing. It had given them all a lift.

Muddy held the match to the bowl of his pipe and puffed away determinedly. Before he took the stem from his mouth, there was a dense cloud of blue smoke above his head and the tobacco glowed like the coals in a blacksmith's forge.

'No change to what I told you this morning as regards pilots I'm afraid. Hopefully, a new flight commander and some replacements on Sunday.'

'A name on the flight commander, sir?'

'Sorry, no Jack. And if no-one turns up, I'm pretty set on moving Alex up. Any dissenters?'

He looked at them both.

'Okay. Until then, we'll stay as we are.'

Jack had assumed that that would be it. But he was wrong.

'The AOC did have one bit of new gen though. A major change in tactics, partly due to the high flying formation you met this morning. From tomorrow, they're going to try and launch us paired with a Hurricane squadron. We'll concentrate on going high for the fighters, while they make for the bombers.'

'Makes sense,' Jack said. 'They'd never admit it, but we are better at height. Who are they going to pair us up with?'

'Well, he hopes the Station'll be back on its feet shortly so they can move 79 back in. Until then, I have no idea. We'll just have to play it by ear.'

'No change there then!' Jack said with heartfelt resignation.

They looked at one another and laughed.

The stand down hadn't come early, but they hadn't been scrambled either. When the release finally came, they used a selection of vehicles, including the Station

Commander's staff car, to make for the White Hart.

It turned into a great night. Alex drank more than he should have, and they finished with a tremendous sing-song, the Station Commander not only joining in, but teaching them a few songs of which his mother would not have approved.

Although Alex had been thinking about his mother and the look on her face, he hadn't been as homesick since his return to Biggin. The Station had become more like home, the Squadron more like a family, not a replacement for the one in Ludlow, but a family nonetheless. The relationships were more complicated, but, in some ways, no less intense.

Chapter 13 – Friday 6th September 1940

'Four thirty, sir. Four thirty.'

With the lengthening nights, their early morning call was half an hour later. It didn't seem to help, especially after a night on the beer.

'Four thirty, sir.'

'Thank you, Jenkins.'

'Your tea's on the side, sir.'

The bloody man never gave up.

'Thank you, Jenkins.'

Alex eased himself onto one elbow and groaned. His head throbbed, and his mouth and tongue were lined with foul tasting felt.

'Glad it's not just me.'

Reluctantly, he opened his eyes. Jenkins was just disappearing round the door, and Piers was looking at him, bleary-eyed.

Fifteen minutes later, Alex looked round the dining room. In many ways, it was a very different scene from his first Squadron breakfast. Compared with the gloomy room in the Officers' Mess, the conservatory of Sambrook House was relatively small and bright, footfalls echoing off the stone floor and high ceiling. And many of the characters from that first breakfast - S to Z in his pyjamas, Birdy with his head on the table – had gone.

But, in other ways, it was remarkably similar: the haggard looks, the lack of conversation, and the sense of foreboding as they waited for the steward to announce the arrival of their transport.

The major difference, though, was that then, Alex had felt like an outsider, sitting on the edge, trying to understand why everyone looked and acted as they did.

Now, he knew only too well why only Muddy, Piers and Bunter seemed able to eat, and why they all looked so bloody awful, even those who'd joined only recently, like Bomber and the Admiral. Okay, it was partly the late night and the beer, but mainly, it was cumulative mental and physical fatigue, and fear of what the day might hold. Always that. The fear that this might be your last breakfast.

A steward clumped in and walked up to Muddy. They all knew what he was about to say, but they remained seated until forced to accept the inevitable.

'Transport's outside, sir.'

Jack's rigger shouted above the din. 'Stokesy's been sent on a 48, Flight.'

'Good for him, Smudger. Who's in the cockpit then?'

They were both looking up at a hunched figure completing the engine checks.

'LAC Geordie Hale, Flight.'

'Don't think I've met him.'

'One of the replacements, so he hasn't been around long.'

Jack patted the wingtip. 'How is she?'

'Seems fine, Flight, if the engine's okay.'

Jack hoped it was. They were down to nine kites. For the first time, they didn't seem to have received any overnight replacements. Another indication of how difficult things were getting perhaps. And they could have done with them.

The sky was clear, full of stars, and he had no doubt the hint of brightness on the eastern horizon heralded another beautiful day.

The engine was shut down amid backfires and

clouds of smoke. Aircraft in other pens were still running up, but at least you could hear yourself think now.

The engine fitter climbed down the wing and walked up to them. 'Seems fine, Flight.'

'Thanks, Geordie. See you in a minute.'

Alex and Jack met as they walked back to the hut.

'How's the head this morning, Alex?'

'Not so bad thanks, Jack. Great stuff oxygen.'

'Still all set for tonight?'

'I think so. I spoke to Sophie yesterday afternoon and she still seemed keen.'

'Good. Caroline's really excited. Says she hasn't been to Town for ages.' Jack said Town with Caroline's BBC pronunciation.

'Well, apart from passing through, I've never been *to Town* either, so I'm really looking forward to it as well.'

'Good, well that makes four of us then.' They approached the hut. 'Right, let's see how much shut-eye we get.'

They stepped inside, tiptoeing round the prone bodies, just as the Adj came out of the CO's office.

'Wake up, you 'orrible lot. The CO wants a word.'

Muddy briefed them on the change of tactics. The positive line was that they could attack the enemy fighters on their own terms, without the distraction of trying for the bombers first.

But Alex couldn't help thinking they'd be engaging the more potent enemy aircraft earlier, with all the added danger that entailed. He kept his thoughts to himself, but he could see he wasn't the only one with reservations. Theirs not to reason why,...

Even before the briefing, Alex had doubted he'd get any sleep. Now there was no chance. He settled down and waited for the dawn.

A few hours later, he stepped from the hut and flinched at the sight of Ginge devouring a bacon doorstep oozing fat. It activated his gag reflex and he had to look away. He couldn't face anything solid himself. It was all he could do to sip at his tea.

As expected, it was a beautiful morning. He wished it was late evening, that he would shortly be leaving to prepare for his night out. If events ran their normal course, there was no guarantee that he and Jack would be there. His earlier pessimism hadn't been dispelled by the appearance of the sun.

The CO was walking back from the flight line. He stopped in front of them.

'No more aircraft I'm afraid. So, if it's a squadron push, we'll go as three sections as planned. Any questions?'

He was greeted by a glum silence.

'Okay. Let's hope for a quiet day.'

Looking at the sky, Alex knew it was a forlorn hope.

Sophie returned Kelvin Rice's smile.

'Good morning, sir'

'Morning, Sophie. How are you?'

She'd really enjoyed her walk in the crisp morning sunshine, her heart sinking only on entering the shop. 'Very well, thank you, sir. It's a lovely day.'

'Yes, it is. Unfortunately, the Hun's noticed as well.' He nodded at the map.

A black counter was sitting over the French coast. Sophie steeled herself. She looked at the faces of the other WAAFs. They all betrayed fatigue and tension, fear for what the day might hold, none more so than Angela. Why don't they just leave us alone, horrible Nazis?

She sat, exchanged the usual pleasantries with her flight sergeant, and waited. Kelvin Rice divided his attention between the map and Sophie. She met his glance a couple of times and they exchanged smiles.

After 15 minutes, the large formation, estimated at 300 plus, was approaching the English coast between Dover and Dungeness.

The Uxbridge line rang.

Alex waved away Dev and Jock and turned into line behind Bunter. The pessimism and fear had been submerged by the race to the aircraft, the interaction with the groundcrew and the activity of strapping in and setting off. Now, the negative feelings were bubbling just beneath the surface again. He hoped he could keep them there.

Muddy turned into wind and taxyed forward before stopping, Ginge and Bunter halting to either side of his tailplane.

Alex turned to follow and stopped 50 yards behind them. He looked back over his shoulders, watching the Admiral and Bomber stop beside him, and Jack and Woody behind them, to either side of Piers.

A green light shone from the caravan.

'Dragon, here we go.'

Red Section set off and Alex progressively opened the throttle, exhilarated by the rising growl of the engine and the acceleration. He looked to right and left to see the Admiral and Bomber holding in nicely. Ahead, Muddy's tailwheel lifted and he eased the stick forward, feeling his own tailwheel rise and the mainwheels skipping ever more lightly over the grass. With Muddy airborne, it took only the merest backward pressure for his own Spitfire to leap into the air. He tweaked the brakes and swapped hands.

As he pumped with his right hand, his left remained almost completely steady. He was flying serenely on, while Bomber and the Admiral both bounced madly to either side of him. His lips spread into a broad smile.

'At last.'

The lift in spirits seemed out of all proportion to the achievement, almost as potent as when Sophie had expressed her love for him.

He wondered if Jack and Piers had noticed.

The large formation must have split before it reached the coast. Now, elements of various sizes were fanning out over south eastern England. The Observer Corps were hard pressed to keep up, as were the Controllers at Uxbridge.

Having launched Dragon, Kelvin Rice hoped Group wouldn't take too long choosing which element they wanted them to attack, not least because he had to coordinate their arrival with a Hurricane squadron operating out of West Malling. In the meantime, he'd directed them to climb to the south east.

The Uxbridge line rang again.

'Dragon, this is Bastion, fifty plus bandits, angels one six passing east abeam Ashford, vector zero seven zero.'

'Bastion, this is Dragon Leader, wilco passing angels ten.'

Sitting at the back, Jack felt the old pride. He

weaved away to the right, lowered the left wing and looked across at the other eight Spitfires. He still felt a strong bond, even with those who'd only been around a few days, like Woody. And on the calendar, it was no time since Piers and Alex had been sitting as novices on his wing, yet here they were, one already a flight commander, the other likely to be one in the next few days. They'd been through a lot together, and no doubt today would provide more of the same.

'Griffon, this is Bastion, vector zero six five.'

An unfamiliar voice replied. 'Bastion, this is Griffon leader, wilco, passing angels eight.'

Ten Hurricanes he presumed were Griffon were to his left, well below and behind. All being well, Dragon would have time to distract the fighters before they reached the bombers.

Alex lost sight of the Hurricanes as they dropped back beneath him.

'Dragon, this is Bastion, bandits in your low one o'clock ten miles, turn left vector zero four zero.'

Crispy was turning them to intercept from above and behind.

'Bastion, this is Dragon Leader, wilco, passing angels one seven.'

They were still climbing and ought to end up well above the fighter escort. He looked down and right, more in hope than expectation. Ginge was bound to spot them first.

The tension was mounting, but time seemed to pass desperately slowly. He knew it was an illusion that would be shattered as soon as the enemy were sighted, from which point everything would be a blur.

'Dragon, line abreast, line abreast, go.'

Alex edged his section forward and watched Piers ease Green Section into position to the left of Ginge. They were accelerating, levelling at 20,000 feet. Now where was the enemy?

'Dragon Leader from Green 2, bandits one o'clock low.'

Jack had spotted them.

'Roger, Green 2, looking.'

Alex saw them as Muddy spoke to Ops.

'Bastion, this is Dragon, tally-ho, tally-ho, twenty 88s plus forty escorts.'

The bombers were 4,000 feet below, the 109s split high to either side, the 110s even higher, probably no more than 2,000 feet below Dragon.

'Roger Dragon Leader, good luck, Bastion out. Griffon, this is Bast…'

Alex ignored the rest of the transmission and followed Muddy towards the Messerschmitt 110s, who still seemed unaware of their presence. But not for long.

Tracer set out from some of the rear gun positions. He eased Yellow Section right and picked a 110. As he'd anticipated, time accelerated exponentially. No sooner had he chosen his target than he was approaching 250 yards.

He fired, but flashed past the twin tail of the German fighter without registering any hits. After a moment's hesitation, he pulled hard towards the right hand 109s. Too hard.

Although he avoided blacking out, it took an age for his vision to return. When it did, he was confronted with empty sky. The battle was taking place behind and below him.

'Come on Alex. Get a grip.'

He pulled left, squinting down on a chaotic scene. Way below, the bombers were surrounded by Hurricanes and 109s. Closer, but still a thousand feet below, was a jumble of Spitfires and Messerschmitts, 109s and 110s.

He was hot and disorientated, arms already aching as he continued to pull round looking for another target. Then, low to his left, he saw a 110 roll in behind a Spitfire.

Jack saw the 110 in his rear view mirror.

'No way, Butt.'

He made to turn, but rods of light flashed in from the right. Chunks flew off his engine cowling, his canopy shattered and he felt a burning pain in his right calf. He screamed and reached down. A black shadow passed above, momentarily darkening the sky.

The pain subsided, but not the sudden flush of panic.

He raised his hands. Soaked in blood.

Uncharacteristically, he remained paralysed, looking at his bloodied hands.

Alex knew who it was. The 109 had fired and flown on. But the 110 was still closing.

Why didn't Jack do something?

He rolled inverted and pulled. Arcing down over the pair, he eased his Spitfire's nose clear of Jack's tailplane and pressed the gun button.

Nothing. He pressed again.

'Damn!'

The 110 was still closing.

Alex set his jaw. Coldly, he estimated the lay off.

Would he be in time? He had to be.

A voice.

Piers.

'Pull, Alex, pull.'

But Alex was pushing, making a last minute adjustment as he looked down into the terrified faces of the German pilot and gunner.

Epilogue

The pain seemed as fresh as the day the cannon shell had torn through his calf. There had been other wounds since, other losses, but in the sunlit corner of the churchyard, it was that day in September 1940 that was thrust to the fore.

The simple white headstone could have marked the final resting place of any one of the millions that had fallen in either the Great War or the second global conflict just ended. And, although the RAF badge narrowed the field, it was still chiselled into tens of thousands of similar Portland Stone blocks. Even the words, ONE OF THE FEW, could have applied to any one of over 500 fighter pilots killed in the Battle of Britain. No, it was the name and the date that brought a face to mind, a smiling countenance that would be forever youthful.

Warm fingers meshed with his, and a head leaned against his shoulder. Jack gave the hand a squeeze, a silent thank you, but her closeness could not diminish his sadness on this occasion.

It must have been several minutes before he squeezed the hand again. She leaned down, placed a single red rose on the neatly manicured turf, straightened and wiped her cheek. After another brief period of silent contemplation, they turned and walked hand in hand down the tarmac path, the tap, tap of her heels drawing him back to the present.

The visit, too long delayed, had given him a renewed sense of his own good fortune, and of his friend's sacrifice.

While she rummaged about in the boot, Jack leaned on the driver's door and looked back into the corner of the cemetery. The headstone was still visible.

Next to it, stood a young man. He was tall and blond, dressed in a rumpled blue uniform, white silk scarf and flying boots. Above the ribbon of the Distinguished Flying Cross, pilot wings shone out from his left breast. He raised his right arm and waved, smiling broadly.

A dull thud rocked the car, and footsteps crunched on gravel.

'Alright, Jack.'

'Yes, darling.'

With the distraction, the image had faded.

But not the memories.

Historical Note

Phase 3 of the Battle of Britain lasted from August 24th to September 6th 1940. For Fighter Command, it was the most dangerous and intensive period of the Battle. Over its 14 days, the RAF lost over 466 fighters destroyed or damaged, and six of the seven Sector Airfields in 11 Group were severely mauled, as were five of the forward airfields.

Two hundred and thirty one pilots were killed, wounded or missing.

On 7th September, Hitler launched massed daylight attacks on London, relieving the pressure on 11 Group and its airfields. There were still terrible losses to be borne, both in the air and on the ground, but ten days later the plan to invade the British Isles was postponed, never to be resurrected.

Officially, the Battle of Britain lasted until the 31st October 1940, but it was won in the last week of August and the first week of September.

Author's Note

When I was a lad, my friends and I used to take a short cut through a local cemetery. One of the graves had a simple, but distinctive, white headstone. This book is dedicated to the Battle of Britain pilot buried beneath it.

I've seen many such headstones since, some of them dedicated to friends and acquaintances killed in flying accidents, but I still visit the one in Ludlow. It was part of my inspiration for joining the Royal Air Force, and the major inspiration for this book.

I'm especially indebted to Squadron Leader Tony Iveson DFC RAF (Retired), a Battle of Britain pilot who spared the time to talk to me early in my research. Other major sources of information and inspiration included the staff of the Battle of Britain Memorial Flight at RAF Coningsby; the books Fighter by Len Deighton; The Most Dangerous Enemy by Stephen Bungay; Fighter Boys by Patrick Bishop; and First Light by Geoffrey Wellum, another Battle of Britain veteran I was privileged to meet. On the internet, I found the sites battleofbritain.net and raf.mod.gov/ BofB1940 most useful. The cover design is based on Paolo Camera's Spitfire In Cloud.

For their feedback on my weekly readings, I'm grateful to the members of Cardiff Writers' Circle, and I offer special thanks to Rebecca Dalley, the Business Development Manager at the Royal Air Force Museum, for her helpful comments on my early drafts.

Although, in the main, I tried to follow the pattern of events at Biggin Hill during the last week of August and the first week of September 1940, Wings Over Summer is entirely a work of fiction, as are its characters. Where the facts did not fit my requirements, I changed them to suit. In addition to these wilful alterations, I'm sure there will be many unintentional errors, and these are solely my own.

Glossary and Abbreviations

Angels: codeword preceding height in thousands of feet (eg, angels one five = 15,000 feet).

AOC: - Air Officer Commanding - the Air Vice-Marshal commanding an RAF Group.

Bandit: enemy aircraft.

Buster: full throttle.

Clock Code: the pilot imagines himself sitting at the centre of a clock face, with twelve o'clock dead ahead and three o'clock ninety degrees right, etc. He reports sightings accordingly (eg, bandits ten o'clock high = enemy aircraft 60 degrees left of the nose and above the horizon).

CO: Commanding Officer.

DFC: - Distinguished Flying Cross - medal awarded to officers in recognition of gallantry in the air.

DFM - Distinguished Flying Medal - equivalent of the DFC awarded to ranks other than officers.

Flight: 646 Squadron comprises two flights of six aircraft - A and B.

g: the effect of gravity on pilots in a manoeuvre, making them feel heavier or lighter. Pulling 3g makes them feel three times their normal weight and drags blood from their brains, while pushing to 0g makes them feel weightless.

IntO: Intelligence Officer.

Line Abreast: a formation in which aircraft fly side by side, their wingtips generally no more than a few yards apart.

Line Astern: a formation in which aircraft fly one behind the other, generally no more than a few yards apart.

MT: - Mechanical Transport - an RAF station's fleet of vehicles.

NCO: non-commissioned officer.

OTU: Operational Training Unit.

Pancake: return to base and land.

RDF: - Radio Direction Finding - the early name for Radar.

Roger: message heard and understood.

Section: 646 Squadron's two flights each have two sections of three aircraft (eg A Flight comprises Red and Yellow Sections and B Flight, Green and Blue).

Snapper: Messerschmitt Bf109E.

Vic: a formation adopted by a section of three aircraft, the two wingmen sitting to either side of the tailplane of the leader.

Vector: codeword preceding the course to steer in degrees (eg vector zero nine zero = steer a course of 090 degrees).

WAAF: member of the Women's Auxiliary Air Force - pronounced Waff.

Wilco: I will comply with your instructions.

Printed in Great Britain
by Amazon.co.uk, Ltd.,
Marston Gate.